Too late to lock the door . . .

"She walks in beauty, like the night," Zach quoted from the darkness.

Tess's eyes grew wide and she turned toward the sound of his voice. She could barely discern his figure emerging from the shadows.

He tilted a bottle to his lips, drank, then setting it aside, strolled toward her. His bare feet were soundless on the hard-packed earth, his gait, that of a night creature stalking its quarry. He halted in front of her. His faded denims rode low on his hips, the top buttons unfastened. His shirt hung open, exposing a torso sculpted of taut muscle and bronzed flesh. Tess swallowed, hard. *Run, hide, lock the door,* her inner voice entreated.

"It's late," she murmured. "I probably should go to bed."

"Fraidy cat." He traced a finger along the line of her jaw. "You could take me with you."

She blinked, certain she must have misunderstood. "W-what?"

"You heard me, darlin'." A wicked smile curved his mouth. Lazily he worked the woven strands of her hair free from the confining braid.

"We could be lovers."

Zach caressed her cheekbone with the pad of his thumb, then dragged his fingers through her hair and cradled the back of her skull. "You remind of a curious little kitten. I want to find out if you'll bare your claws or purr with pleasure when we make love." His warm breath fanned her cheek. "Which will it be, little cat?"

The kiss was slow and seductive. A kiss meant to arouse and inflame. A kiss that gave, yet one that demanded in return. Tess became lost in its magic, melting against him, savoring a heady draught of desire. She wrapped her arms around his lean waist and held fast. The entire world seemed to quake and heave, and he was her rock. Eyes closed, Tess arched her neck and welcomed the host of sensations that flooded through her.

And she purred, a low, throaty, feline sound deep in her throat. . . .

BOOK YOUR PLACE ON OUR WEBSITE AND MAKE THE READING CONNECTION!

We've created a customized website just for our very special readers, where you can get the inside scoop on everything that's going on with Zebra, Pinnacle and Kensington books.

When you come online, you'll have the exciting opportunity to:

- View covers of upcoming books
- Read sample chapters
- Learn about our future publishing schedule (listed by publication month *and author*)
- Find out when your favorite authors will be visiting a city near you
- Search for and order backlist books from our online catalog
- Check out author bios and background information
- Send e-mail to your favorite authors
- Meet the Kensington staff online
- Join us in weekly chats with authors, readers and other guests
- Get writing guidelines
- AND MUCH MORE!

**Visit our website at
http://www.kensingtonbooks.com**

REBEL'S TREASURE

Elizabeth Turner

ZEBRA BOOKS
Kensington Publishing Corp.
http://www.kensingtonbooks.com

ZEBRA BOOKS are published by

Kensington Publishing Corp.
850 Third Avenue
New York, NY 10022

All Kensington titles, imprints and distributed lines are available at special quantity discounts for bulk purchases for sales
promotion, premiums, fund-raising, educational or institu-
tional use.

Special book excerpts or customized printings can also be
created to fit specific needs. For details, write or phone the
office of the Kensington Special Sales Manager: Kensington
Publishing Corp., 850 Third Avenue, New York, NY 10022.
Attn. Special Sales Department. Phone: 1-800-221-2647.

First Printing: January 2002
10 9 8 7 6 5 4 3 2 1

Printed in the United States of America

For Joyce Flaherty,
a very special agent.
Finding you was finding a treasure.

Prologue

Gettysburg, Pennsylvania
July, 1863

"Drop it, you thieving rebel."

Zach McClain froze. He felt something hard jab the narrow space between his shoulder blades. Sweat trickled beneath the gray homespun of his Confederate uniform.

"Don't make me shoot, Johnny Reb." The soft spoken threat was punctuated by another sharp poke.

Zach dropped the loaf of bread to the kitchen floor.

"Good. Now keep your hands where I can see them."

Slowly, Zach raised his hands above his head. Silence stretched between the pair. Zach considered his options. The voice belonged to that of a young girl—nervous, uncertain. Determined. Should he challenge her, she might make good her threat. Even if her aim was poor, at close range she could inflict serious damage. He decided instead to appeal to her sympathy.

"Have a heart, ma'am," he drawled, summoning every ounce of Southern charm. "The cherry trees have been picked clean. My friend and I haven't eaten for days."

"Save your explanations for the authorities."

Faced with the prospect of being turned over to blue-bellies, his decision came easily. Zach pirouetted on his uninjured leg and jerked the weapon from the girl's hands. Blinking in disbelief, he stared at the object he now held. "A broom?" he asked, torn between laughter and disgust.

The girl backed away, her eyes enormous in her pale face. "I—I don't like guns."

Tossing the broom aside, Zach darted his eyes toward the door leading to the rest of the house. "Who else lives here?"

She took another step backward, but was brought up short against a cast-iron cookstove. She eyed him warily. "Just my mother," she said, then added, "and my uncle, and my three older brothers. If you don't leave this instant, I'll scream."

Her attempt at bravado brought a smile, his first in weeks. "You're not a very convincing liar."

Moonlight streaming through the window above the dry sink allowed him to see the girl more clearly. She was a pretty little thing with long, brown hair and solemn gray eyes. All prim and proper in a white cotton nightdress that covered her slight form from chin to toe. "How old are you, darlin'?"

"Thirteen."

Thirteen, Zach mused. And she looked even younger. But in this trying period, boys hardly much older than this girl were being blown to smithereens by enemy gunfire. He had witnessed more than his share of their wounded, broken bodies sprawled across bloody battlefields. But Gettysburg had been by far the worst.

"What are you going to do?"

The girl's timid question recalled Zach to the moment at hand. "I'm going to finish what I started." He took an awkward step forward, then bent and picked up the bread he had dropped and stuffed it inside his jacket.

"You're hurt."

He glanced up to find her staring at the bloodstained bandage wrapped around his thigh. He flinched at her unsolicited sympathy. "I'm alive."

"But your leg . . ."

He shrugged off her concern. "My friend's injuries are worse by far."

"How bad?"

"Bad enough."

She narrowed the gap between them. "Take me to him. Perhaps I can help."

"You?" Zach snorted. "You're hardly more than a child."

She raised her chin a fraction. "After the battle, I helped tend as many as I could—regardless of the color of their uniforms, and in spite of Mother's protests."

Zach pondered her offer. Jed Duncan, the grizzled sergeant who had befriended him, could use whatever help was available. He had caught a bullet at Pickett's Charge. Zach worried that the wound was starting to fester. "How do I know you can be trusted? That you won't turn us in?"

She drew a hasty cross over her heart. "I won't tell a soul. I promise."

For some reason, Zach believed her. "All right," he agreed. "But what about your mother?"

The girl flashed a smile that changed her from pretty to almost beautiful, a smile hinting at the beauty she would someday become. "Mother takes a sleeping potion every night. She sleeps like the dead."

They were halfway across the barnyard when it occurred to Zach that he hadn't asked the girl's name. "What's your name, darlin'?"

She shot him a sidelong glance before answering. "Tess. Tess Montgomery. And I'm not your darlin'."

Zach swallowed his second smile of the evening. The girl had mimicked his Southern accent perfectly. "Pleased to make your acquaintance, Miss Montgomery. I'm Private Zachary McClain from the fine state of South Carolina, Thirty-third Infantry. Friends call me Zach."

Jed Duncan winked at her. "Good lookin' devil, ain't he?"

Tess blushed furiously, but silently agreed. Without the dark-gold beard, Zach McClain looked dashingly handsome. Seeing his transformation made her glad she had remembered to bring her father's razor and strop.

"Your turn, you mangy ol' buzzard." Wiping off the last of the shaving soap, Zach offered the razor to his friend.

"No way!" Jed held up his hands in protest. "Not until Grant surrenders to Lee."

"Mr. Lincoln will never let that happen," Tess replied with spirit. "You'll have a beard long enough to trip over."

Jed chuckled and bit off a hunk of tobacco. "Talkin' about whiskers, did I ever tell you the story about my great-grandpappy . . ."

Zach rolled his eyes and Tess stifled a giggle while Jed launched into another of his tales.

Later, Zach offered to walk her to the house. "You know, don't you, that we'll be leaving soon," he said as they strolled across the barnyard in the moonlight.

Nodding, Tess swallowed the lump in her throat. "I'll miss you. Both of you," she said.

"It's mighty kind of you to keep us hidden all this time."

"Mother leaves all the chores to me. She never goes near the barn." She paused and scuffed a clump of sod with a bare toe. "Besides, I promised not to tell."

Catching her chin in one hand, he raised her face to his. "Nevertheless, Jed and I appreciate all you've done: the food, the bandages, but most of all the kindness."

Nothing in her young life prepared Tess for what came next. With a slow smile that lighted his eyes, Zach bent his head and brushed a fleeting kiss across her lips. A kiss so brief, Tess wondered if she had only imagined its gossamer touch.

"Be careful, darlin'," he warned. "Don't let anyone break your heart." With that final, cryptic remark, Zach turned and left her standing in the moonlight.

Her emotions in turmoil, Tess picked up the skirt of her dress and ran the remaining distance to the farmhouse.

She failed to notice a solitary figure watching from the shadows.

One

Tucson, Arizona
April 1873

Nothing in the dime novels she faithfully devoured had prepared her for this moment.

After thousands of miles by rail, then coach, Tess Montgomery had finally arrived in Tucson. Stepping down from the stagecoach, she looked up and down the dusty thoroughfare—and felt a twinge of disappointment. Not a single gunslinger, desperado, or soiled dove in sight.

The stagecoach driver clattered down from his perch. Jerking his tobacco-stained beard toward the adobe buildings that served as headquarters for the Butterfield Overland Stage Company, he asked, "You stayin' at the Buckley House, miss?"

Tess clutched a battered valise that had once belonged to her father, unconsciously protecting her small cache of funds. "Ah, no, I won't be needing a hotel."

The driver raised a bushy brow. "You have family or friends in Tucson?"

"No," Tess confessed with a vigorous shake of her head. "No, I don't know a soul here."

The man stared at her intently. "If yer lookin' fer work, I might know a place or two."

"Thank you, but that won't be necessary." Tess beamed at him, bursting to tell someone, even a stranger, of her good fortune. "I'm here to collect an inheritance."

"An inheritance, eh?" The driver grinned back, revealing large, yellowed teeth. "Seems like you struck the mother lode."

Tess made a mental note to add that phrase to her journal. All the colorful expressions she heard were painstakingly entered into a frayed notebook in the hopes that someday a story of her own might be published. "Would you happen to know where I might find Abner Smith?"

"Smith?" The driver rubbed his jaw, his callused fingers rasping against bearded stubble. "Ain't he the lawyer feller?"

Tess nodded. "Do you know where I might find him?"

"Try lookin' fer his office down near City Hall at the corner of Ott and Court Street."

After thanking the man, Tess arranged for her trunk to be kept at the Buckley House until her return and headed off to find the lawyer's office. As she made her way along the dusty street, she gazed at her new surroundings. The city of Tucson, if the crude enclave of adobe buildings could be called such, sat on the floor of a high desert valley ringed by mountains. Overhead, the sun blazed from a sky of such an intense shade of blue it hurt her eyes. A modest collection of saloons and small businesses lined the thoroughfare.

Tess found the town's citizens every bit as fascinating as the scenery. The population was as varied as a bouquet of wildflowers. Disreputable men dressed in faded denim and others in proper business attire blended with dusky-skinned, black-eyed men and women of obvious Spanish ancestry wearing wide-brimmed hats and colorful garb.

She felt as though she had entered a different world. Arizona was a far cry from the rolling Pennsylvania countryside she had left behind. She found the strangeness frightening, yet at the same time, oddly exhilarating. After years spent caring for her ailing and demanding mother, she was hungry for a taste of adventure. To explore the world beyond the small village of Gettysburg—the only world she had ever known.

Halfway down Court Street, she paused to read a sign mounted on a wrought-iron bracket: *Abner Smith, Attorney at Law.* Tucked inside her valise was the Tucson lawyer's letter. A letter that had upended her world. A letter declaring her an heiress, bequeathing her freedom and adventure.

Drawing in a deep breath to steady her nerves, Tess pushed open the door and stepped across the threshold. Compared with the bright sunlight outside, the office was swathed in gloom. Tess stood just inside the door and waited for her eyes to adjust to the dim interior.

"May I help you?"

She blinked at the sound of a man's brisk tone. Suddenly conscious of her travel-stained appearance, she moved toward the figure seated behind a large desk near the rear of the room. "I'm Tess Montgomery," she began.

Upon hearing her name, the man rose to his feet and came around the desk to welcome her, hand extended in greeting. "My dear Miss Montgomery, at last we meet. I'm Abner Smith. Welcome to Tucson."

"I came as quickly as I could after receiving your letter." Tess shook the man's small, soft hand. The lawyer was slight in stature, with thinning brown hair neatly parted in the center and slicked down with Macassar oil. In contrast to the sparse hair on his head, he sported a luxurious mustache that covered his upper lip and bracketed his mouth. He was much younger than she had imagined, probably not much more than thirty.

"Please sit down; make yourself comfortable." He indicated two chairs positioned in front of his desk. "You must be tired after your long journey. Allow me to offer you something cool to drink. Lemonade, perhaps?"

Tess sat down and accepted his offer. After Abner Smith excused himself to go in search of refreshments, Tess tried to summon a measure of composure. She ran her hand over the skirt of her rose-brown skirt in a vain attempt to smooth the wrinkles. At the outset of her journey, she had been so proud of her smart traveling costume—her single extravagance—with its small, fashionable bustle. But endless days of travel had taken its toll. Even the silk flowers on her little straw hat seemed to have wilted during the journey. Her stomach felt jittery, her palms sweaty, now that the actual hour was at hand. Soon she would learn the exact terms of Jed Duncan's will. She had been staggered at the unexpected generosity of a man she had known only briefly.

Abner Smith returned with a tray holding an earthenware pitcher and several glasses. He poured a glassful of lemonade, then handed it to Tess. "For a modest sum, Angelina Cardoza provides refreshments for thirsty travelers."

"I'm very grateful to Mrs. Cardoza," Tess murmured as she took a sip, finding the drink deliciously cold and slightly tart.

"Señora Cardoza is an enterprising woman when

there's money to be made." Abner Smith resumed his place behind the desk and poured a second glass for himself. "Did you know Mr. Duncan well?"

"No, not very." Tess traced the rim of her glass with her index finger. In fact she hardly knew Jed at all, which was why hearing that he had named her beneficiary had been so surprising. "We met briefly following the battle at Gettysburg."

"If memory serves, Gettysburg took place nearly ten years ago. You could hardly have been more than a child."

"Thirteen." She smiled slightly at the recollection. "I discovered that Jed, along with a friend, was using my family's barn as a hiding place until they were well enough to rejoin their units. I did whatever I could to help."

"Even though they were the enemy?"

Her spine stiffened at the underlying rebuke. "I thought of them simply as two men, far from home, wounded and hungry . . . and frightened. If the situation had been reversed, Mr. Smith, and it had been my father trapped behind enemy lines, I pray a Southern woman would have done the same."

"Excuse me if I sounded unduly harsh. I'm a Northerner myself, originally from Ohio. I was merely curious as to what had prompted your concern for those men." Smith leaned back in his chair, his light-brown eyes watchful. "And what about since the war ended, Miss Montgomery? Have you and Mr. Duncan maintained contact?"

"Not really," she replied. "Over the years, I received an occasional letter, thanking me for my help and relating some of his adventures. I always wrote back, but I don't know whether or not he ever received them."

Propping his elbows on the desk, the lawyer rested

his chin on steepled fingers. "News of Mr. Duncan's bequest must have come as quite a surprise."

"I was both surprised *and* saddened to learn of Mr. Duncan's passing. I happened to grow quite fond of Jed during the short time we spent together. Under his gruff exterior beat the heart of a true Southern gentleman."

"You must be most anxious to learn the terms of Duncan's will."

"Of course, I am." Tess leaned forward in her chair, eager to get to the business at hand.

"All in good time, Miss Montgomery, all in good time." The lawyer's mustache twitched in what would have passed for a smile had his mouth been visible. "While I was getting refreshments, I took the liberty of summoning the other party involved."

"The other party . . . ?" she echoed, thinking she must have misunderstood.

Abner Smith nodded complacently. "As soon as the second beneficiary arrives, I'll go over the terms of the will."

The second beneficiary? Had Jed accumulated enough wealth for several people? Smith's letter had mentioned "extensive" property. On that basis alone, she had sold everything she owned and headed west. The sale of the farm at Gettysburg and its few remaining acres had been used to finance her trip. She had risked the entire amount in the belief that her anticipated inheritance would provide for her. Had she been mistaken?

Nervously she sipped her lemonade. "You failed to mention a second party in your letter, Mr. Smith."

"A deliberate omission—at Mr. Duncan's request. He was quite specific in the terms of his will. The old codger was far craftier than most gave him credit for."

Tess's mind reeled under Abner Smith's revelations. Not only had the lawyer deliberately misled her, but he had done so at Jed's insistence. "May I ask the identity of this other person?"

"You'll meet him shortly. He's a guest at the Buckley House." Abner drained his glass, then refilled it. "I trust you didn't suffer overly much on your long journey. Or find us too uncivilized?"

Tess barely heard the lawyer's polite inquiries. She had just come from the Buckley House. Had the person in question silently witnessed her arrival? Had this mysterious second party been as startled as she to learn he had been named as beneficiary? Had he, too, gambled everything on coming to Tucson to claim his inheritance? And, she wondered, did he also labor under the misconception that he was the sole heir?

Her thoughts scattered at the clatter of boots on the wooden walkway outside the lawyer's office. She tensed as they slowed, then stopped.

Abner Smith rose from his chair to acknowledge the newcomer.

Tess stood also and turned toward the door, curious to see the man Abner Smith had named as second beneficiary. Limned in brilliant golden sunlight, the man paused on the threshold just as she had done earlier. His tall, broad-shouldered frame blocked light from spilling into the room, casting it into even deeper shadow. Tess sucked in a sharp breath. Though she couldn't see the man's face, he personified the dime-novel hero of her dreams. He was dressed simply in a plaid shirt, open at the throat, tan leather vest, and faded denim pants. A gun belt draped his trim hips. Lean and lethal, he embodied the type of man wise mothers cautioned their daughters against.

And the sort that made foolish daughters disregard such sage advice.

Tess felt her pulse quicken as he sauntered farther into the room. She stared. She couldn't seem to help herself. Something about the man struck a familiar chord. Tipping her head to one side, she strained to see the features hidden by a flat-crowned hat, its brim pulled low.

"We've been waiting for you, McClain."

The glass of lemonade slipped from her nerveless fingers and crashed to the floor. Tess failed to hear the sound of breaking glass over the buzzing in her ears. *McClain? Zachary McClain? It couldn't be. It just couldn't be.*

"Miss Montgomery?"

The lawyer's voice seemed to be coming from the end of a long tunnel. Her head felt weightless as a balloon. It had been ten years since they had last seen each other. Ten long years since her very first kiss. She had been a young girl then, a girl hopelessly infatuated with a tall, dashing Confederate soldier. That they were on opposing sides made their plight seem all the more romantic—forbidden and exciting.

Abner Smith came out from behind his desk. "Are you all right, Miss Montgomery? You've grown quite pale."

"Yes, yes, I'm fine. Thank you," she managed for the lawyer's benefit. But she wasn't fine at all. Once again, Tess sensed that her life had taken an unexpected detour. Gradually, she became aware that Zach McClain maintained his distance.

And remained silent.

Tess took a hesitant step forward, heedless of glass crunching beneath the soles of her shoes. "Zach? Is it really you?"

Zach McClain stood unmoving, boots firmly planted

in the center of the room. "What the hell are you doing here?"

Tess froze, stung by his curt tone. "Why, the same as you. I'm waiting for Mr. Smith to inform us of the terms of Jed's will."

Zach swore softly under his breath. "I haven't heard them yet, but I dislike them already."

Rubbing his hands together, Abner adopted a false cheerfulness. "I had no idea the two of you were old friends."

"We're not." Zach's reply left no room for doubt.

The lawyer glanced uncertainly from one to the other. "I'll find Angelina and have her clean up this mess so we can get on with the business at hand."

Abner hastened from the office, leaving the two of them alone. Unsure how to respond to Zach's blatant hostility, Tess studied him warily. The man standing before her bore only a superficial resemblance to the gangly Confederate youth of her memories. All traces of softness had been erased, washed away by life's vagaries. She remembered Zach McClain as open, friendly, charming. The man the boy had become was none of these things.

The intervening years had weathered Zach's features just as sun, wind, and rain sculpted even nature's hardest substances. His jaw looked granite-firm, and just as unyielding. His wonderfully wide and mobile mouth had become stern and unsmiling. Eyes a startling shade of green glittered as coldly as twin emeralds in the deeply tanned face.

"It's been a long time," she ventured.

"Not long enough."

Tess's eyes widened at the rude retort. She blinked back the sting of tears. "You've changed. I think I liked you better before."

"You, on the other hand, have hardly changed at

all." Zach took off his hat and rifled his sun-bleached hair with impatient fingers. It was all he could do not to wrap his hands around Tess Montgomery's pretty little neck. She hadn't changed at all. She still oozed the same sweet innocence she had at thirteen. Anyone observing her initial surprise at seeing him again would have been taken in by it. But he knew it was guilt, not surprise, that had drained the color from her cheeks.

He was relieved when Abner Smith returned seconds later, accompanied by a plump woman with merry black eyes. Maintaining a constant volley of Spanish, she quickly cleaned up the mess on the floor, then left, still chattering.

The lawyer motioned toward the chairs in front of his desk. "If you two will be seated, we can begin."

"After you, Miss Montgomery." Zach made a sweeping gesture toward the places indicated. With exaggerated courtesy, he waited for Tess to take a seat before lowering himself into the chair next to her and stretching out his legs. This close, he couldn't help but catch a faint whiff of violets that seemed to cling to her. Sweet, delicate, innocent—the scent suited her perfectly. Unless one knew better, he quickly amended.

Smith assumed the role of host. He turned to Zach, his mustache twitching in another ghost of a smile. "May I offer you a glass of Angelina's lemonade?"

"Quit wasting time, Smith."

"Very well." Smith opened his top desk drawer, pulled out a pair of wire-rimmed glasses, and slipped them on. Next, he brought out a sheaf of official looking documents. After pompously clearing his throat, he began, "Mr. Duncan wished for me to express that both of you held an enduring place in his affections."

Zach brushed a smudge of dust from his hat. "Get on with it."

The lawyer shifted in his chair, apparently discomfited by the other man's blunt manner. "Jedediah Duncan possessed no surviving kin. In the event of his death, it was his final wish that the sum of his total wealth become the possession of you, Mr. McClain, and you, Miss Montgomery."

"Are you sayin' ol' Jed finally struck it rich?"

Smith shuffled papers and avoided looking at Zach directly. "At the time of his death, Mr. Duncan owned a ranch. . . ."

"A ranch?" Tess made no attempt to contain her excitement.

Nodding gravely, the lawyer sent her a reproving look at the interruption. "Besides the ranch known as Casita de Oro, Mr. Duncan also owned a silver mine."

Now it was Zach's turn to sit up straight and pay attention. "A mine? The old codger owned a silver mine? A ranch for her, a mine for me. That's mighty generous of Jed."

"Er, um . . . that's not exactly what Mr. Duncan intended."

Zach and Tess exchanged looks.

"Kindly explain, Mr. Smith, just what Mr. Duncan did intend," Tess said quietly.

With uncanny accuracy, Tess seemed able to read his mind. She had just voiced the question he had been about to ask—but more diplomatically. Zach let out an impatient breath. The little attorney was quickly getting on his nerves with his constant pussyfooting about. Zach couldn't dismiss the uneasy feeling that something was about to spoil his good fortune. Not that the situation wasn't bad enough already. It had brought him face-to-face with a woman he hoped never to see again in his lifetime.

"Mr. Duncan was quite specific. The ranch and mine are to be held jointly."

"What the hell is that supposed to mean?" Zach surged to his feet. He didn't wait for Smith to answer. "In that case, Miss Montgomery can sign over her half of the mine to me, and I'll sign my half of the ranch to her."

"I'm afraid it's not that simple, Mr. McClain." His face flushed, Smith ran a finger around the inside of his starched collar. "Mr. Duncan specified the two pieces of property must be owned jointly. Unless a buyer for both can be found, they are not to be sold separately. If this contract is violated by either party, both properties revert to the United States Government."

Furious, Zach shoved a lock of sun-bleached hair from his brow, only to have it fall back almost immediately. "So each of us owns half of a ranch and half of a mine?"

"Precisely."

Tess shook her head in dismay. "Whatever possessed Jed to do such a thing?"

"The answer's simple, darlin'." Zach's sugar-coated drawl was tainted with bitterness. "Poor, misguided Jed had simply taken leave of his senses."

Abner Smith rose, signaling that the meeting was concluded. As he escorted them from his office, he congratulated both of them on their good fortune and supplied directions to their newly acquired properties.

Tess hesitated near the threshold and turned to the attorney. "You failed to mention, Mr. Smith, what precipitated Mr. Duncan's untimely demise. I hope he didn't suffer."

"Oh, no, Miss Montgomery." Smith hastened to assure her. "Doc said the bullet killed him instantly."

Tess paled visibly. "He was shot?"

Smith nodded. "Murdered."

Tess opened her mouth to speak, but no sound came out.

"A bullet right between the shoulder blades." Relishing the tale, Smith rocked back on his heels. "Whoever committed the deed dropped Jed like a sack of flour. Never even had time to draw his gun."

TWO

Tess stood on the boardwalk outside Abner Smith's office and stared at Zach McClain's retreating back. What on earth was the matter with him? Why was he acting so strangely. Almost as though . . .

. . . he hated her?

An invisible band tightened around her heart. Zach had always occupied a special place in her affections. With the passage of time, her girlhood crush on the dashing Rebel had become a faded photograph in her book of memories. Whenever she scanned the pages of her youth, thoughts of Zach McClain never failed to prompt wistful smiles and summon sweet *I wonder*s. Inevitably, reality intruded—usually in the form of her mother's strident voice—and she would reluctantly return to the present.

She watched Zach disappear through the swinging doors of a saloon. Surely she was being fanciful. He had no reason to harbor enmity toward her. People changed all the time, she reasoned. Zach wasn't the only man who had returned from war a far different person than the idealistic boy who had enlisted.

The thunder of galloping hooves drew her attention. At the sound, Tess took an involuntary step backward until her spine pressed against rough adobe. A half-dozen soldiers rode past, churning up a brown cloud of dust in their wake. She found their presence alternately consoling and alarming. Fort Lowell, she had learned from fellow travelers, had been established in Tucson to protect its residents from the Apache. The people she had spoken to thus far seemed of one opinion. They felt that if civilization were to come to the Arizona territory, the Apache needed to be eradicated. If recent newspaper accounts could be believed, the Apache had no intention of allowing that to happen. Tales of their raiding, killing, and burning sprees abounded. Shuddering at the thought, Tess wished she were braver.

"Whatsa matter, honey?"

At the sound of a woman's voice, Tess swung around and found herself face to face with a buxom blonde dressed in a sapphire silk gown cut daringly low. The woman's china blue eyes were alight with humor.

"Don't let this place scare you," the woman continued, her manner friendly.

Tess raised her chin a notch. "Not in the least."

"Good for you." The woman nodded approvingly. "Our boys in uniform are here to defend and protect— but seem better at raisin' hell. Caused quite a ruckus a couple years back when they shot ol' man Pennington's favorite hound along with a couple o' citizens."

Tess's eyes widened with horror. "I hope the injuries weren't serious."

"Unfortunately, the men survived. Pity about the dog, though," the woman said with a shake of her head, which sent her daffodil yellow curls dancing.

Not sure how to respond, Tess cleared her throat and changed the subject. "Could you kindly direct me to the livery stable?"

"Down the street a block—can't miss it." She nodded over her shoulder. "Thought you must be new in town. Bet you're fresh off the afternoon stage, aren't you?"

"Yes, ma'am. My name's Tess." She extended her hand politely. "Tess Montgomery from Pennsylvania."

The woman enfolded Tess's hand briefly in her own before releasing it. "Well, Tess Montgomery from Pennsylvania, it's a pleasure. I'm Lily—Lily London from the Silver Sequin just down the street." She pointed a manicured finger at the saloon Zach had disappeared into minutes earlier.

"Ohh . . ." Tess knew her response was woefully inadequate, but it was all she could manage. *The Silver Sequin?* Could Lily London be a "soiled dove"? If so, she was nothing like Tess had imagined. Not at all painted or brazen as portrayed in the dime novels. Actually, Tess rather admired the woman's direct, friendly manner.

Lily glanced around. "No family here to greet you, hon?"

"I don't have any family." The words came out with difficulty. Now that her mother was gone, Tess was truly alone. All alone.

Lily's eyes took on a speculative gleam as they swept over Tess, from her modest little straw hat to her scuffed leather shoes. "It ain't so bad, dearie. Families ain't all they're cracked up to be. You look like a smart girl. Ought to do all right on your own."

Tess fervently hoped the woman wasn't mistaken. She had risked everything on coming out west.

Tipping her head to the side, the woman continued to study Tess. "Pretty face, nice figure; with the right clothes and a little makeup, maybe a different hairstyle, you could make a decent living for yourself. Face and figure's all I had to start with, and now look at me. I own my own place."

"I already have a place of my own." When Lily raised one elegantly arched brow in obvious skepticism, Tess hastened to explain. "I just inherited some property along with a few head of cattle. I thought I'd try my hand at ranching." As she spoke the words aloud, her nebulous future suddenly crystallized. No longer vague or uncertain, Tess felt a new sense of purpose and direction. After all, she had grown up on a farm. She knew how to care for livestock. How different could ranching be?

"Raising cattle's no easy way of life, especially for a woman. Come see me if you change your mind. I'll find a job for you at the Sequin."

Tess watched the woman sashay off. So intent was she on observing the exaggerated sway of Lily's hips that she failed to notice two women approaching until they were nearly alongside. Tess summoned her friendliest smile, expecting it to be returned.

"Humph!" the taller of the two sniffed. The other pretended not to see Tess at all as she swept past.

Rebuffed by the pair's odd behavior, Tess continued down the street in search of the livery stable. She found it, next to the blacksmith shop. After she introduced herself to Sam Wilburn, the stocky, ruddy-faced proprietor agreed to lend her a wagon.

"This skewbald here used to belong to Jed," Sam explained as he slipped a harness over the neck of a docile-looking horse with a coat of large, irregular patches of white and brown. "Guess it now rightly belongs to you."

Tess mumbled a reply as she stroked the horse's dark muzzle. In truth, the horse was only partly hers. The other half, and she refused to dwell on which half, belonged to Zach. At any rate, it felt good to own a horse again. She'd been forced to sell her mare, Daisy, after her father's death at Fredericksburg.

"After you're settled, come back into town for the rest of your livestock. Then you can pay what you owe me for feed." Sam folded his brawny arms across his thick torso and gave her a hard, unblinking look that dared her to refuse.

Tess gulped. "Ah . . . I'm sure we can make some kind of arrangement." Her small cache of money was rapidly dwindling. First her trip out west, and now the bill from the livery stable would eat up still more. Then she remembered that Zach was equally responsible for the debt. For the first time since the reading of the will, she was happy that she wasn't Jed's sole heir.

Sam nodded, apparently satisfied with her response. "You'll find my prices fair," he said as he assisted her onto the wagon, then watched her drive off.

A short time later, Tess left the town behind. Rather than worry over her depleted funds, she concentrated on the passing scenery. Arid and brown, Arizona bore no resemblance whatsoever to the verdant rolling countryside that she was familiar with. Instead of trees, tall, strangely-shaped cacti, which she had learned from a fellow traveler were called saguaro, raised their prickly arms toward a cloudless sky. A pang of home-sickness struck her, the sudden longing rapier-sharp. She tried to convince herself that the desert's strange-ness made it all the more fascinating. But in spite of her best efforts, all she felt was an encroaching sense of alienation.

The afternoon sun beat down mercilessly, far hotter than previous April days she remembered. Shrugging out of her jacket, Tess unfastened the top buttons at the neck of her simple white shirtwaist. She had been thrilled and excited to receive Abner Smith's letter hinting of extensive properties. A whole new way of life had appeared before her eyes. She had leaped at the opportunity. Now doubts assailed her. She wondered if her decision had been too hasty, too impulsive. All of her earlier optimism deserted her, leaving her besieged with doubt.

Maybe it had been foolhardy to sell what remained of the farm. Perhaps she should have been resigned to an existence raising chickens and selling produce, content to remain a spinster, watching life pass from a creaking rocker on the front porch.

But she wasn't resigned. Wasn't content. She wanted more. She wanted to expand her world, to experience adventure, not merely live it vicariously from the pages of dime novels.

Feeling more resolute, she sat straighter and looked around with renewed interest. The horse strained to pull the wagon as the road began a steep ascent. Saguaros marched up granite mountain slopes. A hawk circled overhead, a dark silhouette against a cobalt blue sky. Short, scruffy bushes dotted the barren landscape at regular intervals. Meanwhile, the relentless sun burned through her thin cotton shirtwaist. Yes, Arizona was different, much different, from the gentle Pennsylvania countryside.

But, she reminded herself, different didn't necessarily mean wrong or bad—only different.

Following Abner Smith's directions, she veered from the trail and up a winding path marked by boulders on either side. The path twisted upward, then dipped slightly. Tess reined to a halt. A flat-roofed, stucco-covered adobe house—her house—sat in a shallow basin, shaded by a small copse of cottonwood trees. Behind it were several outbuildings. Not even the neglected air of the small ranch could stem the tide of optimism Tess felt at the sight. Instantly, she pictured how the house would look with boxes of bright-colored flowers beneath the three deep-set windows covered by iron grillwork. Clay pots overflowing with blooms would flank the double doors of rough-sawn wood.

Eager to discover the house's secrets, Tess gave the reins a gentle slap. The wagon rolled forward, then came to a stop in front. Tess barely waited until it came to a complete halt before climbing down. Looping the reins over a hitching post, she went to the door, which stood slightly ajar, and pushing it open, peered inside. Heavy shutters barred the light from entering. As she stepped across the threshold for a closer look, she tripped over an object in her path and fell headlong.

In spite of the leather gloves she wore, her palms stung from the abrupt contact with the rough wooden floorboards. Her small hat, which had perched so jauntily atop her brown curls, was knocked askew, the brim now dipping rakishly over one brow. Scrambling to her feet, Tess brushed the dirt from her skirt, then cast a backward glance over her shoulder. Reassured that only the stately saguaros had witnessed her graceless entry, she returned her attention to the house's interior.

Now that her vision had adjusted to the dim light, chaos was clearly evident in what she assumed was the parlor, or *sala*, as she had heard some call it. Furniture, most of it broken, was strewn about like a child's carelessly discarded toys. Shattered pottery littered the floor. Books were scattered everywhere, their spines splayed open, the pages torn.

Sick with dread, Tess wandered further inside. Carefully skirting a pile of debris, she drifted from room to room. The house was U-shaped, making it larger than it appeared from the outside. In addition to the parlor, which ran along the entire front of the structure, there were two bedrooms in one wing, and a kitchen and what appeared to be a dining room in the other. All the rooms flowed from one to the other through a series of doorways. A second door in each room opened onto a small patio. The thick, whitewashed adobe walls made the temperature inside the house surprisingly comfortable.

The vandals hadn't left a single inch undisturbed. Stuffing trailed like entrails from mattresses and pillows. Drawers had been yanked free of cabinets, their contents dumped. Clothing and personal items were strewn everywhere. In the kitchen, cupboard doors stood open. Burlap sacks of flour, rice, and beans had been eviscerated, their contents a gritty carpet beneath her feet. Who could have committed such senseless destruction? she wondered.

Apaches? Had they been the ones who murdered Jed?

Dazed, Tess stepped outdoors and into the small patio. A porch with an earthen roof wrapped around two sides of the enclosure and provided welcome shade from the relentless sun. Wooden benches had been upended and hurled against a well, which occupied space in the far corner near a chinaberry tree. A worn path led away from the house toward a crude stable with a small corral and several lean-tos.

Righting one of the benches, she dragged it under the porch roof and sank down on it. She rested her head against the adobe wall and tried to think calmly, rationally. She needed to plan a course of action, needed to decide what to do next. If Indians had ransacked the house, were they likely to return? And was she safe here alone? The sun was already beginning to lower in the sky. The ring of mountain peaks assumed a duskier hue, becoming a little menacing, more isolating. Civilization seemed a long way off. The thought of returning to Tucson after nightfall was a daunting one.

A slight sound from the front of the house penetrated her preoccupation. She tensed, every sense alert and straining. Then she heard the noise again, this time louder, more distinct. Her heart pounded wildly. She had left the door ajar. Could it be an animal foraging for food? A mountain lion? Or had the vandals returned?

She rose to her feet, her eyes frantically searching the patio for something—a rock or stick—to use as a weapon. She spied an upended clay pot nearby, snatched it up with both hands, then pressing her back against the wall, raised the pot above her head and stood poised to attack.

"Tess?"

Tess felt her knees turn to jelly at Zach's familiar drawl. Seconds later he stepped from the house onto the patio.

Feeling foolish beneath his chill green gaze, she slowly lowered the clay pot to the ground. From the scowl on his face, he didn't seem any happier to see her now than he had in Abner Smith's office.

"What are you doing here?"

"You're forgetting half this hovel is mine." He made a sweeping gesture toward the house. "For God's sake, Tess, were you so disappointed Jed's dyin' didn't make you a wealthy woman that you tore the place apart?"

A bubble of laughter threatened to break loose. The hilarity was quickly snuffed by a gust of righteous indignation. "Don't be ridiculous. This is how I found the place when I arrived."

"Casita de Oro? House of Gold? Jed sure picked himself a fancy name for a crumbling pile of adobe." Tipping back the brim of his hat with a thumb, Zach let out a low whistle of disgust. "Whoever did this sure left one helluva mess."

She struggled to keep the fear from her voice. "Do you think it was Apaches?"

"Doubt it." He dismissed her fear with a snort of

derision. "Folks tend to blame everything on the Indians. I've known Apaches to burn a place to the ground, but slashing pillows and breaking dishes isn't their style."

She digested this information in silence, then pursued the issue from another angle. "If not Indians, who would do so much damage? And why?"

He studied her upturned face with narrowed eyes. "Maybe the same ones who shot Jed in the back."

Tess ran the palms of her hands up and down her arms to erase a sudden chill. "Whoever did this must have been searching for something important. Do you think they'll come back?"

He shrugged. "Maybe, maybe not. Anything's possible."

Uncomfortable under his cynical regard, she dropped her gaze to her hands. She discovered that her sole pair of leather gloves had been ruined beyond repair by her earlier fall. Frustrated by their loss and the lack of funds to replace them, she stripped them off and tossed them onto the bench behind her. Conscious that Zach's sharp gaze followed her every movement, she latched onto the first thought to enter her head. "I recently read a story in the *Fireside Companion* about a detective called Old Sleuth. In the story, the killer kept coming back to the scene of the crime."

"Old Sleuth?" A sandy brow quirked. *"Fireside Companion?"*

She bristled under his mockery. "I'll have you know the *Fireside Companion* is a perfectly reputable publication. It boasts thousands of readers."

"My mama used to say there was no accountin' for taste."

Tess ignored his sarcasm. "Do you suppose the culprits who ransacked the house found what they were looking for?"

"No way we'll ever know for sure—unless, of course, they decide to pay us another visit."

His offhand remark heightened Tess's apprehension. Her mouth felt as parched as the Sonoran desert. "If they do come back, what then?"

Zach rested one hand lightly on the butt of the Colt fastened at his waist. "They'll get a reception they weren't expecting."

Tess chased down her fear with a draught of indignation. "If you're trying to scare me, you're succeeding."

He pinned her with a hard stare. "Anyone with a lick of sense should be scared. Apaches, murderers, thieves, gunslingers, the Arizona Territory is crawlin' with 'em. If you knew what was good for you, Tess Montgomery, you'd head home on the next stage out of Tucson."

If you knew what was good for you.

Her mother had repeated that same phrase countless times. Over the years, Tess had grown to hate every syllable, and all it implied. Drawing herself to her full five feet, three inches, she met his look, a grim but determined glint in her gray eyes. "Maybe I don't have a lick of sense. Maybe I'm too stupid to know what's good for me. But one thing you can count on, Zachary McClain, I'm not going to let you—or anyone—run my life."

"This land will chew you up and spit you out."

"I'm not leaving." She raised her chin a fraction. "Nothing you say will change my mind, so you might as well save your breath."

"A rundown ranch and an abandoned mine hardly qualifies you as an heiress. Why stay?"

She'd sooner cut out her tongue than admit she had nowhere else to go. "I could ask you the same question," she countered. "Why stay when you could be living in that grand house in South Carolina you used to talk about all the time?"

"After Savannah fell, your fine Yankee general, William Tecumseh Sherman, marched north through the Carolinas. Thanks to him that grand ol' house is nothin' more than a pile of rubble."

"I'm sorry," she murmured. And she truly was. She remembered listening spellbound as he talked about the splendid plantation that had been in his family for generations.

Zach took off his hat and tapped it impatiently against his denim-clad thigh. "At least consider finding a place in town."

"I'm staying right where I am." She glanced meaningfully at the steadily darkening sky. "It's nearly sundown. Shouldn't you be getting back yourself?"

He gave a mirthless laugh. "And why would I do that?"

Her eyes widened at his rejoinder. "I recall Mr. Smith mentioning you were staying at the Buckley House."

"Was," he corrected, "but no longer. I plan to bunk here until the place is sold."

"Here . . . ?" Her voice squeaked. "Where do you propose to sleep? Surely you don't intend . . . ?"

"I have as much right here as you do."

Unable to dispute his claim, she quickly chose another tactic. "Yes, but it's hardly proper for the two of us to share the same roof."

"You won't leave, and neither will I. Not too many alternatives remain. My finances are presently a bit—how shall I put it—strained?"

And so were hers, she wanted to fire back, but didn't. It seemed at last they had found common ground. "But what will people think?" she asked after a lengthy pause.

"I couldn't care less. In a town where citizens get murdered for no apparent reason, how can anyone object to two people living under the same roof? After all, its only temporary until we can locate a buyer, split the proceeds, and move on."

He made it sound so logical that she couldn't mount an adequate argument to the contrary. "Even so . . ."

"Look here, Tess," he said impatiently. "It's not as though we were sharing a bedroom. If it eases your mind, think of me as your boarder."

Tess could only imagine what her mother would have thought about having Zach McClain as her boarder. Mary Montgomery had been extremely protective of Tess and her reputation. She had been the sort who worried constantly about others' opinions. She would turn over in her grave if she knew Tess was about to share a house with a man without benefit of clergy.

And, to add insult to injury, the man in question was a Confederate!

Tess's gaze darted about the patio, coming to rest on the well in the corner. "Don't you have a wife or sweetheart who might . . . object . . . to this sort of living arrangement?"

"No wife, no encumbrances. What about you, darlin'?"

Darlin'? Years before he had called her that. What had been once been a term of endearment, now seemed infused with sarcasm. She also noticed that his sugary drawl could become exaggerated with mockery and contempt. She swung her gaze back to him and saw only a ghost of the boy she once knew.

"What's the matter, Tess?" he goaded. "Cat got your tongue? No husband, no cryin' babies waitin' back home?"

Her throat felt tight. "No husband—no babies." Not now, probably never. Only a handful of men had returned from the war to farm the fields in and around Gettysburg. The ones young enough to seek a wife didn't want to be burdened with a demanding invalid for a mother-in-law.

Zach shifted his weight from one foot to the other. "See here, Tess, I don't like this situation any more than you, but it looks like we're stuck with each other. Let's make it as painless as possible. One simple rule. You stay out of my way; I'll stay out of yours. Agreed?"

"Agreed," she said.

"Good, then we ought to get along just fine."

He started to turn away when her next question stopped him cold. "Zach, what happened to you? You never used to be like this."

"In case you've forgotten, darlin', the war happened."

Tess closed the narrow gap between them, resisting the impulse to lay her hand against his cheek. He seemed so angry, so bitter. Filled with pain and rage. She felt the need to offer comfort, ease his suffering. "The war was a horrible time for everyone, but it's over now. Sins of the past are best forgotten."

As she watched in morbid fascination, a subtle change occurred. His features tightened, hardened, becoming as formidable as the encircling mountains. A trick of the waning light? She wondered. But before Tess could find the answer, Zach grabbed hold of her shoulders. From the strength of his grip, she knew the inner battle he waged to control his temper.

"One last rule, darlin'. Never—I repeat—*never* bring up the subject of war."

Tess stared at him wide-eyed, then swallowed loudly. Gradually his grip relaxed, and he released her, stepping back.

"I hope we understand each other."

"Perfectly." Tess bit down on her lower lip to keep it from trembling. "I have a rule, too."

Zach raised a sandy brow and waited.

Blinking back tears, Tess gathered the tattered remnants of her courage. "Don't call me darlin'. Never . . . ever."

Three

Tess Montgomery. The person he hated most in the entire world.

Zach kicked a rusty bucket and sent it tumbling across the hard-packed earth. Fate had played a cruel, perverted prank by depositing her back into his life. No, he corrected, it wasn't fair to rail against fate when the fault lay with Jed Duncan. Ever since Gettysburg, he and Jed had held vastly different opinions about the woman. Jed had insisted that she was an angel in disguise and had refused to listen to reason any time Zach had attempted to convince him otherwise. Zach had told Jed outright that Tess Montgomery was a lying, traitorous little bitch, but the man had refused to believe him.

Well, Zach thought, at least he had been wise to lay ground rules between the two of them. He'd stay out of her way; she'd stay out of his. The less they had to do with each other, the better off he'd be. He didn't trust himself around her. It took every shred of willpower not to shake her senseless. What a conniving little actress. She had managed to look the picture of innocence as she questioned him about the war. As if she didn't know what had happened to him.

As if she cared.

Hooking his thumbs into the waistband of his denims, Zach stared over the ridge of mountains silhouetted like a jagged scar against the darkening sky. Scars were funny things, he mused. Some were visible reminders of past agony; other scars, like the ones he carried, were well hidden from the naked eye. He sighed, the sound a sad whisper from the depths of his soul. Hell, instead of blaming Tess Montgomery for all the misery she had caused him, maybe he should get down on his knees and thank her. Hatred for her had kept him alive while others around him died like flies.

Damn! What had possessed him to ask her if she was married, had kids? He couldn't care less if she had married a dirt farmer and had a half-dozen snotty-nosed brats. It was no business of his. None at all. He tried to block the memory of pain mirrored in her silver-gray eyes. For a moment—just a moment—it had weakened his resolve. He had no intention of lowering his guard around her. She couldn't be trusted.

A handful of stars were making their debut in the evening sky when Zach finally returned to the house. He closed the door firmly behind him and then, after tugging a heavy bar across it to keep out uninvited guests, made his way through the darkened house.

"Tess," he called. "Where in blazes are you?"

"Out here in the back," she answered.

He followed the sound of her voice to the patio. "What are you doing sitting in the dark?"

"Look what I found." She held a kerosene lamp up for his inspection. "The globe is cracked, but I think its still usable."

"Then what the devil are you waiting for?" he asked, making no effort to mask his annoyance. "Why not light it?"

"I don't have any matches."

Zach let an impatient breath hiss between his clenched teeth. Digging through a vest pocket, he produced a match. A loud scratch was followed by a flare of yellow light and the pungent smell of sulfur. He hung the lantern from a hook on an overhead beam. In the mellow glow of lamplight, Tess's slender form was illuminated, outlining every soft curve, each gentle swell. While he had been cooling his temper, she had removed her hat and taken the pins from her hair. Loose chestnut-brown curls cascaded down her back and over her shoulders. Damn, she was a pretty sight! His eyes roamed over her heart-shaped face with its delicately sculpted cheekbones and obstinate little chin with a tantalizing cleft. Her most striking feature, however, were her large, luminous gray eyes. Soft as a newborn kitten's, mysterious as summer fog. The promise of beauty hinted at years ago had been fulfilled, he thought with grudging honesty. Like a butterfly from a cocoon, Tess had emerged from girlhood into a beautiful woman.

"Are you hungry?"

The typical female question snapped Zach back to the present. He was angry at himself for being snared by her beauty. Angry at the primal tug of attraction he felt in spite of his resolution to distance himself. "Don't worry about me. I can take care of myself."

"Worried?" Her chin lifted defiantly. "Don't flatter yourself. I simply thought, since we find ourselves in the same predicament, that it might be helpful if we worked together as a team. For instance, I found the lantern; you had a match."

"As I see it, the fewer dealings we have with each other, the better."

She linked her fingers together, then studied them, her expression downcast. "I know I must seem forward. I didn't mean to imply . . ."

Zach felt an unexpected spurt of contrition. He had been raised to be a gentleman in the true Southern tradition. Now circumstances had reduced him to bullying a defenseless woman. Who would he target next? Widows and puppies? He tried to soften his tone. "Tell you what. Why don't you scout around and see what you can find in the way of food? In the meantime, I'll fire up the estufa."

At her blank look, he pointed behind the kitchen to an item that resembled a rectangular box made from adobe that stood approximately two feet high. "The estufa is our cook stove. Because of the heat, most meals here in the Southwest are prepared outdoors. That beehive-shaped object next to it, an horno, serves as an oven."

Tess eyed the crude pair dubiously.

"I'll cook tonight," he offered gruffly. "Afterwards we'll take turns."

Tess leaned her back against the rough adobe and shot Zach a surreptitious glance. She never would have guessed the dime-novel hero of her dreams would possess culinary skills. And yet, using a single iron skillet, he had managed to prepare a simple but tasty meal with the items she had unearthed from the chaos. He had also possessed the foresight to bring some supplies along with him, which was more than she could say for herself.

Turning his head, he caught her staring. "What's wrong? Did I drip beans down the front of my shirt?"

Embarrassed, she glanced away. "I'm just surprised at how good everything tasted. I never met a man who could cook."

He grunted an acknowledgment. "Well, tomorrow's your turn. I've been thinking," he continued. "Sharing the workload might not be such a bad idea. That applies to all the chores, including taking care of the house and the animals as well."

"All right," she agreed. "That seems fair."

Leaning back, Zach stretched out his long legs, crossed them at the ankles, and stared up at the sky. A thick silence descended, then stretched, and stretched. Tess shifted uncomfortably on the bench next to him. Clearing her throat, she asked, "Did you find anything of interest when you looked around earlier?"

He shrugged. "Not much. A stable of sorts with a small corral and a couple of lean-to shelters."

"Do you think anything has been stolen?"

"Jed's tools were scattered everywhere, but whoever did this wasn't after tools."

Tess felt a chill chase down her spine. "If not robbery, why would anyone do this?"

"Way I figure, they must have been searching for something. Something of value."

"What could Jed possibly own that would drive someone to murder?" She spoke softly, the question directed more toward herself than Zach. She couldn't chase away the thought of how Jed had died. Abner Smith's words echoed in her ears. *"Right between the shoulder blades. Never had time to draw his gun."*

"I don't know who killed him, but I intend to find out."

The quiet conviction in his voice left no room for doubt. He meant every word. "Poor Jed," she murmured. "To survive the war only to fall victim to murder."

Zach stood suddenly and dragged his hand through his tawny locks. "Look, Tess, you being here really isn't a good idea. If you won't consider returning to

Gettysburg, at least think about finding a room in town."

Feeling at a disadvantage with him towering over her, she stood also. "Don't worry about me," she replied, unconsciously repeating his words from an earlier conversation.

"Fine, but don't expect me to save your hide when you find yourself in more trouble than you can handle."

"I can take care of myself."

"You're being stubborn instead of sensible. If the men who did this come back, how do you expect to defend yourself? I bet you don't even know how to load a gun, much less aim one."

"Then I'll learn," she snapped.

"You don't even like guns."

For a long time, the two simply stared at each other while their minds pinwheeled back to a summer night nearly ten years ago. The night a young girl and Confederate soldier first met and formed a tenuous bond. Tess stared into Zach McClain's face. As she watched, a transformation crossed his handsome features. Much to her regret, they hardened once again, becoming aloof—the face of a stranger.

"I heard rooms at Hodges Hotel were reasonable. Maybe you could try there."

"What about at the Silver Sequin?" she retorted. "Maybe I could get a room there."

His green eyes narrowed into slits. "What do you know about the Silver Sequin?"

It took all her willpower not to squirm or glance away. "I chanced to meet Lily London after leaving Mr. Smith's office. She offered me a job."

"A job!" The single word burst out like an expletive.

"Yes, a job." His manner instantly put her on the

defensive. "I thought the offer very generous of Miss London."

"Darlin', from what I've heard about the lady, Lil boasts many virtues, but generosity isn't one of them." He caught her chin between thumb and index finger. "I don't suppose Miss London mentioned exactly what sort of job she had in mind."

"Ah . . . um . . . she wasn't specific." Having him this close wreaked havoc on her train of thought. The scent of leather and musk clinging to him seemed more exotic than an expensive perfume. The feel of his callused fingers against her skin scrambled her senses.

"You wouldn't last ten minutes waiting tables or tending bar," he scoffed.

In the far recesses of her brain, she knew she should pull away from his touch, but couldn't seem to summon the willpower. "I can do whatever I set my mind to."

"Lil took one look at fresh goods and had only one particular job in mind. You'd be flat on your backside keepin' a mattress warm."

Hot color suffused her cheeks. She wanted to jerk free of his touch, but his grip tightened.

"Granted, you don't look the type, darlin', but where women are concerned I've been fooled before."

The timbre of his voice was seductive, smooth, and sweet as honey; his meaning, however, was bitter as quince. Scalding tears welled in her eyes, and she furiously blinked them away. Placing both hands against his chest, she pushed him away. "And where men are concerned, especially Johnny Rebs, I've been known to be wrong, too. You're nothing at all like the boy I once knew."

Picking up her skirts, Tess beat a cowardly retreat.

* * *

Nothing at all like the boy I once knew.

Tess's choked words echoed in the thick silence that
followed her departure. Zach pinched the bridge of his
nose and tried to block the ache that was beginning to
build behind his eyes. Tess was right: he was nothing
like the boy he had once been. Nothing at all.

Seeing her again stirred up old memories. Memories
he had tried to keep buried. Sometimes he succeeded.
Most times—like tonight—he failed. His transition
from idealistic boy to embittered man had been brief.
It had begun and ended with his incarceration in two
Union prison camps, first at Point Lookout in Mary-
land, then at Elmira Prison Camp in west-central New
York, six miles north of the Pennsylvania line.

Elmira—or Hellmira as it was dubbed by its in-
mates—had nearly destroyed him.

Later, after the war, Zach had learned that Elmira's
death rate topped that of its infamous Confederate
counterpart, Camp Sumter, more commonly referred
to as Andersonville. At times during his stay, he had
almost envied those who died. At least they had escaped unspeakable horrors.

Elmira had wrought changes, none of them good.
Zach removed a half-empty whiskey bottle from an
inner pocket of his vest and took a long pull. The liquor
burned his throat, heated his belly. A second swig followed. The raw whiskey was nothing like the fine
bourbon his father once favored, but it helped to soothe
frayed nerves. Helped sleep come more readily. Sleep
that was often elusive, and all too brief. Sleep haunted
by dreams of a living hell.

Zach brought out a thin cigar and, after lighting it,
sank down on one of the wooden benches, propped his
back against the wall, and stared up at the star-filled
Arizona sky. The distant howl of a coyote disturbed
the uneasy quiet. Zach restrained a wild impulse to tip

his head and howl right back. Maybe it would help to rid him of some of the anger and frustration that were bottled so tightly inside him, he felt ready to explode. He felt like a keg of blasting powder, primed and ready for someone to light the fuse. And he feared that someone had appeared in the guise of little Miss Sweet-and-Innocent herself, Tess Montgomery.

Only Tess wasn't innocent at all.

She was the person responsible for sending him to that hellhole prison. She had vowed not to disclose their whereabouts. Promised not to tell a soul. But she had lied. No one else had known where he and Jed were hiding.

He drew in a puff of smoke, then exhaled. Fortunately Jed hadn't been present when the authorities had arrived to capture him. Later, he learned Jed had eventually headed west, where he then joined a group of Confederate bushwhackers headed by William Clarke Quantrill. The group known as Quantrill's Raiders had terrorized citizens throughout the South and Southwest. Tales of their bloody rampages had become legendary. Zach had been relieved to learn that after the war Jed returned once again to a peaceable life. Many others, however, refused to change their lawless ways.

When the cigar burned to a nub and the whiskey bottle was empty, Zach stretched full-length on the hard wooden bench, pulled a blanket around his shoulders, and drifted into an uneasy slumber.

A sleep—as so often happened—haunted by images of hell.

"Get up, Reb!"

The lieutenant's command was accompanied by a shove that knocked Zach from the uppermost bunk onto

*the floor. He was hauled to his feet by two burly prison
guards.*

"Don't think you and Potts can makes fools of us. I
know you both planned the escape."

"Potts acted alone," Zach tried to explain. "I tried
to tell him it was no use, but he wouldn't listen." *The
image of Potts's bloody, bullet-riddled body was still
vivid in his memory. A. P. Potts had vainly attempted
to rush one of the guards and scale the stockade wall.
Realizing the futility of his effort, he was limping back
toward the barracks when another guard filled him
with buckshot.*

"Yer lyin'!" one of the guards barked.

*Zach's protests earned him a blow to the side of the
head that left his ears ringing.*

"You're gonna set an example, boy. After the rest of
the prisoners see what happens to anyone caught planning an escape, they'll reconsider."

"I didn't do anything, I swear."

*Zach's denial went unheeded. He was dragged un-
ceremoniously from the barracks to the center of the
compound. Once there, he was forced into a sitting
position on the ground with his knees drawn up to his
chest.*

"See how brazen you are after you've been bucked
and gagged."

*Dread flooded through Zach upon learning the pun-
ishment he was about to undergo. He opened his mouth
to lodge a protest, only to have a stick the size of a
man's thumb wedged between his jaws and secured in
place. Next his wrists were bound together with a thick
rope and slipped over his drawn-up knees. A second
stick, larger and longer than the first, was wedged under his knees then over his forearms. Unable to move,
Zach was forced to maintain this uncomfortable position while his cramped muscles screamed in protest.*

The August sun blazed unmercifully from a cloudless sky. Sweat trickled down his back and under his arms. Zach felt his skin blister under the intense rays. Flies buzzed around his head and crawled over his face and arms, yet he was helpless to knock them away. A raging thirst soon added to his misery.

As the day drew on, he was subjected to further indignity. Word of his punishment had traveled beyond the walls of the stockade. Townspeople jostled for position along the two observation platforms that had been constructed immediately outside the prison walls. For a nominal sum of fifteen cents, the citizens of Elmira and the surrounding countryside could watch him suffer. Zach was acutely aware of the barrage of insults and disparaging remarks from the onlookers. Humiliated, powerless, he teetered at the limits of his endurance.

The muscles of his arms, legs, and back felt as if they were twisted into tight knots. Zach offered a silent prayer of gratitude as nightfall approached and the crowd dispersed. A cool breeze replaced the burning sun. But soon he was beset with a problem of another sort. The temperature plummeted as boiling, dark clouds filled the sky. A summer storm broke with the fury of a woman scorned. Zach was pelted with large, frigid drops of rain that seemed to flay his sunburned flesh.

Morning found him shivering so violently he had nearly severed the wooden bit lodged between his jaws. Atop the observation platform, people were already beginning to gather, eager witnesses to his agony, his defeat. His profound and abject loss of pride and dignity.

When his bonds were finally severed and the gag removed, tears of pain made dirty tracks down his cheeks as he rocked back and forth, doubled over. The

*pain was unbearable. Spasm after spasm rippled
through him.*

"On your feet, Johnny Reb," his nemesis barked.

*Zach made a feeble attempt to stand, but his legs
buckled and refused to support his weight. He was
dragged to the barracks accompanied by the jeers of
the townspeople.*

Zach bolted upright. Disoriented, he looked around.
The dream, the insults and jeers, had seemed so real,
he expected to find a row of smug, vindictive faces
staring back at him. Instead, he saw Tess standing just
outside the door of her bedroom, her nightgown a mere
smudge of white against the darkness.

"Zach, are you all right?" she asked, her voice filled
with concern.

"What are you doing out here?" he snarled.

"I heard a noise. It sounded as though someone were
crying."

Zach's hand shook as he raked his fingers through
his hair. His whole body ached as though from ague,
but he knew well enough that the ache had to do with
the dream rather than an illness. "Can't you see no
one's crying? Now leave me alone."

She took a tentative step forward. "I only want to
help."

"Go back to bed." A thread of steel undermined the
soft command.

Tess hesitated, then retreated, disappearing like a
wraith into the shadows. Zach squeezed his eyes shut.
Shame coursed through him at his own weakness. The
nightmares, the irritability, the temper, all of these
things seemed beyond his control. He hadn't always
been like this.

Only since Elmira . . .

Seeing Tess again, hearing her ask about the war,

had stirred up a hornet's nest of memories. Zach pulled out another cigar and lit it with hands that weren't quite steady. Ever since his release, he had deliberately avoided any discussion of the war. He didn't want to think about it, didn't want to remember. That was the way he could cope with everything that had happened to him. The only way to keep sane. Otherwise, he would soon be as loony as his brother, who was only content when he was hoeing a pitiful patch of cotton.

A capricious twist of fate had brought Tess Montgomery back into his life. Tess, the woman singularly responsible for the all the pain he had suffered. Damn her to hell and back!

Four

The first thing Tess noticed the next morning was Zach's revolver on a chair next to her bed. A hastily scrawled note was propped alongside it. Carefully avoiding any contact with the gun, she picked up the slip of paper. Zach's words flowed across the page in bold, masculine script: "In the case of intruders, point gun, squeeze trigger."

She eyed the pistol much the same way she would a coiled rattlesnake. She hated guns. Loathed them. In Gettysburg's aftermath, she had witnessed their deadly destruction firsthand. She had seen how bullets ripped blood vessels, tore muscle, shattered bone. Did Zach think, even for an instant, that she could actually pick up a firearm and shoot another human being?

Turning away, she slipped into a gown of faded homespun and dressed quickly. As she reached for her hairbrush, her gaze fell once again on Zach's revolver. It was probably a Colt .44, the type referred to in stories of the Wild West that filled dime novels. Fascinated in spite of herself, she stepped closer. The gun looked heavier, larger than she had imagined. Its blue-steel barrel was oiled and slick, the walnut grip shiny and smooth. She wondered if Zach had used this gun against another. And if so, how many times? How would she react if her life were at stake—or Zach's? Would she feel differently then about picking up a gun, aiming, then firing? She hoped she never had to find out.

Then, even more disturbing thoughts slithered through her mind. Though her gaze remained fixed on the weapon, she unconsciously retreated a step. Was this the same type of weapon that had killed Jed? What kind of monster would shoot a man in the back? Intuitively she knew the answer. Only someone totally devoid of a conscience would commit such an evil, reprehensible act.

Deliberately closing her mind on the disturbing notion, she twisted her hair into a knot and left the bedroom—and the gun—behind.

Although she found no sign of Zach, she did find an orange waiting at the spot where they had eaten dinner the previous night. The small, thoughtful gesture brought a smile to her lips. Perhaps, just perhaps, there was a glimmer of softness beneath his hard exterior. A trace of gentleness, or innate kindness, that the war had failed to destroy.

The orange in her hand forgotten, she sank down on a bench, a faraway expression on her face. The changes in Zach had at first shocked, then saddened her. The Zach McClain she had encountered yesterday in Abner Smith's law office bore little resemblance to the one who inhabited her memory. This newer, changed version of Zach McClain uttered hateful words and chilled her with a glance. The charming young Confederate she remembered had lavished smiles and compliments upon her until, instead of a plain little Pennsylvania farm girl, she had felt like a princess in a fairy tale.

Slowly she began peeling the orange. Though she still might be plain, she was no longer a child who believed in fairy tales. She was a grown woman who had abandoned the security of a simple albeit unexciting existence to go in search of a new life. A woman willing to take risks. She wouldn't turn coward now no matter how intimidating she found Zach McClain.

The crackling call of a bird dragged Tess back to the present. Glancing toward the chinaberry tree tucked into a back corner of the patio, she saw a bird with brilliant yellow-and-black plumage. Upon finding a satisfactory perch among the uppermost branches, the bird began warbling a series of lazy notes. The odd sounds reminded her vaguely of the cries that had awakened her from a sound sleep the night before.

At first she had tried to convince herself the noises were those of nocturnal animals who prowled the mountainside. When they persisted, however, she had gotten out of bed to investigate. Instead of an animal she had encountered Zach—angry and defensive and lashing out. She still had no idea what had precipitated his outburst. Shaking her head, she doubted that she'd ever understand the man.

Setting thoughts of Zach aside, Tess realized the time had come to start chores. Finishing the last section of her orange, she slipped an apron over her dress, tied a kerchief over her hair, and set to work.

Caught up in a frenzy of housework, the hours passed quickly. Tess barely noticed as morning slid into afternoon. It was late afternoon when the house was finally cleaned to her satisfaction and order restored. Weary and covered with grime, she wandered through each of the rooms with a critical eye. She was pleased with the results of her labor. Although nothing fancy, she had managed to create a comfortable, homey place in which to live. She was about to take off her apron when a slight sound drew her attention. She paused to listen, her head cocked to one side.

From the patio she heard the unmistakable crunch of stealthy footsteps.

"Zach . . . ?" she called, hoping for but not really expecting an answer.

She drew in a shaky breath and tried to convince herself she had only imagined the noise. Then the sound repeated, and she knew with certainty that she was no longer alone.

"Who is it? W-what do you want?"

Her questions were met with silence. Had Jed's murderer returned? If so, he probably wouldn't hesitate to kill again. Would she be next? She pictured Zach's gun lying next to her bed exactly where he had left it and silently cursed her own stubbornness. He had tried to warn her of the dangers, but she had refused to listen.

Flattening her back against a wall, Tess turned her head and cautiously peered out a window. A shadow cast by the late afternoon sun steadily advanced toward the house. Frantically her eyes darted about, looking for something with which to defend herself, and landed on a scrub bucket half-filled with soapy water. Edging closer, she curled her fingers around the rim and hoisted the pail above her head.

She held her breath. And waited.

At last, the intruder stepped across the threshold. Tess gaped in surprise. A young Indian woman stared back, appearing, if possible, every bit as terrified as Tess.

"You like?" The woman held out a woven basket for Tess to see, heaped with dried fruits and vegetables.

Tess slowly lowered the bucket as the fear dissolved into an absurd impulse to laugh. The woman came as a peddler, not a cold-blooded killer. She had allowed her imagination to run rampant.

"You trade?"

Tess studied her uninvited guest with unabashed curiosity. Long, ink black hair rippled down the woman's back like coarse silk. She wore a simple cotton shift stretched taut across an abdomen distended in the final stages of pregnancy. Crude sandals bound with string protected the woman's feet. Tess's attention returned to the woman's face. Although she knew it was impolite to stare, she couldn't seem to drag her gaze from the double row of blue lines that extended from the corners of the woman's mouth down to her chin.

"Who are you?"

The woman ignored Tess's question.

Tess tried again, pointing to herself. "My name is Tess. What's yours?"

"Pi nyi maach."

Tess nodded, pleased at the progress. "Do you live nearby?"

"Pi nyi maach." Again the woman offered the basket for Tess's inspection.

Tess sighed. Apparently, the woman's command of English was limited. At any rate, she decided, the items Pi nyi maach had brought would make a welcome addition to the evening meal. Some of the food items she recognized; others were foreign to her. She selected squash, beans, and a handful of dried berries. "How much do I owe you?"

"Pi nyi maach," the woman returned.

Tess smothered a sigh of frustration and motioned for the woman to remain where she was. "I'll be right back."

As she hurried to retrieve coins from her purse, Tess had no way of knowing whether or not the woman understood her. When she returned moments later, however, she found Pi nyi standing exactly where she had left her.

The woman solemnly accepted the coin Tess offered, then left as quietly as she had entered. Tess stared after her, silently congratulating herself on her encounter with an Apache. If Pi nyi maach were any indication, the Apaches weren't nearly as fearsome as she had been led to believe.

The setting sun streaked the desert sky with molten gold, fiery orange, and rich vermilion. The surrounding foothills were bathed in mauve shadows, while tall spikes of saguaro cactus appeared as purple sentinels in the twilight.

Tess sighed. "I never would have believed a desert could be this beautiful."

Zach set his plate aside. He and Tess sat on adjacent benches on the patio after just having finished their evening meal. To his chagrin, he found scenery other than the desert sunset beautiful—and infinitely more distracting. He had returned to the ranch to find Tess in the kitchen, her back turned, stirring the contents of a shallow wooden bowl. Long tendrils of hair had escaped the tidy knot and trailed the slender column of her neck. Afternoon sunlight slanting into the room had burnished her chestnut locks with red and gold. He had restrained the urge to ease up behind her, place his hands at her waist, and nuzzle aside the curling wisps with a trail of kisses until she shivered with pleasure.

Tess turned to him with a smile. "Though Arizona is vastly different from Pennsylvania, it has its own unique type of beauty, don't you think?"

Zach felt as though a fist had slammed into his gut. *Damn,* he swore silently. What the hell was wrong with him? The impact of her smile jolted him clear to the soles of his feet. A purely physical reaction, he assured himself. The type any red-blooded man gets when he's gone too long without a woman. It didn't mean a thing, not a damn thing. Nevertheless his unguarded response to a woman he professed to hate rankled.

Tess ignored his scowl. "It almost makes me hope that it will take a long time to find a buyer for Casita de Oro."

"Don't go getting attached to this place," he growled. "Remember, it's only temporary. Soon as a some fool shows up with cash in his pockets, this place is history. I'll be gone so fast all you'll be able to see is my dust."

She dropped her gaze, but not before he saw hurt darken her gray eyes to the color of slate. Awareness of his ability to inflict pain brought no satisfaction. Angrily he reminded himself that her feelings were no concern of his. None at all. Still he squelched an urge to apologize.

"Supper was good," he muttered in a halfhearted attempt at amends. "Lucky for us, I caught a rabbit, but we would have had a good meal without it. You never mentioned where you found the fixings."

"I bought them," she replied smugly.

"Bought them, eh?" He tipped his head to one side and studied her through narrowed eyes. "You're one fast worker if you had time to set this mess in order, then ride into town for food."

Tess shifted uneasily. "That's not exactly what happened."

His gaze narrowed with sudden suspicion. "S'pose, then," he drawled, "you tell me *exactly* what did happen."

She took her time before answering, first setting her plate aside, then carefully brushing crumbs from her skirt. "An Indian woman, an Apache I think, came by while I was cleaning. I bought some vegetables from her."

"An Apache?" His voice sharpened. "I hope you had sense enough to have my revolver close at hand."

"No, I didn't," she admitted grudgingly. "Your gun is exactly where you left it. Though I appreciate your concern, Zach, I could never turn a gun on another."

"An Apache?" He plowed his fingers through his hair. "Don't be a fool, Tess. If you don't want to shoot somebody, fine, but at least keep a gun handy so you can fire off a round if you find yourself in trouble. Sound carries a long way in the desert. It'll bring me running on the double."

"Except for scaring me witless, the woman didn't pose a threat. In fact, she seemed rather nice." Tess stood and began gathering the dishes. "She said her name was Pi nyi maach."

"Pi nyi maach?" he repeated slowly.

Tess watched a genuine smile break across Zach's face. The change was startling. Years dropped away as she glimpsed the boy she once knew. While she looked on in amazement, Zach threw back his head and laughed, a rich, mellow sound. A wonderful sound.

Finally, he sobered, though amusement still danced in his eyes. "Darlin', I hate to tell you this, but that wasn't the woman's name."

"But," Tess protested, puzzled, "I'm sure that's what she told me."

"By any chance did your mysterious guest sport blue markings on her face?"

"Yes." Tess nodded eagerly. "Do you know her?"

"I think it can be a safe assumption the woman wasn't Apache." He pulled a cheroot from his vest pocket and lit it. "There are several peace-loving tribes in the area. The Pima and Papago refer to themselves as the Tohono O'odham, the People. According to their custom, women over the age of sixteen consider those blue lines a sign of beauty. I've also been told," he continued, "that the People do not think it wise to talk with strangers, so they answer most questions with *'pi nyi maach.'* "

"What does that translate into?"

"I don't know."

"Oh . . ." she said, disappointed at his answer. "You seem so knowledgeable, I just assumed . . ."

"I don't know."

"Of course you don't. Why should you?" She collected their dinner dishes and carried them inside.

"That's not what I meant."

Tess half-turned to find Zach standing behind her, one shoulder braced against the door frame, ankles crossed. Did he have any idea what an attractive picture he presented? He could pose for the cover of a dime novel. Tall, broad shouldered, with a rangy build. Casual grace and cool confidence. The type men wanted to emulate, the type women just plain wanted. And she was no exception. The sensation was foreign to her, made her uncomfortable. Especially the way he looked now, animosity set aside, amusement tugging the corner of his mouth. It gave her hope, made her dream.

With a supreme effort, she picked up the thread of their conversation. "Exactly what *did* you mean?"

"Pi nyi maach translates as *I don't know."*

"Ah," she said, her eyes lighting with comprehension. "I *didn't* know."

He grinned at her quip.

Anxious to prolong the camaraderie, she asked, "Tell me about your day. I assume you spent it at the mine. Did you find anything of interest?"

"Not really." He raised his shoulder and let it fall in a diffident shrug. "A played-out mine—just like Smith said we'd find. Doubt it ever showed much profit. Strange, though . . ."

"Strange? In what way?"

He stared thoughtfully at the glowing tip of the cheroot in his hand, then swung his gaze back to hers. "Can't imagine why Jed bought it in the first place."

"Maybe someone convinced him that he'd find a fortune in silver there."

"Could be," he returned, his tone ripe with skepticism. "Jed was pretty canny when it came to spending money. The mine doesn't look like he ever worked it."

"But why buy a silver mine unless you plan to look for silver?"

"Funny you should ask. That's the same question I asked myself." Drawing on his cheroot, he walked away, leaving her alone to mull over the puzzle.

The next morning, Zach announced they were going into town. He told her that while she stocked up on supplies, he would see about the livestock and settle the debt at the livery stable.

For the umpteenth time during the ride, she tugged on the narrow brim of her hat. Though pert and fashionable, the small scrap of straw afforded little protection from the glaring Arizona sun. Glancing at Zach, who rode alongside the wagon, his face shaded, his hands protected, Tess felt a flicker of envy. She fretted that her complexion would soon be ruined, with her nose sunburned and peeling and freckles splattered across her cheeks. She looked down at her hands on the thick leather reins. They would fare no better. With her only pair of gloves ruined, blisters were already starting to form.

Zach's voice interrupted her sorry inventory. "Zeckendorf's Mercantile on Main Street ought to carry just about everything we need. If not, try E. N. Fish and

Company a couple doors down. Explain who you are and tell them you want to open an account."

"What about you?" she asked.

"I'll catch up with you later."

Tess resented his high-handed attitude, but she kept her comments to herself. She couldn't help but wonder if a visit to the lush Lily London of the Silver Sequin was included on Zach's list of errands.

Leaving the wagon a short distance away, Tess entered the dry-goods store. Zeckendorf's appeared to do a brisk trade. Pausing just inside the door to take stock, she found it not much different from stores back home. Shelves were stocked with every conceivable item one might need. Barrels of rice and beans vied for floor space alongside sacks of flour and cornmeal. A display case housed an assortment of fancy buttons, ribbons, and lace. She gave the items a lingering glance, then turned away to attend to more practical matters.

"Welcome to Zeckendorf's Mercantile."

Tess glanced from the list in her hand into the smiling face of a clerk. The man appeared to be in his early thirties, of medium height, with nut brown hair combed away from a wide brow, and a full beard and mustache. A crisp white apron covered an even crisper striped shirt.

"I don't recall seeing you before. You must be new to Tucson." Shrewd brown eyes gauged her with a combination of curiosity and speculation.

Tess gave him a tentative smile. "I'm Tess Montgomery. Pleased to meet you, Mr. . . ."

"Davis," the clerk replied. "Cal Davis. I trust you'll find Zeckendorf's has everything you might need. How can I be of assistance?"

"I was hoping you'd be kind enough to allow me to open an account."

"The store will be happy to oblige, ma'am. Whereabouts are you staying?

"At the Casita de Oro, Jed Duncan's former home."

"Shame about Duncan." Cal Davis wagged his head sympathetically.

"Yes, it is," she murmured.

"Hadn't been for the buzzards circlin', no tellin' when they'da' found his body."

A shudder rippled through Tess at the image.

"Sorry, Mrs. Montgomery. Guess you didn't know all the details."

Tess picked up a can of peaches, frowned at the price, then set it back on the shelf. "And, Mr. Davis, it's *Miss* Montgomery. I'm not married."

Cal Davis scratched his beard. "Don't mean to scare you none, miss, but Duncan's ranch is a long ways outta town. It's no place for a lady all by herself."

"She's not alone."

Tess stiffened at the sound of Zach's voice directly behind her.

"Sorry, ma'am." Flustered, Cal Davis glanced from one to the other. "Guess I misunderstood. Thought I just heard you say you weren't married."

"I'm not." Tess felt heat suffuse her cheeks. She flung out her hand toward Zach. "I mean we're not."

Her explanation only seemed to make matters worse. Now it was the clerk's turn to color; whether from embarrassment or anger it was hard to tell.

"Well, I never!" A woman customer sniffed.

Tess swung around to find the same woman who, after seeing her with Lily London the day she arrived, had passed her on the street without a greeting.

"You, brazen hussy!" The woman pointed an accusing finger at Tess. "Not married and openly living with a man without benefit of matrimony. How dare you flaunt yourself in front of God-fearing folk?"

"Now, now, Miz Josie, don't get all riled. You don't want to set off one of your spells." Cal Davis, sensing they were drawing a crowd of onlookers, took the woman's arm and tried to steer her away. "Got some real nice canned goods just arrived from California."

But Josie Goodbody wasn't about to be sidetracked. She jerked free and whirled on Tess and Zach. Bright splotches of color dotted her pinched cheeks. Her pale eyes, blazing with righteous fervor and razor sharp, darted from Tess to Zach, then back to Tess. "Shame on you." She clucked her tongue in disapproval. "Tucson is struggling to become a respectable town, a place where folks will want to settle and raise families. We don't need people like you with loose morals blackening our reputation."

"Enough!" Zach stepped forward, his voice soft, his warning loud. "What we do, or don't do, is none of your damn business."

"Well, I never," she bristled. "Just because this is still frontier, young man, don't think we're uncivilized. The good citizens of Tucson will refuse to turn a blind eye to such goings-on."

Without further ado, she turned and marched out of the store in a huff, leaving a buzz of gossip in her wake.

Zach took off his hat and raked his fingers through his hair. Mortified, Tess stared at the floorboards, wishing she could sink through the cracks and disappear. Cal Davis made a shooing motion with his hands and the small crowd that had assembled reluctantly dispersed.

"Wouldn't want Josie Goodbody as my enemy," Cal muttered. "Miz Josie holds a lot of sway over the womenfolk. Everyone seems to lack the backbone to stand up against her once she's on a crusade."

Zach offered his hand and introduced himself to the

clerk. "You seem like a reasonable man, Davis. It's not the way Miss Goodbody seems to think. Miss Montgomery and I have jointly inherited Jed Duncan's property. Until a buyer is found, we're stuck living under the same roof."

Frowning, Cal tugged his earlobe. "Harmless or not, folks are apt to draw certain conclusions about you living together."

"We can't be responsible for what others think," Tess said, adopting a reasonable tone. "All we want to do is open an account."

The clerk continued to look discomfited. "If it was up to me, folks, I'd be happy to oblige, but my boss might see things differently."

"Forget about credit." Zach dug into his pocket, produced a wad of cash, peeled off several bills, and tossed them on the counter. "Before you pack up our things, there are a couple more items I want to add to our order."

Zach strolled over to a corner devoted to ladies' apparel. His gaze swept over the items on display before finding what he was looking for. "This ought to do," he said, plucking a straw hat from a hook and thrusting it at Tess.

Her brows drew together in a puzzled frown. The hat was perfect, she realized, with a wide brim and pale-blue ribbon, something she would have chosen herself. She tried to catch Zach's eye for an explanation, but he was studying the contents of a display case.

"I also need gloves, leather ones." He caught Tess by the wrist and held up her hand. "About this size."

Cal Davis sorted through a box and produced a suitable pair. The clerk's manner, Tess noted, had become almost deferential after seeing Zach's money. "Will there be anything else, sir?"

Zach nodded. "A pistol. Something small enough to

fit a lady's hand, yet powerful enough to get the job done."

"No!" Tess caught his sleeve. "You know how I feel about guns."

Ignoring her outburst, Zach shook off her touch as easily as he might a pesky fly. "Show me what you have."

Reaching beneath a counter, Cal brought out a felt-lined box containing a variety of firearms. Fascinated in spite of herself, Tess looked on as Zach selected several for closer inspection. After testing their weight in the palm of his hand, he looked down the sights and examined the grips.

"We'll take this one," he said at last.

"Good choice. Can't go wrong with a Smith and Wesson." Cal slapped a box of shells next to the pistol. "I'll even throw in the ammunition."

While the clerk tallied up the amount, Tess drew Zach aside. "You have a lot of nerve," she whispered angrily. "What will people think when they find out you've been buying me gifts?"

"Same thing they think already." A muscle worked in his jaw, the only indication of temper. "That we're living in sin."

Tess bit her lower lip to keep it from trembling. "Maybe your reputation doesn't matter to you, but mine matters to me."

Zach folded his arms across his chest, unmoved. "Then find another place to stay."

"I can't," she blurted, her voice choked.

"Can't?" He quirked a sandy brow. "Or won't?"

"Both." His green eyes bored into hers, but she stubbornly refused to look away. "Casita de Oro is as much mine as it is yours. No one is going to drive me away. No one," she repeated, then stormed out of the store.

Zach hefted the box of supplies onto one shoulder and followed.

Tess ignored him as he loaded the items into the back of the wagon. Finally, Zach had had enough. "Stop behaving like a fool."

"A fool?" She rounded on him.

"Yes, you heard me, a fool." Fine, Zach thought, if she was hankering for a fight, so was he. "Where do you think you are, at a garden party?"

"I don't want you to buy me things. I don't want a gun. And," she practically spit the words, "I don't want people thinking we're sharing a bed."

He stepped closer, but she retreated, until her back was pressed against the side of the wagon. "Let's set matters straight. I don't care what a bunch of strangers think. Survival is the name of the game. And when it comes to being a survivor, darlin', I'm an expert."

She opened her mouth to speak, but he cut her off. "Like it or not, we're in this together. I'm not about to sit back and do all the work because your hands are blistered and bleeding, or you're too sick from sunstroke to do your share. I don't want to find buzzards circling your dead body because you were too damn ignorant to defend yourself. Understand?"

"Fine," she agreed, her expression mutinous. "After we sell the ranch, I'll pay back every cent."

"Damn right you will." He swung into the saddle, leaving her to climb into the wagon unassisted. "First thing tomorrow, be ready to learn how to use that gun."

Five

His eyes steady on hers, Zach placed the Smith and Wesson on the scarred table between them. His expression defied her to challenge him. Her lower lip jutted mutinously, but Tess decided wisely to keep her comments unspoken.

Zach stuffed a box of shells into his pocket, then picked up the gun and headed out the door. "No sense putting it off."

There seemed little else for Tess to do but follow him across the patio, past the corral and outbuildings and into the hills beyond.

Traces of snow lingered in the uppermost peaks of the distant mountain range. Saguaro, prickly pear, and ocotillo studded the desert floor. Here and there she passed paloverde trees bedecked with tiny yellow blossoms. An otherwise perfect morning, Tess mused, were it not for the approaching lesson.

"Stay close behind me," Zach fired back over his shoulder. "Don't expect me to be around every time you land in trouble. Time you become responsible for your own safety."

"Funny, I don't recall appointing you as my bodyguard."

"Don't flatter yourself. I've got better things to do than baby-sit a stubborn female."

"Until now I've managed to fend for myself quite nicely," she reminded him.

He skirted a tall stand of cactus. "Not to mention Jed's killer still on the loose, have you considered how you'd defend yourself against an Apache raiding party? There are few folks in these parts who haven't lost a friend or relative to an Apache arrow."

She nearly stumbled. Although she knew it foolish, her eyes scanned the distant hills as though half-expecting to see a horde of Indians descending.

"And it's not just humans you should fear," Zach continued, warming to the subject. "What would you do if you met up with a bobcat? Or came across a rattlesnake?"

Tess held up her hands in defeat. "All right, enough. You convinced me."

"Took long enough," he muttered.

For their initial session, he selected a relatively flat stretch of terrain. He waited until she reached his side before beginning his lecture.

"Yours is a thirty-eight-caliber Smith and Wesson. You'll see it's noticeably smaller than the one I carry." His hand rested lightly on the butt of the gun strapped to his waist. "Mine's a Colt forty-four commonly referred to as Peacemaker. But big or small, it doesn't matter. Even a derringer can be deadly at close range."

She tried not to think of Jed, who had been ruthlessly gunned down in his own home—her home now—his body left for the vultures. "Tell me what to do," she said resignedly.

"That's a good girl."

Tess tried to convince herself that the flutter in her stomach was caused by nerves, and not by the warm note of approval in his voice.

He adopted a businesslike tone. "Now pay close attention while I show you how to load a revolver."

Tess inched closer until her arm brushed his. Her brow wrinkled in concentration as she watched him break open the cylinder and slip the bullets into the chambers. He had beautiful hands, she thought, distracted by the long, tapered fingers that seemed better suited to playing a piano than loading a gun.

He glanced up suddenly and caught her staring. He was close, so close she could see flecks of gold in the green of his eyes. He had beautiful hands—and beautiful eyes. Once they had laughed together, shared secrets, dreams. She had dared consider him a friend. She suddenly wished it could be that way again.

"If you dislike me so intensely, why do you care whether or not I can protect myself?" The question came straight from her heart, bursting free before she could stop it.

"Good question, darlin'. Damned if I know." Squinting slightly, he stared down the barrel of the gun and squeezed the trigger. In the distance, the blossom at the tip of a spindly ocotillo cactus exploded in a flurry of orange.

Tess wordlessly watched petals drift to the ground like specks of blood. Zach's cold indifference flayed like a knife. He had erected a wall around his feelings that was impossible to scale. A feeling of hopelessness washed over her, along with a profound sense of loss.

"Guess you could blame my temporary lapse of judgment on my upbringin'." He blew on the smoking barrel of his Colt. "My mama raised her sons to be defenders of the fairer sex. Chivalry lives on, so it seems. It's an inbred flaw in most of us Southerners," he drawled, "even when the woman happens to be Yankee."

She sucked in her breath at his deliberate cruelty,

then succumbed to the urge to strike back. "How many times do I have to remind you, Johnny Reb, the war's over?" she said coldly. "Quit wasting my time. Let's get on with the lesson."

His eyes narrowed, but not before she read the surprise at her curt rejoinder. Seeing it gave her a small measure of satisfaction.

"Fine," he grunted, handing her the gun he had purchased for her.

The Smith and Wesson felt heavier than she had expected. Heavy and cold. Ominous.

While Zach lined up a series of small rocks to use as targets on a nearby ledge, Tess surreptitiously wiped her sweaty palms on her skirt. As much as she had opposed the idea of firing a gun, now she found herself equally determined to learn. It was obvious that Zach considered her a burden. And that was the last thing she wanted to be. She'd prove she could take care of herself—even if it meant learning how to shoot a pistol.

"Don't be afraid of it," he snapped. "It's not going to bite."

She gave him a resentful look. In spite of her resolve, some of her squeamishness must have shone through. "Point gun and squeeze trigger," she quoted the instructions he had left along with his Colt. "How difficult can it be?"

With a muttered oath, he positioned himself behind her. "Rule number one, keep your finger off the trigger until you're ready to shoot."

"What's rule number two?"

He ignored her question. "Raise your right arm. Not so fast, slower," he cautioned. "Like this."

The beat of her heart doubled as his body lightly molded itself alongside hers. She found herself wanting to lean closer, press even more firmly against his whipcord strength. Her reaction shocked her. Appalled her. Maybe she was no better than the brazen hussy Josie Goodbody assumed she was. Intuitively sensing the danger of such proximity, she started to pull away, but Zach's left arm wound around her waist, holding her firmly in place.

"Don't be skittish."

His voice poured over her, thick and slow and rich as molasses. His breath softly fanned her cheek. Suddenly consumed with heat, she shifted position. She glanced up at the sky. Had the sun suddenly grown hotter? Although the morning was warm, she realized the heat she was experiencing came from deep within. Dear Lord! Did Zach have any idea of the effect he had on her?

"Steady, now," he coached. He adjusted his stance slightly, then, with his hand over hers, raised her arm until it was extended in front of her. "Just look straight down the barrel and line up the sight with your intended target."

She drew in a breath to calm her nerves and inhaled his essence instead. Leather and soap and sunshine mingled with the slight tang of tobacco. His scent had a potent effect on her senses, made her forget everything but the man behind her. Her eyelids drifted shut; her concentration evaporated.

"C'mon, Tess," he said, his tone no longer cajoling but impatient. "Keep your eyes shut and you won't come within a hundred yards of your target."

Embarrassed, she renewed her effort to pay attention. "Maybe this isn't such a good idea," she murmured.

Zach continued as though she hadn't spoken. "Zero in on your target, then curl your index finger over the trigger . . . and squeeze."

The loud blast echoed in her ears.

All the targets remained untouched.

"I missed."

"All things considered, that's not surprising."

After firing off six shots without striking a target, Tess refilled the cylinder while Zach observed. "Good," he said with a nod of approval. "Let's try a two-handed method until you get accustomed to holding a gun."

He stood directly behind her, widened his stance, then pulled her back against his chest, her head tucked beneath his chin. "See if this works any better."

Having to learn how to shoot a gun was bad enough, but being this close to Zach was sheer torture. Tess was acutely aware of his hard-muscled length pressed along her spine. And the unmistakable bulge of his manhood. Desire coiled like a serpent in the pit of her stomach, waiting to sink its sharp fangs. Even without being bitten, she knew she'd find its venom sensual and erotic. It would make her want what she couldn't have. Make her feel things she shouldn't.

Holding his arms parallel with hers, Zach placed his hands over hers and took aim. "Shooting a gun's not all that difficult if you just focus on your target."

Tess forced herself to concentrate. Gritting her teeth, she squeezed the trigger. And could have wept with relief when a bullet ricocheted off one of the rocks with a satisfying *ping*.

Flushed with success, she turned to Zach with a smile. Instantly he released her and stepped back. Her smile quickly faded into concern when she saw the fine bead of moisture lining his upper lip. "Are you all right?"

"Blasted heat," he muttered. Taking out a handkerchief, he wiped the perspiration from his face. "I think you've got the idea. All you need now is practice. Lots and lots of practice."

Careful to remember Zach's instructions, Tess reloaded the revolver and took aim. Her efforts were rewarded by the whine of a bullet striking rock with increasing regularity. By the time Zach decided she had had enough for one day, her arms quivered with fatigue.

"Not bad for the first time," he grudgingly conceded. "We'll try this again tomorrow."

"Tomorrow?"

"Tomorrow," he repeated firmly. "And every day after that until you can hit the broadside of a barn with some degree of proficiency." He turned in the direction of the ranch.

Tess followed. "In case you haven't noticed, there aren't any barns."

"This isn't some kind of joke. Your life could depend on how seriously you take these lessons."

"And I think, Zach McClain, you take everything much too seriously. You seldom smile and rarely laugh. You've changed over the years, and not for the better."

He stopped so abruptly that Tess skidded to a halt to avoid crashing into him. He turned and glowered at her. "Maybe there's a damn good reason for the change."

His green eyes blazed with fury. Tess felt herself shrivel under their force. His gaze drilled into her, through her. He seemed to be waiting for her to say something, do something, but she had no idea what that could possibly be. Almost as though he expected an explanation, a confession. Or an apology.

"I don't understand you anymore. Tell me what's wrong."

His breath hissed between his teeth as he visibly fought to control the demons raging within. "I can't look at you without remembering the worst years of my life," he said, his voice raw with emotion. "The less time I'm forced to be in your company, the happier I'll be."

Tess watched his long strides carry him down the incline. The day no longer seemed bright and beautiful. Zach's hatred of her was a living, breathing entity. A monster that struck with cruelty and cunning. She raised her hand in a gesture of helplessness, then let it drop to her side. "What did I do?" she asked in an agonized whisper.

But Zach was a long way ahead of her and either didn't hear her question or refused to reply. One thing was blindingly clear to Tess: She needed an answer. Needed to know what had caused this rift between them.

Picking up her skirts, she raced after him. Her feet slipped on a patch of loose gravel, and she slid toward a tall cactus with myriad irregular, protruding branches. She reached out to halt her slide. Suddenly, she let out a sharp cry of pain. Her arm burned as though it were on fire, the agony so intense that tears streamed down her cheeks. Through a haze of tears, she saw a cluster of three-inch-long needles protruding from her upper arm. Blood dotted the sleeve of her cotton blouse where they had pierced the fabric.

Zach, upon hearing her cry, stopped and turned. "What's wrong? A rattler? Did it bite?"

Stinging, fiery pain robbed her of speech. Mutely, she shook her head. She attempted to jerk her arm free, but to her horror, the cactus assumed a life of its own. It seemed to spring toward her with diabolical glee. Within seconds another cluster of needles was imbedded next to the first. Tess bit her lower lip to keep from screaming.

Zach ran to her side and assessed the situation in an instant. "Good Lord, girl, didn't anyone tell you to keep away from jumping cholla?"

She sniffed back tears but couldn't keep the tremor from her voice. "You warned me about murderers, Apaches, bobcats, and rattlers, but you failed to mention cactus."

"That, darlin', was lesson number two," he said as he picked her up and carried her toward the house.

Zach, careful not to jostle her injured arm, placed her on the bed. "Stay put and don't try to move. I'll be right back."

As if she was about to dance a jig when her arm felt as though it had been stung by a dozen hornets, Tess thought with a trace of resentment. How was she to know an innocent-appearing tree would unexpectedly attack and turn her into a human pincushion? Glancing downward, she saw six long needles protruding from her arm just above the elbow.

Zach reappeared in the doorway with several objects in his hands. "I know, darlin'," he commiserated. "It hurts like the devil."

She exhaled a ragged breath. "Do whatever you have to do, but get them out of my arm."

Setting the items on a small table next to her bed, he stared thoughtfully at her injured arm, then nodded. "The first thing we need to do is get you out of that blouse."

"You want me to undress?" In spite of her discomfort, her voice rose in disbelief.

He rubbed his chin. " 'Course I could cut the sleeve off, but it seems a damn shame to ruin such a pretty garment."

Her resolve wavered. She didn't want to lie exposed beneath Zach's gem-green gaze, but neither did she want her favorite blouse sliced to ribbons. "Can't you just jerk them out the same way you would a thorn or a sliver?"

" 'Fraid not, sweetheart. Cholla have little barbs that bury themselves beneath the skin. If they're not completely removed, they can set up an infection."

"Fine," she snapped, the pain making her irritable.

"Here." Zach handed her a blanket. "Use this to protect your modesty."

Using her uninjured arm, Tess covered herself with the blanket, then slowly unfastened the long row of tiny buttons. When she was finished, Zach ignored her half-formed protest and eased her into a sitting position. Keeping his expression impassive, he carefully removed the blouse from one shoulder, then slowly but firmly eased the sleeve down the other.

Tess bit back a scream of pain as the thin, sharp needles slipped through the fabric. Zach tossed the blouse aside. He studied her face for a moment in silence, frowned, then left the room only to return moments later with a bottle of whiskey.

She eyed the bottle suspiciously. "If you think for one minute I'm going to . . ."

He uncorked the bottle with his teeth and held it to her lips. "Drink."

"But . . ." She opened her mouth to object only to have Zach pour it full of the vile-tasting spirits.

"Take your choice, darlin', you can either swallow or choke." He levered her backward and tipped the bottle higher. "I suggest you swallow, 'cause one way or another you're going to take your medicine. And you can thank me later."

She struggled frantically, using her good arm to push against his chest, but he was relentless. At last, she ceased fighting him and swallowed noisily, then gasped for air. The whiskey scalded her throat, burning its way to her stomach. "Just you wait, Zach McClain," she wheezed. "I swear I'll get you for this."

"I like a woman with spirit." Again he held the bottle to her mouth and tilted it, forcing her to drink until whiskey dribbled out the corners of her mouth. Satisfied she had had enough, he set the bottle aside and perched on the edge of the mattress. Using the corner of the blanket, he dabbed whiskey from her chin. "Trust me, I'm not one to waste good alcohol. Removing cholla needles isn't going to be a pleasant experience for either of us."

Eyes streaming, stomach aflame, Tess glared up at him with all the venom she could muster. If her arm didn't hurt quite so much, she would have told him in no uncertain terms what she thought of his caveman tactics.

Zach wiped the tears from her cheeks with the pads of his thumbs. "If it helps, think of the whiskey as an anesthetic. During the war, soldiers would have sold their own mothers to lessen their pain."

Gradually the discomfort in her arm became more tolerable. Though it still burned and stung, she felt somehow detached from it. She began to feel as though she were floating, drifting on gentle currents of air. And sleepy; she felt very, very sleepy. "Let's get rid of the cholla," she said, stifling a yawn. "I want to take a nap."

"Fine by me, darlin'. You've had a busy morning."

Tess shrank back into the mattress when she saw him reach for the whiskey, but this time instead of forcing it down her throat, he poured it over the puncture sites. She sucked in a sharp breath at the sting. Blinking a sheen of moisture from her eyes, she saw him take a pocket comb from his vest.

While she observed in wide-eyed fascination, he skillfully inserted the teeth of the comb under the cactus spine and flicked it away. "The trick is to do this so that the needle doesn't flip back into your skin. Now hold real still, while I pull out the rest."

Tess bit her lip and stared at the ceiling as he repeated the process. Each time he tugged one of the barbs free, she felt a spurt of gratitude that he had forced her to drink the spirits to ease the pain. It galled her to realize he had been right when he predicted she'd thank him later.

At last, he leaned back, the task completed. "There," he said, "your arm ought to feel better already."

"Much," she admitted, giving him a watery smile. "I'm sorry for being such a baby."

"You did just fine." He brushed a damp curl from her cheek, then absently ran his fingers down the length. "You should have seen the way I carried on first time I met up with a cholla."

She studied him curiously, uncertain whether he was serious or simply teasing. "I can't imagine a man like you ever screaming or carrying on."

His expression hardened into a cold, aloof mask. "A little more alcohol to stop any infection . . ."

Just as he raised the whiskey bottle, a feminine voice trilled, "Hello, there. Anybody home?"

Tess and Zach turned immobile, so still their figures could have been carved in marble. Before they recovered from their initial surprise, Josie Goodbody poked her head into the bedroom. Her eyes darted from one to the other, absorbing every detail: Tess half-clothed, Zach bending over her, a whiskey bottle in one hand.

Josie clutched her handbag to her chest. "Oh my, oh dear!" she exclaimed. "It's worse than I thought. Much worse."

Tess grabbed for the blanket, which was bunched around her waist, and held it to her chest. Ignoring the pain in her arm, she wriggled herself into an upright position. "Mrs. Goodbody," she managed. "What a surprise."

Josie Goodbody entered the room followed by a tall scarecrow of a man dressed in a shiny black broadcloth suit. Long sideburns framed his angular features, and a pencil-thin mustache decorated his upper lip.

Zach rose to his feet and, clearly annoyed, faced his unexpected visitors. "What do you two want?"

Josie Goodbody straightened her narrow shoulders and thrust out her chin. "I brought Reverend Tobias Miller, who happens to be a preacher traveling through these parts, to talk sense into you. Help you see the error of your ways." Her noise wrinkled as she sniffed the air like a bloodhound in pursuit of its prey. "What's that smell?"

"Spirits," Reverend Miller intoned solemnly. "The root of all evil."

Josie's eyes rounded in horror. "Can you pray for them, Reverend?"

"Oh, sweet Jesus," Tobias Miller cried, rolling his eyes heavenward. "Help these sinners repent of their disgraceful behavior. Help them see Thy light."

Quivering in righteous indignation, Josie pointed an accusing finger at Zach. "Mr. McClain, have you been plying this young woman with liquor, then having your way with her?"

Before he could reply, Tess hiccuped. Loudly. The single syllable dropped like a stone in a still pool.

All eyes shifted to her flushed face. And she hiccuped again.

"An abomination!" Josie declared in disgust.

The clergyman bestowed the full power of his wrath on Zach. "Are you prepared to do the right thing by this young lady? Make an honest woman of her?"

"Get out," Zach ordered, his voice low, his temper tightly leashed.

"You don't understand," Tess tried explain. "It's not the way it looks."

"I have eyes in my head, Miss Montgomery. Don't think I'm fooled for a minute. We find you half-clothed, in bed with a man, the room reeking of whiskey. And, to make matters worse," she said, shaking a bony finger for emphasis, "it isn't even noon yet."

Tess gaped at the woman in astonishment. Then did the unforgivable. She giggled.

"Well!" Josie's face went from red to an unflattering shade of purple. Pivoting on her heel, she flounced from the room, the preacher close at her heels. "Never in my born days."

An odd combination of sounds erupted from Tess, part hiccup, part giggle. Embarrassed, she clapped her hand over her mouth to muffle her merriment. The harder she tried, the more impossible they became to control.

Zach shot her an amused look and shook his head. "Some people just can't hold their liquor."

For some unknown reason, his comment sparked a new series of giggles. When they finally subsided, she slunk down on the mattress and rolled onto her side, facing the wall. "Go away," she mumbled. "I'm tired. When I wake up, I want to find this has all been a bad dream."

"Sleep tight, darlin'. You've had an eventful day—and it's not even noon yet."

As Tess drifted off to sleep, she wondered if she imagined the sound of Zach laughing.

Six

Before riding out to the mine, Zach looked in at Tess one last time. She was sound asleep, rolled into a ball, one hand tucked beneath her chin, the other stretched on the pillow. Soft and defenseless as a kitten. He wondered if she'd purr if petted. He caught himself about to graze her cheek with his fingertips, and pulled back in self-disgust.

Living under the same roof day in and day out was straining his resolve to maintain an emotional distance. Tess had a way about her that constantly chipped away at the wall he had erected. A sweetness, an innocence, that eroded barriers. A physical appeal that hit him with the force of a sledgehammer. He could still remember how she had stared at him, the cholla needles protruding from her arm. Shock and pain had glazed her eyes, making them appear molten silver. Her mouth, pink as a rosebud, had quivered ever so slightly, captured his unwilling attention. And now, even in her sleep, she tempted his willpower. Her skin, pale and satiny-smooth, reminded him of the magnolias that once graced Briarwood, his family's home. Her breasts, rounded and full, strained the tissue-thin cotton chemise and threatened to overflow their confines. His manhood hardened at the teasing glimpse of nipple clearly visible. Summer berries sprang to mind, wild and sweet. He fisted his hands to keep from touching. But more than touch, he wanted to taste.

Disgusted with his wayward thoughts, disgusted with himself, he left the house with long angry strides. He quickly saddled his horse and rode off. The road, little more than a trail, wound westward, then climbed into the Tucson Mountains. Had it not been for Abner Smith's directions, a passerby could easily miss the turnoff to the mine.

Zach let his thoughts wander. Ever since the days of the California gold rush, Arizona had attracted prospectors. Though dreams of gold first attracted miners to the area, the promise of silver kept them here. A steady parade of hopefuls pried and poked their way through the Sonoran desert with the persistence of prairie dogs. Expectation soared with new strikes reported in the central part of the territory. Prospectors investigated every rocky ridge and crevice, willing to take risks and sometimes losing their scalps in the bargain. Not even the Civil War had deterred their efforts.

Had Jed purchased the mine in the hope of finding a mother lode? Or had some unsavory character salted the mine to convince a gullible victim to part with his life savings? From what he had seen thus far, Zach suspected the latter was true in Jed's case.

Upon reaching his destination, Zach dismounted and tossed the reins over a low hanging branch of a paloverde. He stood for a moment, hands on hips, and surveyed the area. Nothing appeared changed from his last visit. Rough-hewn timbers formed a lopsided frame around the narrow opening gouged into the mountainside. Giant monoliths flanked either side of the entrance.

Zach approached slowly and, upon entering, found the lantern just inside the opening—exactly where he had left it. The mine was a seemingly endless maze of tunnels, some relatively short, others long and meandering. None had turned up anything of particular interest thus far. Today, he decided, he'd explore a branch running perpendicular to the main artery.

Within minutes, the temperature took a noticeable plunge, the air cool and clammy after the dry Arizona heat. Blackness closed around him like a tight glove, making him grateful for the lantern's jaundiced glow. Somewhere in the distance Zach heard the faint drip, drip, drip of an underground spring. Ignoring the scrabble of rodents, he advanced farther into the passageway. The beam of light fell on a metal wagon directly in front of him. A pickax stood propped against one wall. Chunks of rocks were strewn everywhere. He felt a glimmer of excitement. Was this where Jed had hoped to strike it rich?

Thumbing back the brim of his hat, Zach studied the scene in front of him. His initial optimism vanished, replaced by a nagging sensation something was wrong. Raising the lantern above his head, he peered into the cart only to find it empty. Next, he swept the shaft of light over the floor. Rocks were scattered in a random pattern rather than piled ready for loading. And why not just put them in the wagon in the first place? He rubbed his jaw. Odd, he thought, if he didn't know better he would think the cart had been unloaded instead of waiting to be loaded. But who would do such a fool thing? And why?

Squatting on his haunches, he set the lantern down, picked up one of the rocks, and examined it. He turned it first one way, then the other, trying to solve the puzzle. He didn't claim to know all that much about silver, but he was determined to learn all he could. He remembered once hearing a prospector claim silver was much more difficult to recognize than gold. Frowning, he tried to recall that conversation. If memory served, it had something to do with its color. Depending upon what other ore silver combined with, its color could range anywhere from white to dark blue. The clump of rock he held gave no hint of any value. Frustrated, he dashed the chunk to the ground. Much to his surprise, instead of shattering into fragments, the rock flattened but otherwise withstood the impact.

"Interesting," he muttered, picking up the rock and staring at it thoughtfully. "Damn interesting."

As he got to his feet, a plan began to form. He tossed the rock into the air, then caught it. He'd ship it off to an assay office, maybe even one all the way in California. It was worth good money to find out if this was a useless chunk of rock, or something far more valuable. For the time being, he would keep this to himself. No sense mentioning it to Tess. Granted, she was an equal partner in this venture, entitled to a half share of the profits, but this was pure speculation. He had no reason to trust Tess to keep his secret. He had trusted her once before—in another place, another life—and she had failed miserably.

Stepping out of the mine into the bright sunshine, Zach paused, waiting for his eyes to adjust. His earlier question came back to taunt him. Why would anyone unload a cart and carelessly discard its contents? He nearly dropped the rock he held as the answer became glaringly obvious.

Unless that person was searching for something else.

Something far more valuable than silver.

Yawning broadly, Tess stretched, then winced. Her eyes flew open and rested on the bandage tied around her upper arm. Events of that morning flooded back and she groaned aloud. The cholla. Zach's brusque yet gentle treatment. Josie Goodbody's untimely visit. Her own series of embarrassing hiccups and giggles. It hadn't been a nightmare after all.

Her gaze shifted to the blouse draped over the back of a chair, one sleeve speckled with rust-colored stains. No wonder Josie Goodbody and her friend, Reverend Miller, had leaped to their conclusions. What else could they have thought at finding her half-naked with a man in her bed, and the room smelling like a distillery? And in the middle of the day? In the woman's mind, being caught fornicating was just cause for condemnation, but being caught fornicating in the middle of the day was unpardonable.

Tess swung her legs over the edge of the bed and sat up. Except for a dull headache, probably the result of the whiskey Zach had forced down her throat, she felt fine. She caught sight of her reflection in the mirror above a small chest and winced again. With her hair streaming wildly about her shoulders and wearing a chemise worn thin by numerous launderings, she matched her own description of a loose woman. Lily London would take one look and hire her on the spot to service her customers.

Tess cocked her head to one side and listened, but the house was quiet. She had no notion of where Zach had gone, but was grateful that he was occupied elsewhere. After washing her face and hands, she felt immeasurably better. She slipped into a lavender-blue dress sprigged with tiny yellow flowers, then brushed her hair and tied it neatly in the back with a yellow ribbon.

Feeling immeasurably better, she decided to enjoy what remained of the beautiful spring day. This was the perfect opportunity to indulge in her favorite pastime. Sorting through her collection of dime novels, she selected one of her all-time favorites, *Street and Smith's New York Weekly.* She settled on a shaded bench on the patio. Within minutes of opening the worn cover, Tess was immersed in the adventures of Buffalo Bill, the King of the Border Men.

She was so engrossed in the tale that she failed to hear riders approaching. The dime novel fell from her lap at the sound of pounding on the front door. Her heart pounding equally hard against her ribs, she leaped to her feet. She stood gnawing her lower lip in indecision. She hadn't seen the Smith and Wesson since morning and, even if she had, she was far from proficient with it. Apaches wouldn't knock on doors. Murderers probably didn't either, she reasoned, but she had little personal knowledge on which to base her opinion.

The knocking sounded again. She approached the door cautiously, knowing whoever was on the opposite side could easily gain entry. "Who is it?" she called out, hoping her voice didn't betray her nervousness.

"No call to be afraid, ma'am," replied a male voice heavy with an accent from the deep South. "We're old friends of Jed Duncan. Come to pay a visit."

Tess felt her pulse steady. She eased open the door a crack and discovered two men standing on her doorstep. One was tall and rather handsome with wavy brown hair and bright blue eyes. The other stood considerably shorter with a wiry build, mousy blond hair, and small, deep-set eyes of no particular color.

"How do you do, ma'am?" A dimple flashed in the taller man's cheek as he grinned boyishly. "Sure hope this ain't a bad time to call."

"No," she said, summoning a smile. "Not at all."

"Name's Jimmy Jerold." The good-looking one doffed his hat. He motioned toward his companion.

"This here's my friend, Moe Black. We rode with Jed during the war."

"I'm Tess Montgomery. Any friends of Jed are always welcome here. Please, come in." She stood aside and invited them to enter.

The pair stepped inside and looked around, silently cataloging the lack of furniture in the small parlor in a way that made her uneasy.

His curiosity appeased, Jimmy bestowed another of his charming smiles on Tess. "Ol' Jed was one lucky cuss. How did that ol' buzzard manage to attract such a fine looking woman as yerself?"

Tess felt her cheeks grow warm. "Jed and I were friends. Nothing more."

"Where is that ornery codger, anyway?" Jimmy glanced over his shoulder expectantly.

Tess experienced a sinking sensation in the pit of her stomach. Neither of Jed's friends knew about his murder. She cleared her throat, took a deep breath, then tried to break the sad news as gently as possible. "I'm sorry to be the bearer of bad news, but Jed is dead."

"Dead . . . ?" Jimmy's jaw dropped in disbelief. Moe simply lowered his gaze and studied the floor.

"I know this must come as a shock."

"I can't believe it." Jimmy slowly shook his head from side to side. "Jed was always the picture of health. Never knew of him to take sick."

"Why don't you step out on the patio while I fetch us something cold to drink?" Tess suggested. "It'll give you a little time to get over the shock of Jed's death. Afterwards, I'll be happy to share what little I know about it."

"That's mighty kind of you, ma'am, but my friend and I don't want to be a bother."

"You're not in the least."

After ushering them through the house and onto the patio, Tess went into the kitchen, where she set three mismatched glasses and a chipped pitcher with lemonade on a wooden tray. She wished she had something more to offer her guests—fresh baked cookies or cake—but this was the best she could do. Jimmy rose to his feet the instant he saw her return with a heavy tray. Following a pointed look from his friend, Moe Black belatedly did likewise.

"Please, gentlemen, be seated."

Jimmy took the tray from her and set it on the bench. "Mighty thoughtful of you, ma'am. We're awful parched after our dusty ride up from Mexico."

Tess smiled as she poured lemonade and handed each man a glass. "What part of the South are you from, Mr. Jerold?"

Moe Black snickered at the formal use of his friend's name. Once again Jimmy shot him a silent rebuke, and he ceased.

"We hail from the fine state of Tennessee. And"—his dimple winked with wicked impudence—"friends call me Jimmy."

"And some folks call 'im 'Gentleman' Jimmy," Moe volunteered with a sly smile.

"You didn't say if you preferred to be called Miss or Missus." Jimmy regarded her with frank admiration.

Tess realized with a start that the man was actually flirting with her. Jimmy Jerold possessed an engaging charm, and from his manner, Tess guessed he was well versed in its effect on women. It was hard to take offense, however, when he flashed that choir-boy grin. She sat down and sipped her drink. "It's Miss, but please call me Tess."

"Miss?" A speculative gleam brightened Jimmy's bright blue eyes at the announcement. "I guess this here is my lucky day. No business of mine, of course,

Tess, but what's a pretty little thing like you doing so far from town? It isn't safe for a woman, what with Apaches still running wild."

"She's not alone."

The three people on the patio turned in the direction of Zach's voice. Moe's hand flew to the handle of the gun riding low on one hip. For a man whose movements could only be termed sluggish until this moment, his reflexes proved amazingly quick.

Tess held her breath. Her eyes nervously darted from one man to the other. Zach stood, feet lightly planted, his right hand brushing his holster. While his stance appeared relaxed, she sensed the coiled tension, the wariness, the alertness. Malice glittered in Moe Black's small eyes, along with an eagerness to pull the trigger. Tess looked to Jimmy for help in controlling his friend's impulsive behavior. Instead of finding an ally, he seemed to be enjoying the spectacle of two men pitted against each other.

"Z-Zach," she stammered. "These are friends of Jed."

At last, Jimmy came to her rescue. "Now, now, boys," he drawled. "No reason why we can't all be friends. No reason t'all."

"Tell your watchdog to back off." Though Zach addressed Jimmy, he kept his eyes fastened on Moe.

"Who you callin' a dog?" Moe snarled.

Jimmy clucked his tongue. "Don't go scarin' the little lady, Moe. Now tell her you don't mean no harm."

"Sorry," Moe grunted, his expression sullen.

Tess let out a deep breath when Moe's hand left his gun and reached for his drink. She did't realize until then that her hands were shaking. "Gentlemen, this is Zach McClain, my partner."

"Partner . . . ?" Jimmy raised one brow. "My, my, isn't that interestin'?"

Heat cascaded through her at his tone. Tess felt herself flush from the roots of her hair to the tips of her toes.

"Yes, partners," Zach snapped. "As in *business* partners."

Moe muttered something unintelligible under his breath but subsided at a warning glance from Jimmy.

Tess rose to her feet and stood beside Zach. "According to the terms of Jed's will, Zach and I inherited equally."

"So you each own half, eh?" Jimmy tugged his earlobe. "Strange sort of arrangement if you ask me. What do you suppose made ol' Jed do somethin' like that?"

"I don't see where that's any of your concern." Zach's voice was as cold as his eyes.

"Ah, but it does matter," Jimmy corrected smoothly.

Folding his arms across his chest, Zach leaned against the doorway. "And how's that?"

Jimmy drained his glass, then stood. "Now that I've been assured you and the pretty Tess are strictly business partners, you can't object if I pay her a social call from time to time."

Tess's mouth parted in surprise at the man's boldness. Zach, however, merely shrugged. "None of my business. I couldn't care less how she spends her time."

Jimmy's smile widened. "Well, honey, I hope you don't object if I come calling. I'd consider it an honor."

Jimmy Jerold's outright flattery was soothing balm against Zach's stinging indifference. Aware that the three men watched her closely, expectantly, she raised her chin and smiled. "No, of course I don't mind. You're welcome any time."

Triumph flickered in Jimmy's blue eyes as he bent low over her hand. "Until next time, Miss Tess."

Moe smirked, but refrained from further comment as Tess escorted him and his friend to the door.

Doubts assailed Tess even before the dust settled after their departure. She already regretted that she hadn't discouraged Jimmy Jerold. The man was much too smooth, much too practiced, for someone with her limited experience. His unflagging confidence undermined her own. And in spite of his smiles and flattery, something about him made her a trifle uneasy. Moe Black was another matter entirely. Her dislike had been spontaneous—and strong.

A thought struck her as she slowly turned and went to rejoin Zach. Neither Jimmy nor Moe had expressed any curiosity about the circumstances surrounding Jed's death. She tried to find a logical explanation for this, but finally gave up, attributing it to Zach's sudden arrival and the ensuing hostility. Along with irritating her, Zach's animosity toward their visitors had surprised and shocked her. She had no idea what had prompted him to be not only rude, but downright surly. After all, they had been friends of Jed's, and as such, had been entitled to a warmer welcome.

When she returned to the patio, she found Zach, his back turned, staring out at the distant mountains. "You could have been a little friendlier," she remarked. "Or is Southern hospitality only a myth?"

"What do you know about that pair?" he asked without turning around.

"They said they were Jed's friends, and that they rode with him during the war."

Zach gave a snort of derision. "That alone should have told you they weren't to be trusted."

"You needn't be sarcastic, Zach McClain." Tess picked up the empty glasses and started for the kitchen. "This is my home too, and I can invite whomever I please."

Turning abruptly, he crossed the space separating them, took the glasses from her hand, and set them on the bench with a distinct thud. "Woman, are you that naive?"

Instinctively she stepped backward, coming up hard against the adobe wall. He braced a hand on the wall on either side of her head and leaned forward. She felt the heat from his body mere inches from hers. Her mind blank, she forgot the question he had just asked.

"Do you have any idea who Jed rode with after Gettysburg?"

She swallowed hard and shook her head. "I asked Jed once or twice when I wrote to him, but he never answered my question."

"Does the name Quantrill ring any bells? William Clarke Quantrill?"

Her throat suddenly went bone dry. "Yes, of course. He was a Yankee who fought for the Confederacy. The newspapers were full of his exploits."

"How much do you remember?" Zach's mouth set in a grim line.

Tess frowned, trying to recall everything she had read, gossip she had overheard. Tales of murder and mayhem. "Surely most stories were grossly exaggerated. No one could be that evil—or that deranged."

"Ever hear of a place called Lawrence, Kansas?"

"Yes," she said, her voice scarcely above a whisper. "Even after all these years, I still remember the name of the town."

"Jed wrote me that he joined Quantrill's bushwhackers just before the massacre took place. I don't think he realized what he was up against. At any rate, by the time he did, it was too late. It was either kill or be killed."

"All those innocent men and boys . . ."

"Quantrill's orders were to kill every man big

enough to carry a gun. While he ate a hearty breakfast, his men slaughtered innocent civilians. A preacher was shot milking his cow. Others were gunned down as they stood in their own doorways. Some burned to death when their homes were set on fire."

A series of gruesome images paraded through her mind. Worst of all, Jed Duncan, her friend, had been part of the unspeakable horror. Tess wanted to press her hands over her ears and beg Zach to stop.

But his grim recitation continued. "Quantrill's reign of terror didn't stop at Kansas. Countless men, soldiers and civilian alike, were brutally slain, their bodies mutilated, until Quantrill finally met his Maker."

"Enough!" she cried. "Why are you telling me all this?"

Zach sighed. His hands dropped to her shoulders, his grip firm, but surprisingly gentle. "After the war, some of his guerrillas were able to return to peaceable lives. But not all. Quantrill attracted notorious cutthroats, men like Bloody Bill Anderson, Jesse James, Cole and Jim Younger. By their own admission, the two who just paid us a visit said they rode with Jed. I'd bet my last dollar they also rode with Quantrill."

She thought of Jimmy Jerold's disarming smile. Could he really be a devil in the guise of a choir boy? Moe Black, however, was a different entity. She had sensed a certain cold ruthlessness about him. "Even if they were members of Quantrill's Raiders, that doesn't necessarily put them in the same category as Jesse James or the Youngers. You said yourself some resumed peaceable lives."

His grip tightened ever so slightly. "No, but it does mean we should proceed with caution till we know more about them."

"Very well, then." She met his look without flinching. "I'll have ample opportunity to learn more about Mr. Jerold when he comes calling."

"You just do that, darlin'." A muscle ticked in Zach's jaw. He stepped away from her, his expression hard. "And when you do, ask him how many innocent people he murdered in cold blood."

Seven

The Silver Sequin hummed with activity. Smoke hovered in the air like thick, gray fog. The tinny notes from a piano were nearly drowned out by a raucous chorus of male voices. An occasional trill of feminine laughter punctuated the din. Men in various modes of attire stood three-deep at the bar. Others occupied tables, cards fanned in one hand, a drink nearby, a pile of crumpled bills in the center. No one paid any attention to the two latecomers huddled at a table in a far corner.

"Think they're tellin' the truth?"

Jimmy Jerold poured whiskey into a glass from the bottle sitting between them. "It's our job to find out—one way or another."

Moe mulled this over in silence. His small, colorless eyes restlessly scanned the crowed. "What do you make of 'em?" he asked at last.

"Tess Montgomery is a right pretty little thing. Never met someone like 'er I couldn't get around."

Moe grunted. "How can you be sure she doesn't have a thing goin' with McClain? After all, the two of 'em are livin' together."

Jimmy pulled out a fat cigar, struck a match, and puffed it to life. "Livin' together don't necessarily mean sleepin' together."

"That right?" Moe let out a snort of disgust. "What kinda man lets a woman share the same roof but not the same bed?"

"Could be McClain don't like women."

"Could be." Moe sounded doubtful.

Leaning back, Jimmy studied his companion through a blue cloud of smoke. "Or, could be he just doesn't fancy this particular woman. 'Cause if'n he does—an' I was watchin' the whole time—he sure don't act it."

"And that's where you come in." Moe smirked, revealing a row of crooked, yellowed teeth. "Charm the pants off her while stealin' her blind."

Jimmy grinned back. "Somethin' like that."

"What's the next step?"

"First, there's some groundwork to be done."

"Such as?"

"Such as spend a little time gettin' to know the lady, win her confidence. Gifts and flattery don't hurt much, either."

Moe gave Jimmy a hard look over his raised glass. "Hope you ain't plannin' on spendin' the last of our cash on useless trinkets to impress some dumb bitch."

"Gotta stop thinkin' that way, my friend. Instead, look at every penny spent as an investment. If this pays off like the man says, we'll soon be rollin' in dough."

Lowering his voice, Moe leaned forward, resting his arms on the scarred pine table. "And after we find what we're lookin' for. What happens to the lady then?"

This time when Jimmy smiled, his eyes were cold as glass. "When the lovely Miss Montgomery—and her business partner—are no longer of any use, we'll let the buzzards pick their bones clean."

"Then sit back and watch the authorities blame their

deaths on the Apaches." Moe lifted his glass in a toast. "To success."

Jimmy did likewise and clinked his glass against that of his friend. "To fortune."

Tess tried to blame the dull ache in her arm for keeping her awake. Impatiently she flung the dime novel aside. Instead of making her sleepy, Deadwood Dick's wild adventures left her more wide-awake than ever. Absently massaging her sore arm, she stared up at the saguaro cactus ribs and wood beams that formed the ceiling.

A cool breeze swept down the mountainside and drifted through the partially open door. In the distance, a coyote howled; its notes lingered, sorrowful, eerie. Tess felt loneliness well from the depths of her soul. She had hoped—prayed—that Arizona would mark a new beginning to her life, and an end to the old, but nothing had changed. She had simply exchanged one lonely place for another.

She had, however, learned one valuable lesson in the process. Having someone share the same roof didn't necessarily make a house a home. There had to be mutual respect, and if not love, at least the bond of friendship. She doubted that would ever be the case with Zach. It saddened her to know how little regard he had for her. Saddened—and confused her.

Knowing any attempt to sleep would be futile, she swung her legs over the edge of the bed and reached for her shawl. She padded across the room and pushed the door wider. Her eyes widened at the beautiful sight. Millions of diamond-bright stars studded an ink black sky. A moon dangled like half of a broken locket above the ragged ridges of mountains.

Midnight beckoned, and she slipped outside, walked

to the edge of the porch, and leaned against a post. The visit from Moe Black and Jimmy Jerold replayed over and over in her head like half-remembered lyrics of a song. Wouldn't good friends want to know the details of a friend's untimely demise? Strange, she mused. As far as they knew, Jed could have succumbed to pneumonia or a rattlesnake bite as readily as a bullet in the back.

Instinct told her that the pair weren't to be trusted. She wasn't as naive as Zach liked to think. Neither was she stupid. Zach might not like her, but he had nothing to gain by lying to her. She had believed everything he had told her about Quantrill and his vicious band of cutthroats. He had told her that some of Quantrill's band had returned to law-abiding ways after the war, but not all. For the time being, she'd withhold judgment on Jimmy and Moe.

Gradually, she became aware that the night breeze gently ruffling the folds of her cotton nightdress carried with it the aroma of tobacco. Tess turned slowly as Zach stepped from the shadows into the moonlight. He stood silent, watchful. His shirt was unbuttoned, revealing a broad expanse of hard-muscled chest, burnished by the sun to a rich bronze. His tousled hair spilled across his brow like a tangled skein of amber silk. He held a thin cigar negligently in one hand; a bottle dangled from the other. Tess swallowed hard. He looked dangerous—and very, very attractive.

"I—I thought I was alone." She clutched her shawl more tightly around her. His presence made her feel curiously off balance, nervous. Excited. "I didn't realize at first that you were out here."

"That was my intent."

"I'm not sure I understand."

"I hoped you wouldn't notice and would go back to bed."

She gave a small shrug. "I couldn't sleep."

"Neither could I," he admitted, "but that's hardly anything new."

It wasn't much, this fragile thread of conversation, yet she was reluctant to break it. "Have you always had trouble sleeping?" she ventured.

With inherent grace, he raised the cigar to his lips and drew on it, letting out a long stream of smoke. "Not always, darlin', just since the war."

Tess frowned. There was a rough edge to his usually smooth drawl. "You've been drinking, haven't you?"

He let out a harsh laugh. "How observant of you, but unfortunately I'm still quite sober."

Tess raised her chin a notch, refusing to be intimidated by his sarcasm. "Do you drink often?"

"Only when I can't sleep."

"Which you claim is often."

"You're smart as a whip, as you Yankees say." With a wicked smile curling his mouth, he held out the bottle. "Care to join me?"

"No, thank you." She couldn't repress a shudder, remembering how the vile liquid had burned her throat when he had insisted she swallow some before removing the cholla barbs.

He chuckled at her reaction.

"Enough whiskey for one day, eh?" Not waiting for her answer, he raised the bottle and took a long pull.

She wondered briefly how he would react if she accepted his offer. It might almost be worth it to wipe the smug look off his handsome face. He was baiting her, she knew, deliberately trying to get rid of her. But his words had the opposite effect. Instead of leaving, she perched primly on one of the benches lining the shaded porch. She pulled the shawl more snugly around her shoulders and gazed up at the sky. "I never realized before how beautiful the desert can be at night."

"What if I told you to get the hell out of here?"

"Then I'd simply remind you that this is my home too, and I have as much right to be here as you."

He studied her insolently. "Jed must have been loco to think this would work," he muttered.

She toyed with the loose braid that hung over one shoulder. "I've been thinking about Jed. . . ."

"What about him?" Zach's tone was clipped with impatience.

"I'm having a hard time reconciling the Jed I remember with Quantrill and his bushwhackers. Jed always impressed me as decent, kind."

"He was."

"Then why would he take up with Quantrill?"

His expression remote, Zach flicked ash from his cigar. "Everyone has a dark side to their nature," he said at last, giving her an oblique look. "Even a Miss Goody Two-Shoes like yourself."

His answer made her pause to consider. What was her dark side? It had to be her long-standing fascination with a certain rebel soldier. She had experienced it first as a young girl; she was experiencing it again as a grown woman. But this time it was darker, deeper, more intense. Unruly sensations and erotic thoughts rippled through her each time he touched her. He had only to look at her a certain way, speak in a certain tone, and her insides began to melt.

Linking her fingers together, she tried to discipline her wayward thoughts. "I always admired the way Jed had taken a young recruit under his wing, giving him the full benefit of his experience. Never for one minute, did he doubt that the South would emerge victorious."

Zach wandered closer. He stared down at the glowing tip of his cigar. "Jed was frustrated that the war was becoming a long-drawn-out affair."

"No one expected the war to last as long as it did," Tess replied quietly. "I remember Father boasting that the backbone of the Confederacy would be broken before spring planting."

"And my Daddy was convinced the Union would be brought to its knees before tobacco harvest." Zach's smile was tight. "Fools, both of them."

"Fools," she repeated with a trace of wistfulness. "Or optimists."

"Instead, the bloodbath continued for four long years."

"Father against son, brother against brother. Thousands upon thousands of lives."

Zach remained silent, caught up in memories.

"Historians call Gettysburg the worst." Tess rested her head against the adobe wall. The past burned into the present like acid. "As long as I live, I don't think I'll ever forget watching Lee's and Grant's armies descend on the town, endless ribbons of blue and gray. If I close my eyes, I can still smell the bloodshed, feel the earth shudder from the cannon fire . . . hear the screams."

Zach, too, would always remember it. He had been a cog in that wheel of death and destruction. If he closed his eyes, it all came back to him in vivid detail. He could taste that odd mix of fear, anticipation—and inevitability. He took another swallow of whiskey as though it could wash away a nightmare that had been all too real. Clearing his throat, he said, "Even before Gettysburg, Jed was growing impatient. He feared the conflict would grind on for years, blamed the lack of resolution on West Point-educated generals. He chafed under their command."

"I don't understand." She stared at him, trying to

read his expression, but his face was veiled in shadow. "Why did he think that?"

Zach puffed thoughtfully on his cigar. "To Jed's way of thinking, when it came to war tactics, all the officers, the generals in particular, had read the same textbooks. Jed believed the situation called for leaders cut from a different cloth."

"And William Quantrill was such a man?"

"Could be." He shrugged. "Hard to say what was going through Jed's mind once our paths parted."

Tess rose and went to stand next to him. "I don't understand how anyone could justify such heinous acts. How could they live with that on their conscience?"

Zach stared down into her upturned face. What irony, he thought. Tess Montgomery had sent him to hell. Now, she, of all people, questioned how others could live with guilt on their conscience. All she had to do was hold up a mirror. But what would she see? The same as he did? Guileless gray eyes, a face so pretty it made his heart ache. Some people, he knew, had the God-given talent of being able to block even the worst experiences from their minds, to convince themselves certain events never occurred. Perhaps Tess numbered among these. He envied that ability. His days would be simpler, his nights less haunted, if he, too, could lock away the horrors of Elmira.

"Can't tell from the outside what someone's heart is like," he drawled. "Take yourself, for instance, darlin'. In your chaste nightgown all buttoned to the chin, you could be mistaken for an angel on a Christmas tree. Underneath that pretty exterior, might be nothin' more than a lump of coal."

His barb stung sharper than that of a cholla. "Can't we ever have a single conversation without you turning hateful?"

Zach steeled himself against her appeal. Suddenly, he found himself wanting to press his mouth against hers to still its slight quiver. He wondered how the soft curves and gentle swells of her body would fit against the hard planes and angles of his own. Ruthlessly he tamped down the surge of desire. "It's way past your bedtime, little girl. Go to sleep."

"It pains me to see how bitter you've become." She placed a hand lightly on his arm. "Let me help you. Tell me what happened to change you so."

The touch of her cool fingers was as unwelcome as that of a tarantula against his flesh. He resisted the urge to shake free. Instead, his eyes glacier cold, he stared pointedly at her hand until she removed it. "Haven't we had this conversation before, darlin'? The war happened."

"Isn't it time you stop acting as though you were the only one affected?" Tess held her ground, clasping her shawl even tighter in her earnestness. "The war happened to everyone. There are few people alive today whose lives weren't turned upside down. Who didn't experience a loss."

Zach flicked his cigar away, the lit end making a glowing red arc in the darkness. He wanted to grab her shoulders and shake her until her hair came loose from that damn braid. Didn't she know she was playing with fire? Didn't she care? "You don't listen very well, do you?" he asked through clenched teeth. "In case you've forgotten, I warned you never to mention the war."

She swallowed. "I remember, but this time I'm not going to let you intimidate me. You weren't the only one who suffered, Zach."

He inched forward until his body brushed hers. "That right?"

Her eyes widened at the contact, but her chin firmed

in determination. "The war's over and has been for years. Don't you think it's time to pick up the pieces and get on with your life?"

Anger burned away the alcoholic haze he had carefully nurtured. What the hell gave this woman the right to give him advice? If she were a man, he'd settle the matter with his fist. Or his Colt .44. But she wasn't, and he had never been as painfully aware of the fact than he was at this moment. "Easy for you to say, darlin'," he growled. "Tell me how you suffered."

"I lost my father at Fredericksburg," she said, her voice breaking, "but you don't find me wallowing in self-pity."

"And you're implying I do?"

"I'm not implying; I'm telling you outright." Her own temper ignited. She jabbed a finger against his chest for emphasis. "You're so busy feeling sorry for yourself, you can't think straight. Rather than hold everything inside, you might find it helpful to talk about your problems."

In spite of his own simmering fury, Zach couldn't deny a grudging admiration. Little Tess Montgomery had more guts than he imagined. Grown men often backed off when they sensed the explosive violence beneath his cold rage. Tossing the whiskey bottle on the ground, he snagged her shawl and hauled her against him. "There's only one kind of talkin' I feel like doin' tonight."

Her lips parted, whether in surprise or protest, he didn't know; then it was too late for rational thought. His mouth covered hers, hard and demanding. He wanted her; it was that simple, that basic. But there was nothing either simple or basic in the desire that swept over him with the force of a dam breaking. Need washed away years of resentment, drowned bitterness in honeyed sweetness.

In the far recesses of his mind, he was aware of her clenched fists pressed against his bare chest. He expected her to resist, rebel against this onslaught of sheer physical lust. Then, once again, she surprised him. Rather than push him away, her arms crept upward and circled his neck. Wrapping his arms around her, he held her tightly, molding her small, slender body against his. She was a perfect fit, just as he had hoped, better than he had dared dream.

He changed the angle of the kiss, then deepened it. She made a throaty purr of approval. The small sound fueled his already inflamed senses. Quick to take advantage of her involuntary response, he slid his tongue into her mouth, stroking, teasing, seducing. Pleasure, almost painful in its intensity, tore through him when her tongue shyly met his.

His hand found her breast, cupping its fullness in a callused palm. Warm, round, ripe. Exquisite. Her breathing changed, quickened, became ragged as his thumb flicked across her taut nipple, once, twice . . .

Tess broke free. Eyes glazed and unfocused, she stared up at him. Nervously she ran the tip of her tongue across lips reddened from his kiss.

Zach kept his gaze fastened on hers, mentally bracing himself for the anger, the denial, the indignation that was sure to come. He should feel ashamed of himself for taking unfair advantage of an innocent. Should, but didn't. All he felt was regret. A strange, lingering sorrow that the interlude had ended prematurely—and the knowledge that it would never be repeated.

"You shouldn't have," she whispered. "I shouldn't . . ." Head high, she turned and slowly walked away.

Fragile, Zach thought as he watched her leave. She reminded him of spun glass—delicate and fragile, as though she might shatter at a harsh wrong word or unexpected movement. Damn! He shoved a hand through his hair. What had he gone and done? What had he been thinking? He had almost seduced the woman he had sworn to hate.

His eyes fell on the whiskey bottle lying near his feet, and he muttered a curse. He couldn't blame his actions on the alcohol. Though his plan had been to drink enough to court a night's sleep, he was far from inebriated. The simple truth was, he hadn't been able to keep his hands off her. For days, thoughts of her had crept into his mind at odd times. He'd remember how her eyes turned to liquid silver when she smiled, the pleasing sound of her laughter, the stubborn tilt of her chin with its tempting dimple.

Maybe he should plan a visit to the Silver Sequin. He was long overdue for a little recreation, needed to let off a little tension. Tess Montgomery could tempt a saint.

And no one had ever labeled him a saint.

Eight

During the ensuing week, neither Tess nor Zach referred to the midnight kiss. It was as though, by unspoken agreement, as long as neither mentioned it, both could pretend it had never happened. If Zach caught her stealing frequent looks at him, he refrained from comment. If Tess discovered him studying her with brooding intensity, she kept silent. Cowards, the pair of them, she reflected with a rueful smile.

Though they were careful to maintain a safe distance after nightfall, their days fell into a routine. Each morning before the sun grew too warm, Zach supervised Tess's target practice. While firing a steady barrage of instructions, he avoided any direct contact. Tess offered no objections. With Zach's physical presence less of a distraction, her skill increased rapidly.

"I'm going into town this afternoon," Zach announced after one of their lessons the following week.

"I'll go with you," Tess offered, excited at the prospect of a trip into Tucson. "I've got a list started . . ."

Zach cut her off. "Not this time."

"It'll only take me a minute to get ready."

"Don't bother. I plan on going . . . alone."

"Ohh." She tried to mask her disappointment, but the attempt was transparent.

"I've got business to attend to and don't need you tagging along." He tugged the brim of his hat lower to shield his eyes from the sun's glare. "You should be safe enough on your own for a few hours. Just make sure to keep your pistol within reach."

"You needn't worry about me," she informed him, adopting a casual air. "I'll be quite all right by myself."

Did he think her a child in need of a nursemaid? She wondered irritably. She wasn't afraid to stay at the ranch by herself. After all, she wouldn't always have Zach to depend on in time of trouble. For years she had managed to take care of herself, as well as her ailing mother. She had managed then, and could again, with or without the help of Zachary McClain.

On the pretext of checking the supply of feed, she followed Zach into the lean-to and watched while he saddled his horse. Secretly, she hoped he would renege and invite her to accompany him. She'd gladly brave an encounter with Josie Goodbody for the chance to procure a recent issue of Beadle and Adam's latest dime novel at Zeckendorf's. When it appeared that Zach wasn't about to relent, she turned to leave. It was then that she noticed Zach do something that struck her as odd.

From the corner of her eye, she saw him slip a small package wrapped in plain brown paper into his saddle-bag. If that wasn't enough to capture her curiosity, his furtive manner was. When he caught her watching him, she could have sworn a guilty expression crossed his face before being quickly veiled.

He scowled at her, defying her to question his actions. She returned the look, then asked calmly, "Will you be home in time for dinner?"

"Don't bother waiting for me." He swung into the saddle and rode off without a backward glance.

Tess stood in the dirt yard and watched Zach head

toward Tucson. He was acting strangely. What was he hiding from her? In the short time they had shared the same house, she had come to know when something was amiss. And something, she sensed, was definitely amiss. At first, she thought she might have imagined the sleight of hand, but the telltale bulge in the worn leather saddlebag told her differently. Had the small parcel precipitated the solitary trip into town? Somehow, she suspected it did. But why the need for secrecy?

As she went about her chores, Tess pondered the question but failed to find a satisfactory explanation. Over the years Zach had become a man with many secrets. Prized, painful secrets he kept locked in a vault to which only he carried the combination.

Picking up a broom, she vented her frustration on sweeping the patio. In the ten years since their initial meeting, he had changed from an open, straightforward youth into an enigma. She recalled listening to him speak freely, affectionately, of his home in the Carolinas. He often mentioned his parents and older brother, his beautiful green eyes aglow with warmth and humor. Whatever fate had befallen him in the final two years of the war, he wasn't about to share. Least of all with her.

But in spite of his harsh words, she couldn't deny the certainty that traces of the gentle Southerner remained hidden beneath his surly manner. At times, a glimmer of a kind, thoughtful man shone through the granite exterior. He had surprised her when he insisted she have gloves and a wide-brimmed hat as protection against the elements. He showed concern for her safety by his frequent warnings and his insistence that she learn how to fire a gun. No, she decided, she wasn't ready to give up and turn her back on him. Weren't gold and silver embedded in rock? Didn't finding them require faith and perseverance? And, in the end, wasn't the treasure worth the effort?

Feeling immeasurably better for having resolved this in her mind, she put away the broom and went into the kitchen. Even though Zach had said he might not be home for supper, she decided to make a pan of cornbread. Besides, baking would help pass the time. As she reached for a bowl, she caught sight of the Indian woman standing in the doorway less than three feet away.

Startled, Tess nearly dropped the bowl. Recovering, she clutched it to her chest as though it might steady the rapid beat of her heart. "You were so quiet that I didn't hear you arrive."

"Papago learn quiet."

Hands shaking, Tess set the bowl on the table. "Next time, please, make noise."

The woman gave her an uncomprehending stare. "Why you want noise?"

Tess stifled a smile. "Noise serves as a warning, a sign of danger."

The woman considered this, then nodded solemnly. "Papago not harm you. The People live in peace."

Tess hurried to make amends. "I'm sorry if I offended you."

"Not worry," the Papago woman replied. She held out an object for Tess's inspection. "You like?"

Tess examined the intricately woven basket. Narrow white coils had been sewn together to form a shallow basin into which a black geometric design had been incorporated. "Yes," she said. "It's quite pretty."

The Indian woman's coal black eyes sparkled with pleasure. "You trade?"

"Trade?" Tess repeated while her mind worked rapidly, selecting, then discarding various items that might be suitable for barter.

"Devil's claw." The woman pointed toward a plant growing in a corner of the small, enclosed patio. "Worth much."

Frowning, Tess looked from the shrub, then back to the woman. "You're willing to accept that bush in exchange for this basket?"

The woman nodded eagerly. "Yucca make white straw. In summertime, Devil claw make black. Much needed, much admired by the People for baskets."

"Very well," Tess agreed, feeling she had gained the better half of the bargain. "Gather all you like."

The woman smiled for the first time. Gesturing at the sack of cornmeal, she asked, "You make bread?"

Tess made a face. "I'm afraid I haven't quite mastered how to do it well outdoors."

"You like I show you Papago way."

The next hour passed pleasantly as Tess observed her new friend. After heating the estufa, the woman made a thick batter out of cornmeal, then shaped a portion into a ball, patting it between her palms until it resembled a pancake. When she was satisfied with the shape, she gingerly dropped it on the hot surface of the stove. After allowing it to cook for a minute, she turned it over, then carefully removed it and handed it to Tess.

"Bread," she announced proudly.

The thin round was identical to a Mexican tortilla, she noted, which was used to wrap around anything and everything from eggs to meat. "Thank you," she murmured, not sure what the woman expected from her.

Nodding and smiling, the woman rested her hand on her swollen belly. "Now you make."

Taking care not to burn her fingers on the hot griddle, Tess imitated what she had seen the woman do. The process was repeated until the last of the batter was finished, and she had a neat stack of round, flat bread.

"I appreciate you teaching me."

"You, Tess," the woman said, pointing first at Tess, then at herself. "The gray-robes baptize, call me Amelia."

"Don't matter what she calls herself," a male voice sneered. "She's still just a dirty injun."

Startled, both women looked up to find Jimmy Jerold standing on the porch. They had apparently been too busy becoming acquainted to hear his arrival.

"Amelia is a welcome guest in my home." Tess gave him a reproving look. "I trust you to keep a civil tongue."

"You're still new to these parts, sugar." Jimmy ignored her rebuke and advanced toward Amelia. "Injuns are nothin' but trouble. A bunch of thievin', lyin' no-goods."

"That's quite enough, Mr. Jerold!"

Tess might as well not have spoken for all the effect her rebuke had on him. Jimmy narrowed his gaze and kept it fixed on Amelia, who slowly retreated in the opposite direction.

"Go on, git!" At a menacing move from Jimmy, the woman whirled and fled.

"You had no right!" Tess said, outraged by the man's audacity.

"Sorry I ruffled your feathers, sugar," Jimmy smoothly interrupted her tirade, "but believe me, you'll thank me later."

"Amelia meant no harm," she said stiffly, struggling to control her temper. "She only came to barter."

"Barter?" He snorted in disbelief. "Before she's through, she'll steal you blind. You're too green, too trusting, to know their shiftless ways. Pardon the plain speech, but I'd be derelict in my duty if I neglected to warn you of the dangers."

This time Tess failed to succumb to Jimmy Jerold's overt charm. He was revealing another side of his personality, and she didn't like what she saw. "To what do I owe your visit, Mr. Jerold?"

"Now, now, Tess, honey, shame on you." His light-blue eyes twinkled with good humor. "I thought we settled this matter last time. Call me Jimmy."

Tess found herself wishing Zach would suddenly appear. She didn't relish the prospect of being alone with Jimmy Jerold for any length of time. Something about him made her uncomfortable. She cast a look over his shoulder toward the door, half-expecting to see Moe's smirk. "And what about your friend, Mr. Black? Didn't he accompany you this afternoon?"

"Moe? I told him to find another way to occupy his time. I don't need his help when I pay a pretty lady a social call." He took off his hat and smoothed a hand over his dark, wavy locks. "It's a long ride from town, sugar. S'pose you could offer a weary traveler a cold drink?"

"Of course," she replied, remembering her manners. She had quickly learned upon her arrival in Arizona that in the desert offering a guest a cool drink was much more than a social courtesy; often it was a matter of survival.

She returned to the patio shortly with two tall glasses of lemonade, and renewed determination to lecture Jimmy on his treatment of Amelia. In her absence, he had made himself at home. He was seated on a bench, his legs stretched out comfortably, ankles crossed. Her irritation was forgotten, however, the instant she spotted the fluffy creature on his lap.

"A kitten!" she squealed in delight. Shoving the drinks at him, she scooped up the small bundle of fur.

The kitten was the color of soot, with a white face and four white paws. The tiny creature studied her through inquisitive green eyes.

"Thought you'd forgive me once you saw the present I brought."

Jimmy looked impossibly smug, but Tess forgave him when the kitten licked her cheek with its raspy strawberry-pink tongue. "He's adorable!"

"She," Jimmy corrected, idly taking a sip of lemonade. "It's a girl. I've been told her name is Smoky. Not surprising," he chuckled, "considering she was born in a bar room."

Tess sank down next to him, cradling the kitten in her arms. "Is she mine?"

"All yours, hon." He grinned at her over the rim of his glass, enjoying her reaction.

Tess smiled in return. She gently stroked the kitten's soft gray fur, enchanted by her new pet. The kitten purred, contented. "I don't know how to thank you,' she murmured.

"No thanks necessary. Only reward I need is knowin' I found this little critter a good home. Bartender claimed the cats outnumbered the mice. Fact is, he threatened to drown 'em unless someone offered to take one or two off his hands."

Tess decided that, though Jimmy Jerold might have his share of flaws, she couldn't fault his love for animals. His kind rescue of the imperiled kittens raised him a notch in her estimation. "It was very thoughtful of you."

His gaze was bold as it fastened on her. "The color of her fur made me think of your eyes. Sort of soft and smoky."

Tess blushed. The man's blatant flattery made her feel flustered and self-conscious. To hide her embarrassment, she concentrated on the kitten in her lap, continuing to stroke its silky coat.

Her telltale flush was all the response Jimmy needed. He flashed a dimpled smile. "Ain't that just like a female," he drawled, watching her pet the kitten. "Women always like being petted."

Tess felt her color deepen. "R-really, Mr. Jerold," she stammered, "such talk isn't proper."

"Sorry, sugar. Didn't mean no offense. Got a bit carried away seein' the pretty picture you make holdin' that little critter."

Though Jimmy Jerold's words were contrite, he failed to look repentant. Tess's uneasiness increased knowing full well she was alone with this man while Zach was miles away and not due back for hours.

Jimmy seemed attuned to her thoughts. "Speaking of friends, where is your Mr. McClain? I fully expected your partner to put in an appearance."

She considered inventing a falsehood, but she had never been a convincing liar, so she opted for the truth instead. "Zach went into town on business."

"Business, eh?" Jimmy idly studied the toe of his dusty boot. "What kind of business?"

"He didn't say."

Jimmy clucked his tongue and wagged his head in disapproval. "You're much too trustin', sugar. Don't go forgettin' you're half owner of this place. That gives you the right to know what's goin' on. Take my advice; don't let the man railroad you."

"Zach doesn't tell me very much," she admitted, her eyes fixed on the kitten dozing in her lap. "I'd be the last person he'd confide in."

They sat for awhile in silence while overhead a flock of swallows drifted on air currents searching for insects. A light breeze ruffled the yellow blooms of a paloverde tree.

Jimmy observed the slow, ponderous progress of a desert tortoise making its way across the hard-packed earth at the edge of the patio. "Havin' nuthin' to do must get borin' for a man," he said at length. "What's McClain do all day?"

Tess shrugged, then took a sip of her drink, which had grown warm. "I'm not sure exactly. I think he spends most of it at the mine."

"Now that's mighty interestin'." Jimmy reached over and scratched behind the kitten's ears. "Heard the mine was worthless. People claim the small vein of silver never amounted to much."

"That was my understanding, too," Tess confessed.

Jimmy lapsed into silence again. Turning her head to study him, Tess found his handsome face uncharacteristically somber.

"Shame about Jed." He shook his head mournfully. "Damn shame."

Tess expelled a sigh of relief. At last he'd expressed a measure of sorrow at the death of a friend. Perhaps her initial impression of him had been too harsh.

"A prospector at the Silver Sequin said Jed had been shot in the back. That his place had been ransacked. Is that true?"

"Yes, I'm afraid it is." Her throat clogged with emotion. "Poor Jed, he didn't stand a chance."

"Do you have any notion what his killer mighta' been lookin' for?"

Thoughtfully she traced a finger down the kitten's spine. "I've given the matter a great deal of thought, but I can't imagine what it could be."

Jimmy tugged his earlobe. "Hard to imagine Jed ownin' anything valuable enough to get himself killed over."

"Whatever it was, I'm convinced his murderer found what he was searching for."

"Why is that?" he asked, his tone uncharacteristically sharp.

"It's just simple logic," she said, attempting to explain her theory. "I put this place back together piece by piece. I cleaned every square inch. If there was anything of value, I would have found it."

Jimmy relaxed visibly, unable to refute her reasoning. "Makes sense, I s'pose," he muttered, then flashed a dimpled grin. "Beside findin' Smoky a good home, I had another reason for visitin' this afternoon."

Tess looked at him expectantly.

Jimmy kept her in suspense while he leisurely finished his drink and set the glass aside. "There's gonna be a fiesta next week. I was wonderin' if you'd like to go."

"You're too late, Jerold." Zach strolled through the open kitchen doorway and onto the patio. "Miss Montgomery is already spoken for. She agreed to come with me."

Tess rose so abruptly, the kitten nearly tumbled from her lap. Jimmy stood, too, his movements slow and deliberate. Feet braced, expression belligerent, he confronted Zach, then dismissing him, focused his attention on Tess. "That true, sugar?"

"Isn't it time you head back to town, Jerold?" Zach kept his tone mild as he sauntered over to Tess and casually draped an arm around her shoulder. "The desert can be a dangerous place after nightfall. All kinds of varmints prowling around."

Tess tensed beneath Zach's possessive embrace. Her initial instinct to pull away had been swiftly replaced by others far more treacherous. A yearning to stay, the desire to press tighter. She chastised herself. Foolish, fanciful feelings for a foolish, fanciful woman. Zach was only using her as a pawn in a game he and Jimmy played. A game powered by masculine pride.

"Let the lady speak for herself, McClain. Unless," Jimmy sneered, "you're afraid to hear what she has to say."

"You heard the gentleman, darlin'," Zach all but purred. "He's waiting for your answer."

Tess was tempted to contest Zach's claim, but changed her mind when she felt his fingers bite into her arm in an unmistakable warning. Reluctantly she set aside thoughts of rebelling against his dictatorial manner. Truth was, she didn't relish an evening spent in Jerold's company. "I'm sorry your trip here was wasted, Jimmy, but Zach's right. I already promised I'd go to the fiesta with him."

"And you never break a promise, do you, Tess?"

Though Zach smiled, there was neither approval nor warmth in his eyes. In spite of the day's heat, Tess felt chilled by their coldness. She started to draw away, but his steel-like grip imprisoned her at his side. She stared sightlessly at the sleeping kitten cradled in her arms and wondered what she had done to warrant such hatred.

Slowly she became aware of Jimmy Jerold's watchfulness. "I don't know how to thank you for Smoky," she said, stroking the kitten's soft fur.

Jimmy treated her to more of his patented charm. "Why, that's easy, sugar. Just save me a dance at the fiesta with the prettiest girl there."

Ignoring Zach's scowl, Tess jerked free from his hold and, still holding her new pet, escorted her guest to the door. Jimmy gave her a broad wink before swinging into the saddle. Then, tipping his hat at a jaunty angle, he headed toward town.

Zach came out to stand beside her as she watched Jimmy ride off. "What was he doing here?"

"Can't you make noise like a normal person when

you approach?" she asked irritably. "You're as bad as Amelia."

"You're avoiding answering my question," he growled. "And who the hell is Amelia?"

Tess sighed with exaggerated patience. "Amelia is my Papago friend. And what makes you so sure Jimmy wanted something?"

"His type always wants something."

"He gave me a gift," she said, shifting the kitten, who was now wide awake and curious. "And invited me to a fiesta. Must you always be so cynical?"

"Chalk it up to . . ." He halted mid-sentence, frowned, then dragged a hand through his hair.

"Chalk it up to what?" she persisted.

"Forget it," he snapped, hooking his thumbs in the waistband of his denims. Damn! he cursed silently. He wished—no, he prayed—he could forget his years spent in a wretched Union hellhole. Elmira would have transformed even the angel Gabriel into a cynic. He felt like throttling Tess. She was forever poking her pert little nose into things she should keep out of. The blasted woman seemed on a mission to make him remember untold horrors. When would she learn to leave him alone?

He blew out a breath, then cursed again. Tess stood gazing up at him with guileless gray eyes, the picture of innocence. She looked as sweet and defenseless as the tiny kitten she held.

And just as soft.

The traitorous thought streaked through his brain like lightening. Just as swiftly, he recalled the feel of her in his arms. Soft and yielding. And beneath all the softness, a firestorm. A passion that he surmised had surprised her as much as it had him. Passion that made him yearn for more than just a kiss.

He clenched his jaw as he willed away the lustful

images that danced through his head. Images of her straining against him, her pale body naked and gleaming in the moonlight. Her long chestnut locks twined around them like silken bonds. Her lids lowered over eyes of liquid silver, lips parted, sweet as honeysuckle. What was wrong with him, anyway? She was becoming an obsession.

At times he even forgot he hated her.

"You look angry." Tess absently scratched the kitten behind its ear. "I hope you don't object to my having a pet."

"Of course not," he ground out. What kind of ogre did she think he was? But what did he expect after his callous treatment of her? He heaved a sigh, partly of regret, partly of frustration. "I almost forgot. I brought you something from town."

"Something for me?" Her eyes lit with pleasure.

"Don't get all excited," he cautioned. "It's not really a gift, but something purely practical." Leaving her to follow, he strode across the yard to the corral where he had left a small crate. He picked it up off the ground and held it up for her inspection. The motion was accompanied by a noisy flapping of wings and frenzied squawking.

"Chickens?" A slow smile spread across her face. "You brought me chickens?"

Setting the crate back down, he studied her closely, trying to gauge her degree of sincerity. In his book, a crate of poultry didn't exactly equal a cute and cuddly kitten. "Figured they might come in handy, seeing how far we are from town and all."

Tess put down the kitten and removed the wooden peg from the lid of the crate. A rooster strutted out, followed by a hen and her brood of chicks. Before Zach could read her intent, she flung her arms around his neck and gave him a hug, then quickly stepped away. "Sorry," she said with a self-deprecatory laugh. "I must have been carried away by the thought of fresh eggs."

Zach caught himself grinning in return. Embarrassment stained her cheeks a becoming shade of pink. At that moment, it would have been very easy to let down his defenses and relax his guard. Almost too easy. But he wasn't about to let that happen. Clearing his throat, he kept his expression bland. "Thought maybe a country girl would appreciate the idea of chicken dinner on Sundays."

"There's a hen coop behind the lean-to. I'll clean it out first thing tomorrow morning. Thank you," she added with a shy smile before turning away.

Zach watched the gentle sway of her hips as she returned to the house with the kitten scampering close at her heels. Under normal circumstances, he and Tess would have been friends, might even have been lovers.

If things had been different . . .

He brought himself up short. What the hell was he thinking? He might as well be wishing pigs could fly. Or that the moon was made from green cheese. All the ifs, buts, and maybes in the world wouldn't change the irrefutable fact that she had betrayed him.

And that betrayal had nearly cost his life—and his sanity.

Nine

True to her word, early the next morning Tess went about the task of cleaning the henhouse. Smoky, the kitten, scampered about while the chickens pecked at bits of dried corn scattered in the dirt. The chicken coop was filthy and, judging from its appearance, probably hadn't been used for quite some time. Wrinkling her nose in distaste, she reached inside and removed a pile of straw.

"The poor chickens," she muttered under her breath. With the large amount of dirty straw stuffed inside, they had little room to roost.

She continued to pull out straw until it formed a small mound at her feet. Using the back of her hand she wiped the sweat from her brow, leaving a long smudge of dirt in its place. "Almost finished," she said aloud as her fingers groped for a final wad lodged at the back of the coop almost beyond her reach.

"What on earth . . . ?"

To her surprise, instead of straw, she encountered something solid. Grasping the object with both hands, she pulled it free. Dumbfounded, she found herself holding a rectangular-shaped package wrapped in heavy oiled paper and tied with string.

The henhouse forgotten, she sank down on a nearby

rock and stared at the item in her lap. Someone had gone to a great deal of trouble to conceal whatever was inside. The item, she concluded, must be quite valuable to warrant such measures. Excitement and anticipation bubbled through her veins like vintage champagne. Very carefully, she brushed the dust and grime from the package, then paused as a more sobering notion struck her. What if the contents of this parcel had cost Jed his life? This could very well be the treasure his killers had searched for—and failed to find.

Knowing she was being overly suspicious but unable to stop herself, she cast a nervous glance over her shoulder. Reassured no one was around, she tugged the string loose. Her fingers trembled with eagerness, but she forced herself to proceed with slow deliberation as she removed the outer wrapper.

Dime novels, a dozen at least, tumbled to her feet. She stared at them for a moment in blank confusion, then laughed out loud at her own foolishness. A fine treasure she had uncovered. She had been prepared for gold or silver, or perhaps a fortune in jewels. But dime novels?

Still smiling, she bent to retrieve them. She scanned the tattered covers: *Tip Top Weekly, Fireside Companion, Frank Leslie's Boys of America,* many dating back more than five years. Some she recognized as having read; others were unfamiliar. She smoothed a hand over a worn cover. Though they might not be gold or silver, she mused, they were, indeed, a treasure of a different sort. Jed had apparently shared her love of popular fiction. This morning's find would provide countless hours of enjoyment. She had enough reading material to last for months.

After arranging the magazines in a neat stack, she went about her chores. Humming to herself, she lined the bottom of the henhouse with clean straw, then poured water into a chipped pottery dish. True, the chickens had been a simple gift, but they were appreciated all the same. Zach's thoughtfulness never failed to surprise her. She only wished he would be more open, more willing to discuss his troubles. Instead, he hoarded secrets like a miser hoards his gold.

Tess paused in the task of sweeping the stoop. She wasn't even certain how Zach spent most of his time. She assumed it was at the abandoned silver mine, but that was only a guess, nothing more. Did the mine, she wondered, have anything to do with his mysterious trip into town the previous day? Somehow she was convinced it did. Not for one minute did she believe he had ridden all the way into Tucson to purchase chickens. No, his trip had been prompted by a more clandestine motive. Though he had tried to be secretive, she was certain he'd slipped a small package into his saddlebag.

You're much too trustin', sugar. Don't go forgettin' you're half owner of this place.

Jimmy Jerold's warning came back in a rush. Maybe there was some truth in what the man said. Until now she hadn't made any effort to visit the mine. Perhaps that had been a mistake. Though Zach would probably try to discourage a visit, she didn't need an engraved invitation to explore what was already hers. Somehow, she doubted that he'd welcome her intrusion into what, until now, had been his exclusive territory. She resumed sweeping. Well, if he could be sneaky, so could she. She'd simply time her visit to coincide with his absence.

As though conjured from her thoughts, Zach picked that time to ride in. Swinging down from the saddle, he looped the reins over a post, then sauntered toward her. Heat crept into her cheeks as his gaze traveled from the kerchief on her head down her soiled apron to the stack of old magazines at her feet. His bold assessment left her feeling self-conscious and defensive. She knew she couldn't possibly look less attractive than she did at this moment.

He gave her a crooked smile. "You look like a chimney sweep."

She brushed aside a wisp of hair that had escaped its confines and succeeded in adding another streak of grime to her face. "I've been cleaning."

"So it appears." Reaching out, he rubbed a thumb over the smudge on her cheek.

Her pulse jerked in response to his touch, then took off at an unsteady clip. Her tongue tangled in knots and refused to utter an appropriate retort.

He nodded toward the pile of dime novels. "What's all that?"

"N-nothing." She was so grateful his attention was no longer focused on her that she stammered in relief. She couldn't seem to think coherently when he was touching her. "Just some old issues of dime novels I found while cleaning."

"Looks like trash." He nudged them with the toe of his boot. "Maybe you can use them to line the chicken coop."

"Absolutely not." Horrified by the notion, she scooped them up and clutched them to her chest. "Jed apparently shared my fondness for dime novels. I intend to read every last issue—and probably more than once."

He snatched several from the pile in her arms. "The Lady of Egypt," he read, arching one sandy brow. He continued to look amused as he scanned the contents. "Ned Buntline? Deadwood Dick? Old Sleuth? Do you actually waste your time reading this trash?"

His superior attitude rankled. "For your information,

Mr. McClain, these stories happen to be very entertaining."

She tried to grab them back, but he held them just beyond her reach while he perused more of the titles. "What kinds of stories are these for an intelligent person?" he scoffed.

Raising her chin a notch, she glared at him. "I assure you they're perfectly respectable in every way. Dime novels happen to be quite popular with thousands and thousands of readers."

"So I've heard," he said dryly.

"People even as far away as England enjoy this type of literature," Tess added, feeling compelled to defend her choice.

"Literature?" Zach snorted in disgust. "I've heard people in London commonly refer to this type of *literature* as 'penny dreadfuls' and 'shilling shockers.' "

"Perhaps if you tried one instead of simply poking fun, you might change your opinion." This time when she made a grab for the dime novels he held, she succeeded. Turning on her heel, she marched toward the house.

Zach fell into step alongside her. "I prefer a different sort of reading material."

"Such as?" To her chagrin, Tess found she was interested in spite of herself.

"I was raised on the classics."

"Different people have different tastes," she replied acerbically. "That doesn't necessarily make either choice wrong, only different."

He held open the door and she swept past, nose in the air. "Did your mother approve of your reading habits?"

Tess shrugged, but avoided meeting his eyes. "She preferred that I use my money on other things."

"On reading material such as the classics?"

She shot him a telling glance. "Don't you have something more important to do than criticize my reading tastes?"

He propped himself against a wall and watched as she set the magazines aside, poured water into a basin, and began to scrub the grime from her face and hands. "I stopped by Abner Smith's office when I was in town yesterday."

She stopped scrubbing to glance at him over her shoulder, unmindful of the soapy water dripping on the floor. His tone had been casual, almost too casual. "And may I ask why?"

"I wondered if anyone had expressed any interest in buying this place."

Her mouth went dry at the thought of selling Casita de Oro. In the short time she had lived here, she had grown fond of the little ranch house, and already dreaded the thought of leaving. "And had they?"

"Not a buyer in sight." Zach thumbed back the brim of his hat. "Smith did mention he met up with a pair Jed's old buddies."

"Jimmy Jerold and Moe Black." Tess reached for a towel and dried her hands.

"From the way Smith talked, he was the one who informed them that Jed had been shot. He said after their talk they asked for directions on how to find this place. Said they wanted to take a look around."

"That's odd," she murmured. "They acted as though they hadn't heard about Jed's death until I told them."

"Well, at least that explains why they didn't appear unduly upset over the death of an old friend. And that's not all."

Turning, she leaned against the counter so that they stood facing each other. "There's more?"

Zach's relaxed pose was at variance with the tension

around his mouth and eyes. "He said Black and Jerold were awfully nosy about the terms of Jed's will."

"Maybe they felt Jed should have bequeathed his property to them instead of us. They might resent the fact that we own everything."

"That's a good possibility." He nodded agreeably. "According to Abner, they seemed pretty disappointed when they learned both pieces of property had to be sold as one. I can't get rid of the notion they're up to no good. Why else would they resort to lies?"

"It could be that you're making too much of this."

"Could be you're not making enough," he countered.

They seemed to have reached a stalemate. Zach took off his hat, hooked it on the back of a nearby chair, then raked his fingers through his hair. "Look, Tess, we each own half a run-down ranch and played-out mine, but they're our only assets. I don't know about you, but I aim to protect what's mine."

"Not everyone has ulterior motives, Zach. It could be nothing more than idle curiosity on the part of Jimmy and Moe."

His mouth set in a stubborn line, Zach pinned her with a cold-eyed stare. "I don't trust either one of them. Until I figure out what they're up to, I'd advise you to stay away from them. Especially Jerold."

"That won't be easy without appearing rude." She absently twisted the towel she still held in her hands. "I did promise Jimmy a dance at the fiesta."

"We both know promises are made to be broken, don't we, Tess?"

His words cut like a whip, the edge in his voice sharp enough to draw blood. "I—I don't know what you mean."

"Always the innocent, aren't you?" he sneered. "You play the role to perfection."

Her mind became mired in hurt and bewilderment. Tears pricked the backs of her eyelids, then mercifully anger rose to the fore. Suddenly she had had enough. Zach had brought her to the verge of tears too many times. But no more. She was tired of his sly innuendos and snide remarks. "You have no right to tell me what I can and can't do," she flared. "No right to say who I can dance with. No right to insult me."

She hurled the wadded-up towel at his head, but he caught it easily with one hand. "If you've got a half a brain in that pretty head of yours," he growled, "you'll heed my warning and stay away from Jerold. He's nothing but trouble."

"And so are you," she fired back. They stood toe to toe, glaring at each other, neither willing to back down. "Stop treating me like a dim-witted child. I'm entitled to do whatever I choose, see whomever I please. Remember, Zach, I'm merely a partner in this venture, not your wife."

A muscle ticked in his jaw. "A fact for which I'm eternally grateful."

As he stalked off, she stomped her foot in frustration. Zachary McClain had to be the most infuriating, most aggravating man she had ever encountered. She had always considered herself even-tempered—until now. Zach seemed to possess a God-given talent when it came to getting her riled.

A plaintive meow diverted her attention. Glancing downward, Tess found Smoky rubbing against her skirt in a bid for attention. With a sigh of resignation, Tess bent down and picked her up. Holding the kitten in her arms, she gently stroked its back as her anger begin to dissipate. It seemed impossible to have a single conversation with Zach without having it end in an argument. The constant tension between them wore on her nerves. Every time she thought she was making pro-

gress, something unforeseen would trigger his temper.
She didn't want Zach as her enemy. She wanted him
as a friend. As a . . .

. . . *lover?*

Shocked by the unbidden thought, she stood stock-
still. Where had that idea sprung from? The very notion evoked erotic images, unleashed indecent urges,
made her yearn for forbidden pleasures. What had
come over her? She wasn't the sort of woman to casually take a lover. She wasn't the sort to take any lover
at all. She had been raised to be a woman of sound
character, to possess unquestionable morals, high stan-
dards. Definitely not the sort to invite a man into her
bed without benefit of matrimony. Yet, she admitted,
nuzzling the kitten, aside from the temper he provoked,
Zach McClain was capable of eliciting a wild array of
responses from her. He spelled trouble, all right,
trouble written in bold letters.

Supper that night was a silent affair. Tess and Zach
kept their heads bent over their dinner plates, giving
the mundane meal of beans and tortillas their undi-
vided attention. Topics of conversation flitted through
Tess's mind like fireflies on a summer's eve, then were
judged for merit and, found lacking, discarded. The
atmosphere between them felt electrically charged,
thick and heavy and ominous, a storm about to break.

As soon as the dinner dishes were washed and put
away, Tess excused herself and retreated to her room.
She undressed in the dark and slipped between the
sheets. She drifted into a fitful asleep, worn out by a
day of emotional turmoil.

Sometime later she wakened. The room was pitch
dark without even a sliver of moonlight to relieve the
blackness. Coyotes howled from the foothills, their

cries louder and closer than usual. Eerier. Though she had no concept of the time, she guessed it to be well after midnight.

Wide awake, Tess got out of bed and, drawing a shawl around her shoulders, stood in the doorway leading onto the patio. Wrapping her arms around herself, she stared up at the heavens. Clouds shrouded the moon and blanketed the stars with inky velvet. Tess discovered that the darkness, contrary to being oppressive, imbued her with an odd sense of freedom. It made her feel invisible, invulnerable, invincible—as though she could say or do anything and no one would see, no one would know. No one would judge. She ventured farther onto the patio, tipped back her head, closed her eyes, and invited the kiss of the gentle night breeze across her upturned face.

"She walks in beauty, like the night," Zach quoted from the darkness.

Tess's eyes grew wide and she turned toward the sound of his voice. She could barely discern his figure emerging from the shadows. "I—I thought you were asleep."

"Sleep is no longer a friend, but an enemy."

A small inner voice urged her to retreat, to ignore the beguiling sugar-coated baritone. She dismissed it. "Why do you call sleep an enemy?"

He tilted a bottle to his lips, drank, then, setting it aside, strolled toward her. His bare feet were soundless on the hard-packed earth, his gait that of a night creature stalking its quarry. He halted in front of her. His faded denims rode low on his hips, the top buttons unfastened. His shirt hung open, exposing a torso sculpted of taut muscle and bronzed flesh. Tess swallowed hard. *Run, hide, lock the door,* her inner voice entreated. Again, she turned a deaf ear.

"You still haven't answered my question," she

prompted in a husky voice that she didn't recognize as her own.

He stared at her, his eyes heavy-lidded, while the seconds ticked past. Even in the dim light she could discern their emerald glitter. They made her nervous. Made her reckless. She moistened her lower lip with the tip of her tongue . . . and waited.

"Blame my sleeplessness on the war."

She wondered what it would feel like, how he'd react, if she smoothed her hand over his sleek chest. "You tend to blame everything on the war."

"S'pose I do." Reaching out, he tugged the ribbon loose from the end of her braid.

"It's late," she murmured. "I probably should go back to bed."

"Fraidy cat." He traced a finger along the line of her jaw. "You could take me with you."

She blinked, certain she must have misunderstood. "W-what?"

"You heard me, darlin'." A wicked smile curved his mouth. Lazily, he worked the woven strands of her hair free from the confining braid.

He was only toying with her, she assured herself. Only testing to see if she would rise to the bait. Yanking her braid free, she flung it over her shoulder with a toss of her head. "Stop teasing, Zach. Be serious."

"Thought I was," he said with a rueful grin. "Must be losing my touch."

Her heartbeat bolted like a skittish mare, then raced at a gallop. Zach McClain was having a devastating effect on her senses whether she wanted to admit it or not. Tall, muscular, with tousled, sun-streaked locks, he embodied the dashing dime-novel hero of her fantasies. She made one last, desperate attempt to corral her wayward thoughts. "I don't like it when we argue," she managed. "If we can't be friends, I hope we can refrain from being enemies."

"We'll never be friends." He cupped her face in his hands, his touch gentle, his gaze fierce. "That matter was settled years ago."

She lost the battle for control. "Must we be enemies?" she asked, barely able to speak above the pounding of her heart.

Dipping his head, he lightly brushed her lips with his. "We could be lovers."

Tess felt the air leave her lungs in a rush. She let out a strangled laugh and fought to regain her equilibrium. "W-what did you say?"

"You heard me." His mouth moved over hers in a series of soft, fleeting, playful kisses. "We could be lovers."

She shivered violently beneath his sensual assault.

"Cold?" he whispered against her ear.

"Yes—er, no." In truth, she felt both. Was that possible? she wondered dimly.

Lifting his head, he smiled down at her. "Does the thought of being lovers frighten you, Tess?"

A lump the size of an apple seemed lodged in her throat. "You frighten me," she admitted, her voice a whisper.

"I want to do more than frighten you, darlin'. I want to make love to you."

Tess couldn't have moved if she had tried. His startling declaration immobilized her body, stunned her brain. She felt besieged by myriad emotions, most of them new and unfamiliar and not quite welcome.

Zach caressed her cheekbone with the pad of his thumb, then dragged his fingers through her hair and cradled the back of her skull. "You remind me of a curious little kitten. I want to find out if you'll bare your claws or purr with pleasure when we make love."

His warm breath fanned her cheek. "Which will it be, little cat?"

This time the kiss was different: slow and seductive. A kiss meant to arouse and inflame. A kiss that gave, yet one that demanded in return. Tess became lost in its magic, melting against him, savoring a heady draught of desire. She wrapped her arms around his lean waist and held fast. The entire world seemed to quake and heave, and he was her rock.

His lips left hers to trail kisses down her neck, pausing to torment the wildly beating pulse at the base of her throat. Eyes closed, Tess arched her neck and welcomed the host of sensations that flooded through her.

And she purred, a low, throaty feline sound deep in her throat.

At the sound, Zach raised his head. Before the haze cleared from her senses, Tess found herself being swept off her feet. A triumphant smile spread across Zach's handsome face as he carried her toward the bedroom.

Ten

Tess heard Zach kick the bedroom door shut behind them. Shadows black as night veiled the bedroom. Shadows that concealed, condoned. Sanctioned. Crossing the room, he deposited her on the mattress, then straightened. She gazed up at him. He stared back, his eyes hooded. Moments ago he had seemed so confident and assured, but now his earlier assurance was gone, leaving him oddly hesitant. Panic blossomed deep within her. Had he changed his mind? Didn't he want her?

She needed him, she realized, needed him to fill a void. An ache only he could ease. Barely daring to breath, she offered a silent prayer that he found her attractive, alluring. That he needed her as desperately as she needed him. In an invitation as old as Eve, she held out her arms.

After what seemed a small eternity, he sank down next to her and crushed her against him. "God, help me," he rasped. "I'd have to be either a saint or a fool to refuse what you're offering. I'm neither."

His mouth found hers, hot and hungry, demanding and seeking. Any misgivings she might have had evaporated like a puff of smoke. She clung to him, her ardor matching his, eager to give, eager to take. Desire spun a silken web, wrapped around them, binding them together. When his tongue engaged hers in a delightful foray, she met each advance with enthusiasm and delight. Reality whirled away, taking with it life's myriad troubles. The entire world seemed contained in one tiny room.

She was barely aware of Zach nimbly unfastening the tiny buttons at the yoke of her nightdress. At the touch of chill air against heated flesh, her nipples furled into tight buds. A fact Zach quickly discovered. She drew in a sharp breath as his hand closed over the firm mound of one breast. This time, however, unlike the previous one, she did not draw away in fright, but welcomed the undeniable tug of pleasure.

Encouraged by her small whimper of encouragement, Zach nudged the thin cotton gown from her shoulders, leaving her naked to the waist, her breasts exposed to his heated desire. Tess was torn between the urge to shield them from his predatory stare and a wanton desire to flaunt them.

Zach's green eyes were no longer cold and remote, but smoldered with passion. Bending his head, he laved one rosy aureole with the tip of his tongue while lightly squeezing the other between his thumb and forefinger. A soft moan escaped Tess when he drew the distended and supremely sensitive nipple into his mouth, and sucked.

An exquisite sensation, sharp as a spear, ripped through her entire body. Tess arched her spine, unconsciously offering her breasts to be feasted upon. Threading her fingers through his hair, she held him against her.

"Zach . . ." His name seemed the only word her dazed mind was capable of forming.

He trailed tender, moist kisses from the cleft between her breasts, down her midriff to her navel. Tess shivered with pleasure at the warm rasp of his tongue, then gasped as it dipped into that shallow recess. A strange restlessness began to claim her. Her body shifted and moved, no longer able to remain quiescent.

Zach, too, must have experienced that same building urgency. With ill-concealed impatience, he swept off her nightgown, tossed it to the end of the bed. Next, he tugged the ribbon at the waist of her drawers and pushed them over her hips. His hand leisurely explored her slender frame, examining, fondling, caressing.

"Your skin is like satin," he murmured. "Warm and soft and smooth."

Every place he touched, every place his glance lingered, Tess burned. Burned and grew bolder. "I want to see you, too," she whispered, stunned by her own brazenness. "All of you."

Zach's momentary surprise gave way to approval. "Whatever you want, darlin'." With a feral grin, he quickly shrugged off his shirt, slipped out of his denims, and kicked them aside. His manhood sprang free, engorged and ready.

Tess's eyes widened at her first sight of a man's naked splendor. But before she could react more fully, Zach stretched on the bed next to her and pulled her into his arms. Reveling at the imprint of a hard, masculine body branded against hers, she buried her face in the curve of his neck. His scent, a heady blend of soap and leather, tobacco and whiskey, surrounded her, intoxicated her. Made her senses swim.

She shivered with delight when his elegant but callused hand stroked her spine from nape to hip, then settled on the curve of her buttock, urging her closer, tighter. Their bodies fit together.

Perfectly.

"So, kitten, you like being petted, do you?"

Playfully Zach nipped the juncture where her neck

and shoulder joined. She sucked in a sharp breath, then let it out in a slow sigh as his tongue gently anointed the small wound.

"Mmm," he growled, low in his throat. "Soft and sweet as a ripe summer peach. Someday—someday soon—I'm going to taste you all over."

And, Tess promised herself, she'd do the same to him. Heat surged through as erotic images of them touching, tasting, savoring each other frolicked in her head.

Zach's wonderful, magical hands lightly traced the curve of her hip, skimmed along the silken flesh of her inner thigh, then slid between her legs. Instinctively she shrank from this invasion. "There, there, kitten, it's all right," he soothed. "Let me love you."

He kissed her then, an unhurried, drugging kiss that numbed her fear, quieted her doubt. Gently, carefully, he parted the folds guarding her feminine vault and circled the tiny bud with the tip of his index finger. A tiny flame curled at that precise spot, burning hotter, brighter, with each tantalizing caress. She rotated her hips, straining to be closer to the source of this sweet torment. "Zach . . ." she cried, his name a broken whisper.

Her body no longer seemed hers to control, but his. Coherent thought was impossible. The very act of breathing became more and more difficult. Her entire being was centered on a wondrous tension cresting deep within her. Indescribable pleasure, so intense it bordered on pain. Helpless in its throes, Tess felt herself hurtle faster and faster toward a nonexistent shore. She clutched the bedclothes with both hands, her fingers alternately flexing and relaxing.

While his clever fingers teased the slick, hot nub of her femininity, his mouth and tongue wreaked further havoc on her senses. Desperately seeking release, her body writhed with need. A throbbing ache mounted deep inside her, an ache so acute it consumed her. An ache only he could assuage.

Tess wound her fingers through his hair. "Zach, please, please . . ."

His eyes locked with hers. He hesitated then, his handsome features etched with uncertainty. "Tess, are you sure?" he asked, his voice a strained whisper.

Tess felt as though she had waited her entire life for just this moment. The past and future merged into the present. Everything else ceased to exist. Speech nearly impossible, she nodded. "Yes, oh yes . . ."

His features taut with passion, he spread her legs and positioned himself between her thighs. Bracing his elbows on either side of her head, he entered her with slow deliberation. Closing her eyes, Tess prepared herself for the ultimate invasion. She tensed as her insides stretched to accommodate the unfamiliar fullness of his male organ.

"Open your eyes, Tess," Zach murmured. "I want to see my reflection in them when I make you mine."

Tess did as he asked. All the wonderful, heady sensations that had brought her to this point vanished. Left in their place was doubt—and fear.

Zach smoothed an errant curl from her cheek with gentle fingers. The simple act, tender yet possessive, helped soothe her qualms. She hazarded a smile, and failed. Still poised above her, Zach rested his forehead briefly against hers, then kissed her. He deepened the kiss in agonizingly slow increments. And annihilated any lingering reservations she had harbored.

Sliding one hand between their bodies, he found the slippery, sensitive bud nestled between her folds. With infinite patience and finesse, he stroked and teased until once again she was fully aroused.

He began to move his hips, thrusting and withdrawing, thrusting and withdrawing, until her body was no longer tense, but pliant and accepting. Then in one smooth stroke, he ruptured the delicate membrane guarding her inner vault.

Tess cried out at a sharp rending pain, her nails biting into his bronzed back.

"Hush, darlin'." With the pad of his thumb, Zach wiped away a solitary tear that trickled down her cheek. "I'm told it only hurts once. Afterwards, when a man makes love to you, you'll feel only pleasure."

Confirming his words, the pain began to subside. Zach gradually resumed his earlier motion, alternately thrusting and retreating, until flames of desire erupted once more. Angling her hips to better receive him, she wrapped her legs around his waist and held fast. She strained against him, needing, searching for a mysterious something almost within her grasp.

He drove her higher and higher with each powerful stroke. The muscles within her contracted, convulsed around his manhood. Her entire being seemed focused on a distant star, the ultimate rapture, that grew brighter, hotter, closer as she zoomed heavenward. Then, with a gasp of wonder, she shattered into a million tiny pinpricks of blinding light.

With a hoarse cry, Zach threw back his head and, shuddering, emptied his seed.

Slowly, gently, Tess floated back to earth. The moment had been so perfect, she wanted to weep. So perfect, she wanted it to last forever. The joining of a man and woman had far exceeded any expectations. There could be no greater intimacy, no greater sharing, than what had just taken place between them. She had never felt so close, so special. Only with Zach. Since her girlhood, Zach McClain had occupied her mind. Now he had claimed her body and, in the process, had captured her heart as well. The cycle was complete.

Zach eased his weight from on top of Tess. Groping about, he found the blanket and drew it up around her shoulders. He should leave. Should, he knew, but somehow he was reluctant to part just yet. With a contented sigh, Tess turned on her side, one arm lightly draped across his chest.

Guilt wriggled through Zach's conscience, making him squirm. Tess was soft and sweet and giving. Every man's dream. *Damn!* Why should he feel guilty? He had only taken what was offered. Hadn't he warned Tess he was no saint? Yet the woman had practically thrown herself at him. What was a red-blooded man to do? He wasn't a gelding, for Christ's sake.

Yet she had been a virgin. That fact didn't surprise him. What did amaze him, however, was that after all the hateful things he had said to her, she had generously given him a precious gift reserved for one's beloved. A priceless treasure only bestowed once in a woman's lifetime. But why should he let that bother him? He hadn't used force. He had merely accepted what was freely offered. Besides, he rationalized, she owed him. Considering all the pain and suffering she had caused him, Tess Montgomery's virginity seemed a small price in return. What was so terribly wrong collecting an old debt?

Absently, he picked up a silky curl that spilled across her bare shoulder and wound it around one finger. Such pretty hair, he mused. When sunlight struck it a certain way, red and gold highlights burnished the dark chestnut strands. Holding Tess, making love to her, seemed as natural as breathing. Tess was a beautiful woman with a body designed for a man's enjoyment. Besides physical beauty, she also possessed other fine qualities as well. She had spirit, courage, generosity, passion. She was everything he could hope for in a woman, everything he dreamed of finding. Regret surged through him, harsh and bitter. If only things had been different . . .

If she hadn't betrayed him . . .

If she hadn't sentenced him to hell . . .

If she hadn't condemned him to memories that haunted . . .

"Why?"

The question burst forth of its own accord. Suddenly, after all these years, it was no longer enough just to know that she had revealed his hiding place to Union officials. He needed to know why. Needed to know what had prompted her to break a promise. True, it had happened long ago, and nothing could alter the subsequent chain of events. Still, he wanted to hear the explanation from her own lips. Maybe then, and only then, he could start to put the past behind him.

"Why, Tess?" he repeated. "What made you do it?"

"Because I wanted to be close to you." She ran a finger along his collarbone. A dreamy quality infused her voice. "Because I wanted you closer to me."

Zach wrapped his fingers around her wrist and pulled her hand away. Squeezing his eyes shut, he sighed. Was she cleverly avoiding the real issue between them? Or was she simply responding to the present? Whichever the case, maybe he should take his cue from her. Maybe it would be wiser to let sleeping dogs lie.

"Zach?" A tentative note had crept into her tone. "Is something wrong? You sound . . . angry."

Opening his eyes, he turned his head to stare at her, and that was nearly his undoing. Her eyes shone like liquid silver; her mouth, lush and sweet from his kisses, reminded him of summer berries. But it was the tenderness in her expression that scared the hell out of him.

"Don't make this into something it isn't." His words came out harsher than he intended.

"What do you mean?" Hurt tarnished her silvery gaze, darkening the hue.

Zach felt guilt surge anew, and ruthlessly ignored it. "What just happened between us was nothing special. It was simply two healthy people satisfying a mutual physical urge."

She bit down on her lower lip to still its quiver. "It was special to me."

Belatedly, he realized he still held her wrist, and dropped it like a red-hot branding iron. He swung out of bed and searched for his denims in the dark, cursing softly when he couldn't find them. "Set any romantic notions aside," he growled. "Blame them on reading too many of those damn dime novels."

Tess drew the blanket higher under her chin. "The way I feel has nothing to do with my choice in reading material."

Zach steeled himself against the pain in her voice. "A man and a woman living under the same roof is only asking for trouble. Jed should have known something like this was bound to happen."

"You're absolutely right," Tess agreed, her voice strained. "The blame lies entirely with Jed—and the dime novels."

Zach, who had finally succeeded in finding his pants, paused. "Maybe the word *blame* is a bit too strong," he conceded.

"You're more experienced in these things than I am." She cleared her throat, her gaze fixed on the ceiling. "Perhaps *blame* is too strong a word. Maybe you should have chosen something milder, such as *fault,* or *error,* or even *mistake?*"

Balancing on one leg, he inserted a foot into a pant leg only to discover it was inside out. He swore again, louder this time. "Look, Tess, what just occurred wasn't rape."

"I never said it was."

"I didn't force myself on you. You could've stopped me anytime."

"Now you're telling me what happened between us was *my* doing?"

"No, of course not," he snapped. He succeeded in wriggling into his denims, but decided against wrestling with the buttons. "I just wanted to remind you I never would have laid a hand on you if you hadn't wanted me to."

"I see," she returned in a small voice. "That makes me little better than Lily London and her girls at the Silver Sequin."

He snatched his shirt from the floor. "You're getting too emotional—just like a woman."

"You idiot!" she cried in a choked voice. "I *am* a woman."

"That's exactly what got us into this predicament." He scooped his wrinkled shirt from the floor and slapped it against his thigh in agitation. "Look, where's the harm? What's so terrible about two people sharing a bed now and then? Can't we just enjoy each other's company without trying to turn this into something complicated?"

"Get out!"

He dodged an object aimed at his head and beat a hasty retreat. *Women,* he thought in disgust as he slammed the door behind him. He paused just outside her room to draw a deep breath of night air. Even after leaving her, he could still smell the faint, lingering scent of lilacs. He needed to rid his senses of her scent, needed to clear his head. A breeze carried the screech of a night owl. Then he heard another sound, a more disturbing one. A small whimper, followed by muffled sobs.

Tess's cries clawed his conscience, ripped apart his glib attempts to cast blame, shredded his lame excuses of vindication. He hung his head, shamed. He had willfully seduced her, stolen her innocence. He had taken unfair advantage of her naïveté. Then, to salve his pride, he had tried to assign the blame to Jed, dime novels, and even Tess herself. Anywhere but the real culprit—himself.

Unable to bear the heartwrenching sobs any longer, he crossed the patio in long strides, entered the kitchen, and rummaged through a cupboard for a bottle of whiskey he had stashed away. Upon finding it, he pulled out the cork and took a long swallow. Not even the burn of alcohol could cleanse the remorse he felt. He stood for a long moment, debating whether he should go back and apologize. He wanted to take her in his arms, offer comfort, and beg forgiveness. He took a step in her direction, then halted. He didn't trust himself. He was afraid that a look, a touch, and he'd want to make love to her all over again. *Damn!* Just thinking of her made him hard.

Disgruntled, he shoved his fingers through his hair, swore, then took another swig of whiskey. What he had done to Tess Montgomery defied every principle drummed into his head. He had been taught to honor women, not defile them. That had been an unwritten code of honor where he had grown to manhood. He had betrayed her trust, degraded her reputation, destroyed her innocence.

Betrayed, degraded, nearly destroyed.

Didn't she do the same to you? an insidious voice whispered. Why, then, did he labor under a heavy yoke of guilt? Why not mark her debt as paid in full and get on with his life? He stared at the bottle in his hands as though hoping to find the answer etched in the glass.

Starting with their first kiss, revenge had been the furthest thing from his mind. Making love to her—and that's the only way he could describe what had just happened between them—had far surpassed any of his past experiences with women. The intensity had unnerved him. At the time, he had tried to dismiss it as lust, pure and simple. But in retrospect, there was nothing simple at all about the feelings she had evoked. Along with the passion, he had felt a profound sense of homecoming—and peace.

He replaced the cork in the whiskey bottle. After years of torment, he wondered bleakly, was he finally beginning to heal? And if so, at what cost?

Eleven

Sunlight spilled into the room like lost gold, but not even the brilliant sunshine could penetrate the heavy gloom that surrounded her. Curling into a tight ball, Tess pulled the blanket over her head.

Coward, fool, idiot, tramp, slut, whore.

The litany went on and on until she finally ran out of names to call herself. After last night, how could she face Zach again? How could she pretend nothing out of the ordinary had happened when her whole world had changed? And more important, how had something so beautiful, so precious, been transformed into something ugly and tawdry?

Tess felt a tug on the blanket. "Go away," she muttered. She wanted to be left alone to wallow in her misery.

The tugging persisted. She shrank from the thought of how she must look after a night spent crying herself to sleep. Her eyes felt swollen and gritty, and she knew her hair must be hopelessly snarled and matted. She wasn't prepared to see Zach just yet—maybe never. "Leave me alone." Even to her own ears, she sounded like a petulant child.

When there was no reprieve from the gentle prodding, she flung the bedclothes aside. "There," she cried. "Satisfied?"

When there was no response, she cautiously peered over her shoulder. Smoky, the kitten, meowed back. Daintily the little cat lifted one paw and gave an impatient swipe at the blanket. Tess groaned at her own foolishness. Apparently, when it came to Zach McClain there was no limit to her own stupidity. Had she really expected to find him hovering over her this morning? That he'd beg forgiveness, then pledge his undying devotion?

Well, there would be no more cowering beneath the covers. With a weary sigh, she shoved the blanket aside and sat up. A dull hammering pounded against her skull. Grains of sand seemed embedded in her eyeballs. Inside she felt hollow, empty.

Tess wearily massaged her throbbing temples. She had learned a valuable, if painful, lesson last night. It was possible for bodies to mate in the most intimate of human acts while their hearts never touched. Possible for one heart to melt, and the other to remain hard as stone. Tears clogged her throat, and she willed them away. *Enough,* she silently rebuked herself. *No more tears.*

"Let this be fair warning," she addressed the inquisitive kitten. "Don't let someone the likes of Zach McClain ever break your heart."

Smoky cocked her head to one side and studied her through bright, green eyes—eyes nearly the color of Zach's. A look that could only be described as feline sympathy crossed the kitten's small face.

Glancing around, Tess noticed her nightgown neatly draped over the back of a chair. An uncomfortable warmth surged through her at the thought that Zach had returned while she slept and carefully arranged the garment. Another small thoughtful gesture that, under different circumstances, she might have found endearing. As it was, however, she steeled herself against a treacherous softening toward him.

As she went about dressing, she felt a twinge of discomfort between her legs, an unwanted token of the night before. Turning her attention to chores, she started to strip the bed linen, then froze. Dark-red stains contrasted vividly against stark white cotton. Yet another vivid reminder of lost virtue. Averting her gaze, she gathered the sheets into a bundle. She peered at her reflection in the mirror before leaving the room. A pair of solemn gray eyes, their lids puffy, the whites bloodshot, stared back from a face pale and drawn. She looked sadder, she concluded, if not wiser.

Tess busied herself scrubbing and sweeping until both bedclothes and house were immaculate. When there was nothing more to clean, she filled a tub with hot water. After bathing and washing her hair, she luxuriated in the tub until the water grew cold and her flesh was pebbled with goose bumps. Then she dressed in a simple blue-and-white gingham dress, leaving her hair loose around her shoulders while it dried.

To while away the rest of the afternoon, she brought out the stack of dime novels that she had found hidden away and began to sort through them. Stories of cowboys, detectives, unrequited love. Wonderful, magical tales. During her mother's lengthy illness, they had saved her sanity. Each week, she'd purchase one with her egg money. Then, when chores were completed and her mother settled for the night, she'd immerse herself in harmless fantasies. In the halo of a kerosene lamp, she'd indulge her hunger for romance and adventure. For a few hours, she'd forget about doctor fees, leaking roofs, and the bill at the butcher shop. Forget she had no strong shoulder to lean on—and, in all likelihood, never would. Though Zach might disparage her taste in reading material, it had proved her salvation.

She ran her hand over a tattered cover. Had Jed derived the same enjoyment from dime novels that she had—searched for the same escape? But what she didn't understand was why he had gone to such lengths to protect and hide them. Most people, herself included, preferred to keep their books close at hand—not in a chicken coop, of all places. Yet Jed had painstakingly bundled the dime novels, wrapped them in waterproof paper, and stored them in the far recess of a henhouse. She had almost missed finding them because of all the straw stuffed around them. No, it was all very strange indeed.

Unless Jed had grown senile.

Tess rested her back against the adobe and considered the possibility. People, she had observed, often developed eccentricities as they aged. Some did odd things that made absolutely no sense to anyone else. If that theory was true, in fact, it might explain the unusual terms of Jed's will. And yet, she thought, frowning, no one mentioned Jed losing his mental faculties. She made a note to ask Abner Smith a few subtle questions about Jed's state of mind the next time she was in town.

Idly she began to leaf through back issues of *Fireside Companion,* but at first none of the stories captured her interest. Finally, she selected a dime novel featuring her favorite serial detective, Old Sleuth. The story was one she hadn't read before, and she was quickly lost as the mystery unfolded. Time slid away. At a low feline growl, she glanced up from her story. In the far corner of the patio, Smoky crouched on her belly, eyes glued on a butterfly with iridescent blue wings flitting around the bush of devil's claw.

Bemused, Tess returned her attention to the novel in

her lap. Suddenly the plot ceased to make sense. At first she blamed it on her temporary distraction at the kitten's antics. Flipping to the previous page, she re-read the last several paragraphs and turned the page. The story still failed to make sense. Belatedly, she realized the reason for her confusion. Pages were stuck together, thereby eliminating two entire pages of text.

Her brows knit in concentration as she tried to separate the two without tearing either of them. To her amazement, she realized they weren't simply stuck together, but securely glued.

"What on earth?" she said aloud.

Lightly, Tess ran her hand over the page and was surprised to detect a faint bulge beneath the print. On closer inspection, she noticed a delicate slit along the bound edge. Smooth, straight, and deliberate, the cut was barely visible unless one looked closely. Her heart began to hammer with excitement. Someone, probably Jed, had cleverly hidden something between them.

Her hands trembled as she carefully pried the slit apart. Using her thumb and forefinger as pincers, she withdrew a folded sheet of paper. For a long time, she simply stared at it, regarding it as she might a strange, hairy insect. She wondered if this was how Pandora felt before opening the fabled box. Then, slowly, she unfolded the delicate sheet of paper and spread it across her lap.

It was a map of sorts, she noted, with several crude diagrams and spidery print. Tess held it up and examined it more closely. The words weren't written in English, but another language, possibly Spanish. She stared at one of the drawings consisting of a series of lines and curves, but nothing looked familiar. She couldn't escape the feeling that her discovery was significant. Otherwise, why would Jed have gone to such great lengths to conceal its whereabouts? Had this rudimentary sketch cost him his life?

"Tess," Zach's voice rang out. "Where are you?"

She quickly folded the map and returned it to its hiding place. "Out here on the patio," she called, trying to blame the fluttery sensation in her chest on her discovery rather than on Zach's arrival.

He emerged through the kitchen. His sweat-dampened shirt clung to him like a second skin. His clothes were covered with grime, and dirt streaked his face. She knew without asking that he had spent the day exploring the mine. He stood quietly in the shade of the overhanging roof while his gaze wandered over her, then lingered on her face.

Careful to keep her expression schooled, Tess rose to her feet and returned his look. The dime novel slid to the ground, momentarily forgotten. She should hate him for seducing her, she told herself. Not for what he had done, but rather for the emotions he had evoked. She'd never be able to look at him again without remembering the night spent in his arms. And admitting that, regardless of the personal cost, she would gladly do it again. He had not only awakened her body, he had touched her heart.

She cleared her throat and broke the silence. "There's hot water if you want a bath before supper."

"Thanks." He gave her a crooked half-smile. "Guess that's your way of telling me I need one."

She summoned a smile in return. "I'm sure you would've reached the same conclusion on your own."

He jerked his head toward the dime novels scattered about. "Looks like you did some reading."

"A little." Belatedly she recalled the craftily concealed map she had found. Kneeling, she began gathering the dime novels.

"Here," he said as he knelt next to her. "Let me help."

"It isn't necessary."

"Never like to argue with a lady, but I beg to differ with you." He handed her a dog-eared copy of *Boys' Life*.

Careful to avoid touching him, she snatched the book from his hand. His proximity was playing havoc on her senses. Her emotions threatened to become volatile, chaotic. Hurt, anger, betrayal, love, and longing all tumbled inside her. She wanted to shove him away one instant and draw him closer the next. Pushing her conflicting feelings aside, she concentrated instead on retrieving the magazines. "Thank you for your help," she said as she scrambled to her feet.

"You're quite welcome," he replied, straightening, his tone equally formal.

Tess hated the tension between them. Zach seemed as ill at ease in her company as she did in his. Neither of them it seemed knew how, or was willing, to bridge that gap. Too many words had been left unspoken. Too many feelings unexplored. They had been lovers but couldn't be friends. The realization left her bereft.

"Did you find anything of interest at the mine?" Tess asked, struggling to keep her tone light.

Zach's eyes narrowed with sudden suspicion. "What do you mean?"

"You spend a lot of time there is all." She shrugged her shoulders. "You needn't get defensive. I was simply making conversation."

He relaxed visibly. "No treasure in silver, if that's what you want to hear."

"None at all?"

"Talk has it the mine was played out years ago."

"Then why go there?"

Now it was his turn to shrug. "Not much else to do.

Who knows? Maybe there's still a vein or two waiting to be discovered."

"But so far you haven't found them?"

"No, nothing but rocks and dirt."

She bit her lip to keep from asking about the package she had seen him slip into his saddlebag and take to Tucson. Obviously, it was a secret he wasn't ready to share. Well, she decided, two could play this game. She had a secret, too. For the time being, she wouldn't mention the strange map she had found. At least not yet. She wanted a chance to solve a mystery just like her favorite detective character, Old Sleuth.

The kitten, who had grown weary of terrorizing butterflies, trotted over to Zach and rubbed against his pant leg. Before Tess could scoop it out of the way, Zach bent down and picked it up.

"Looks like I've got a new friend," he drawled, stroking the tiny ball of fluff. Smoky purred in contentment.

Tess's mouth went dry at the sight of Zach petting the kitten. She shifted her weight from one foot to the other. Only last night, those long, tapered fingers had played across her body as skillfully as a pianist, striking chords with unerring precision, making her resonate. Making her purr. Just thinking about it made her feel flushed, feverish. "I—ah . . . I'll fix supper while you wash up," she said as she began to turn away.

"Tess . . ."

"Yes." She held her breath and waited.

Zach held the kitten gently against his broad chest. Two pairs of eyes, the same remarkable shade of green, regarded her solemnly. "Nothing," he said at last. "By the way, the fiesta's the day after tomorrow. We might as well take the wagon and load up on supplies while we're there."

"Might as well," she said, her voice flat.

Too many words unspoken. Too many feelings unexplored, she repeated silently as she hurried inside.

The day of the fiesta dawned bold and bright. The sun blazed from a brilliant blue canopy dotted with puffy white clouds. By the time the wagon rolled into town, Main Street teemed with people in a festive mood.

"I didn't think there were this many people in the entire Arizona Territory," Tess commented as her gaze swept the throng.

"Word of a fiesta travels. Families in all the outlying ranches make the trip into town for special occasions."

Zach found a place near the livery stable to leave the wagon. He tossed a coin to an eager boy of eight or ten with black hair and sparkling dark eyes, then fired a stream of instructions in Spanish.

"Sí, señor." With a wide grin, the boy slipped the coin into his baggy pants.

Zach leaped down from the seat and came around to assist Tess. "I didn't know you spoke Spanish," she said, trying to think about the mysterious map with its indecipherable lettering, and not on the strong hands at her waist.

"A little," he admitted. He swung her to the ground but didn't release her. "You look pretty in that yellow dress."

At the unexpected compliment, Tess ducked her head and hoped the wide brim of her hat hid her flushed cheeks. Knowing that Zach rarely resorted to flattery made any rare praise even more precious. It made her glad she had chosen the sunny, lemon yellow muslin sprigged with tiny lavender flowers. Zach, too, had taken time with his appearance. If possible, he looked more strikingly handsome than ever in his chambray shirt and buff-colored leather vest. His hat had been thoroughly brushed, his boots polished to a high gloss. "You look nice, too," she said, suddenly shy.

"Tess?"

"Yes . . ." She tilted her head back so she could decipher his expression.

"About the other night . . ."

The commotion on the street dimmed, then faded. The hands gripping her waist tightened spasmodically as he seemed to stumble over what he wanted to say. His gaze settled on her mouth in a way she found disconcerting. Nervously, she moistened her lower lip with the tip of her tongue.

"You have the sweetest mouth," he murmured. "Soft and luscious as a Georgia peach."

Tess knew he meant to kiss her right then and there in the middle of town. Her lips parted as her body swayed toward his in an unconscious invitation.

"Bold as brass, the two of you!"

Tess and Zach sprang apart at the sound of Josie Goodbody's voice. Turning as one, they found the woman charging toward them, her face livid with outrage.

"Don't you have any shame? Any decency?"

Zach recovered first. "Mrs. Goodbody," he said with a smile and tipped his hat in a courtly gesture. "You're looking lovely today as always."

Josie pursed her lips and peered at Zach through narrowed eyes. "Are you mocking me, boy?"

He gave her a smile that rivaled Jimmy Jerold's for charm content. "Why, Miz Josie, what a suspicious nature you have."

"Suspicious, my foot" she sniffed. She wagged her index finger under his nose. "You ought to be ashamed of yourselves. Not only are you living in sin, but now you're flaunting your lust in public. And in front of innocent children."

Tess had forgotten the young boy whom Zach had charged with the care of their wagon and horses. She glanced over to find the lad watching the scene with avid interest. A pair of prospectors with tobacco-stained beards and a small group of enlisted men from nearby Fort Lowell had gathered as well to listen to the woman's diatribe.

"The ladies of my sewing circle were shocked, absolutely shocked, when I told them what I found the morning of my visit."

From the corner of her eye, Tess saw one soldier nudge another. She felt her cheeks burn. "It isn't the way you think, Mrs. Goodbody. Zach was only trying to—"

"Hah!" Josie snorted. "I wasn't born yesterday, missy. I know *exactly* what that man was trying to do."

Zach took Tess by the elbow. "Look here, Miz Josie, anything that goes on between Miss Montgomery and myself is between the two of us. I told you before, it's none of your damn business."

"Such profanity!" Indignant, Josie Goodbody pressed a hand against her flat bosom. "Must I remind you, young man, to keep a civil tongue in your head when you're addressing a lady."

Tess cast a sidelong glance at Zach. His jaw clenched tight; his lips thinned. He was clearly torn between temper and tradition. From everything she knew about him, he had been raised to be a proper Southern gentleman. Josie Goodbody, however, clearly tried both his patience and good manners.

Zach let out a long sigh. "Sorry, ma'am."

"And another thing," Josie continued, unfazed. "Any man with a good upbringing would do the honorable thing. You've already stolen her virtue, destroyed her reputation. Marry the girl and make an honest woman of her."

"Yeah," one of the prospectors chimed. "Marry 'er, or step aside and give one of us a chance."

His bearded friend nodded in quick agreement. "Me and Pete would be right grateful to have a woman to cook and clean up after us. We'd treat 'er like a queen."

"Hell with cookin' and cleanin'; if she was my woman, I'd let her stay in bed all day." A ruddy-faced private gave Tess a lewd wink. "Flat on her back."

Before he knew what happened, the private found himself flat on his back in the dusty thoroughfare with Zach looming over him, his fists bunched. The onlookers grew very quiet; apparently none of them wanted to further test Zach's temper.

Zach took Tess by the arm and steered her away. "If you'll kindly excuse us . . ."

"Heed my advice, Miss," Josie called after them. "Men are weak when it comes to ways of the flesh. They don't always know better, but women should. Make sure McClain puts a ring on your finger before he puts a baby in your belly."

"Don't pay any attention to the bunch," Zach said in a low voice as he hustled Tess down the street. "Josie Goodbody is a self-righteous prude. Ignore her."

But though she tried, she couldn't dismiss the way those men had looked at her, their expressions rife with speculation. They had undressed her with their eyes, made her feel dirty, cheap. The fiesta no longer held its original appeal. She would have much preferred a quiet afternoon on her patio, miles from ugly accusations and lascivious glances.

Tess was still struggling to recover from the unpleasant assault on her character when she spied Lily London sashaying down the boardwalk in their direction.

As on their previous encounter, Lily was dressed in a stylish but revealing gown, this time in deep purple, designed to showcase her generous bosom.

"My, my," she cooed upon drawing closer. "If it isn't Miss Tess Montgomery, one of Tucson's newest citizens."

"Good afternoon, Miss London," Tess replied.

"Call me Lily, hon; everyone does." Though Lily addressed Tess, her blue eyes feasted on Zach as though he were a box of bonbons. "Aren't you going to introduce me to your friend?"

Tess hastily made the required introductions.

"Pleasure to make your acquaintance." Lily extended a soft, manicured hand to Zach. "I don't think we've met. I never forget a face, especially one as handsome as yours."

It was more than Zach's face that captured Lily's interest, Tess thought with a flash of irritation. The blond saloon owner boldly assessed his body as thoroughly as a tailor measuring him for a new suit. With a start, she realized that what she felt wasn't irritation, but jealousy.

"The pleasure's all mine, ma'am," Zach drawled, giving her a slow smile.

"I should have known better than to worry about clever little Tess. Looks like she's done all right for herself by finding a strapping, good-looking man like yourself to protect her."

"Zach and I are partners," Tess explained stiffly.

"Of course you are, hon." Lily's tone had grown condescending. "After all, a girl's gotta do what a girl's gotta do to survive."

Zach's smile faded. "What Tess meant to say was that we're business partners. Jed Duncan left his property to us jointly. So like it or not, until a buyer is found we're stuck with each other."

Lily shrugged her shoulders, the action causing her breasts to rise and fall like twin mounds of bread dough. "From where I'm standing, that doesn't seem too much of a hardship."

Tess fumed inwardly. Lily London's attitude was just as disturbing as Josie Goodbody's had been. Even though one condoned what the other condemned, both had been quick to leap to the wrong conclusions. Both failed to recognize the situation for what it really was.

Or did they?

Perhaps both women were right in an odd, convoluted way. She and Zach were drawn to each other by a strong physical attraction. Even knowing it was wrong, somehow its lure was impossible to resist. But was what she felt toward Zach purely physical? asked a small voice at the back of her mind. The situation would be far less complicated if the answer was yes, but her heart refused to cooperate.

Lily, oblivious of Tess's dilemma, moved off with a cheerful wave. "Next time you're in town, Johnny Reb, stop by the Silver Sequin and ask for Lily. The first drink's on the house."

Twelve

"Wait here," Zach muttered. "I want to get some cigars." He disappeared inside a small shop wedged between a butcher's and blacksmith's, leaving Tess on the boardwalk.

Tess eyed the wooden sign above the door with skepticism: *U.S. Postmaster.* This seemed an unlikely place to purchase cigars, but here in the territory stores often served multiple purposes. Still she couldn't erase the suspicion that Zach was interested in something other than tobacco. And that something had to do with the package he was so secretive about.

She had been tempted on numerous occasions to tell him about the map she had found hidden among Jed's dime novels. Each time, though, she had suffered a change of heart. Part of the reason she had kept the discovery to herself could be attributed to sheer stubbornness. Why should she confide in Zach when he refused to confide in her? Why share when he hoarded? Yet, she admitted, she was no closer to solving the riddle. After learning that Zach spoke Spanish, she was more tempted than ever to enlist his help.

At the sound of lively music, Tess swung around and saw a large throng of people round the corner. It was a procession, she realized, led by a half-dozen altar boys wearing white surplices over scarlet cassocks. Their leader, a boy of twelve or thirteen, carried a large crucifix. These were followed by a priest attired in intricately embroidered garments. Men, women, and children of all ages dressed in colorful garb trailed behind. Last of all came the musicians, several with guitars, one waving a tambourine, and another shaking dried gourds. What the band lacked in sophistication they made up for with enthusiasm. Up and down the street, people swarmed out of stores and businesses to watch the noisy contingent wend its way toward San Agustin Church in the plaza.

Even without turning, Tess sensed Zach's presence behind her. She began to move aside, but his hands resting lightly, possessively, on her shoulders stopped her. The gesture was surprisingly intimate and spontaneous, and seemed the most natural thing in the world. It took all her willpower not to lean against him and invite his embrace. Instead, she stood perfectly still, afraid to move, unwilling to do anything that might shatter the rare bond between them.

"Its the Feast of the Ascension," he said, his voice a low, pleasing rumble in her ear. "Most Mexicans are very devout Roman Catholics. See how the women hold their rosary beads and recite the prayers as they follow along?"

Tess kept her eyes fastened on the passing procession, but her mind was elsewhere. All her senses centered on Zach: the light pressure of his hands, the heat emanating from his hard-muscled body, his smell. She could remember the taste of his mouth, the texture of his skin, the warm cocoon of his arms around her. The magic he evoked when he moved deep inside her. She closed her eyes and tried to staunch the flood of memories—and failed. Maybe she was the brazen sinner people assumed, but God help her, she wanted Zach McClain so much it terrified her.

"Ready?"

Her eyes flew open. "Ready?" she repeated, fearful that he might have divined her unruly thoughts.

"For the bullfight." He gazed down at her in bemusement. "It's quite an event around here. Folks have talked of little else for weeks. Of course, if you're squeamish . . ."

"No." Tess shook off the last remnants of the sensual fog. "By all means, I'd like to attend."

Together they joined the steady stream of people making their way toward a makeshift bullring constructed near the Tully and Ochoa corral. Children's laughter punctuated the noisy blend of Spanish and English and contributed to the festive atmosphere. Tess found the gaiety infectious.

Zach steered her toward the entrance. "Later, after sundown, there'll be music and dancing. And, of course, food of every sort imaginable."

The mention of dancing brought back her promise to Jimmy Jerold. She'd much rather dance with Zach. She wondered if he'd even ask her, or choose to remain aloof. Jimmy, on the other hand, was overly friendly. Aside from the blatant flattery, the way she caught him looking at her made her decidedly uneasy.

She and Zach filed into the bullring, which consisted of crude bleachers on either side of a large circular area of sunbaked earth. Participants in the event could enter the ring through a sturdy gate at the far end. Zach, his hand at her waist, guided her to a spot along the righthand side of the arena that would allow a clear view of the proceedings. "Are you sure you want to do this? It's still not too late to change your mind."

Her brows drew together as she scanned the bullring. Men far outnumbered the women, but that in itself wasn't unusual here in the Arizona Territory. Any misgivings she might have had vanished the minute Josie Goodbody and a lady friend entered the ring and planted themselves in the front row on the opposite side. If prim and proper Josie could witness the sport, so could she. "I wouldn't miss the opportunity to see a real bullfight for the world. I've read all about them."

"In dime novels, of course," Zach said dryly, lowering himself onto the bleacher next to her. He gave her a long, considering glance. "You may not feel the same after you've witnessed one for yourself."

Tess barely heard the subtle warning. "Why is that?" she asked.

"You'll see."

Tess gave him a quizzical look, but when no further explanation was forthcoming she returned her attention to the festivities. The bleachers were soon jammed with spectators, young and old, men and women, dark-skinned and light. A well-dressed gentleman who, Zach informed her, was the mayor of Tucson, arrived and took a seat that assured him an excellent view of the event.

At the sharp, staccato notes from a bugle, an expectant hush fell over those assembled. Her heart knocking against her ribs in anticipation, Tess craned her neck for a better look at the gate.

Two horsemen in plumed finery burst into the ring at a full gallop. Turning in opposite directions, they circled the ring at a fast pace. Tess held her breath when it appeared that their paths would collide. At the very last moment, they veered away. The maneuver was greeted by enthusiastic clapping from the crowd.

Next, the gate swung wide to admit all the participants. Some men were mounted on magnificent high-stepping horses; others entered on foot and wore elaborate costumes in bold colors trimmed with sequins and braid. Another group were plainly dressed and astride heavy work horses. Slowly, and with all the pomp and pageantry at their command, they strutted around the perimeter of the arena. Tess joined the others in a wild display of applause.

Leaning closer, she raised her voice to be heard above the crowd. "Where is the matador?"

Just as she posed the question, a solitary figure stepped into the ring. Tall and reed slender with snapping black eyes, he carried a sword in one hand and, in the other, a short red cape lined in yellow satin draped over a stick. The afternoon sun glinted off the gold braid trimming his green silk costume.

Haughty, his manner bordering on arrogance, the matador approached the mayor and saluted. The mayor rose to his feet and, raising his right arm, granted permission for the bullfight to begin in earnest. A loud roar of approval went up from the crowd.

An expectant hush fell as a bull was herded through a chute into the ring. The animal, an enormous creature bulging with muscle and exuding vigor and power, charged to the center of the ring. Lowering its head until the wide expanse of its mighty horns nearly swept the ground, the bull pawed the earth. Tess felt the ground vibrate beneath its sturdy hooves. The sensation was intensified by the heavy thud of her heart against her ribs.

Immediately, a group of four sprang into action. The men approached the animal with an odd mix of caution and bravado as they waved colorful capes to snare the bull's attention.

"The men you see now are *peones*," Zach explained, assuming the role of instructor. "It is their duty to tempt the bull into a series of charges so that the matador can observe its movements and gauge the quality of its charges."

Tess watched, fascinated, as the *peon* closest to them flicked his cape. Tess couldn't be sure whether the loud snap or the bright color had enraged the bull, but with head lowered, it attacked. Waiting until the last possible second, the man sidestepped and narrowly avoided being gored with one of the long, pointed horns. She sucked in a breath at the near miss, mindless of Zach's bemused glance.

After the matador had studied the bull's movements to his satisfaction, the *peones* retired to the sidelines. This was the cue for the men on horseback to spur their mounts forward.

Zach leaned closer. "These men who carry lances are called *picadores*."

As Tess watched, a *picador,* lance poised above his head, charged the bull. Waiting until he was nearly alongside the animal, he drove the sharp point into its back. The bull let forth a loud bellow of pain and rage. Not giving the wounded beast time to recover, a second *picador* imitated the actions of the first. The bull shook its massive form, sending a spray of ruby red droplets into the moisture-starved earth. The crowd erupted into an angry furor.

Tess clutched Zach's sleeve, shocked by the men's blatant cruelty. "Why are those men tormenting that poor animal?" she demanded.

"It's the *picadores'* job to weaken the bull, to tame its energy."

"Didn't they hear how the people object to such barbaric tactics?"

"It's just the opposite, darlin'. If the bull is too weak, he won't put up a good fight. The crowd fears they won't get their money's worth. The matador, on the other hand, feels quite differently. He likes the odds more firmly in his favor."

As though to test the veracity of Zach's statement,

the matador stepped forward. Careful to maintain a comfortable distance, he shook a yellow cape in front of the bull to further provoke it. Enraged almost beyond endurance, the animal dove at the fluttering satin, then twisted, turned, and charged again. Each time, the matador gracefully dodged the attack. Acknowledging the audience's applause with a slight bow, he strutted to the edge of the arena.

Zach pointed to a trio of men. Each of them held two long darts with steel hooks attached at one end. "The *banderilleros* are the next ones to prepare the bull for its fight with the matador."

Tess absorbed this information in silence. She suddenly was besieged with renewed doubts about the wisdom of attending a bullfight. The stories she had read in the dime novels had glorified the contest between man and beast, making it seem daring and noble. In them, the matador's bravery had assumed almost mythical proportions.

Unable to drag her gaze from the spectacle, she watched the *banderilleros* take their positions. One by one, in rapid succession, they ran at the bull and hurled their darts into its unprotected back. The darts viciously pierced the animal's thick hide and clawed their way into muscle and tissue. Horrified, Tess pressed her hand against her mouth.

Snorting and bucking, the bull ran about the arena in a futile effort to dislodge the painful spears embedded in its flesh. Dark rivulets of blood matted the bull's once-glossy red-brown coat. Tess cast a longing glance toward the entrance of the arena and was dismayed to find the way barred by a solid wall of spectators.

Again, the matador stepped forward. With a flourish, he waved the red-and-yellow satin in front of the bull, teasing and taunting until, in a maddened frenzy, the animal charged. Proudly, the bullfighter executed a series of deft maneuvers, demonstrating his mastery over the wounded beast to the delight of those assembled. Crazed with pain and weakened by blood loss, the bull's movements were becoming increasingly erratic. Loud cheers from the crowd signaled their approval. Even Josie Goodbody, Tess noted in amazement, joined in the applause.

The heat, the smell of blood, and the certainty that worse was yet to come combined to make Tess's stomach queasy. She didn't know how much more she could tolerate before embarrassing herself. A small sound escaped, signaling her distress.

Zach turned to her, his brow knit with concern. "Damn," he cursed softly. "I should have known this was going to be a bad idea. You aren't about to get sick, are you?"

In spite of the balmy temperature, a cold sweat beaded her brow. "No," she replied, her voice choked.

"Liar," Zach drawled. He handed her his handkerchief while he scanned the arena for the nearest exit.

But it was too late.

The matador exchanged his wooden sword for one of steel. Unable to witness the ultimate cruelty, Tess buried her face against Zach's broad shoulder. Her entire body shuddered as a deafening cry went up from the crowd. She burrowed against him, shamed by her need for comfort, helpless to refute it. In spite of her misery, she was conscious of Zach's arm securely around her.

"Don't watch," he murmured, his voice low and soothing. "It'll be over soon."

A final burst of applause signaled the crowd's approved of the mayor's decision to reward the matador with both of the bull's ears for his bravery and skill. Bile burned the back of her throat. Once again she feared she would disgrace herself by being sick.

When she finally opened her eyes minutes later, the dead animal was being hauled from the ring. The *banderilleros'* darts, still deeply embedded in its thick hide, waved back and forth like macabre wands. The mutilated, blood-encrusted carcass bore no resemblance whatsoever to the healthy, robust animal that had entered the arena a short time ago.

Never again, Tess vowed as, dazed and disillusioned, she trailed Zach from the bullring.

Never again, Zach vowed as he peered down at Tess. Her face looked as pale as paper, her pretty gray eyes glazed. He cursed himself for a fool for ignoring his better judgment and taking her to a bullfight. What had he been thinking?

You don't have a lick of common sense, boy.

In his mind, he heard his mother's stinging rebuke as clearly as he had more than ten years ago when he enlisted in the Confederate army. Nothing she had said had dissuaded him from following his father's and brother's example. No amount of tears, pleading, or reasoning could sway his decision. He had been determined to acquit himself with valor and honor. Instead, he had spent most of the war rotting in a Union prison camp. Stripped of everything he prized: valor, honor, and dignity. No, he thought grimly, he didn't have a lick of sense then, and still didn't.

Tess dabbed the perspiration from her temples. "The bullfight was nothing like the stories I read. I had no idea it would be so vicious—so unfair."

"Many things are unfair."

He dug a coin from his pocket, paid a vendor for a gourd of cold water, and thrust it at Tess.

Tess drank thirstily, then returned the gourd. "The

poor bull never stood a chance to survive. He was doomed the moment he entered the ring."

"Some would argue it was fate. Destiny."

"You weren't always this cold, this dispassionate. I remember the fervor in your voice whenever you spoke of your home and family. I remember the fire in your eyes when you championed the Confederate cause. Even though I disagreed, I admired your conviction."

He silently admitted the truth of her words. He used to be much different from the man he was now. While imprisoned at Elmira, hunger, cold, and abject humiliation had eroded his fervor. Pestilence had ravished his idealism until only cynicism remained. No, he acknowledged, he'd never again be the same. Aloud he said, "Ten years is a long time. Everyone changes."

Glancing down at her, he was glad to see some color had returned to her cheeks. Tess, he reflected, seemed to have changed very little from the girl he had once known—and trusted. A fact that never failed to surprise him. Knowing she had betrayed him, he expected to find her tougher, more resilient, even callous. Yet here she was, upset over the demise of a dumb animal to the point that it made her physically ill. How could anyone that sensitive, that tenderhearted, turn her back on a fellow human being and commit him to hell? It just didn't make sense.

"If I live to be a hundred," Tess continued as she returned his handkerchief, "I swear I'll never go to another bullfight."

Taking her arm, Zach steered her toward the plaza. "Arizona is too harsh for a girl fresh off the farm. Once we find a buyer for the place, you oughta consider moving back east."

* * *

The remainder of the afternoon passed pleasantly as they browsed the streets surrounding the plaza, stopping frequently to examine the handcrafted items that were for sale. The merchandise was spread on blankets, displayed from donkey carts, or carried by the vendors themselves. Tess paused to admire a dress similar to ones she had seen many of the Mexican women wearing. Embroidered yellow and blue flowers trimmed the wide ruffle that circled the scooped neckline; the sleeves were short and puffed, the skirt full. It looked pretty, yet practical for the hot summer months ahead. Remembering her limited resources, however, she reluctantly returned the dress to a plump, brown-skinned woman who looked as disappointed as she by the decision.

The setting sun was beginning to streak the sky with varying shades of vermilion when Zach suggested they eat dinner. He found two empty places at one of the long tables that had been constructed specifically for the fiesta, then went off in search of food. He returned a short time later with two plates heaped with slices of beef, roasted potatoes, and a variety of unfamiliar delicacies. He set a plate in front of Tess, then sat down next to her.

"Tamales, enchiladas, and tacos," he said, identifying the items he had selected for her to sample.

Zach dug into the meal with gusto. Now that her earlier queasiness had subsided, Tess's appetite returned. After a few bites of the traditional rice and beans, she cautiously tasted some of the Mexican favorites. "Umm," she murmured after tasting the enchilada. "Delicious."

"Are you enjoying our fiesta, Tess?"

Tess glanced up to find Abner Smith beaming down at her. She noted with wry amusement that the lawyer's plate was stacked nearly as high as Zach's.

"This seat taken?" Not waiting for a response, Abner plunked himself down next to her. "The food's reason enough in itself to come to a fiesta."

Tess bit into something so hot and spicy it stole her breath away. "Yes," she agreed in a raspy voice, her mouth on fire.

Abner chuckled. "Like most things around here, the food takes some getting used to." He tore off a piece of tortilla. "How did you like the bullfight? I spotted you in the crowd and thought you looked a little green toward the end."

"I hated it," she replied vehemently. "I never want to see another bullfight as long as I live."

"All the ladies say that, then can't wait for the next one." He dismissed her words with a careless wave of his fork. "Even Josie Goodbody likes them. Matter of fact, if Josie had her way, we'd have them more often."

At the mention of the bullfight, Tess's appetite fled. She felt Zach's gaze settle on her, but refused to meet his look. Thankfully, just then three men in rough garb claimed the bench opposite them and forestalled further discussion of an event she had found repulsive.

The first, a burly man with a sunburned face and a red-gold beard, regarded Tess and Zach with avid interest. "Hey," he said at last, "ain't you the pair livin' at Jed Duncan's old place?"

Zach leveled a cold stare at the man, his mouth hard and unsmiling. "Miss Montgomery and I inherited the ranch and mine jointly."

"Yeah, sure," he mumbled. "Meant no harm, just curious is all."

The trio exchanged uneasy glances, then took a renewed interest in the food on their plates.

"Jed was an old friend of ours," Tess explained, hoping to ease the awkward situation.

"Heard the two of you was old friends, too," one of the men said, not looking up from his plate.

Tess felt her cheeks grow warm. She wondered who had disclosed details of her previous relationship with Zach. Jimmy Jerold or Moe Black? Lily London? She cast a sidelong glance at Abner Smith. Was the lawyer the culprit? Regardless, she disliked being the subject of idle gossip. She could only imagine the tongues Josie Goodbody had started to wagging after her unexpected visit.

Abner Smith stopped chewing long enough to study the three seated across the table. "Don't suppose any of you gentlemen are interested in buying them out? According to Duncan's will, the mine and ranch have to be sold as one." He winked at Tess. "Probably could get them real cheap."

A horrified expression spread across the homely face of the third man in the group. His drooping eyelids gave him a permanent look of melancholy. "Hell, no. Money's scarcer than hen's teeth right now."

The third man, short and round with salt-and-pepper wiry hair and sporting sidewhiskers and mustache, reached across the table and pumped Zach's hand. "Name's Fritz Kemper. The big ugly one is my brother Henry; the older ugly one's my brother Leo," he said by way of introduction.

"None of us could figure out why Jed kept hanging around Tucson." Henry shoveled a fork-full of beans into his mouth. "Some folks were beginning to get suspicious. Others just joked about it."

"Why was that?" Zach asked, his tone neutral.

Henry chewed, swallowed, shoveled in more. "People thought ol' Jed was the last of the fools who still believed the crazy notion about the lost gold shipment."

Lost gold shipment?

At the mention, Tess felt her pulse quicken. Her mouth went dry. Next to her, she felt Zach's body grow taut with sudden tension.

"That old story?" Abner scoffed. "If there were any truth to the rumor, the gold would have been found years ago. Miners scoured every inch of the territory. Looked under every rock."

"Damn right." Leo nodded in dour agreement. "War's been over eight years. Someone would've found it by now. No way they could keep it a secret."

Zach speared a piece of meat with his fork. "We're still new to these parts. Care to enlighten a couple strangers as to what all of you are talking about?"

"And Jed's role in this," Tess added.

Fritz, the most talkative of the Kemper brothers, seemed only too happy to oblige. "If you remember, France ruled Mexico back in those days. Napoleon III appointed Maximilian as emperor. According to legend, Napoleon secretly instructed Maximilian to deliver a shipment of gold to Robert E. Lee."

"Why would Napoleon III want to aid the Confederacy?" Tess asked, puzzled but intrigued by the tale.

"Spoken like a true Yankee," Zach replied, pushing his plate aside.

Abner picked up the story. "Seeing as how the United States was embroiled in a civil war, France felt free to ignore the terms of the Monroe Doctrine, which, if you recall, forbids European interference in the Western Hemisphere. In the interim, France gained control of Mexico. At the time, Lincoln was too busy defending the Union to launch much of a protest. France hoped that if the Confederacy was victorious, they would be more lenient than the North and allow further expansion. The Frenchies weren't above offering a bribe. The gold would cement an alliance with the new government in the United States."

Henry bit into a chili pepper, causing his ruddy face to become even ruddier. "It's rumored Lincoln constantly worried about French troops bein' so close to the border."

"Honest Abe feared the power-hungry French would try to annex Louisiana or parts of the Southwest." Fritz paused in his eating long enough to explain.

Abner removed his gold-rimmed glasses and polished the lenses with his handkerchief. "Once the war ended and the Union had won, the United States was free again to enforce the Monroe Doctrine. France was forced to withdraw its troops, leaving Maximilian with no support. Shortly afterwards, Mexican troops rallied against French rule and brought Maximilian before a firing squad. Napoleon III, of course, denied ever attempting to aid the Confederacy."

"This gold, I assume, was supposedly shipped through Arizona?" Zach kept his expression neutral.

"Yep," Leo nodded glumly. "But it never arrived."

Tess pushed the food around on her plate and tried to contain her mounting excitement. Was the map she had found related to the lost gold? It was almost too much to hope for, and yet . . .

"A fortune in gold," she murmured, unaware that she had spoken the thought aloud.

"Ain't no such thing." Using a tortilla, Leo mopped up the last of his beans. "A tall tale is all."

"Supposedly, a small contingent of soldiers was sent to guard the gold, which was hidden under the false bottom of a wagon," Fritz said before biting into a tamale. "No sign of them or the gold."

"Gold's never been found, but it ain't fer lack of tryin'." Henry stole a chunk of meat from Leo's plate when his brother's head was turned. "First couple of years, the territory crawled with fools hunting lost treasure. Finally most of 'em gave up, either settlin' here or movin' elsewhere."

"For a while folks thought Jed Duncan might be one of them." Pursing his lips, Abner held up his glasses and peered through the lenses, then, satisfied, slipped them back on. "But Jed surprised everyone by buying the old Montoya place along with that petered-out mine. He began to talk about ranching and started a small herd."

"Too bad about Jed." Leo wagged his head in sympathy. "Nice ol' man. Never harmed a fly."

"Do you have any idea who might have shot him?" Zach swept an encompassing look over the three brothers.

Henry stifled a belch. "All kinds of men roamin' about who'd shoot a man for the change in his pockets. No tellin' who might've done it."

Frowning, Abner consulted his pocket watch. "If there was such a shipment, I'd blame Quantrill and his bushwhackers."

"Why Quantrill?"

Zach's voice was calm, deceptively calm. Tess knew him too well by now to be fooled by this show of indifference.

"Who else?" Abner gave a dismissive shrug. "Seems to me they'd be privy to any information on Confederate activity."

Leo nodded in solemn agreement. "Quantrill and his men were no more'n a bunch of thievin' cutthroats."

"Hard to believe anyone could be worse than Quantrill, but Bloody Bill Anderson was the dirtiest bastard of them all," Henry said around a mouthful of food.

"Bloody Bill found Jesus afore he died," Leo observed.

"Yeah," Leo snorted. "And St. Peter himself personally escorted him through the Pearly Gates."

Fritz ignored his sibling's sarcasm. "Bloody Bill ain't the only one who found religion afore he died. "Jed spent so much time out at the mission, people joked he might have a callin'."

"What mission is that?" Tess asked quietly, breaking her lengthy silence.

Abner gave her a benign smile. "San Xavier del Bac, about ten miles south of town. The priests left years ago, but the Indians still take care of the place."

"Funny," Zach mused, "as well as I knew him, Jed never showed much of a tendency toward churchgoing."

"No tellin' why folks do what they do." His meal finished, Fritz rose. His brothers did likewise, and the three ambled off. Minutes later, Abner made his excuses and left.

Tess remained perfectly still while her mind raced. After riding with Quantrill had Jed found himself in need of salvation? Did that explain why he had spent so much time at the mission? And, if that wasn't enough of a mystery, there was the unsolved matter of the lost gold. She chewed her lower lip in concentration. Were the two connected somehow? Excitement thrummed through her bloodstream—an excitement that was quickly squelched when she thought of the map she had found. A map that may have cost Jed his life. Unless she exercised the utmost caution, it might endanger hers as well.

The notion was a sobering one.

Thirteen

The music started at nightfall. The notes from a flute and fiddle lured the crowd to the plaza as predictably as moths to flame. Tess and Zach eased their way through the crowd to a spot near the musicians.

"See how everyone watches us?" Tess whispered to Zach. The curious stares of the men and the condemning ones from the women were making her increasingly uncomfortable.

She wanted to flee. She found herself longing for the little house tucked into the foothills. "No decent woman dares speak to me. As far as they're concerned, I'm the same caliber as Lily London."

"You're making too much of this." But Zach's denial failed to carry any conviction.

As the musicians struck up a familiar tune, a group of soldiers standing across the plaza nudged one another. Finally, the bravest of the bunch, a fresh-faced corporal barely out of his teens, approached them. He cleared his throat loudly. Tess couldn't be certain whether it was to gather his courage or to draw her attention.

"Pardon me, ma'am, but I'd be honored if I could have this dance."

He looked so young, so earnest, Tess found herself

smiling back at him. "My pleasure, Sergeant," she replied, deliberately promoting the young man.

He reddened to the tips of his ears and held out his arm. Ignoring Zach's frown, Tess allowed the corporal to sweep her onto the dance floor. When one dance ended, another of the young man's comrades, emboldened by his success, claimed her as a partner. Much to her surprise, Tess discovered that in spite of her initial misgivings she was enjoying herself. The only thing that would have made her enjoyment complete would have been if Zach had asked her to dance. She peered over the shoulder of her current partner and looked for him, but he was nowhere in sight.

Jimmy Jerold separated himself from the crowd and tapped the soldier she was currently dancing with on the shoulder. "Excuse me, Private," Jimmy Jerold drawled. "I believe Miss Montgomery promised this waltz to me."

The young soldier relinquished Tess with obvious reluctance, then left after eliciting her promise to save a dance for him later.

"With half of Fort Lowell clamoring for your attention, I thought I'd have to fight off an entire regiment to get one dance." He pulled her into his arms and twirled her around the floor. "Must say, I can't blame the soldiers. I happen to share their taste when it comes to beautiful women."

"Please, sir, such flattery will make my head swell," Tess replied, hoping to keep the mood light.

"You most certainly are the belle of the ball this evening." Jimmy glanced toward the sidelines as he guided her in slow, sweeping circles. "Where's your business partner?"

"Some men don't care for dancing. I fear Zach may be one of them." Even as she spoke the words, she doubted their veracity. Zach, she sensed, would prove an excellent dancer. Whether on horseback or walking across a room, he moved with an innate grace that would be displayed to advantage when executing the steps of the waltz.

"Shame on McClain for deserting you. The man needs to be taken to task for ignoring a woman of your considerable charms. Or, perhaps, he's to be pitied for having taken leave of his senses."

Jimmy Jerold, Tess reflected, oozed charm as effortlessly as others breathed. She would feel more relaxed, however, if he weren't holding her quite so tight. The smell of liquor on his breath added to her unease.

"What do you say we try to find us a little privacy. Don't you think it's high time we get better acquainted?"

Warning bells clanged inside her head. Where was Zach, anyway? she wondered in growing panic. She could have used him to fend off Jimmy's advances. She was a rank amateur pitted against an accomplished flirt and ladies' man. "I don't think that's a good idea."

"And might I ask, why not?" The amused glint in his blue eyes signaled that he was not only aware of her discomfort, but delighted by it.

"Because leaving with you would only confirm what people already suspect."

He arched a dark brow and feigned innocence. "And that is?"

She wasn't in the mood for games, so she went straight to the heart of the matter. "Even though I fear my reputation is ruined beyond repair, I refuse to fuel any more gossip. Going off with you, or any other man, regardless of how innocent, would only confirm their suspicions."

"Look me in the eye if you can." He lowered his voice. "Convince me McClain has never been your lover."

Only his arm firmly around her waist kept her from stumbling. Blood rushed to her cheeks, branding them with shame and embarrassment.

"I thought as much," Jimmy chuckled. "No need to go gettin' all upset. Preacher or not, it's perfectly natural for two healthy people livin' under the same roof to share a bed. But what bothers me, sugar, is McClain doesn't treat you right. I know how to please a woman. You won't be disappointed, I promise."

Chest heaving, Tess shoved him away. She could hardly believe what he was suggesting. His boldness momentarily robbed her of speech.

"Do I frighten you, sweet Tess? I'm not the big, bad wolf you know."

"And I'm not Little Red Riding Hood," she retorted. Slowly she became aware that the music had ended and people were drifting away.

"Since you no longer have a reputation to worry about, what harm can it do if we disappear for a little while. No one will miss us. McClain's nowhere in sight." He gave her a melting smile, full of dimples and boyish charm. Reaching into his pocket, he pulled out a key and dangled it in front of her. "My room is just around the corner. If it makes you feel better, you can meet me there."

Tess had heard enough. She spun around and walked away, mindless of the direction. People stood about in small clusters, talking, laughing, exchanging gossip. She caught snippets of conversation as she passed.

". . . living in sin."

"No better than a whore . . ."

"But she looks a decent sort," a woman protested.

"Don't be a twit, Em. Josie Goodbody caught them together—"

"And in broad daylight."

She berated herself. What had she expected others

to think? An unmarried man and woman sharing the same house was fertile ground for gossip. And yet, she had foolishly refused to think of the consequences. Finances had left her little choice in the matter. Finances and the terms of Jed's will. However, she could have been as chaste as a nun and people would still have drawn the same conclusion. Still, she could have tolerated the derision of Tucson's citizens if it hadn't been for one thing: Zach's indifference She had surrendered more than just her virginity. She had lost her heart to a man who had none to give in return.

Blinking back scalding tears, she nearly collided with Abner Smith.

"Tess, dear, you look upset." Abner took her elbow to steady her.

Her attempt to smile faltered. "I—I have a terrible headache," she improvised. "I just want to find Zach and leave."

"What a shame," Abner commiserated. "You'll miss the fine exhibition of Spanish dancing, but if you're not feeling well . . ." He fell into step with her. "I'll help you find McClain. Thought I saw him enter the Congress Hall Saloon a while back—a place unsuitable for a lady like yourself."

"Few people in this town consider me a *lady*." She was unable to keep the bitterness from her voice. "In fact, they're convinced the opposite is true."

"Don't take it to heart." He pulled a thick cigar from his vest pocket, struck a match, and puffed it to life. "Decent, upstanding citizens are making a concerted effort to bring civilization to Tucson. We've got a school, a first-rate newspaper, and Alexander Levin's talking about constructing a theater. You can't blame folks for frowning on your . . . er, living arrangements. After all, they are a trifle unusual."

"But you of all people know the circumstances that prompted these 'arrangements.' "

"Now don't get upset. It'll only make that headache of yours worse." Abner blew out a pungent stream of cigar smoke. "In all fairness, Tess, talk was bound to happen. An attractive woman such as yourself openly living with a man who isn't her husband. Can't say I blame McClain for taking advantage of the situation. Under similar circumstances, I admit even my willpower would be sorely tested."

She stared at him aghast. Surely she had misunderstood. Was Abner Smith implying he wanted to bed her? First Jimmy Jerold, now Abner Smith? Her headache suddenly became quite real.

"Don't look so shocked, Tess," he chided gently. "My intentions are honorable. I would, of course, offer you the protection of my name. You could do far worse than to marry me."

She stopped in her tracks. "Marry you?"

His luxuriant mustache twitched in a smile. "I see my proposal comes as a surprise."

Tess shook her head in confusion. "Doesn't my sordid reputation, my lost virtue, make me less than desirable as a wife?"

He flicked ash from his cigar, then shrugged his narrow shoulders. "You're quite attractive, and besides, women are in short supply in these parts. It would be a fine match. Eventually, talk of your alliance with McClain will cease, and gossips will find fresh fodder to chew."

"I—I'm afraid that's quite impossible. I don't love you."

"What I'm suggesting has nothing to do with love. I look upon it as a sensible solution to a delicate problem. I'm offering you a chance to regain respectability, while I, on the other hand, as a married man of means, establish myself more firmly in the territory."

Her tongue seemed to cleave to the roof of her mouth. Abner Smith's marriage proposal was the culmination of a day she longed to wipe from her memory. "Thank you, Abner, but I'm sure you'll understand if I decline."

"Don't be too hasty, my dear." Abner eyes glittered behind their polished lenses. "Rest assured, I won't embarrass either of us by repeating my offer. However, should you experience a change of heart, please feel free to contact me."

Abner half-turned at the sound of footsteps bearing down on them. Tess's gaze followed the direction of his. Zach strode toward them, his jaw clenched and lips compressed. He looked furious, but at that moment Tess was so happy to see him, she wanted to throw herself into his arms.

"Where the devil have you been?" he barked. "I've searched half the town looking for you."

She linked her arm in his. "Let's go home."

Abner Smith thoughtfully puffed on his cigar as he watched them merge into a milling crowd.

In the week since the fiesta, Zach had watched Tess grow more and more withdrawn and increasingly despondent. But never once did she complain. Never once did she cast blame. That she did neither made him feel lower than a worm. "Everyone knows," she had whispered brokenly during the long ride home. "Everyone thinks I'm a whore."

"Don't pay any attention to those people," he had advised that night. "They don't know us. They don't know you."

He leaned his head back against the adobe and stared

up into the night sky. Tess Montgomery was far too sensitive for her own good. She needed to toughen up in order to endure the rigors of life in the Arizona Territory. He had watched her during the bullfight, seen her shifting expressions capture every nuance of her emotions. He had found her more entertaining than the pageantry inside the ring. He smiled in wry amusement. Tess had probably been the only person in the entire arena rooting for the bull. Then his smile faded, died.

How could a woman so sensitive to the plight of an animal trade a man into hell? And hell was the only word that could accurately describe a prison camp so brutal that one out of four left in a pine box.

But she had been a child then, barely into her teens, an inner voice counseled.

He raked his fingers through his hair. If he couldn't trust the child, what made him think he could trust the woman? He couldn't. Wouldn't. Doing so would weaken him, make him susceptible to betrayal and loss. He didn't think he could survive another trip through hell. He still carried the scars from the first one. The miserable journey had left him irritable and short-tempered, unable to sleep, and afflicted by nightmares when he did. Not even alcohol could drown the memories of torture and suffering and humiliation.

Something soft and furry brushed his pants. Glancing down, he found Tess's kitten, Smoky, rubbing against his leg. He scooped Smoky up and set her in his lap. Absently he ran his hand over the downy fur that almost matched the color of Tess's eyes. Something inside him seemed to melt each time she gazed up at him with those guileless silver eyes of hers. And her smile—it was lethal, disarming. Then, just for an instant, a mere fraction of time, he would forget past hurts.

Though he had never intentionally set out to seduce her, the results were the same. He hadn't been surprised to discover she was still a virgin. Ever since that fateful night, guilt dogged his footsteps. He blew out an impatient breath. He should have exercised restraint. Should have clamped down on that hot, heady surge of desire. Should have turned and hightailed it to a place like Lily London's. Should have done all those things, but didn't. Instead, like a complete idiot, he had succumbed to his baser instincts when he should have known better.

Zach set the kitten down and began to pace. He had been raised to be a gentleman. It had been ingrained in him since birth that women deserved the utmost respect, honor. They were to be accorded unfailing courtesy. Yet he had grievously ignored these tenets. He had robbed a young woman of her innocence. Such actions were reprehensible. They would have shamed his parents.

Are you going to do right by the girl?

He could almost hear his father's admonition from the grave. Blinded by lust, he had callously destroyed a young woman's reputation, then turned his back on her. Abandoned Tess to the censure of every respectable woman in the territory. Made her the target of lewd and lascivious comments from the men. Hell, how stupid could he be? It didn't take a gypsy fortune teller to predict that sleeping with her would cause trouble.

Are you going to do right and marry the girl?

That would have been his mother's greatest concern. Zach hung his head and pinched the bridge of his nose. Tess Montgomery had once betrayed him. He should feel satisfaction at avenging his pain at her expense. Yet all he felt was guilt.

Damn it to hell! He felt guilty, and it was her fault

he felt that way. Well, he was sick and tired of guilt gnawing at him day and night, worse than a toothache. Tired of watching Tess mope around, seeing her long face. He could have coped better if she had ranted and raved. But no, she chose to play the martyr instead. Meanwhile, his conscience didn't give him a moment's peace. Even his parents nagged from their graves.

. . . marry the girl?

Maybe the notion wasn't so farfetched after all. He stopped pacing, jammed his hands in his pockets, and stared out toward the mountains. Marriage? Five minutes before a judge would fix the problem. Five minutes would end his guilt and restore her reputation. Damn! The solution had been right under his nose the whole time. A simple ceremony, a signature on a document, and their troubles were over. Satisfied, he rocked back on his heels. Marriage—a practical, sensible solution. After all, it was only a piece of paper. Later, after the ranch was sold and Jed's murderer found, he'd go one way, Tess another. Divorce was no problem here in the territory.

"Why are we coming here?" Tess asked as Zach drew up in front of the squat adobe building that served as the Pima County Courthouse.

He avoided meeting her look. "We have some unfinished business to settle."

Something in his tone made her wary. He had been acting strangely ever since this morning, when he had informed her they would be coming into town. "Is it a legal matter of some kind?"

"You might say that." He climbed from the wagon, looped the reins over a hitching post, and came around the side to lift her down.

Tilting her head to one side, she studied his shuttered

expression from beneath the brim of her bonnet. "Zach McClain, why are you being so secretive?"

Instead of releasing her, he continued to keep his hands at her waist. His expression was grim as he stared down at her. "We're getting married."

Stunned, she could only stare uncomprehendingly. The ground seemed to drop from beneath her feet, sending her plummeting through space. Her fingers spasmodically dug into his shoulders to stop the fall. "M-marry?" she whispered.

"You heard me."

A cyclone of thoughts and emotions whirled through her mind, scattering logic, annihilating reason. Her single thought was that Zach wanted to marry her. To make her his wife. Until this moment, the possibility had existed only in her dreams. Now, it appeared, her dreams were about to become reality. She alternately wanted to laugh and shriek with joy, to fling her arms around his neck and weep.

"We can't continue living the way we are indefinitely. I'm tired of the way the townspeople keep sticking their noses into our business. Besides, I owe it to you."

"Owe me?" She recoiled as though he had struck her.

He dropped his hands from her waist, but didn't retreat. "I'm more experienced than you. I should have known better than to take advantage of your innocence. What I did was wrong, and I'm prepared to do the honorable thing."

Her joy had been premature. A brief moment of insanity. She had allowed herself to hope. To dream. Now wasn't the time, or so it seemed, for either hope or dreams, but hard practicality. She moistened her lower lip with the tip of her tongue and tried to marshal a semblance of rational thought. "Correct me if I'm mistaken, but you decided to marry me because you feel guilty?"

A dull flush crept across his cheekbones, and he couldn't quite meet her gaze. "Damn right I feel guilty—and it's all your fault."

Several men came out of the courthouse, arguing loudly. Tess turned her back to them and lowered her voice. "I don't understand, Zach. You made it clear from the beginning that you don't like me. Now you want to marry me?"

"It's the smart thing to do."

"I'm not a charity case," she fired back. "I don't need you to marry me out of pity." Her voice had raised several notches, attracting the attention of a passing woman with a young child.

"I've given the matter some thought, and marriage is the only sensible solution." He took off his hat, absently twirled the brim. "For Christ's sake, Tess, it's just a piece of paper."

Just a piece of paper? Maybe she was greedy, Tess thought, but she wanted more than just a piece of paper. She wanted a marriage—a real marriage.

"This is only temporary," Zach continued. "Just until we sell the damn place."

"I see," she said. "Then what do we do? Go our separate ways?"

He shrugged. "You'll be free to do whatever you want. As for me, I plan to hang around long enough to find Jed's killer."

"Another debt to be paid," Tess murmured.

"Yeah, I guess," he admitted grudgingly. Reaching out, he caught her chin and raised her face to his. "Be honest with me, Tess. If you don't want to marry me, just tell me now, and I promise I'll never bring up the subject again."

Tess felt her heart lodge in her throat, where it

threatened to choke her. Zach's clear, bottle-green eyes seemed to plumb the depths of her soul. *No.* That was all she had to say. Such a simple word. Such a complicated man. She had given herself to him freely, unconditionally. She had been prepared to accept the consequences of her actions, but had never anticipated this.

His thumb lightly trailed the line of her jaw. "Well, Tess, which is it going to be? Yes, or no?"

No. Such a simple word. Such an impossible one. Suddenly, the answer became painfully obvious. She had fallen in love with Zach McClain the night she had caught him stealing food from her kitchen ten long years ago. She had fallen in love with him all over again the moment he had stepped into Abner Smith's law office. Now she had the chance to make him love her in return. *People change,* she thought. *I can help him change. I can make him love me.*

"Yes," she whispered. "Yes, I'll marry you."

Fourteen

Tess leaned forward and studied her reflection in the mirror. Same eyes, same hair, same mouth. Outwardly nothing had changed, but inwardly, she'd never again be the same. How strange, she mused, to wake up one person and go to bed another. And all because she had become a wife. Zach's wife. Five minutes spent before a justice of the peace had altered the entire course of her life. She and Zach had exchanged simple vows. Ageless vows. Solemn promises to love and honor and cherish. They had signed documents that made the arrangement legal and binding.

"Man and wife," she whispered, enjoying the sound of the phrase.

She could never remember being this happy. She wanted to dance, sing, shout. *Mrs. Zachary McClain. Tess McClain.* She wanted to loudly proclaim her new status to the world. As she turned from the mirror, her eyes rested on the flowing white dress spread across the foot of the bed. While Zach took care of the legalities before the wedding, she had remembered the dress she had admired the day of the fiesta and bought it. It had been worth every hard-earned dollar to see the look on Zach's face when he saw her in it. Even

Abner Smith, who had been recruited as their witness, had stared with frank admiration.

Upon learning she was about to get married, the Mexican woman who owned the tiny shop had insisted on helping her prepare for her wedding. The woman, Carmela, had removed the pins from her hair, tied the sides back with blue ribbon, and left the rest to fall in loose curls around her shoulders. Standing back to inspect her handiwork, Carmela had clapped her hands in delight. "Ah, señorita, beautiful."

And Tess had felt beautiful. Had felt like a bride.

Lovingly, she folded her wedding dress and put it away, then turned back the covers on the bed. She wondered what was keeping Zach. Surely, he'd be coming to her soon: after all, this was their wedding night. He might not love her—yet—but she knew he desired her.

Zach had been unusually quiet ever since leaving the courthouse. Abner had insisted upon treating them to dinner at the Shoo Fly Restaurant. Much to her relief, the lawyer acted as though nothing out of the ordinary had ever taken place between them. Nothing in his manner indicated that the week before, he, too, had proposed matrimony. Abner had kept the conversation centered on happenings in and around Tucson. No further mention was made of the gold shipment that had mysteriously disappeared.

Tess blew out the single candle that sputtered in a tin holder. She stood for a time in indecision, absently twirling the wide gold band that graced the third finger of her left hand. Then, before she lost courage, she flung the door wide and stepped onto the patio.

The beauty of the night was breathtaking. Millions of stars were sprinkled across the sky and twinkled like diamonds. A crescent moon bathed the rugged mountains in silvery fairy light. Nocturnal creatures created a unique-sounding symphony all their own: the screech of an owl, the howl of a coyote, the lonesome *whip-poor-will* of a nightjar. Under a cloak of darkness, the desert teemed with activity as bobcats and mountain lions hunted unsuspecting prey. Life in the desert, Tess was learning, could simultaneously be beautiful and harsh.

"Zach . . ." she called softly, tentatively.

A small movement drew her attention to the solitary figure standing in the shadow of the paloverde tree.

"Zach?" She approached him with measured tread. "Are you all right? I was starting to worry."

"If you know what's good for you, darlin', you'll run along to bed and leave me alone."

"I know exactly what's good for me." Reaching out, she took his hand in hers. "You're good for me."

"Ah, Tess, how many times have I tried to warn you. I'm not the man you think I am—not the man I used to be."

"For better, for worse, Zach. I didn't take our vows lightly."

He smiled then, a smile so sad it tugged at her heart. "I wonder," he mused, "if you're destined to be my ruination . . . or my salvation. Which will it be, Tess?"

She shook her head. "Neither, Zach. I just want to be your wife."

"And my lover?"

"Yes," she whispered. "I want that as well." Keeping her hand firmly in his, he didn't resist as she led him away.

Once inside the bedroom, he stopped, forcing her to turn and face him. "I want to see how you look wearing nothing but moonlight. Show me, Tess."

His voice, usually so silky-smooth, sounded husky, sensual. She felt shy under his penetrating stare, yet at the same time strangely confident. Slowly, as though in a trance, she unfastened the tiny buttons of her nightdress, then, with a shrug of her shoulders, let the filmy fabric float to her feet.

His pent-up breath escaped in a soft hiss. Wordlessly he raised one elegantly shaped hand and trailed a fingertip from her earlobe down the column of her neck to the wildly fluttering pulse at the base. "Touch me, Tess; feel my heart beat to the rhythm of yours."

Gently, she pressed her hand to his chest. The strong, rapid pounding of his heart vibrated against her palm. The knowledge that his desire echoed hers brought with it a surge of power. Pleasure keen enough to taste. Her entire body tingled with heightened sensual awareness. Her breasts ached for the feel of his hands, his mouth. Heat formed in the pit of her stomach, trickled downward to pool between her legs. She yearned to touch. To be touched in return.

The tension between them coiled tighter. Inch by tantalizing inch, Zach drew an imaginary line between her breasts. Displaying no apparent haste, he lightly traced the sensitive skin surrounding the aureole, around and around, until her nipples hardened in response. Need prompted her unconsciously to lean closer to increase the contact.

His eyes never leaving hers, he continued this maddening foray, outlining her navel, skating across her flat abdomen, setting the muscles quivering with anticipation. Her breath caught in her throat as his finger strayed lower still. In her mind, she could already imagine his stiff shaft gliding into the cleft between her legs. She was slick and wet, ready to receive him. Her body shifted of its own accord to accommodate his invasion. But again he made her wait, made her want.

"Zach . . ." His name came out a plea, a sigh.

"Impatient, kitten?" One corner of his mouth quirked in amusement, but his eyes remained serious, intent. Passion deepened their hue to the dark and mysterious green of a primal forest.

With the tip of his finger, he drew tiny concentric circles on the inner flesh of her thigh. Tess caught her lower lip between her teeth and fought the urge to rub against him like a cat in heat.

"You like this?" he asked, his voice a low, seductive rumble. "Or do you want something more?"

"Yes, yes . . ." Standing in the dark naked, her hand over his heart, while he played her body like a musical instrument, was sheer torture. The most exquisite torture imaginable. At each skillful stroke, her body resonated. Each masterful touch struck powerful, erotic chords.

When he slid his finger smoothly inside her, she gasped at the wild burst of desire that rocketed through her. His actions slow and deliberate once again, he brushed the pad of his thumb back and forth over the sensitive bud of her femininity.

He had assumed total command of her body. Tess could no longer meekly stand idle. Helpless to resist, she arched her mound against his hand and rotated her hips, wordlessly pleading, seeking.

He feathered a kiss across her temple. "Ah, sweet Tess, are you ready to be mine?"

Biting back a moan, she closed her eyes as the sensations threatened to spiral out of control. Desire and need pumped through her blood, roared in her brain. A desire only he could sate. Her inner flesh clenched spasmodically, relaying her frantic need to hold him tighter, pull him deeper.

Relenting at last, he swept her into his arms and placed her on the bed. She opened her eyes and stared up at him. Strong and powerful, he loomed over her, a phantom lover of moonlight and shadows. Fully aroused, she moved restlessly. Her hair fanned across the pillow in tumbling disarray. Her entire being throbbed and trembled for his touch. "Please," she whispered, prepared to beg if necessary. "Please don't stop."

He gave a harsh laugh, then sank down on the bed. "It would be easier to keep the earth from spinning."

Reaching out, she tugged at his shirt with fevered haste, sending buttons flying. Abandoning the final remnants of patience, he divested himself of the remainder of his clothing, then stretched out next to her and pulled her against him. Tess molded her hips against his pelvis, desperate for the feel of his manhood. Her hands roamed up and down his back, eager to learn the texture of his skin, to savor the play of underlying muscle. She reveled in the feel of her breasts, their nipples exquisitely sensitive, pressed against the hard planes of his chest. She shifted slightly, sinuously, and was gratified by his groan of pleasure.

"You little minx," he murmured, his voice husky.

He captured both her wrists in one of his hands and pinned them to the mattress above her head. She gazed at him with longing. His dark-gold hair fell across his brow. Desire sculpted his handsome features. His bottle green eyes held a reckless glint.

"You almost made me forget something the preacher back home used to say: 'Patience will yield its own reward.' "

He kissed her then, a kiss that started slow and drugging, but quickly turned hungry. While his mouth ravished hers, his free hand traveled over her body, stroking, caressing, teasing, inciting. He wedged a knee between her thighs, and she surged against it. Another woman, a stranger, seemed to inhabit her body. A woman with fierce appetites, one unafraid to make her demands known. She teetered on the brink of fulfillment. She was close, so close to the ultimate rapture. . . .

"Don't, Zach," she rasped. "Don't make me wait. I can't . . ."

He released her hands and cradled her face. "This time, kitten, I promise no pain."

Positioning himself, he entered her with a single, smooth thrust. For an instant, Tess marveled at how her body stretched to accommodate the hard length of him, marveled at the pleasure. Then, as Zach began to move, she ceased to think at all. With each thrust, inner tension coiled tighter and tighter until she thought she would surely explode. She moved with him, urging him on.

Suddenly, and without warning, she unwound like a tightly coiled spring. Rocked by a violent explosion of ecstasy, Tess sobbed out his name. Zach uttered a hoarse exclamation of fulfillment as his release followed hers.

In the aftermath of passion, they lay sated, their limbs entwined. Gradually, their ragged breathing smoothed and their racing hearts rates slowed. Overcome with tenderness for the man she had married, Tess whispered, "I love you."

Every fiber of Zach's body tensed at the declaration. "What did you say?"

"I love you," she repeated sleepily. "I think I always have."

He disentangled himself from her and swung his legs over the edge of the bed. "I don't want your love. Not now, not ever." Ignoring her sharply indrawn breath, he located his pants and stepped into them.

"Damn!" he muttered, cursing his own stupidity. The last thing he wanted—the last thing he needed—

was Tess Montgomery's undying devotion. He should have known better. This was what he got for seducing a virgin. He snatched his shirt from the floor and pulled it on as he strode from the room. Why couldn't she simply enjoy the physical aspects of marriage? If it was enough for him, why couldn't it be enough for her?

Once outdoors, he took a cheroot from his shirt pocket and found a match. He inhaled a lungful of pungent smoke, then blew it out. Wasn't it enough that he had given her his name? Restored her reputation? Why must she muddy an already complicated situation with emotion?

He heard Tess's quiet approach, but purposely kept his back turned. For a long moment she said nothing, just stood staring up at the stars. At last, she cleared her throat. "I don't expect you to love me in return. At least not yet," she amended. "Many marriages start as ours did, but in time . . ."

"All the time in the world won't change the way I feel."

She flinched at the coldness of his tone, but doggedly continued, "You must care at least a little. Especially after what we just shared."

He turned to her with a pitying glance. "Darlin', we need to set something straight. You're confusing lust with love. Trust me, what just happened between us was nothing special." He half-expected a bolt of lightning to strike him dead for his blatant lie.

"I see," she said in a small voice.

He gave her a sidelong glance while pretending to study the tip of his cigar. Tears shimmered on her lashes like beads of crystal. Seeing them, knowing he had caused them, made him feel lower than a snake. In her haste to dress, he noticed she had missed the top two buttons on her nightdress. Desire stirred anew at the memory of the sweet bounty awaiting beneath the thin layer of cotton. "Go to bed, Tess," he said, his tone harsher than he intended. "It's late."

She drew her shawl more firmly around her shoulders. "I had hoped your feelings might have undergone a change, softened. I know in the past you disliked me—"

"Dislike?" He gave a bark of laughter. "That word's a little weak to describe my feelings toward you. *Hate* would be far more accurate."

She took half a step backward as though physically assaulted. "Hate," she echoed. "What have I ever done to earn your hatred?"

He crossed the patio in long strides, turned, strode back, and stood in front of her. His chest heaved with the force of his emotions. "I've hated you for years. But maybe rather than blame you, I should be grateful. While others around me died like flies, my hatred for you was all that kept me alive."

"I don't understand what you're trying to tell me. You're not making sense."

"Did you ever think about me after Gettysburg, Tess? Did you ever wonder why I left so abruptly?"

"Yes, of course, I—"

He cut her off. "For most of the next two years, life wasn't worth living. March of 'sixty-five, I even prayed I'd be one of the corpses carried out in a pine box." He didn't like to remember that period in his life. Fellow prisoners, nearly five hundred that month alone, had succumbed either to smallpox or pneumonia. To add to the misery, unusually hard rains caused the Chemung River to overflow its banks, flooding the camp.

He closed his eyes briefly, drew on his cigar, and tried to staunch the flow of painful memories. "If I'm not making sense I guess it comes from spending two years penned up like an animal."

"Penned up?" Tess clutched his arm. "You were in prison?"

"Don't pretend you don't know what the hell I'm talking about."

Her fingers tightened on his sleeve. "Tell me what happened."

"Why? So you can gloat?"

"Tell me," she demanded, her voice low, insistent, determined.

He schooled his expression to remain emotionless. "After my capture at Gettysburg, I was sent to Point Lookout, Maryland, then soon as it was completed, transferred by ship, then train, to Elmira, New York. Some poor devils didn't even survive the ride there because the train they were jammed into collided with another. For days, survivors lay in a makeshift hospital, their wounds unattended, clothing glued to cuts and fractures with dried blood."

"How horrible . . ." she murmured.

Zach stared into her pale face, but felt no mercy. He had to hand it to her. She was one hell of a fine actress. "That was merely the beginning, an omen of worse to come." He had kept this poison bottled inside for too long. Now that its seal had been broken, the venom spilled out. "Ever wonder why I chose to live in a desert?"

Wordlessly, she shook her head.

"While you knitted in front of a blazing hearth, I stood ankle deep in snow for morning roll call with rags wrapped around my swollen, frozen feet. I vowed then and there, if I survived 'Hellmira' as we called it, I'd never again live anyplace cold." Impatient, agitated, he flicked the ash from his cigar. "Did you ever notice that I never leave so much as a crumb on my plate?"

He didn't wait for her response. "We snatched apple

peels from the mud and devoured them like candy. Dogs and cats that strayed into the compound didn't stand a prayer. When rations weren't enough to ward off starvation, we turned our attention on the large rat population that inhabited the banks of Foster's Pond. Broiled rat was considered a delicacy."

"Enough," Tess pleaded, pressing her hands against her mouth. "Please, no more."

"No glory, no honor, no dying for a cause. Just two long, miserable years in the bowels of hell." He flicked his cigar away, watching the red arc as it shot into the air, then fell to the ground. "And all because you failed to keep a secret."

"But I never," she mumbled. "I wouldn't—"

"No more lies, Tess. I've had my fill." The bottle green eyes cut like shards of glass. "Seeing how we have to stay together, at least for the time being, I won't tolerate anything less than honesty."

Tess barely heard him. Her mind was too busy trying to absorb everything he had just told her. God, how Zach had suffered the final years of the war. A dire lack of food, clothing, shelter, surrounded by pestilence. Finally, she knew why he had changed so drastically from the person she remembered. Survival had exacted a high toll. No wonder he was consumed by rage, fueled with bitterness. No wonder he refused to talk about the past. Tears filled her eyes at the thought of all he had endured. "I'm so sorry, Zach, so very sorry."

"It's a little late for remorse, isn't it, Tess? I trusted you with my life, and you broke your promise."

"I didn't tell anyone, I swear."

"Didn't you hear me? I said no more lies."

She caught a fistful of his shirt as he turned away. "Zach, you've got to believe me. I didn't tell a soul."

He jerked free. "If you didn't tell, who did?"

She didn't have an answer.

Numbness encased her as she watched him retreat into the darkened house. Her chest felt tight with unshed tears. She wanted to cry but couldn't. Her grief was too profound.

Fifteen

If you didn't tell, who did?

Tess rubbed her throbbing temples. Zach's question had drummed in her brain all night long and all day. And still she was no closer to the answer.

Absently, she picked up the first item from a pile of mending, which happened to be a shirt of Zach's. She recognized it as the one he had worn the previous night. Three buttons were missing, buttons that she had ripped off in her eagerness to touch him. Was it only last night they had made love so feverishly? Only last night that she had told him she loved him?

And in return, he had told her about Elmira.

Closing her eyes, she buried her face in the shirt and drew in an unsteady breath. Heady, intoxicating, his scent enveloped her. It brought forth memories of a strong embrace, the taste and texture of his skin. Of passion and desire, followed by accusations and rejection.

She lowered the shirt to her lap and opened her eyes. Now that the initial shock had worn off, all she felt was pain. Incredible pain. She had learned that hearts can indeed ache; hearts can break.

How could Zach believe she'd betray him?

But if she hadn't divulged his hiding place, who

had? Her thoughts kept circling back to the same disturbing question. The mending forgotten, she rested her head against the sun-warmed adobe. Smoky leaped onto the bench next to her, and climbed into her lap. Tess idly scratched behind the kitten's ears. Her head hurt from the effort to recall details of ten years ago.

She recalled with clarity that Zach had walked her partway to the house the night before, then gently kissed her. She wondered: did a woman ever forget her first kiss? Tender, sweet, fleeting, it had been what dreams were made from. The stuff of fairy tales. He had been Prince Charming and she, Cinderella or Sleeping Beauty. The next day she could hardly wait to see him again, but her mother had kept her busy with errands.

"Make sure you don't leave the Johnsons' without waiting for a reply."

Mary Montgomery had been very specific with her instructions. Tess had chafed for almost an hour at the Johnsons' kitchen table while waiting for her mother's friend to reply to the hand-delivered note.

Following dinner and chores, she had lain fully clothed on top of the covers, waiting for her mother to fall sound asleep. But she had fallen asleep instead. The next morning, she had raced to the barn in a panic, but she was too late. Zach and Jed were gone. Gone without so much as a note. Without a word of goodbye.

All these years, she had assumed Zach and Jed had returned to their unit. Nothing in the infrequent letters she had received from Jed after the war suggested otherwise. At the beginning of their correspondence, she had asked about Zach, but Jed avoided any mention of his friend. After a while, Tess had quit asking.

Last night she had been stunned to hear he had been taken prisoner. And even more shocked to learn that he held her personally responsible. For ten long years, he had nursed his hatred of her.

She still recalled his exact words from that long-ago night: *"Be careful, darlin'. Don't let anyone break your heart."* How ironic, she mused, that Zach himself was guilty of the very deed he had warned her against.

A sleepless night and the warm May afternoon took their toll. Tess's eyes drifted shut as she finally succumbed to sleep.

"Tess?" Zach halted in his tracks.

Damn! She looked pretty as a picture sleeping in the shade, the furry gray kitten dozing in her lap. His question forgotten, he took time to admire the sight. Chestnut-brown tendrils had escaped the loose knot atop her head to curl at her brow and temples while others trailed at her nape. It took all the willpower he could summon not to brush the wisps aside with nibbling kisses. Her luminous gray eyes were closed. The faint violet smudges beneath attested to a lack of sleep and lent an appealing fragility. One hand rested on the kitten, the other was turned palm up on the wooden bench. Sun slanting beneath the overhang of the porch glinted off the simple band of gold he had given her just the day before.

He felt his gut clench. He had been tempted to forgo the custom of a ring, then changed his mind. Every woman deserved a wedding ring. Even one who couldn't be trusted. His fingers bit into the leather harness he carried. He cursed again. The more time he spent around Tess, the more difficult it was to hate her. There were times that he almost forgot the ordeal she had put him through. Almost, but not quite. Though he hadn't realized it until later, he had half-hoped she would offer a plausible explanation. That she'd plead youth or patriotism or ignorance. Maybe she had felt an overwhelming need to confess her secret to her mother, aunt, uncle, or cousin. While in prison, he had entertained numerous fantasies of her begging forgiveness while he turned a cold shoulder to her plea.

But reality had been nothing like what he had imagined. Instead, Tess had stared at him, shocked, stunned. Rather than offer abject apologies, she had appeared thunderstruck at his revelations. Either she was genuine or one hell of an actress. In all probability the latter. Of course, she had eventually recovered and denied his charges. He had expected no less, so he wasn't swayed by the feeble attempt. As far as he was concerned, her lack of fervor only confirmed her guilt.

Whether she was guilty or not, he couldn't deny the powerful attraction that existed between them. Now that they were legally wed, there were no barriers in the way of a mutually satisfying relationship. Except that she thought she was in love with him. He, on the other hand, resisted the idea of an emotional entanglement. Once this place was sold and Jed's killer was brought to justice, he wanted to be able to turn his back and walk away. He had no intention of becoming enslaved by beguiling gray eyes, a pretty smile, and the face of an angel.

He let out an impatient sigh. Here it was, the middle of the afternoon with work to be done. Instead, he mooned around like a schoolboy in the throes of his first crush. Enough, he admonished himself. There were a lot of repairs to accomplish if Casita de Oro ever hoped to tempt a buyer.

He cleared his throat loudly. "Tess . . ."

She stirred at the sound of his voice, then opened eyelids heavily weighted with sleep. "Zach?" she murmured.

Zach wondered what it would be like to watch her

wake after a night spent in his arms. Though they had made love twice, each time he had left shortly afterward. Now he regretted those hasty departures. He wanted to savor the feel of her body, all soft and warm and yielding, nestled against his. Wanted to smile deep into her slumberous eyes and see her pretty face flush with remembered passion. Wanted to watch that passion rekindle.

Gritting his teeth, he slapped the harness against his thigh, relishing the sharp sting of leather. What he really wanted, but hated to admit, was for Tess to convince him that she really was the innocent she claimed to be. He blew out an impatient breath. What the devil was wrong with him? He might as well hope he'd find the lost gold. Might as well wish for the moon. All three were impossible.

"Have you seen the wire cutters?" His voice sounded more gruff than he intended, and he saw her flinch. "I've searched all over and can't find 'em."

She sat up straighter and tucked a wayward lock of hair behind her ear. "I used them to fix the broken handle of a pot. I think they're still in the kitchen."

"Damn it, Tess, how do you expect me to get any work done if you hide the tools?" Turning, he strode through the kitchen door with Tess close at his heels and began rummaging through a corner cupboard for the missing item.

"I'm sorry," she said to his turned back. "I'm so sorry," she repeated, her voice small and forlorn.

He froze. "Sorry for what?"

"For everything." She nudged him aside, and reaching into a drawer, produced the missing wire cutters, then handed them to him. "Most of all, I'm sorry about us."

I'm sorry, too! Zach wanted to shout. Aloud he said,

"When it comes to us, it's too late. Ten long years too late."

"Ever since last night, I've thought of nothing else." She rubbed her arms as though she were chilled in spite of the unseasonably warm day. "What happened the night you were captured? Why were you taken prisoner and not Jed?"

"Why the interest?" He parried her questions with ones of his own. "So you can gloat?"

He attempted to move around her, but she stepped into his path, effectively blocking his exit. "Humor me, Zach. Remember, I wasn't there to see what happened."

"You have some nerve, darlin'," he sneered. "You want a firsthand account?"

She raised her chin a notch and refused to budge.

Determination was stamped across her face in bold letters. She wasn't going to let the matter rest until he recounted every last detail. Well, he'd prove to her— and to himself as well—that he could talk about the event without reliving it. "Very well," he agreed grudgingly. "There's not much to tell. Jed's leg was nearly healed, so we planned to leave later that night. Jed made some excuse about wanting to reconnoiter. I think he just wanted to give us time alone."

"Time to say good-bye," she said softly.

"You never came." His tone was flat, accusatory, his eyes hard and cold. "Sheriff Earl Johnson and his deputies showed up instead."

Tess opened her mouth, but no words were forthcoming.

"Johnson and his men slapped me in irons and led me away. They paraded me down the center of Main Street like I was some prized trophy. Early the next morning, before dawn, I was shipped off to Point Lookout under heavy guard.

"Jed wrote later that he had watched the whole thing from a distance. He found out where I was being sent, but there wasn't much he could do. He was fed up with things, so he headed west, where he hooked up with Quantrill. We kept in touch through letters. Jed always believed in your innocence. I never could convince him otherwise."

His monologue over, Zach glared at her. "Satisfied? Is that what you wanted to hear?"

She moistened her lower lip with the tip of her tongue. "Zach, believe me, I never—"

"Enough!" he snapped, suddenly tired of her half-hearted apologies. They didn't bring the peace or finality he had expected. Besides, he was tired of her wounded, stricken look. She was beginning to make him feel as though *he* were the villain. He wanted to shake her, make her admit the truth once and for all. Then, maybe, he could put the past behind him. Get on with his life.

Put the past behind him? Get on with his life? The idea caught him off guard. For years he had trudged painful memories around with him like a heavy boulder. Now, the notion of casting the burden aside seemed revolutionary. Its appeal astounded him. He needed time, however, to come to grips with the novel idea.

"*Sheriff* Johnson . . . ?" Her hand trembled as she brushed a strand of hair from her brow. "I—I don't know what to say."

"You don't have to say a damn thing, darlin'. It no longer matters." Taking Tess by the shoulders, he purposely moved her aside.

She ran after him. "Zach! Wait . . ."

Out the door, over the porch, and across the patio, Zach kept moving. He desperately needed to get away. Needed to escape the turmoil she caused. She made him remember when he wanted to forget. One minute he felt like throttling her, and the next, like making love to her until neither could remember their names. His ground-eating strides carried him toward the stables, with Tess close behind.

She wedged herself between him and the rail holding his saddle. "You can't keep running away. We need to talk."

"Can you honestly deny that you had any part in my capture?"

"No, I can't, but . . ."

"Then this is the only kind of talking I'm interested in." Roughly, he hauled her against his chest.

Hot and hungry and seeking vengeance, his mouth descended, ravishing hers. Instead of resisting his rough invasion, she surrendered. Her mouth opened instantly, willingly. He demanded; she yielded. He plundered; she relinquished. Greedily, he explored the smooth, wet inner lining of her mouth, traced the edges of her teeth.

A low, primal growl tore from deep in his throat. He could feel the fullness of her breasts crushed against his chest. Desire surged through him. He adjusted his stance so that she could feel his male hardness against her abdomen. Feel his raging need.

Her hands tangled in his hair, urging him on.

"Well, well," a smooth voice drawled. "What have we here?"

Tess and Zach broke apart, their breathing ragged, to find Jimmy Jerold and Moe Black observing them from atop their mounts and grinning from ear to ear.

Moe smirked. "Bet you didn't even hear us ride up, did ya?"

"Looks like we're interruptin' a pair of lovebirds, don't it, Moe?"

Zach studied the pair with undisguised suspicion. "What brings you two all the way out here?"

Undeterred by the cool reception, Jimmy swung down from his horse. Moe did likewise. Doffing his hat, Jimmy gave Tess a lazy smile. "You, sweetheart, are certainly the picture of a blushin' bride. Can't remember when I've seen a prettier one."

"State your business, Jerold," Zach ordered, putting an abrupt halt to Jimmy's flattery.

"Tsk, tsk," Jimmy chided. He slid his gaze from Tess to Zach. "Careful, now, McClain. You're startin' to make noises like a jealous bridegroom."

"And you're startin' to try my patience," Zach replied.

Tess cast a surreptitious look at Zach's set expression and feared the two men would come to blows. "It's a hot, dusty ride from Tucson. Why not stay and have a cold drink before heading back to town?"

Jimmy pounced on the suggestion. "A right good idea, sweetheart. You lead the way."

The three men waited on the patio while she went inside to prepare refreshments. She could hear them exchange desultory conversation through the open doorway. While not exactly friendly, she was relieved that they were behaving in a civil fashion. When she rejoined them, Jimmy and Moe occupied the corner bench while Zach lounged against a post, his pose relaxed, his eyes alert.

After serving the men their drinks, Tess took a glass for herself, then stood quietly next to Zach. "I gather from your earlier comments that you gentlemen know Zach and I were married yesterday."

"Why, Tess, honey, that's all the whole town's been talkin' about."

She took a small sip of her drink. "Are people here in Tucson that starved for gossip?"

Moe grunted as he reached for a cookie. "Everythin's news in a town this size."

Jimmy flicked a speck of dust from the brim of his hat. "You broke my heart, sugar, by marrying that scoundrel McClain. I wanted you for myself, but I can't blame the man. A pretty little thing like you is rare in these parts."

"Under the circumstances, it seemed the most sensible thing to do." She tried to keep her tone nonchalant. "People were opposed to the idea of us living in sin."

Jimmy nodded knowingly. "Place is gettin' far too civilized, what with being the capital of the territory an' all."

"Tombstone's more to my likin'.". Moe reached for a second cookie. "Now there's a town that ain't scared of a good gunfight."

Zach hooked his thumbs in his waistband. "Did you ride all the way out here to argue the merits of Tombstone versus Tucson? Or did you have something else in mind?"

Moe and Jimmy exchanged glances. Apparently in no hurry to answer Zach's question, Jimmy reached inside his jacket pocket and withdrew a small bag of candy. "Care for a peppermint?" he asked, offering it first to Tess.

"No." A shudder rippled through her. "No, thank you," she managed, her voice faint.

Jimmy popped one in his mouth. "What, no sweet tooth?"

"I love candy," she admitted. "It's just peppermint I can't abide. At least not since Gettysburg."

Moe cocked his head to one side, his small eyes inquisitive. "How's that?"

The memory of that horrible time was still vivid in Tess's mind. Dead bodies and severed limbs. The lingering scent of blood and gunpowder. "After the battle, people used peppermint oil to mask the odor of bloodshed and death. To this day, I can't think of one and not the other."

"Interestin'." Moe deliberately helped himself to Jimmy's peppermints, stuck one in his mouth, and sucked noisily.

The permeating smell of the candy was making her nauseous. Then, as though he sensed her distress, she felt Zach's hand rest on her and gently squeeze. She felt inordinately grateful for the small act of compassion.

"Time's a wastin', gentlemen," Zach reminded their guests. "Tess and I are still waiting to find out why you're here."

"Besides wantin' to congratulate you newlyweds, we came with a business proposition for you to consider."

"What sort of proposition?"

Dropping all pretense of charm, Jimmy assumed a businesslike manner. "Fact is, McClain, Moe and I recently came into an unexpected windfall. It's no secret the two of you want to sell this place and move on. We're prepared to offer you a fair price."

Zach ignored Tess's gasp of surprise and raised a tawny brow. "Interesting," he drawled. "You're aware, of course, that the ranch and the mine must be sold together?"

"Yeah, yeah," Moe replied, his manner surly. "We heard all about it from that lawyer fella."

"Keep in mind, money's hard to come by in the territory right now. It might be a long time before you get another offer." His expression earnest, Jimmy rested his elbows on his knees and leaned forward. "So, are you interested or not?"

"We're not interested," Zach and Tess answered in unison.

They turned to each other, surprised by their mutual accord, the vehemence of their replies.

Jimmy patted his breast pocket. "We've got cash."

"No." Zach's tone left no room for further argument.

"What Zach means, Jimmy," Tess said, trying to cushion Zach's curt refusal, "is that while we appreciate your offer, we're not interested at the present time."

"You'll regret this, McClain," Moe sneered.

Jimmy reached for his hat. "We'll give you folks some time to reconsider."

Zach gestured toward the door. "I trust you gentlemen know the way out."

Neither Tess nor Zach spoke again until the sound of horses' hooves faded; then Zach stopped Tess as she was about to retreat into the house. "Why were you so quick to refuse?"

"Why were you?" she countered.

Zach's face took on the shuttered expression that signaled his reluctance to discuss his reasons. His lack of trust obvious, Tess threw up her hands in frustration. "Let me know when you're ready to talk. In the meantime, I'm going to fix supper."

By nightfall, the wind had kicked up. Cone-shaped dervishes of sand waltzed across the patio while the paloverde tree dipped and swayed. Gusts danced across the dirt roof and rattled the closed shutters. Instead of eating the evening meal outdoors, Tess had served supper in the *comedor,* or dining room, next to the kitchen.

The candle sputtering in its tin holder bathed the room in a benevolent golden glow. A brightly woven cloth covered the battered table. Baskets bartered from her Papago friend, Amelia, decorated the walls and hid places where the plaster needed repair. Though Tess knew she had succeeded in creating a cozy room, at the present time the atmosphere was anything but warm and cheerful.

Throughout the meal, she was aware of Zach's considering gaze. Finally, he pushed his empty plate aside and said, "You're hiding something from me."

"More coffee?" She refilled his cup without waiting for an answer.

He folded his arms across his chest and studied her through narrowed eyes. "I can't help but feel that whatever you're keeping secret has to do with Jerold's offer. Out with it, Tess."

Carefully, Tess set the coffeepot down, then wiped her palms on her skirt. Maybe the time had arrived to tell Zach about the map she had found. "Very well," she said quietly. "On one condition."

Zach's brow shot upward. "Condition?"

"First, you tell me your secret."

He threw back his head and laughed. "Ah, Tess darlin', you drive a hard bargain. You're a hell of a lot tougher than most give you credit for."

"I'm waiting." She folded her hands primly. "What was in the package you slipped into your saddlebag when you thought I wasn't looking? And, more to the point, does it have anything to do with why you turned down Jimmy and Moe's offer?"

He picked up his coffee cup and held it without drinking. "I came across a suspicious chunk of rock at the mine and had it sent to San Francisco to be assayed."

"Why the secrecy?"

He shrugged, then sipped his coffee. "I was acting on a hunch. I didn't want to say anything until I was sure."

"Sure of what?"

"I suspect the assayer's going to tell me it's silver.

But"—he gestured with his cup to avoid a flood of questions—"what puzzles me is why Jed would ignore an obvious vein of silver. Unless, of course, he was searching for something far more valuable."

"Such as gold," she murmured. Excitement raced through her like wildfire. All the pieces were slowly falling into place. A fortune in gold waited to be discovered. And it was close, so close she could almost feel it.

"You forced my hand, darlin', now it's your turn to lay down the cards." His lips curved in a humorless smile above the rim of his raised cup.

Tess accepted the challenge. "Better yet, rather than tell you what I found, I'll show you."

Leaving the table, she hurried to her bedroom and returned minutes later with a dime novel, which she placed in front of him.

He flicked his glance from the cover, then back to her. "You want me to read the adventures of some dime-store detective?"

"Don't be sarcastic. You might be in for a pleasant surprise." Her shoulder brushed his as she leaned forward and opened the book. Very carefully, she extracted the yellowed map from between the glued pages, then carefully spread it out for him to see.

Zach let out a low whistle as he studied the map. All traces of sarcasm vanished.

"Well," Tess prompted. "What do you think?"

He pointed to a crude drawing. "This looks something like the old Spanish mission, San Xavier, due south of here."

"And what about the writing? I know you speak Spanish. Can you make out what it says?"

While Tess chafed with impatience, he moved the candle closer and strained to decipher the faint print. "*Les chauves-souri?*" At last he lifted his head and gazed up at her. A smile, genuine this time, tugged at his mouth. "The words aren't Spanish—they're French."

"French?" Tess gasped. Then the significance struck her. The fabled shipment had been intended as a gift from the French government. Without thinking, she wrapped her arms around his neck and flung herself at him, nearly toppling his chair.

"Steady, now." Zach's voice carried a hint of laughter at her unbridled exuberance. "Don't set your sights too high."

Tess drew back, sobered by the fact she had literally hurled herself into his arms. "What do we do next?"

He smiled into her flushed face. "At first light tomorrow, I leave for the mission to do some investigating."

"*We* leave for the mission in the morning," she corrected, returning the smile. "Remember, it's my map."

Sixteen

"It's not far," Zach said as he swung into the saddle. "Only about ten miles or so south of here."

Tess adjusted the brim of her hat against the sun's rays, then mounted her mare. "Have you been there before?"

Zach nudged his horse into a lazy trot. "I've ridden past a few times, but never stopped. I think you're in for a treat."

"What do you mean?"

"You'll see."

In spite of her persistent coaxing and wheedling, Zach refused to say any more about the mission. Tess eventually grew resigned to his silence and decided to enjoy the outing. The day was a flawless gem. The gusting winds of the previous night had disappeared as quickly as they had arrived. The morning sun shimmered in a sky the pure blue of a robin's egg. Wispy clouds skimmed its surface like a gossamer bridal veil.

Her spirits soared at the day's sheer perfection. And so did her optimism.

Never in her wildest dreams had she imagined she'd be involved in a treasure hunt. She had come to Arizona seeking adventure, but none of the tales in her dime novels could rival reality. A fortune in gold nearby, just waiting to be uncovered. Her excitement built with each dusty mile.

What would she do with her unexpected bounty? Clothes, jewels, travel? The possibilities were limitless. It would be luxury in itself not to worry about a roof over her head or food on the table. In Gettysburg, she had struggled just to pay her mother's doctor bills, let alone have money left over for pretty things. She had eked out an existence by selling farm produce and eggs. Whenever possible, she had taken in sewing or laundry.

Maybe she'd do something wildly extravagant, she decided with a trace of defiance—perhaps visit England or Italy. Wherever she went, she vowed to be so busy that she didn't have time to think. Didn't have time to miss the man who had first stolen her heart. Then broken it.

Her gaze slid to Zach. What would he do with his portion of the money? He had been blunt from the beginning. He wanted as much distance between them as possible. Perhaps he'd return to South Carolina and rebuild his family home.

Suddenly, her horse shied, bumping against Zach's. Tess struggled to control the skittish animal while looking around to see what might have startled it.

"Javelina," Zach said, pointing to a group of animals that resembled slender pigs with grizzly blackish-gray coats and a gray ruff of fur around their necks.

As Tess watched, the leader led her small herd across the road. Twin baby javelinas were the last to cross. An almost overpowering scent of musk marked their passage. Tess wrinkled her nose at the strong smell. "Ugh!"

"Some call them musk hogs," Zach explained. "They use their scent to mark their territory and keep their herds intact."

She studied them dubiously. "Are they dangerous?"

"Only if cornered. Then they become vicious fighters."

Tess gave the javelinas a final glance. They seemed more playful than dangerous as they rubbed up against each other, snorting and grunting. She turned her attention once more on the arid landscape. The countryside they were passing through was relatively flat. Tall saguaros dotted the landscape with an endless variation of shapes and sizes. The ocotillo, she noted, had undergone a change since her arrival. The slender stalks were no longer green and tipped with red-orange flowers, but now resembled clusters of dried brown sticks. Even the paloverde had lost their dainty yellow blossoms.

Zach seemed to divine her thoughts. "The desert comes alive with color in the spring, but mostly it's various shades of brown. It takes some getting used to, especially for those used to seeing a lot of green."

"Have you gotten used to it?"

"Actually, I prefer the desert. After Elmira, I promised myself I'd never live anywhere it snowed."

There it was, another harsh reminder of what he had suffered. And, according to him, it had all been her fault. She could envision a long line of men, emaciated, clothed in rags, ankle deep in snow. The image filled her with sadness. She wished somehow she could erase those bleak memories, replace them with happier ones, but that was impossible.

She also wished she could rid herself of the notion that she was at least indirectly responsible for his imprisonment. Surely the note she had delivered at the sheriff's home had nothing to do with Zach's capture. The note could have been about any number of things: the change in egg prices, the sewing bee at the Lutheran church, a new recipe for bread pudding. It didn't necessarily have anything to do with Zach. Her mother couldn't possibly have guessed that her daughter hid two rebel soldiers. Tess had been so careful . . .

The day no longed seemed as bright or promising as it had earlier. They rode in silence, each lost in thought. Then, as if it had magically sprouted from the desert floor, the mission San Xavier appeared in the distance. As they drew closer, Tess could make out its white bell towers starkly silhouetted against the blue, blue sky.

She couldn't seem to drag her eyes away from it. "It's lovely," she breathed aloud.

"Folks around here call it the White Dove of the Desert. It once marked the boundary of the Spanish Empire."

As they drew closer, details of the mission became more apparent. Tess noticed only one of the bell towers had been completed. She wondered if time or money had run out before the second of the pair had received its domed crown and cast bell. The architecture was a mixture of styles: Spanish and something more ornate—she guessed Gothic or Moorish. The church was composed of a splendid series of domes, curving arches, and flying buttresses.

They turned off the road and up a well-trodden path leading to the mission. Zach assumed the role of guide. "San Xavier is one in a chain of such missions built by the friars. This particular church, I've been told, was completed nearly one hundred years ago."

As they neared a corral, Tess could see telltale signs of neglect and decay on the crumbling adobe. The walls, which had appeared pristine white from a distance, were on closer inspection a pale golden-pink. She stared in awe at the ornate facade, a collection of balconies, pilasters, and niches with statues, that declared San Xavier a labor of love in the midst of a desert.

Zach patiently waited for her to dismount. "I don't see anyone around. Let's take a look inside." The massive oak door opened with a squeak of rusty hinges. Zach stood aside and allowed her to enter ahead of him.

Tess took a step inside, then halted so abruptly that Zach nearly collided with her. He reached out automatically to steady her. "I had expected a simple place of worship, but this . . ."

". . . is more like a fine cathedral." Zach completed her unfinished sentence. He made no attempt to disguise his own amazement.

His hands resting lightly on her shoulders, they stood and admired the visual extravaganza. The church's interior was a riotous profusion of color: the gold of the altar, and blue, yellow, and red geometric patterns on the walls. Every surface was covered with some type of artwork or design. Instead of individual canvases, religious scenes were painted directly on the walls. What wasn't painted was carved, twisted, turned, or filled with statues. Saints, angels, and lions all shared a home beneath the vaulted, arched ceiling.

An old man came out of the sacristy and shuffled toward them. "Welcome to San Xavier. Please feel free to stay as long as you wish."

"Thank you," Tess replied. The man was small and frail. Long, white hair framed a face as brown and wrinkled as a walnut. At first, she couldn't be certain whether he was Mexican or Indian. "The mission is very beautiful."

He beamed with pride. "Many visitors come to admire San Xavier. If you like, I can show you."

"We'd like that very much," Zach said.

"I am Tohono O'odham," the man explained as he

led them down a side aisle. He paused before a wooden likeness of a saint with a bloody gash on its head and a knife thrust through its chest.

Averting her gaze from the carved figure, Tess gave the man a friendly smile. "My friend Amelia is also Papago."

"Amelia is my granddaughter. She just gave birth to a son."

A son? Tess felt an unexpected stab of envy at the news. She'd dearly love a child of her own—Zach's child. But, given his dislike of her, the possibility seemed remote. "Please," she said past the lump of regret lodged in her throat, "tell Amelia I am happy for her. I hope she'll visit soon and bring the baby."

"She speaks well of you." He gave her a nod of approval. "My name is Antonio. The People take care of the church until the priests return."

Tess and Zach exchanged questioning looks before following Antonio as he continued up the aisle. "Are you telling us that there are no priests at San Xavier?" Zach asked.

"No priests." Antonio shook his head sadly. "They have been gone from here for many years—too many."

Zach persisted. "How many years is too many? One, two, ten?"

Antonio scrunched his wizened face in concentration. "Black-robes came back to the mission maybe nine, ten years ago. But after only one year, they go back to California. None have come since, but the People keep watch until they return to stay."

Tess only heard a portion of what Antonio told them about the mission. Her thoughts kept returning to the conversation with the Kemper brothers at the fiesta. One of them had mentioned that Jed had spent a great deal of time here at San Xavier. But if no priests were in residence, what had Jed done while at the mission?

Had he searched for lost gold? Or had he been seeking a more spiritual treasure, such as redemption for his sins?

Antonio took his role as guide very seriously. "The story is told among the People that no expense was spared. Statues were ordered from Mexico. Pigments for the paint came from Mexico and as far away as Europe. Artists received twice the normal pay."

When the tour concluded, Zach thanked the man and pressed money into his hand. "We were told a friend of ours, Jed Duncan, used to spend time here. Do you, by any chance, remember him?"

Antonio shrugged as he tucked the coins in his pocket. "People come; people go. I do not remember all."

"This man wasn't from here. His speech sounded similar to that of my husband," Tess explained. At the word *husband,* her tongue had nearly faltered. She was unaccustomed to referring to Zach in that manner. And even more unaccustomed to thinking of herself as a wife.

Antonio rubbed his jaw. "I cannot be certain . . ."

Then, Tess remembered a comment Jed had made years before. "This friend once refused to shave until the South won the war. By the time you met him, he probably had a long beard and mustache."

Antonio's eyes lit with recognition. "There was such a man, yes, but he never give his name."

"What do you remember about him?" Zach prompted. "Tell us everything you know."

Scratching his head, Antonio squinted into the near distance. "He came long after the priests left. Said he needed to confess his sins. I told him the black-robes were gone, but he stay anyway."

"What did he do while he was here?" Tess tried to contain her excitement.

Antonio tapped his forehead with one finger. "I think maybe the man was loco. Day after day, he sit in the back and stare at the altar. That's all, just stare at the altar."

Zach frowned. "Did you ever approach him and ask what he was looking for?"

"Yes, I ask." Antonio nodded vigorously.

Tess felt as though she were about to explode with impatience. "And what was Jed's answer?"

"He say he was searching."

Without realizing what she was doing, Tess reached for Zach, her fingers biting into his forearm. "Searching?"

Antonio crossed himself before answering. "He say he searching for peace. Say he's trying to find God's forgiveness. After that I leave him alone."

The answer came as a surprise. Jed must have been deeply troubled in order to sit for days in an abandoned church. Had the years spent as one of Quantrill's raiders been to blame for his troubled conscience? And, more important, had his prayers been answered? She could only hope that they had.

Zach cleared his throat. "How long was he here, Antonio?"

The man's brow puckered in thought. "A week, maybe two. I let him sleep on the cot in the father's old room."

After thanking the man again, Zach asked if he minded that they stay a while longer.

"Stay as long as you wish. This is not my house, but the house of the Lord." He started to shuffle off when Tess stopped him.

"Antonio," she asked hesitantly, "do you think our friend found what he was looking for?"

A slow smile spread across the Papago's wizened face. "When your friend left, he wore the look of a man who has found peace. If you wish to visit, he is buried in our cemetery." Then Antonio disappeared into the sacristy, and they were once again alone in the church.

Zach studied a carved lion that guarded the sanctuary. "Think I'll look around a bit. I'll meet you out front later."

It was apparent to Tess that Zach didn't want her company, and so, left to her own devices, she slipped into one of the pews at the rear. When the elaborate artwork failed to hold her interest, her gaze rested on the empty altar. She wished a measure of the tranquillity that Jed had found would be transmitted to her. She felt many different emotions: a deep, abiding sorrow that Zach could never return her love; quiet joy in knowing Jed had found forgiveness; regret that they were no closer to uncovering the lost gold.

Inner peace, however, continued to elude her. She couldn't put Zach's prison ordeal from her mind. She had only wanted to help him, but now she wondered if she had been careless. Had someone—her own mother, perhaps—discovered her secret?

The longer she pondered her problem, the more hopeless the situation seemed. Zach could never forget the past, never love her. The atmosphere inside the church seemed increasingly oppressive. Wanting fresh air and sunshine, she left through a side entrance. She stood for a moment and looked around. A short distance away, the land sloped upward. Shading her eyes, she discerned the shapes of wooden crosses and knew she had found the cemetery Antonio had mentioned.

Following a narrow footpath, she picked her way over the rough terrain. Upon reaching the top of the incline, she found uneven rows of crosses that had been forced into the hard earth. Some graves were ringed with stones; others were decorated with wreaths or hand-carved figures. Still others, like Jed's, were unadorned. She regretted coming to his grave empty-handed. She wished she had flowers to place on his final resting place, but blooms were rare in this harsh land. All she could do was pray that a merciful God had heard Jed's pleas for forgiveness.

Bowing her head, she remembered an old friend with fondness. Jed Duncan had been a man of contradictions. A Confederate sergeant whose gruff exterior concealed a heart that was basically kind and giving. A soldier who had ridden with Quantrill, then repented, spending endless days in a vacant church begging forgiveness.

She heard the crunch of boots on rocky soil and, without turning, knew that Zach had joined her.

"I thought I'd find you here," Zach said as he quietly took his place next to her.

A steel band seemed to tighten around her chest, restricting her breathing. Her eyes burned with unshed tears. "I couldn't leave without saying good-bye."

"Neither could I." Zach removed his hat and bowed his head.

They stood side by side, united for once instead of at odds. Brought together by a man they had known briefly but who, even after his death, had made a large impact on their lives.

Tess cleared her throat. "Jed was a stranger and friend all rolled into one. I wish we'd had time to become better acquainted."

"He was the best friend a man could ask for," Zach admitted, his eyes fixed on the grave. "To this day, I'll never know why he took a green recruit like me under his wing. He taught me everything I needed to know to survive. Wasn't for him, I'd have perished the first time I saw battle."

Something in Zach's tone, a certain melancholy,

drew her attention. Glancing up at him, she watched his handsome face cloud with vulnerability. She found it oddly touching to see such a strong and independent man relax his guard and reveal his true feelings. Wanting to smooth away the sadness, she started to reach out and touch his cheek. But she dropped her hand to her side, knowing the gesture would be unwelcome. Instead, she said softly, "I once heard my father say that in times of war, friends become closer than blood relatives. It must have been that way between you and Jed."

"Wasn't for the war, our paths would never have crossed. Our backgrounds were as different as night and day, but in battle we were equals, fighting side by side for a cause we believed in." His voice grew husky. "I hope he found his peace."

She ceased fighting her impulse to comfort him and slipped her hand in his, willing to risk possible rejection. "I pray you find yours also."

"Don't know if I can, Tess," he murmured. "Too much has happened."

"You have to let go, Zach. You have to find it in your heart to forgive, if not forget. Your anger is eating you alive. It's slowly destroying any chance you might have for happiness"

"I can't seem to forget, not even when I'm asleep."

He made a feeble attempt to pull free from her grasp, but Tess tightened her grip and held on. "Let me help you, Zach. I owe you that much at least. Let me help you forget even if it's just for the night."

He stared into her upturned face, his eyes no longer unfocused, but the pure, hard green of emeralds. "Do you realize what you're saying?"

"Yes," she whispered. "Yes," she repeated, her voice stronger. "I know exactly what I'm saying. I want to make you forget the only way I know how."

"Why?"

Because I love you. The answer should be painfully obvious. She smiled, a sad, wistful smile. "Maybe because I need forgiveness."

"So you're finally admitting culpability?"

"Oh, Zach, don't you know that I'd never deliberately do anything to harm you?" The question was torn from her.

"I did believe that—once." He closed his eyes briefly. When he opened them again, they were filled with pain and confusion. "I trusted you with my life. Can you honestly tell me you had no part in my capture?"

Her courage withered under his intense scrutiny. Unable to meet the censure in his eyes, she lowered her gaze. How could she deny the charge knowing she had hand-delivered a note that might have alerted the sheriff? Whether she had intended to betray Zach's whereabouts or not, the results were the same. Any denial would ring hollow.

Zach let out a weary sigh. "Your silence gives me your answer."

Tess rested her forehead against his chest. "Believe me when I tell you I would never do anything to cause you pain. Never, I swear."

Zach felt himself softening as he stared at her bent head. He wanted to bury his face in her soft chestnut curls. To gather her in his arms and hold her, just hold her. God help him, he wanted to believe every word that fell from her sweet lips. Wanted to trust so badly he ached. "Sometimes I don't know what to believe."

She raised eyes that gleamed like polished silver. Very gently she placed one hand on his chest. "Let your heart be your guide."

Tess made it sound so simple. But as tempting as it seemed, he had held onto anger, hatred, and bitterness so long that they had become entwined in his soul like evil vines. They were so entangled with his character, he doubted he could cut himself free. Absently, he ran his knuckles along the curve of her jaw.

Let your heart be your guide.

"Even if I wanted to, Tess, I don't know if I can."

She caught his hand, pressed a kiss in his callused palm, then stepped back. "Since it's all you have to give, I'll content myself with your honesty—for now."

Zach watched her turn and retreat down the slope toward the mission. He had thought he had it all figured out. There hadn't been a doubt in his mind. For ten long years, he had hated Tess Montgomery with single-minded determination. She had been the source of his untold suffering and humiliation. He cursed himself for a fool, but his feelings toward her were undergoing a change. Hating her had become next to impossible. Instead of being selfish and deceitful, at every turn she displayed an innate sweetness and generosity. She left him weak with longing.

Needing to vent his frustration, he picked up a rock and hurled it as far as he could. She had responded to his accusations by saying she'd never *deliberately* harm him. What the hell was that supposed to mean? She had been barely more than a child at the time. Had someone coerced her into revealing his hiding place? Or had carelessness on her part led to his capture? And, more to the point, why was he trying to justify her behavior?

Muttering an oath under his breath, he turned and trudged after her.

Seventeen

If she didn't find something to occupy her time, Tess was certain she'd go mad. Every inch of the house had been scrubbed and swept. A stack of fresh tortillas was wrapped in a cloth on the kitchen table. Fresh straw lined the chicken coop. The livestock had been fed and watered.

And Zach was in Tucson.

With a sigh, she carefully folded the map she had been studying. The afternoon stretched ahead of her. Hours with nothing to do. If she stayed put, she'd only spend the time brooding about Zach and the fact that he hadn't made love to her since their wedding night. Not even after she had given him an open invitation to do so at the mission cemetery. She didn't understand why he avoided her. She had read the desire written across his face whenever she caught him watching her. He had once told her he'd have to be either a fool or a saint to refuse what she offered, then confessed he was neither. He hadn't seemed averse to enjoying her favors—as long as it wasn't complicated with emotional ties.

She thoughtfully tapped her fingers against the yellowed scrap of parchment. One of the crude sketches vaguely resembled the mission. A faded line, which

she assumed represented a trail, led north, passing near
both the house and the mine before angling in an east-
erly direction. She gnawed her lower lip in indecision,
then returned the map to its hiding place and left the
house with a spring in her step. With Zach away, this
was the perfect opportunity to inspect the mine.

After saddling her mare, she set off in the direction
she had seen Zach take on numerous occasions. A
worn trail twisted its way into rougher terrain. Scrub
oak, juniper, and piñon dotted the landscape. A hawk,
perched on the arm of a giant saguaro, followed her
progress. From a distance, she spotted a mule deer
ambling along a desert wash.

The path ended abruptly when the mountains took
a sharp ascent. Disappointed, Tess looked around. She
must have been mistaken about the mine's location.
There seemed nothing more than a jumbled wall of
granite. Then, nearly hidden by brush, she spied a
small opening outlined in timbers. Swinging down
from the saddle, she draped the reins over a branch
and approached the mine with a mixture of caution
and curiosity. The entrance was so low she had to stoop
to avoid hitting her head on one of the rafters. She
paused just inside to let her eyes adjust to the dim
light.

Beyond the entrance, it was dark as pitch. She realized belatedly that she had come ill prepared for her
investigation. She took a half step backward when her
foot made contact with something metal. Glancing
down, she saw a lantern sitting on the rocky ground
next to a wooden crate of tools. Items Zach must have
left, awaiting his return. Kneeling down, she rummaged through the box and found matches.

"Perfect," she murmured as the lantern spread an
amber glow.

Holding the lantern high, she ventured farther into

the mine. She had gone only a few yards when her feet dragged to a halt. The mine, in actuality no more than a cave, was cold and black. Quiet and eerie. Doubts crept in. For the first time, she began seriously to question whether exploring it alone was a wise idea. Perhaps she should overrule Zach's objections and return with him another time. Then, berating herself for a coward, she squared her shoulders and continued. She wouldn't go far, she decided, and she wouldn't stay long. Surely she could manage to stay out of trouble if she were careful.

As she moved deeper into the mine, the main shaft divided in several directions. Tess choose the branch on the right. The atmosphere grew even more chill and dank as she slowly made her way along. From the dark interior, she heard the musical tinkle of an underground spring. Raising the lantern, she noticed dark wet patches on the rocky surfaces. Just a little farther, she promised herself, then she'd retrace her steps.

Chunks of rock of varying sizes littered the mine floor. She picked one up and turned it over and over in her hand, examining it. Nothing distinguished it from any other rock she had ever seen. How silly to expect to find glittering strands of gold or silver. She tossed it down, disgusted with her childish notions. Occasionally, the lantern light washed over a memento of miners past: a broken handle of a pickax, a rusty bucket, a wheelbarrow minus the wheel. As Tess cautiously made her way along, the floor sloped downward and the passage narrowed.

She ducked under a stout beam and found herself in a much larger chamber, not so much part of the mine, but a cave. The walls reverberated with an odd clicking sound, unlike any she had heard before. The noise, whatever it was, seemed to originate nearby. She stood still, trying to identify the source. *Animal or human?*

she wondered nervously. Whichever, it made her distinctly uneasy.

She drew in a deep breath and instantly regretted it. She reeled from a strong, almost overpowering musky odor. In the enclosed underground space, the smell seemed far more revolting than that of the javelinas. Her thoughts flew to bobcats and coyotes—and the pistol she had left behind. Zach would be furious with her, she knew, for venturing out without it. A rapid series of sharp clicks filled the air. Lifting her lantern high above her head, Tess peered upward. As she stared in horror, the ceiling shifted and swarmed.

Became alive.

Bats . . .

Bats, hundreds of them, swooped back and forth, flapping silent wings. Tess screamed and dropped the lantern. Every tale, every superstition she had ever heard about bats rushed over her. When one brushed against her shoulder, her terror gave way to sheer panic. Holding her arms protectively over her head, she fled. Bat wings chased her into the darkness. Total blackness pressed in around her, smothering her, until her breath sawed in and out of her lungs. Fearful of finding a dark cloud of bats about to descend on her, she hazarded a glance over her shoulder, tripped, and fell. The palms of her hands stung from their contact with the stone floor. Tears sprang to her eyes as she lay motionless, waiting, listening, praying.

Gradually, she could hear above the loud thumping of her heart. No more clicking sounds. Except for the drip of seeping water, the cave was silent. Silent as a tomb. And blacker than night.

She drew into a sitting position, hugged her knees to her chest, and rocked back and forth. Dear God, what had she done? Without the lantern, how would she hope to find her way out of the mine? In her mad flight from the bats, she had lost all sense of direction. When Zach returned from Tucson and found her missing, would it even occur to him to search the mine? Would he look for her at all? Questions somersaulted through her mind like tumbleweeds. Questions, but no answers.

Slowly she climbed to her feet. With her arms extended in front of her, she began to grope her way along the rough, uneven walls. She stumbled and fell a second time and heard her skirt rip, but got up and doggedly continued. Relief burst through her when the wall dropped away. But her relief was short-lived. She had reached a crossroads. Completely disoriented, she had no idea which way to turn. For all she knew, she might have been burrowing farther and farther into the mountainside. Shivering with cold and fear, she sank to the floor.

"Zach," she cried, hoping against hope she'd hear him answer.

"Zach!" she screamed, a shrill edge of hysteria creeping into her voice. "Zach, please. Help!" She called his name over and over, but to no avail.

Time crept passed. Minutes, hours, days. An eternity. Chilled to the marrow, her throat raw from screaming his name, Tess huddled in a tight ball of misery. She prayed the bats were in a remote part of the mine. Prayed someone would find her. At last, exhausted from her ordeal, she drifted into an uneasy sleep.

In her dream, she heard a familiar voice call her name. Arousing herself from her stupor, she sat straighter and listened. She had nearly convinced herself it had been her imagination when she heard it again. It was Zach. He had found her. She had never been happier in her life than at that moment.

"Zach, I'm in here," she called as loudly as her hoarse voice allowed. "Hurry, please."

"Tess!" Zach yelled. "Stay where you are, but keep talking so I can find you."

Tess shoved to her feet and peered into the stygian gloom. She kept up an endless stream of chatter the entire time. Finally, she detected a glimmer in the distance. Picking up her skirts, she raced toward the light. Laughing and crying at the same time, she flung herself into Zach's arms.

She wrapped her arms around his neck and held on. His embrace was equally fierce. "Tess, darlin', you scared the hell out of me."

"There were b-bats. Hundreds of b-b-bats." Her words were muffled against his chest.

"Hush, sweetheart." His arms tightened. "It's all right. You're safe now."

"I was so scared." She burrowed against him, seeking his body heat to thaw her cold, melt her fears. "I dropped the lantern and couldn't find my way out."

His mouth crushed hers and moved over it ruthlessly. Zach had died a thousand deaths when he had returned from town and found her missing. Now he craved her taste, her feel, her touch. He needed to assure himself that she was safe, unharmed. Tess, it seemed, was as hungry for reassurance as he was. As he had come to expect from her, she abandoned herself freely, passionately to his kiss. Sweet as honeysuckle. Wild as a desert storm. And as he had also learned, a simple taste was never enough.

At last, his breathing ragged, he put her from him. He dragged his hand through his hair, trying to regain control. God help him, but another half minute, and he would have been ready to make love to her right here on the cold stone floor. And knowing Tess, her desire would match his, kiss for kiss, touch for touch.

Bending down, he retrieved the torch he had dropped seconds before Tess had shot out from the shadows and into his arms. She had gone through a horrible ordeal, been frightened out of her wits, and all he could think of were his own base needs. What the devil was wrong with him?

"Let's get out of here," he muttered. Holding the torch in one hand, he caught her arm with the other and drew her along with him.

Familiar with every square inch of the mine, Zach led the way with ease. At the entrance, Tess pushed past him in her eagerness for sunlight and fresh air. She held up her hand to shield her eyes, but stumbled backward from the sun's blinding glare.

"Easy, sweetheart. Not so fast." Zach pulled her just inside the mine, where the light was less harsh.

A shudder rippled through her. "I heard a strange clicking noise, then smelled a terrible odor," she told him, apparently compelled to relate the details of her experience.

Zach gathered her against him and brushed a light kiss across her brow. "It's over, Tess."

But the terror still needed to be purged. "When I held up the lantern, the entire ceiling fluttered like an enormous black canopy shaken by a strong wind. At first I didn't comprehend what was happening, but then seconds later, I realized the cave was filled with giant bats. Hundreds and hundreds of them."

He pressed a kiss onto her chestnut-brown curls. "Shh, darlin'," he whispered. He felt an overwhelming urge to comfort and protect. Probably no different than he'd feel toward anyone who had suffered a terrifying experience, he reasoned, trying to convince himself. Yet Tess fit against him perfectly. He was steadily becoming addicted to the feel of her in his arms.

"I don't know what I would have done if you hadn't found me," she admitted in a small voice.

"But I did find you," he murmured. His heart

twisted at the thought of losing her. Only a flimsy piece of paper united them. He knew that sooner or later they'd sell the property and go their separate ways. But right now, with Tess secure in his embrace, later suited him just fine.

Any notion of a future together was ludicrous. Too much had happened; too much separated them. Tess had offered him love, and he had thrown it back in her face. He had told her outright that he didn't love her—in fact, declared his hatred. A woman, any woman, deserved better from life. Still the notion of losing her tore at his moorings.

Reluctantly, he drew back, needing distance. "Let me take a look and assess the damages." Struck by a sudden thought, his brow wrinkled in concern. "You weren't bitten by a bat, were you?"

"No, I wasn't bitten" she said, giving him a wobbly smile in return. "But I must look a fright."

"Terrible," he agreed, but with a trace of good humor. He smoothed back her tangled hair with a gentle hand. "If the bats could see you now, they'd fly off in the opposite direction."

"Must you be brutally honest?" She gave a self-deprecatory laugh, then ran her hand over her skirt, which was hopelessly rumpled and torn, and winced.

Attuned to every nuance of her expression, Zach saw pain flicker across her finely etched features. Catching her hands in his, he turned them palms-up and found them abraded and bloody.

"I fell," she said simply.

Now that he was certain she was safe and unharmed, the enormity of her rash act hit him full force. "Damn it, Tess, don't you have any common sense?" Not giving her time to answer, he continued angrily. "Do you realize the chance you took? You could have been seriously injured in a fall and lain unconscious for days before being discovered. Or you might have been bitten by a rabid bat. Life is fragile here in the West, especially in the desert. Whatever possessed you to go roaming through the mine?"

She avoided his gaze. "I was curious. After all, it belongs to me as well as you. I have every right to come here whenever I wish."

"Let me rephrase my question." He folded his arms across his chest and glared down at her. "What prompted you to pay a visit to the mine this afternoon—and all by yourself?"

She scuffed a shoe against the ground. "You never offered to take me, so I decided to see what it was like on my own."

"Were you afraid I was keeping something from you?" His temper flared anew. "If you wanted to see *our* mine, all you had to do was speak up. I would have gladly given you a tour—one that avoided a cave full of bats."

"Fine," she sniffed. "I'll remember that in the future."

Her face had paled at the mere mention of the bats, and Zach silently cursed his insensitivity. "Let's get out of here."

Tess started toward her mare, but he stopped her. "You look as though a strong breeze would knock you right out of the saddle." Before she could launch an objection, he picked her up, deposited her on his gelding, then swung up behind her. Ignoring her half-hearted protests, he nudged his mount down the trail, leading her mare behind.

Zach gritted his teeth as she leaned against him, sweet and compliant in the loose circle of his embrace. It was sheer torture to feel her warmth against him. She had become a delectable pleasure that he denied himself with monastic vigilance. She tempted him like a ripe fruit ready to be plucked from the vine, waiting to be savored, enjoyed. Yet something held him back. In spite of the anguish she had caused him, some scruples remained intact. He had no desire to further exploit any tender feelings she harbored toward him.

He heaved a sigh of relief when the ranch came into view. Sliding down off the horse, he lifted her to the ground. "You look like hell, darlin'," he drawled, deliberately trying to create a barrier with his insults. "Go take a hot bath and a nap; then make yourself presentable."

He rode off, leaving her staring after him, looking as bewildered as a lost child.

Tess stared at the saguaro ribs that formed the ceiling above her bed. The nap Zach had suggested that afternoon had been a mistake. Now, instead of being sound asleep, she was wide awake. Wide awake and listening for Zach to return. He had been gone for hours. Probably at this very moment, he was enjoying drinks at the Silver Sequin or one of the many saloons that prospered along Maiden Lane. She had overheard whispers of Tucson's infamous red-light district during one of her infrequent trips into town. Apparently, it held more appeal for Zach than she did.

Punching the pillow, she rolled onto her side, closed her eyes, and wished for sleep. Just as she felt herself starting to drift off, a noise from outside brought her wide awake. She bolted upright in her bed and strained to hear the sound again. It seemed to be coming from somewhere inside the house, and from the clatter of pottery, most likely the kitchen. Zach, she concluded, had finally returned and now wanted something to eat. Getting out of bed, she draped her shawl over her shoulders.

Her bare feet soundless, she crossed the patio to the kitchen, then stood frozen in the doorway. Time dropped away, sending her plummeting to a night ten years past. A night when she had discovered a solitary figure raiding her mother's kitchen. Only this time it wasn't a Confederate soldier, but an Indian youth, who stole from her larder.

Shaggy black hair spilled past his shoulder blades. Loose-fitting garments hung from his slight frame like rags on a scarecrow. Even viewed from behind, he looked half starved. Unaware of her presence, he raised the jug of drinking water and drank deeply.

"There are tortillas in the cupboard," she said quietly.

He swung around to face her, his black eyes dilated with fear. The water jug slipped from his hands and shattered on the floor. Then, as she watched with growing concern, his eyes rolled back in his head and, limp as a rag doll, he collapsed in front of her.

Tess knelt beside him and, dipping the end of her shawl in the spilled water, used it to bathe his face. "It's all right," she murmured over and over. "Don't be afraid. You're safe now. No one will harm you."

In spite of her efforts to revive him, he lay still as a corpse on the kitchen floor. Tess reached for his wrist and was relieved to find a weak but steady pulse. She studied him in the pale moonlight that trickled through the open door. Her intruder was still a young boy, probably, she estimated, not more than eleven or twelve years old. He was painfully thin, with burnished skin stretched taut over high cheekbones and a broad, flat forehead and strong nose.

But why was he stealing food from her kitchen? And, more important, how had he become separated from his family? Those were questions she hoped to learn from her Papago friend, Amelia.

She patted his cheek lightly. "Wake up, my young friend."

At last his eyelids flickered, then opened. He stared up at her, his black eyes dull and uncomprehending.

Tess gave the boy a tentative smile which she hoped he'd find reassuring. "I thought perhaps you intended to spend the entire night asleep on the floor."

Fortunately, she had another jug of water stored nearby. After splashing some into a cup, she slipped an arm under the boy's shoulders and held it to his lips. "Drink," she urged. "Then I'll give you something to eat."

He swallowed a small sip, then took a bigger gulp, and another until he drained the cup.

"Do you think you're well enough to stand if I help you?"

At his blank look, she placed one arm under his shoulders and urged him to his feet. After some effort on both their parts, he stood, though he was none too steady. She draped his arm over her shoulder and half carried, half dragged him toward the room Zach claimed as his. Once there, she gave him a gentle shove and he sank down on the mattress, closed his eyes, and was instantly sound asleep, worn out by whatever ordeal had brought him this far.

Tess spread a light blanket over him, tucked it around his shoulders, then pulled a chair alongside the bed. The boy's lips were cracked and dry, his frame thin and malnourished. He had looked frightened out of his wits when he first saw her. What tragedy had befallen the boy? Whatever it was, she couldn't turn her back on him.

Yawning, Tess squirmed in the chair, trying to find a more comfortable position. Eventually, the events of the day combined with the lateness of the hour to exact their toll, and she, too, fell asleep.

Zach returned home an hour later and found her slumped in a chair in his bedroom sound asleep. One hand rested protectively on the bed, *his* bed, next to a long-haired, dark-skinned stranger.

"What the . . . ?"

Tess woke instantly. She blinked at Zach owlishly, then held a finger to her lips for silence. She rose from the chair and motioned him to follow.

"Who's sleeping in my bed?" he demanded the instant they were outside.

She smothered a sleepy giggle. "You sound like one of the three bears after they discovered Goldilocks."

Zach scowled darkly, apparently failing to find any humor in the situation. "Tess McClain," he said in a most ominous tone, "I'm waiting to hear your explanation."

Instead of being cowed by his manner, she gave him a serene smile. "Hush, Zach. You'll waken our very first overnight guest."

Eighteen

"A guest?" Zach gestured impatiently toward the bedroom. "The boy happens to be an Indian."

"Yes, I'm well aware of that, thank you very much."

"Who is he? How did he get here?"

"I have no idea."

Her calm, matter-of-fact manner seemed to infuriate him. He took off his hat, tossed it aside, and raked his fingers through his hair. "What do you plan to do with him?" he asked with ill-concealed impatience.

She raised her chin a fraction. "Why, care for him, of course." The answer should be obvious. "What did you think I'd do? Abandon the boy?"

He stared at her long and hard, then shook his head. "Of course," he said. "Maybe we could adopt him."

Ignoring his sarcasm, she pretended to consider the idea, then nodded slowly. "What a wonderful idea! The thought hadn't occurred to me."

His eyes widened in alarm, then narrowed. "Wait just a minute here, Tess . . ."

Tess choked back laughter, amused that Zach actually thought she had taken his suggestion seriously. Merriment danced in her eyes as she rested her hand lightly against his chest. "Relax, darlin'," she said, mimicking his favorite endearment. "Talk of adoption is a bit premature. At the present all I intend to do is help the boy regain his health and try to reunite him with his family."

Zach blew out a deep breath. His fingers curled around her wrist where it rested near his heart. "Care to tell me what you know about our so-called guest?"

Tess found it difficult to think clearly when his thumb idly stroked the pulse point at the base of her wrist, causing it to bolt, then run at an unsteady pace. "I have no idea who he is or how he got here."

"Start at the beginning, darlin'."

"I found him in the kitchen, stealing food."

Zach went still, absolutely still.

From his arrested expression, Tess knew he remembered a similar incident—one that had irrevocably linked their lives.

"I was almost asleep when I heard a noise. At first I thought you had returned, and went to investigate. Instead I found the boy. I must have frightened him because when he heard me he whirled around and dropped the water jug. Before I could do or say anything, he fainted dead away."

Zach resumed his absent stroking motion against the sensitive skin on the inner side of her wrist. "Poor kid," he muttered.

Encouraged, Tess continued. "The boy was obviously exhausted and close to starvation. Mexican, Indian, or white, it simply doesn't matter. He needs our help."

"But you don't know anything about him."

Tess smiled softly. At Zach's halfhearted protest, she knew she had already scored a victory. There was no way he could turn his back on someone in need any more than she could. "I know all that I need to about the boy—for now. The rest I can find out later."

"You're determined to see this through, aren't you?"

"Yes," she answered without hesitation. "I'm absolutely certain."

"And there's no way I can change your mind?"

"None whatsoever."

Now it was his turn to smile. "Tess, honey, for a sweet little thing, you can be stubborn as a mule."

"My father used to say that too," she said with wry humor. Though it had taken years to accomplish, she could at last recall fond memories of her father without feeling a keen sense of loss.

Tess gazed up at him and found herself wishing that he'd kiss her. Better still, sweep her off her feet, carry her inside, and make love to her. With her hand over his heart, they stood as close as two lovers. But in reality, they were strangers—intimate strangers. She watched his green eyes darken, deepen, to the mysterious hue of a primeval forest. Desire chiseled his handsome features with sharp, pure lines.

She recognized the hunger; it matched her own.

Then, Zach's expression hardened. Dropping her wrist, he retreated a step and jammed both hands in his pockets. "So . . . what do you plan to do with the boy once he's well?"

The desert night suddenly seemed colder. Chilled, Tess drew her shawl more tightly around her shoulders. She, too, dropped back several steps, needing to collect her scattered thoughts, to mask her disappointment. Drawing a steadying breath, she concentrated on how best to help the boy. "I thought perhaps tomorrow morning you could go the Papago village and find my friend, Amelia. She might be able to identify the boy. Perhaps lead us to his family or relatives."

"All right," he agreed. "That sounds like a good place to start."

"And Zach, take the wagon when you go. Amelia

just had a baby, and I don't want her to have to walk a long distance under a blazing sun."

Zach shrugged. "Sure thing, darlin', you're the boss."

But, Zach thought, she didn't look like any boss he'd ever had. What she did look like was an angel. A temptress. Sweet and pure and seductive. Loose curls cascaded around her shoulders and down her back. And her face—it was so pretty, so damned pretty, his heart stuttered just to look at her.

He had gone in search of her immediately after coming from town. He told himself he only wanted to make sure she was safe. Secretly, he had hoped he would find her awake. Awake and needing him as badly as he needed her. Instead, her bedroom had been empty. For a split second, blinding panic ripped through him. All sorts of dire thoughts tumbled through his mind. His relief at finding her slouched in a chair sound asleep was so profound it left him lightheaded.

"I shouldn't have gone off like that and left you alone," he muttered as she started to turn away.

"No need to worry. I'm perfectly capable of taking care of myself." A fleeting smile soothed the sting of her retort. "You're forgetting my Smith and Wesson, and the many hours of target practice."

He caught a strand of her hair, intending merely to brush it from her cheek, but he couldn't seem to release it. The texture fascinated him. He rubbed it between his fingers, memorizing its silkiness, the springiness of the curl. "When it comes to you, Tess, I don't forget anything. Anything at all."

Moistening her lower lip with the tip of her tongue, she gave him an uncertain smile. "A memory like that can be both blessing and curse."

"It is, darlin'. Trust me, it is."

She remained frozen in place. Waiting, wary. Hopeful.

Zach swore under his breath. Silly woman, didn't she have a lick of common sense. Didn't she know she should run from the devil, not welcome him with open arms and a smile on her lips? He looped the strand of her hair around his index finger. "I don't suppose you had your pistol anywhere handy in case you might need it?"

"Well, no . . ." She made a futile attempt to tug her hair from his grasp. "Why would I need my gun if I thought it was you?"

"True," he conceded. A corner of his mouth kicked up. "I do remember a time years ago when you didn't need a gun, either. A broom handle sufficed quite nicely."

"I was scared out of my wits the night I found you foraging through my cupboard."

"If you were scared, it didn't show."

"My knees were knocking together so loudly, I was afraid you'd hear them."

"A lifetime ago." He moved closer and dropped a light kiss to her mouth, unable to resist.

She leaned into him, her hands at his waist, and sighed—a sad, wistful sound. "Do you find me so lacking that you had to go into town? Are other women more appealing to you than I am?"

Her question was greeted with a lengthy silence. He wondered how she could doubt his attraction to her. Every night he waged a fierce battle with himself to stay away from her. It was the kindest thing to do. She fancied herself in love with him. It would be the ultimate cruelty to encourage tender feelings he could never return. "Is that what you think?" he said at last. "That I went into town looking for female companionship?"

She lifted her shoulders, let them fall. "I didn't know what to think," she admitted in a small voice.

His drawn-out sigh brushed her temple. "If it makes you feel better, I did go into town, but it wasn't to seek the company of other women. After you, they hold little appeal." It was true: where other women were concerned, Tess had spoiled him. None were as pretty—or as sweet.

Tess raised her head, her smoke gray eyes probing his. "Is that a compliment or an insult?"

He slid one arm loosely around her waist, pulled her closer still, then crooked a finger beneath her chin. God help him, he had tried, but it seemed he was fighting a losing battle. Chalk it up to a flaw in his character, but he couldn't keep his hands off her, and no longer wanted to try. "If you must know, I went into town with the intention of getting rip-roaring drunk. As you can see, I'm sober as a judge. Even whiskey seems to have lost its appeal. You're ruining me, darlin'. Soon I won't have any vices at all."

He wouldn't—couldn't—deny himself another long, lingering kiss. Finally, with great reluctance, he broke the contact. "Run along to bed, Tess," he ordered gruffly. "Before I do something we'll both regret." She turned, but not before he glimpsed the wounded look in her eyes and cursed himself for a fool. Another two seconds and he wouldn't have been able to walk away from her.

Tess cast a final glance over her shoulder at the room where the Indian youth slept. "What if the boy wakes up during the night?"

"Go." Zach prodded her in the direction of her bedroom. "I'll sleep out here on one of the benches. If the boy needs anything, I'll call you."

"Promise?"

"Promise."

Zach watched her disappear inside, heard the rustle of bedclothes as she settled down for the remainder of the night. Every fiber of his being yearned to crawl into bed next to her, ached to hold her, love her. But, he did none of those. Instead, he stretched full length on the nearest bench, stacked his hands under his head, and stared up at a desert sky speckled with millions of stars.

The Indian youth was a total stranger. Tess's fierce, protective attitude toward the boy had inexplicably touched a chord deep within him. Touched, then troubled. He recalled a time when he, like the boy sleeping inside, had been hungry, desperate, far from home and family. Then, as now, Tess had gladly provided food and shelter. She had nursed his and Jed's wounds and bolstered their flagging spirits. But in the end, she had also betrayed them.

Zach shifted, trying to find a comfortable position on the hard bench. Why would Tess go to such lengths to care for them only to turn them over to the authorities? It didn't make sense. But again the same troubling question rose in his mind. If Tess hadn't told, who had? Jed had always refused to believe that Tess had betrayed them. Jed, may he rest in peace, had tried but failed to convince Zach of her innocence. He pinched the bridge of his nose. God! How he missed that ornery old curmudgeon.

Besieged with unanswered questions, it was nearly dawn before he fell asleep.

Zach left to fetch Amelia early the following morning. The sun climbed high in the cloudless sky, then dipped in its westerly arc. Tess tried to curb her impatience by busying herself with household chores and caring for her patient. Exhausted from his ordeal, the boy woke only long enough to take food and water before falling asleep again.

Her half-peeled orange forgotten in her lap, Tess leaned against the sun-warmed adobe. Smoky growled ferociously as she attacked a sliver of orange peel with a white-tipped paw. Tess smiled at her pet's antics, then stared across the distant mountain tops. Her smile slowly faded.

She wondered what hardships had befallen her guest. Fading yellow bruises along the boy's rib cage gave mute testimony of abuse. But the fear in his eyes spoke even more eloquently of his mistreatment. When she had simply attempted to smooth the bedclothes, he shrank from her touch, his thin frame pressed against the far wall. His dark eyes, filled with intelligence and distrust, watched her every move. And he had yet to speak.

Tess released a long sigh. She prayed she wasn't returning him to the same situation he had tried to escape. If the boy appeared less than overjoyed at being reunited with his kin, she vowed to intercede on his behalf. She couldn't in good conscience return him to people who engendered so much terror, such desperation. He deserved better. Maybe adoption wasn't such a far-fetched idea after all.

The sound of hoofbeats pulled her from her reverie. With the kitten scampering alongside, she hurried to the parlor before unexpected visitors pounded on the door and woke her guest. Peeking through the partially opened shutters, she was dismayed to see Jimmy and Moe swing down from their saddles and approach the house.

Her first impulse was to bar the door and pretend no one was home, but she knew no locked door would deter them. The pair would simply let themselves in through the back and make themselves at home. She'd just have to brazen it out the best she could until Zach returned. Opening the door, she slipped outside to greet them.

Jimmy was the first to spot her. "Well, well, if it isn't the bride herself come to greet us." His dimples winked in and out as he casually looked around. "Where is that husband of yours, sugar? We came to talk business."

Ignoring Moe, who wore his usual sullen expression, she addressed Jimmy. "He's off on business of his own. Sorry you made the long trip out here for nothing."

She had started to turn away, in effect dismissing them, when Jimmy stopped her. "No trouble at all. We'll just come in and sit a spell till he gets home."

Tess felt a strong reluctance to allow them inside. Her dislike of them mounted each time she saw them. She also wanted to keep the boy's presence a secret. Jimmy had been insulting, even threatening, the day he had intruded on Amelia's visit. She didn't want their hatred vented on a defenseless youth.

"Somethin' wrong, Miz McClain?" Moe studied her with his small mud-colored eyes. "You're not bein' very hospitable."

Jimmy cocked his head to one side, his blue eyes alight with a devilish gleam. "With your husband away, you ain't hidin' a lover in there, are you?"

"How dare you!" Tess gasped, outraged. Red flags of color stained her cheeks.

"Now, Tess, sugar, don't get all riled. I was just teasin'." Jimmy's wicked smile belied his effort to appear contrite. "We really do have somethin' of vital importance to discuss with you and your husband. It's in your best interest if you at least hear us out. And," his smile widened, "I promise to behave myself."

"Very well!" she conceded grudgingly. Turning on

her heel, she led the way through the parlor to the patio beyond. "What's so important that it can't wait?"

Jimmy settled himself on a bench, stretched out his legs, crossing them at the ankles, and scooped the kitten onto his lap. Moe, on the other hand, elected to stand instead, with one shoulder propped against the wall, his gaze watchful.

"Aren't you gonna offer us lemonade and cookies?" Moe asked with an insolent smirk.

Refusing to rise to the bait, Tess held her temper in check and adopted a cool, even tone. "I'm afraid not, gentlemen. The best I can offer you before you leave is a cool drink of water."

Jimmy stroked the kitten's soft fur, lingering on the ruff around its neck. "Seems like this little cat isn't the only one with claws. What do you think, Moe?"

"Never cared much fer cats," Moe remarked in an offhand manner. "Too independent fer my taste. When I was a young'n, nothin' I liked better 'an teachin' 'em who's boss." His small eyes glittered with malice as they shifted from the kitten curled trustingly in his friend's lap back to Tess.

An icy shiver skittered down her spine. Considering they had once been part of the infamous Quantrill's Raiders, Moe, and no doubt Jimmy Jerold as well, could be capable of cruelty and violence. Tess fervently wished Zach would hasten his return. And, for once, she regretted not having her Smith and Wesson nearby.

Jimmy chuckled, sensing Tess's discomfiture. "Yeah, as I recollect, some of Moe's *students* didn't survive their lessons."

The message wasn't lost on Tess. Casting a surreptitious glance toward the room where the boy slept, she hoped he wouldn't waken at the sound of men's voices. These two had a mean streak that she wasn't willing to test. "You said you had business to discuss. I'd be only too happy to relay your message to my husband."

"What's the rush, sugar?" Jimmy arched one dark brow in inquiry and slanted her a look. "Where did you say your husband was?

"I didn't." She resisted the urge to wipe her damp palms along the sides of her skirt.

"Maybe he got tired of married life and took off." Moe withdrew a package of chewing tobacco from his shirt pocket. "I recall seein' him at Lil's place late last night."

"I'm tired of your insults." Tess gave him a cold stare. "I think it's time you go."

But both men ignored her request and refused to budge, leaving Tess feeling powerless and frustrated. Short of brute force, there seemed little she could do to change their minds. Recognizing her dilemma, they took obvious delight in her helplessness.

She struggled to maintain a semblance of poise, not wanting to show how rattled she felt inside. "In case you've forgotten, half of Casita de Oro belongs to me. Suppose you tell me why you're here."

"If you insist, sugar." Jimmy uncrossed, then recrossed his ankles. "Since you and McClain have had time to think things over, Moe and I was wondering if you've reconsidered our offer."

"No," she returned without hesitation. "We've no intention of selling at the present time."

"Don't be hasty, now, sweetheart. We're prepared to be generous. If it's more money you're wantin'—"

"It's not for sale."

Moe bit off a hunk of tobacco. "Don't be stupid. Things happen, accidents and such. Place wouldn't be worth much, say, if it caught fire and burned to the ground."

"I don't like being threatened." Tess held her ground. She knew this unscrupulous pair were doing their best to frighten and intimidate her. She should be both, but a hot, cauterizing anger destroyed all shreds of caution. "Get out of here," she demanded, her hands bunched into fists. "Now."

All traces of affability vanished from Jimmy Jerold's face as he set Smoky on the ground. Before Tess could stop him, Moe picked the kitten up by the scruff of its neck. "Cats have such scrawny little necks. Don't take much to break one. Just a little twist, and *snap.*" He laughed into Tess's shocked face. "Bye-bye kitten."

The crunch of wagon wheels heralded Zach's timely arrival. Tess snatched the kitten from Moe's hand and hastened to greet Zach and, hopefully, Amelia. She reached the doorway in time to watch Zach assist the Papago woman from the wagon seat. An Indian pony, with a rope halter, was tied to the rear of the wagon. Amelia paused to adjust a board strapped to her back, then followed Zach toward the house.

"We have visitors," Tess blurted the moment they were within earshot.

Zach gave a brusque nod toward the two horses tethered nearby. "I recognized their mounts. What do they want?"

"They're increasing their offer." *And threatening to burn us to the ground,* she wanted to add, but kept silent, not wanting to frighten Amelia—or provoke Zach to do something that he might later regret.

Zach gave her a grim smile. "Makes a person wonder why the sudden generosity, doesn't it, darlin'?"

Uncertain, Amelia looked from one to the other. "You want I go?"

"No, no," Tess hastened to assure her friend. "As

my husband has probably explained, we need your help."

"You show me to boy."

"Thank you, Amelia." Some of Tess's tension eased at the woman's willingness to cooperate, an ease compounded by Zach's reassuring presence. She felt confident he could deal with Moe and Jimmy much more effectively than she could. "But first I want to meet your son."

The Papago woman smiled with pride and turned her back so that Tess could admire the infant strapped to its cradle board. "He good baby. Eat, sleep, a good baby."

Tess's chest constricted at the sight of the infant. The round little face peeking over the top of the cradle board was that of a sleeping cherub topped with a thatch of silky black hair. Gently, she stroked one miniature fist, and the infant curled his tiny fingers around hers. A fierce longing slammed into her, a force so powerful that it almost knocked her to her knees. She yearned for a baby of her own. A child to love and nurture. Vaguely, she became aware of Zach's hand at her elbow.

"Tess, you look a little peaked. Are you all right?"

Dragging her gaze from the infant, she stared into eyes as green as springtime and knew with absolute certainty she wanted a child with eyes that same bewitching hue.

"Tess . . . ?"

Clearing her throat, she forced herself back to the present and the problems at hand. "Why don't we first let Amelia identify the boy? Then we can assure Jimmy and Moe that we have no intention of selling what's ours."

She led the way while Zach and Amelia followed. When Jimmy spotted the Indian woman, he rose to his feet. Hatred distorted his face into a mask of ugliness. "What's she doin' here?" he snarled.

"She's invited," Zach replied, his lazy drawl laced with steel. "You're not."

"What'd I tell you?" Moe crowed. He spit a stream of tobacco juice, missing Zach's feet by mere inches. "We found ourselves some injun lovers."

A muscle bunched in Zach's jaw, the only sign of temper. "If you *gentlemen* leave now, you can make it back to Tucson while it's still daylight."

"Don't like your mouth, McClain." Jimmy took a menacing step forward. "Maybe you need to be taught some manners."

"And I'm just the man to do the teachin'." Moe drew back his right arm and aimed a punch. Zach neatly sidestepped the blow while at the same time sticking out his leg and sending the man sprawling in the dirt.

Livid with rage and humiliation, Moe scrambled to his feet and dropped into a crouched position, ready to do battle. Before either man could land another blow, however, everyone's attention was diverted by Amelia's sharp cry of distress.

"Amelia?"

But Tess's inquiry went unheeded. The Papago woman's gaze was riveted on the slight figure framed in an open doorway. Curious, Moe and Jimmy looked to see what claimed the woman's rapt attention.

Taking an involuntary step backward, Amelia covered her mouth with one hand. Her dark eyes dilated with fear, brimmed with loathing. The boy, in spite of his weakened condition, drew himself upright and glared back with equal animosity. Perplexed, Tess looked from one to the other.

As though in a trance, Amelia slowly backed away. Her wary gaze remained fastened on the Indian youth.

Sensing the woman was about to turn and flee, Tess clutched her arm and shook her. "Amelia, tell me. What's wrong? Who is he? What has he done?"

"Boy not Papago." Amelia jerked free of Tess's grip. "He Apache."

Nineteen

"Apache!" Jimmy and Moe exclaimed.

"Apache . . . ?" Zach muttered under his breath.

"Apache," Tess whispered the feared name. Tales of Indian brutality she had overheard during her trip west rushed back with clarity.

While the others watched, Jimmy hooked his thumbs into the waistband of his pants and strolled to the spot where the boy stood.

The boy fairly quivered from the effort not to shrink from the man's approach. Worried that his strength would fail the test, Tess took a tentative step forward, only to be restrained by a warning frown from Zach. She hesitated, chewing her bottom lip in indecision. Out of the corner of her eye, she saw a blur of motion as the painted pony trotted past with Amelia and her son on its back.

"You sure know how to pick 'em, Tess, honey," Jimmy drawled. He stood, feet planted, in front of the boy, who clutched the door frame for support. "Your friend here ain't no ordinary Indian like the Pima or Papago. This one's a dirty, murderin,' thievin' Apache."

"He's just a boy," Tess defended hotly. "Hardly more than a child."

Moe sauntered over to join his friend. "Hey, Jimmy,

haven't we seen this kid somewheres? He looks familiar."

Tess shot a startled glance at Zach, but once again at his subtle signal she held her tongue.

"Look familiar?" Jimmy snorted. "Surely you're funnin' me. As far as I'm concerned all redskins look alike."

"What are you doin' here, injun?" Moe snarled. "Why are you botherin' these nice folk? Gonna wait till they're asleep, then rob them blind? Or mebbe kill them and take their scalps fer souvenirs?"

A kaleidoscope of emotions crossed the youth's face: fear, defiance, hatred. Then his expression hardened. Drawing himself erect, he spit in Moe's face.

Quick as a rattlesnake, Moe backhanded the boy, sending him crumpling to the ground. Instantly Moe went down on one knee, grabbed a fistful of the youth's long black hair, and forced his head back so that his neck was arched and vulnerable. "My friend and me know how to deal with Apache scum." He traced an invisible line across the boy's throat with a stubby finger. "You watched us do it, didn't you?"

"Stop it!" Tess cried, racing across the space separating the two. She pummeled Moe's back in a desperate attempt to make him release the boy. "Let him go!"

Moe flung out one arm and sent Tess reeling. She landed on her backside in the dirt. Before she could scramble to her feet, she heard the unmistakable click of a cylinder as it rotated and locked into place. Her eyes darted to where Zach stood, Colt in hand, the barrel leveled at Moe Black.

"Gentlemen, and I use the term loosely, you've overstayed your welcome."

Zach's voice was as cold and deadly as the weapon he held. Tess felt as though she were watching a dangerous stranger. Evidently, Moe and Jimmy were in no mood to dispute a man with a gun. A man whose eyes glittered like shards of green ice. His gaze fixed on the gun, Moe released the boy and climbed to his feet.

Jimmy held up his hands, palms outward in a gesture of peace. "No need to get riled."

"When I'm riled, you'll know it." Zach's smile was as glacial as his eyes. "Now get off my property before I lose my temper—and don't come back."

Jimmy's affability slipped, revealing a cunning, ruthless nature hidden behind the facade of Southern charm. "You'll regret this," he snarled. "We offered to buy you out, but you were too stupid for your own good. Some folks need to learn their lessons the hard way."

"C'mon," Moe mumbled to Jimmy as he headed for the door. His face mottled with anger, Jimmy followed his companion.

Tess scrambled to her feet as Zach shoved his gun into its holster. He gave her a quick, assessing look. "You all right?"

She nodded, too shaken by the unexpected violence to speak. Wordlessly she went to the boy. Kneeling beside him, she dabbed at the blood trickling from the corner of his mouth with a handkerchief. Dazed, the young Apache stared at her, his eyes black pools of misery.

"Kill," he mumbled. "They kill my people. Take me . . ." A shudder convulsed his thin frame, followed by a series of aftershocks.

Tess wanted to weep at the boy's tortured disclosure. Zach swore viciously, then kicked a clod of dirt, sending it ricocheting off the well in the back corner of the patio. Not knowing how to ease the boy's pain, she did the only thing she could think of. She gathered the boy in her arms, cradled him against her breast, and rocked him. "I'm sorry, so sorry," she murmured over and over.

Zach's Colt hung heavy at his waist. He didn't remember when he had felt this helpless or ineffective. His gun afforded little protection from this kind of pain. Late afternoon sunlight burnished Tess's curls as she ministered to the boy. Her gentle nurturing could soothe even the most battered of hearts, he reflected. A fact he had observed firsthand.

Her tender heart acted as a balm even to his war-scarred soul. Although his nightmares hadn't disappeared entirely, they had abated, becoming less intense, less debilitating. All he wanted to do at that moment was to put his arms around woman and boy and offer what comfort he could. But he held back. Beginning at Elmira, he had constructed a dam around his heart, and it had been a long time since he had allowed softer feelings to leak through. So long, in fact, he feared he had forgotten how.

At last, the boy's tremors ceased. Tess smoothed his hair from his face, then helped him to his feet and led him inside.

Impatient, frustrated, wanting to set matters right but not knowing how, Zach paced. He had known Jimmy Jerold and Moe Black were no good from the beginning. Few men who had ridden with Quantrill could claim to be upstanding citizens since the end of the war. Jesse James and the Younger brothers were prime examples of the caliber of men that Quantrill attracted. Robbing trains and banks, shooting and getting shot, seemed all they aspired to. Jed, in Zach's opinion, had been an exception. He had sought forgiveness from a Higher Source, then spent his days searching for a lost treasure. From the beginning, he had wondered if Jerold or Black were responsible for Jed's murder. But from all accounts, the pair hadn't arrived in Tucson until recently.

"He's sound asleep." Tess's quiet voice roused Zach from his contemplation.

"Poor kid. He's been through a lot."

"His name is Gairmo." She sank down on one of the benches, leaned back, and closed her eyes. "He didn't want to talk about what happened to him. The subject is obviously still painful."

With her eyes shut, Zach was free to study her at his leisure. Damn, if she wasn't the prettiest sight this side of the Rockies. Pretty, but she could be ferocious as a tigress protecting her cub. He couldn't help but admire the way she leaped to the boy's defense last night and again today. Gairmo desperately needed a champion, and couldn't have found a better one than Tess. He was proud of the way she stood up for him.

He eased down next to her. A fiery sun was starting to sink behind the mountains, slashing the sky with bold strokes of gold, orange, and red. This was his favorite time of day, this quiet shift from day to night. Usually it brought with it a sense of peace and tranquility, but not tonight. Jerold and Black had spoiled any enjoyment he might have derived from a sunset. "I don't think we've seen the last of Jed's old buddies," he said at last.

Tess's eyes grew wide and filled with alarm. "What do you think they'll do?"

He shrugged. "Hard to say."

"If they come back, I'll be ready."

"And just what do you propose to do?"

"I have a pistol, and, thanks to you, I know how to use it."

Hearing her grim determination, Zach was torn between dismay and laughter. His harmless kitten had indeed turned into a veritable tiger. But she was no match for the likes of Jimmy and Moe. "What happened to the woman who insisted she could never point a gun at anyone?"

"I'll do whatever I have to because no one, *no one*," she repeated fiercely, "is going to harm that boy."

If only she had protected me with that much fervor . . .

The thought streaked across his mind like summer lightning. *If only . . .*

Zach absently rubbed his chest with the heel of his hand to ease the tightness around his heart. A man couldn't linger on what-if's and if-only's, he told himself. A wise man looked at things the way they were, not the way he wanted them to be. But no one ever accused him of being wise.

"Zach?" Tess was watching him strangely.

He rose abruptly, hooked his thumbs in his pockets, rocked back on his heels, then stared at the striated sky. He watched twilight settle a mantel of mauve over the mountainside. "Moe and the boy recognized each other," he said after a lengthy silence.

"But how?"

"It's just a theory, of course, but I think Moe and Jimmy might have taken part in the Camp Grant Massacre."

She came to stand alongside him. "What massacre?"

"It happened a couple years back, Spring of 'seventy-one. I was north of here at the time, working for the railroad, but news of the atrocity even reached Washington. President Grant, it's said, called the attack 'purely murder.' "

"Tell me about it."

He cut her a quick glance. "It's not like a story you'll find in one of your dime novels. Sure you want to hear it?"

No! Tess wanted to shout in protest. She really didn't care to hear a lurid account of a massacre, but if it explained Gairmo's plight, then she'd force herself to listen to every gory detail. "Tell me," she repeated, her voice soft but resolute.

Zach returned his gaze to the mountains. "Lieutenant Royal Whitman at Camp Grant had permitted several hundred Apache to settle near the army post at the junction of Aravaipa Creek and the San Pedro River. He arranged for them to cut hay, which they sold to the post in exchange for clothing. His actions outraged many citizens, who were convinced Whitman sheltered Apache raiders who struck their farms and then scurried back to military protection.

"Matters came to a head that April after more ranches were raided and more people killed. Tucsonans were convinced the Aravaipa Apaches living near Camp Grant were responsible. A group of citizens met secretly and planned to take action. They were joined by nearly a hundred Tohono O'odham."

Night, black and velvety, descended, replacing twilight. Zach paused in his recitation. Tess wondered if he was giving her time to reconsider—or if the details were too horrible to relate. She hugged her arms around her waist. "Don't stop now, Zach. I want to hear all of it."

"They attacked the sleeping village at dawn." Zach's tone was intentionally void of emotion. "When it ended, more than one hundred corpses littered the ground. Only eight were adult males; the rest were women and children. Nearly all had been mutilated."

Tess pressed her hand against her lips and swallowed down bile. "What has this to do with Gairmo?" she asked when she was again able to speak.

"More than two dozen struggling Apache children were carried off and sold into slavery in Mexico."

"You think Gairmo might be one of them?"

He shrugged. "It's possible that the boy escaped his captors and was trying to make his way back to his people."

"It must have been terrifying," Tess murmured. "He couldn't have been more than nine or ten at the time. He's been mistreated; his body is a mass of bruises. No wonder he fled."

"It took courage to escape," Zach agreed.

Something in his quiet tone captured her attention. Wistfulness, admiration, a tinge of regret? Summoning courage of her own, Tess trespassed into hostile territory, following the path where her intuition led. "What about you, Zach? Did you ever try to escape from Elmira?"

He closed his eyes briefly, his face contorted with pain. "Yes," he whispered. "But unlike Gairmo, I failed."

Tess ached for him. Even after all these years, remembered suffering clung to him like tattered silk streamers, frayed yet strong enough to bind. She had never loved him more than she did at this moment when he stood before her, hurt and vulnerable. "Talk to me, Zach," she prodded gently. "Tell me what happened."

He let out a long, shuddering sigh. "Prisoners called turncoats or razorbacks would do anything for extra rations. One of them got wind of my plan to escape and reported me to a guard. All I got for my trouble was the sweat box." His expression grim, he turned from his view of the mountains and slowly began to pace the length of the patio.

Tess watched helplessly. "How long did they keep you there?"

"Long enough." He gave a harsh bark of laughter. "Long enough to make a grown man bawl like a baby."

Her heart twisted painfully at the thought of his suffering, his humiliation. She yearned to go to him, gather him to her breast, and rock him much as she had Gairmo a short while ago. But, fearing rejection, she did none of these.

"A sweat box can be trying at any time, but in the summer it's pure hell. It's a narrow, upright affair, barely big enough for a man to stand in. Then, as if standing in one position for a long period of time isn't punishment enough, a lid is placed over the top. No food, no water. No air." He sank down on a bench and put his head in his hands. "Soon you lose all track of time. You're too miserable to care. When the guards finally released me, I fell down on my knees and thanked them."

She sat next to him and took his hands in hers. "Nothing that happened at Elmira, Zach, makes you less of a man. You survived a horrible experience, and came out a stronger person. And that takes courage—a very special kind of courage"

He gave her a crooked smile. "You really believe that, don't you?"

"Yes," she whispered. Once again she let intuition guide her. Reaching up, she pushed a lock of tawny hair from his brow. Then, when that gesture wasn't repulsed, she grew bolder. Her gaze never wavering from his, she threaded her fingers though the amber-gold strands and cradled the back of his head. As she brought her lips closer, she watched fascinated as desire clouded and darkened the jewel-like emerald of his eyes to the color of jade.

He wanted her.

Zach wanted her. Joy burst within her like fireworks on the Fourth of July. Dazzling, breathtaking, exhilarating joy. Her mouth met his in a kiss heady with delight. No longer tentative or shy, she reveled in the contact. The smooth, warm texture of his lips, the rough, hot, slick feel of his tongue. Every detail was vastly exciting, hers to explore.

Her eagerness quickly communicated itself to Zach, who responded with alacrity. His mouth moved over hers, hungry and ardent, tasting and ravishing. He shifted and tugged her into his lap, then began to fondle her breasts. Tess's moan of pleasure was muffled against his mouth. Instantly her nipples contracted, ached. She arched her back, unconsciously entreating him to touch. Taste.

God, she was on fire with longing. The realization stunned her. She hadn't guessed until now that a woman's need could rival a man's. It not only could, she discovered, but it did.

Her lips traveled the strong column of his throat. Greedily, she licked his flesh. He tasted of salt and musk, the flavor unique, addictive. "Umm . . ."

"Ah, Tess, kitten," he murmured, his eyes closed. "You make me want to rip off your clothes and make love to you right here and now."

She emitted a sound: a low, seductive, feline purr of approval. She caught his earlobe between her teeth and bit gently. "Then what's keeping you?"

Before he could anticipate her next move, she changed position so that she now straddled his thighs. She almost laughed aloud at his startled expression. With a wicked smile playing across her lips, she unfastened his shirt, stopping at every other button to kiss or caress the smooth expanse of sun-bronzed skin stretched taut over muscle and sinew. Zach groaned and tilted his hips so she could feel his engorged shaft nestled in the V between her legs.

The movement stoked fires already raging. An intense need burned even brighter and turned liquid. Hurriedly, she slid the shirt from his shoulders. Restless, fevered in their haste, her hands wandered over his superbly sculpted torso. He sucked in a sharp breath as her fingers encountered his flat nipple. Her smile broadened as she dipped her head. Lazily she laved the little brown aureole with the tip of her tongue. Zach fought for control as he plunged his hands through her hair. The remaining pins fell unheeded to the ground, her hair falling about her in glorious disarray.

"You're breaking all the rules, kitten." He filled his palm with a plump breast, then squeezed, only to bite back a groan when she wriggled against him, enticing, inviting.

Zach didn't know how much more of this exquisite torment he could endure. His blood felt heated to the boiling point. It roared through his veins like molten lava, hot and dangerous. His vision blurred and diminished until all he saw was Tess. Sweet, wonderful, unpredictable Tess, with her wild nimbus of chestnut curls. She moved against him, head thrown back, neck arched, eyes shut. Kitten, tiger, siren. Every man's fantasy. *His* fantasy.

He could barely contain his need. Feeling clumsier than a green lad upon his first sexual encounter, he unhooked the bodice of her dress and slid it off her shoulders. Her chemise was treated with the same careless regard. At the sight of her naked to the waist, her skirt wantonly spread over his thighs, his control almost snapped. Tess had completed her metamorphosis from blushing virgin into sensual woman. As though relishing her newfound power, she gave him an arch smile, then, with a flip of her head, tossed her long hair over her shoulder. Rising on her knees, she rubbed against him, her soft, warm flesh faintly scented with lilac.

"Love me," she whispered.

Zach didn't need further encouragement. Reaching down, he unbuttoned his pants. Already painfully hard, his manhood sprang free. Impatiently, he tore at her undergarments until the cotton parted with a soft ripping sound. His fingers brushed her mound, and he found her hot and wet and perfect. Grasping her hips, he guided her down on himself. When she surrounded him at last, he thought he had surely died and gone straight to heaven. He surged upward in a tentative thrust, and the muscles of her pelvis clamped around him like a velvet fist. He couldn't prevent a harsh sigh of pure pleasure from escaping.

Tess threw her head back and closed her eyes. She rode him hard and fast, her thighs hugging his, matching him thrust for thrust. Zach held on to her hips. His teeth bared in a feral growl as he tried to prolong the inevitable. Finally, almost simultaneously, they shattered in a wild, tumultuous explosion full of shimmering fireworks and glaring rockets. Then, like a fading shower of sparks, they slowly drifted back to earth.

Twenty

"I looked in on our guest." Zach paused at the doorway wearing nothing but low-riding denims. "He's sleeping like a baby."

Tess rolled onto her side and returned the smile. Happiness flooded through her at his return. After their passionate lovemaking on the patio, Zach had carried her inside, deposited her on the bed, given her a fleeting kiss, then left. They had never spent an entire night together, and she feared this one would be no different. Now she felt a surge of confidence, a rush of optimism. "Is your favorite bench uncomfortable?"

He leaned against the door frame and gave her a half smile that never failed to make her heart skip a beat. "Not only is it too hard, but there's a cold breeze sweeping down the mountain."

"Too cold for a warm-blooded Southern boy?"

"Much too cold, darlin'."

"I'm willing to share." Tess scooted to one side and patted the mattress. "I promise you'll find this much softer."

"And warmer." Zach strolled toward her. "You've turned me into a believer, Tess McClain."

"A believer in what?" Her eyes fastened on his bronzed, hard-muscled chest, the lean hips. To her mind, he was a living portrait of masculine beauty, and tonight he was hers. All hers.

"In spite of rumors to the contrary, you've managed to convince me that there really is such a thing as Northern hospitality." He slipped off his pants and stood before her in naked splendor.

"Let me put those rumors to rest once and for all."

With a smile that put every dime-novel hero to shame, he stretched alongside her and pulled her into his arms. Tess joyfully surrendered to the mastery of his kiss, her joy sweetened by the promise of ultimate bliss yet to come.

This time they made love slowly, with long, leisurely kisses that vanquished doubt and fear. Gentle roaming hands discovered and explored intimate zones, eliciting sighs, quivers, soft moans of delight.

Then, trapped in a gossamer web of passion, Tess began to writhe, almost mindless from the pleasure spiraling through her. *Make this last. Let him love me.* These two pleas repeated in her mind like a litany. Then Zach entered her and even these thoughts vanished as together they rode a tidal wave of passion that carried them to breathless heights.

Afterward, Tess lay beside Zach, their bodies still joined. She felt as if she were floating, drifting on a sea of contentment. Zach's lovemaking had been so achingly tender, she could have wept from the sheer beauty.

Dreamily, she ran her index finger along his chiseled cheekbones, then along the angle of his unshaven jaw. Next she ran her fingers through his sun-streaked hair, memorizing the texture as it sifted through her fingers. "Do you know what I thought the first time I saw you in Abner Smith's office?"

He gave a lazy smile as he wound a long curl around

his finger. "I have no idea, darlin', what goes on in that pretty little head of yours."

Darlin'. Tess wondered if she had only imagined it, or had the venom disappeared from the endearment. Now it almost sounded . . . sincere? "You stood in the open doorway with the sun behind you, so I couldn't see your face. But even so, you were the epitome of every dime-novel hero I ever read about."

"I'm not a hero." He withdrew from her, turned on his back, then rested his arm across his brow and stared at the ceiling. "I told you what happened at Elmira. They brought me to my knees, broke my spirit. Nearly robbed my will to live. I'm no hero, Tess. Don't make me into something I'm not."

She ignored the pain, the defeat in his tone. "You're wrong." She brushed a kiss across his mouth, then another until she felt his lips soften beneath hers. Then, knowing she had his full attention, she looked into his beautiful emerald eyes and spoke from the heart. "To my mind, Zach, a true hero is one who overcomes obstacles—often at great personal cost—and emerges a stronger and better man. You're my hero, Zach McClain. Scarred, battered, but a hero just the same."

Zach remained awake long after Tess had fallen asleep. He kept mulling over what she had said about heroes. Had he emerged from his experiences a better, stronger person? Tess believed he had, and, strangely enough, she made him want to believe it, too. He had confided his darkest moments, but she illuminated them with understanding. He had told her about his weakness, and she talked of his strength. He spoke of cowardice, but she saw bravery. Contradictions all of them, but so was she.

Hatred for her had once kept him alive. Now she had become the instrument for his healing. Bit by bit, one by one, she stripped away his defenses. Her gentle persistence coaxed and cajoled him to let go of bitterness, anger. When those tactics failed, she didn't hesitate to unleash her temper, scold, and berate. Against his will, she had provoked him to reveal events he had never told another human being. Elmira was his deep, dark secret, his hidden shame. Since the day of his release, he had never spoken the hated name aloud. She had goaded him into confronting the past. Coming to terms with it. And for that alone he would be forever grateful. A heavy burden had been lightened.

Dawn was only hours away. Zach drew the bedclothes more snugly around them. In her sleep, Tess instinctively sought his body's heat. With a sigh, he feathered a kiss across her brow and pulled her close. Then, weary of trying to reconcile past with present, he, too, fell asleep, finding sweet surcease in her arms.

The following morning, Tess kept casting surreptitious glances in Zach's direction. Instead of spending the day at the mine as he usually did, he seemed content to remain close to the house. The kitten followed him about as he fed the livestock, then repaired a broken shutter. She sensed a change in his manner, but was afraid to do or say anything that might snap the tenuous bond between them. She concentrated, instead, on their young Apache guest.

The boy spent less time sleeping. He prowled about the house, inspecting his surroundings, and eventually ventured onto the patio. He stood on the shaded porch, cataloging Tess's every movement through eyes eloquent with suspicion and uncertainty. Eyes wise beyond his tender years.

Tess, careful to avoid quick movements that might startle him, placed an orange on the bench. "Eat, Gairmo. This is for you."

He snatched it with a grubby hand, his eager fingers digging into the thick peel. He ate it greedily, the juice dribbling down his chin, as though fearful the precious gift would suddenly be taken away.

While he ate, she set a basin of warm water, a sliver of soap, and a towel on a nearby bench. Next to them, she placed one of Zach's clean shirts. "You wash," she said in a quiet tone.

In order to give the boy a measure of privacy while he bathed, she went into the bedroom he had been using and changed the sheets. At a small sound from behind, she turned and found Gairmo less than three feet away. Water dripped from his newly washed hair. Zach's shirt hung on his shoulders, dwarfing his slight frame, the sleeves reaching past his fingertips. Her heart wrenched at the sight. He looked very young, very vulnerable. And hopelessly lost.

She smiled and approached him slowly. "The shirt's a little large, I see. Let me roll up the sleeves for you."

He looked as though he wanted to flee, but instead remained where he was, his thin body ramrod stiff, while she folded the cuffs back, exposing a pair of frail wrists.

"There," she said. "Much better."

His face solemn, he looked straight into her eyes. "Want to go home."

"Of course you do." Her chest constricted with emotion at the boy's poignant plea. She wanted to put her arms around him and hug him, whisper words of reassurance and caring. But, sensing he wasn't ready to accept comfort from a stranger, she did none of these.

"Want to go home," he repeated. The slight quaver in his voice betrayed his attempt at bravado.

Tess gently placed her hand on the boy's shoulder and met his look. "We—my husband and I—want to help you find your people. We'll do everything we can to see you reunited."

She was heartened when he didn't draw away or flinch from the contact. His expression was plainly dubious, yet so hopeful that she could have cried. "Do you understand me, Gairmo?"

He nodded hesitantly.

"You can trust us, Gairmo. We want to be your friends."

He studied her with eyes old beyond his years. "Gairmo trust no one. Only Gairmo."

Trust was something that must be earned, not forced, Tess knew. Gairmo wasn't ready to trust—and might never be. If indeed he had been at Camp Grant during the massacre, his fears were more than justified. As a young child, he had witnessed the brutal slaughter of his family, then been forcibly abducted and sold into a life of slavery.

"Believe me or not, we are your friends," she reiterated firmly. "We will do our best to help you go home."

She felt some of his tension dissolve. She gave his shoulder a gentle squeeze before releasing it. "It'll be all right, Gairmo, you'll see."

The wistful expression on his face told her he wanted to believe her. Wordlessly he went into the bedroom, climbed into bed, and closed his eyes. Soon, the slow, even rise and fall of his chest told Tess he had fallen asleep.

God only knew how long the boy had wandered through the desert without food or water, Tess thought as she discarded the basin full of wash water. It was a wonder he had managed to survive. She only hoped Zach wouldn't object to her having volunteered his services to help find the boy's family. Somehow, she sensed, he sympathized with the boy's plight and would do what he could.

She had just finished making tortillas when she heard Zach call her name.

"Tess, we have a visitor."

Wiping her hands on her apron, she hurried inside the house in time to see Zach usher Lily London into the parlor. Tess was so surprised to see the woman, she came to a dead halt in the middle of the room.

Lily leaned on the handle of a raspberry red parasol that perfectly matched her dress and bonnet, and gazed around the room with interest. "My, my," she murmured. "So this is how an heiress lives."

Tess flushed, recalling their first conversation the day she had arrived in Tucson. Ignorant of the rundown condition of her newly acquired property, she had boasted to Lily of her good fortune. She had been bursting at the seams to tell someone, anyone, even a gaudily dressed stranger she met on the street. How naive she had been. To a worldly woman like Lily London, it must have seemed the prattling of a silly schoolgirl.

"None of my business, hon, but a few pieces of furniture might help dress up the place a bit." The woman's apparent good humor took the sting out of her words.

Tess gestured toward the bare parlor. "I know it isn't much . . ."

Zach stepped into the breech. "Any furniture that might have been here was destroyed by whoever killed Jed."

"Bastards," Lily muttered. "Jed didn't come to my place often, but I liked the man. He was a true gentleman."

Gentleman? Tess mused. Perhaps *gentle man* would be more a more fitting description for the gristled Confederate she remembered with fondness. "Come out to the patio, Miss London, and have a seat while I get us some refreshments."

"Friends call me Lil," Lily said easily. "This place would be considered a palace compared to what I started out with."

While Zach escorted their guest outside, Tess got together a pitcher of lemonade, glasses, and a plate of molasses cookies. When she stepped outdoors with the tray, she found Lily seated on a corner bench, several plump pillows behind her back. Zach stood nearby, one foot braced on a stool.

Lily made a sweeping gesture with one perfectly manicured hand, indicating the patio. "You've got a real knack for making things nice and homey."

Zach grinned. "We've spent many agreeable hours out here." He waited until Lily was contemplating the plate of cookies, then winked at Tess, causing her to blush.

Zach's teasing aside, Tess took a measure of pride in her accomplishment. She tried to view the small patio through a visitor's eyes and was pleased with the result. The small courtyard was neatly swept. An assortment of baskets hung from overhead beams while strings of red peppers dangled from hooks. Carefully tended clay pots overflowed with greenery. A chinaberry tree in the corner provided shade on a warm afternoon. All in all, it gave the effect of a cozy sanctuary.

"Mm," Lily said, taking a sip of lemonade. "Tastes good after a long, dusty ride."

"What brings you this far from town, Lil?" Zach asked, his gaze speculative.

Lily gave him a coy smile. "Why, honey, what makes you think I'm not just being neighborly?"

One corner of his mouth lifted. "Blame it on my suspicious nature."

She brushed a crumb from her silk skirt. "Talk in town is that you've got yourself a boarder."

Tess and Zach exchanged uneasy glances.

"So it's true," Lily said, observing their reaction. "Jimmy Jerold and his sidekick are telling everyone they meet that you're harboring a renegade Apache."

"A renegade?" Tess flared.

Lily got to her feet. "Mind if I stretch my muscles a bit before I head back to town?" Not waiting for an answer, Lily strolled about, peeking into each of the rooms that opened off the small patio.

Tess sent Zach a look, silently pleading with him to do something to stop her, but he merely shrugged. There was little he could do other than physically restrain the woman.

Lily paused outside the threshold of the room Gairmo occupied. For countless minutes she studied the sleeping boy. "Poor little guy," she said in a hushed voice. "He's sleeping as though drugged. He must've been near the end of his tether."

Tess sidled through the opened doorway and insinuated herself between Lily and the sleeping boy. "Yes, he's been through a great deal."

Lily wagged her head and clucked sympathetically. "He's just a kid."

"Yes, he is," Tess said agreeably, looping her arm through Lily's and steering her away from the boy. "We figure he must be about eleven or twelve."

"He's small for his age."

Returning the woman to the opposite end of the patio, Tess refilled Lily's glass and handed it to her.

"Not only is he undernourished, but he shows signs of recent abuse."

"What do you plan to do with him?"

Zach, who had observed Tess's maneuvering with interest, aroused himself to answer the question. "We think he might be one of the children captured during the Camp Grant Massacre. We'd like to see him returned to his people."

Lily settled herself comfortably on the bench amid the cushions. "That was quite a time. The newspapers were full of nothing else for months."

"Mind if I ask you a question, Lil?" Zach asked.

"You can ask me anything, sugar." Lily gave him an arch look. " 'Cept a lady's age."

"Were you living in Tucson back in 'seventy-one?"

Tess perched on the bench next to Lily, her hands folded in her lap, and leaned forward in her eagerness. "What was it like then? Tell us what you remember."

Lily circled the rim of her glass with a manicured finger. She no longer looked pert and sassy, but serious. "Newspapers talked of nothing else for months. John Wasson, editor of the *Arizona Citizen,* kept up a steady stream of editorials. Soon it was hard to separate the facts from his opinion."

"And just what was that opinion?"

"Wasson hated the Apaches. He favored a policy of total extermination. His articles helped incite people to commit the massacre. Later, he claimed it was an act of self-defense. As a result of his editorials, Lieutenant Whitman was court-martialed, not once, but three times before being found guilty of misconduct."

Total extermination? Self-defense? Tess thought, appalled. "Does everyone feel that way about the Apaches?"

"Many, but not everyone." Lily's ample bosom rose and fell as she shrugged. "Some, mostly Easterners, think the government ought to put them on reservations, feed them, clothe them, protect them. Force them to adopt the white man's ways."

"What about you, Lily?" Zach prompted. "Which argument do you favor?"

Lily lifted her face, her china blue eyes steady and sincere. "I'm opposed to killing innocent women and children regardless of the color of their skin. It just isn't right."

Zach nodded his silent agreement. "Do you have any idea where we might find the boy's family?"

"If it was up to me, I'd start by visiting the Indian reservation at White Mountain. Back in February some time, I heard an area was being set aside for the group from Camp Grant. Might be a good place to start asking if anyone remembers the kid."

Impulsively Tess reached out and clasped the woman's hand. "Thank you, Lily. You've been a good friend. Zach and I appreciate your help."

Lily set her empty glass aside. "There's something else you two should know."

Zach's stance was no longer relaxed, but attentive. "I was wondering when you were going to get around to the real reason for your visit."

"Jimmy Jerold and Moe Black are trying to stir up trouble. They're telling everyone who'll listen that you're harboring an Apache. One with a grudge against the white man. They're insisting the boy must be removed by force if necessary, for your protection as well as that of everyone in the territory." When Tess started to protest, she held up her hand. "That's not all. The young man, they claim, is related to an influential chief. One who could rally his braves to retaliate."

Tess and Zach digested this in silence. Then Tess

raised troubled eyes to Lily. "Surely no one can condemn a boy for trying to be reunited with kinfolk?"

"People get carried away, lose sight of the real target. Apaches are feared as much as hated. Aren't too many folks around here who haven't suffered loss of property or loved ones."

Lily's words echoed the same sentiment Tess had heard uttered before. Enmity between white settlers and Apaches was ongoing. The series of attacks and counterattacks left no clear victor.

Lily stood and retrieved her raspberry silk parasol. "I just wanted you to know how things were so you can prepare. The sooner the boy gets on his way, the better."

Zach and Tess walked Lily to her buggy. After Zach handed her inside, she fussed with her skirt, then patted her yellow curls. "I rarely go out in the afternoon. Sun's bad for my skin and gives me freckles." She waggled her fingers at them. *"Au revoir,* as my French maid, Lisette, would say."

With a smart slap of reins, the buggy rolled off in a cloud of dust.

Tess worried her lower lip. "What are we going to do?"

When there was no immediate answer, she glanced at Zach curiously. His distracted expression told her he hadn't been listening. "Zach?"

"Sorry." He shook his head, recalling himself to the present. "What did you ask me?"

"Jimmy and Moe are planning trouble. I asked what we were going to do about it."

"You, darlin', are going to do nothing but stay home and play nursemaid, while I, on the other hand, am going on a little trip."

"The White Mountain reservation." She didn't need Zach to name his destination.

"We need to find out if anyone there knows our young guest."

The thought of Zach riding alone into an Apache stronghold filled her with trepidation. "Let me come with you."

"You must be out of your mind if you think for one minute I'd take you with me." He held a finger against her lips to waylay her objections. "Besides," he said, adopting a placating tone, "the boy isn't fit to travel."

"But I want to help."

"You can." He placed both hands on her shoulders and exerted gentle pressure until he had her full attention. "First thing in the morning, take the boy to the mine and hide him there. I don't want him around if any unwanted visitors happen by. If someone should come asking, tell them he left in the middle of the night. That you have no idea where he went."

"But . . ."

His hands tightened. "Please, Tess, just do as I say. Promise me you won't do anything rash or foolish while I'm gone."

"Very well," she agreed with obvious reluctance. "I promise."

Zach gave her a hard, swift hug, then stalked off in the direction of the corral. Tess watched him retreat with a sinking sensation. She glanced up at the cloudless sky, but couldn't rid herself of the notion that a storm was brewing.

Twenty-one

Tess stirred, then woke as Zach quietly rose and left the bedroom. She had hoped for another night in his arms, another morning at his side. *Only a piece of paper.* It seemed she was expecting more than he was willing to give. Or, perhaps, more than he was able to give. He had been honest from the beginning. Their marriage consisted of a sheet of parchment and physical desire. No caring, no commitment. No love.

Frustrated and unhappy, she rolled onto her side and punched the pillow. Foolish to yearn for the impossible. Yet fool she was because she wanted more than just his body; she wanted his heart, his soul. His love and friendship. But like a beggar at a feast, she'd take whatever crumb he tossed her way. She'd savor it, treasure it, hoard it like a miser his gold. But without love, even gold could tarnish.

Unable to sleep, Tess pulled a wool shawl around her shoulders and went in search of him. She expected to find him sprawled outside on one of the benches, but to her surprise, she saw a glimmer of light in the kitchen. Soundlessly she went to investigate. Zach sat at the table, his head bent over the map she had found. She hovered in the shadows, admiring the sight of him gilded with lantern light. His strikingly handsome profile and tangle of dark-gold hair were limned in its glow. His chambray shirt hung open, exposing a tautly muscled chest that gleamed bronze. Unconsciously she flexed her fingers, wanting to touch that sleek expanse. Touch, then taste, knowing she would find the flavor erotically salty with a flavor uniquely his own.

Wanton! She scarcely knew the woman she had become.

Resolutely, she broke through the sensual cocoon that imprisoned her. "What are you doing?" she asked, moving out of the darkness and into the light. "Did you find something we might have overlooked?"

Without glancing up, he dragged a second chair closer to the table for her to sit on. "I couldn't sleep. I kept thinking about Lily's parting remark."

She looked at him curiously. "About Jimmy and Moe?"

"No." He shook his head impatiently, pointing at a spot on the map. "Look here."

Her shoulder brushed his as she sank down on the chair next to him. She leaned forward slightly to see what had captured his attention. Frowning in concentration, she stared at the map. The incomprehensible series of squiggles and lines made no more sense now than it had the last time she had looked at it. She turned from the map to stare at him accusingly. "Zach McClain, you're imagining things. Have you been drinking?"

He gave her a crooked smile, then held the map up to the light. "If you look real close, you can make out a faint line that leads from here"—he jabbed the paper—"to here."

"I'm not sure. . . ." she said dubiously.

"Got a pencil?"

Tess still had no idea what he meant to show her, but it was simpler to do as he asked. Fascinated, she watched as he went to work, lightly rubbing the pencil lead back and forth until a faint line emerged.

"My brother and I used to do this all the time when we were kids. Back in those days, we were especially fond of spy games with secret codes," he explained as he worked. "A person can use a pointed object such as a stick, or rock, or even a thumbnail to make an almost invisible line or word. The line, or word, becomes visible when you rub a pencil over it like I'm doing now."

"Why would someone go to all that trouble?"

"Maybe that someone didn't have anything better to write with." His eyes met hers and held. "Maybe he didn't want his secret to fall into the wrong hands."

A frisson of excitement scampered along her nerve endings. Could it possibly mean they were getting closer to solving the mystery of the lost gold shipment? She moistened her suddenly dry lips with the tip of her tongue. "Do you really think . . . ?" she whispered. The notion was so staggering, she couldn't complete the sentence.

But Zach was too preoccupied to answer her unspoken question. After more rubbing, he held the map up to the light once again. Tess strained to see the slight etchings that had appeared.

"Looks like a couple more words written in another language," he muttered. Carefully, he copied the letters onto a scrap of paper, then tucked the note into his pants pocket. "If this means what I think it does, Tess, we're going to be rich beyond our wildest dreams. We'll be able to afford clothes, jewels, travel—our heart's desire."

Tess had difficulty grasping the magnitude of such wealth. "But," she demurred, "doesn't the gold belong to France? Won't we have to return it?"

Zach carefully folded the map and replaced it in its

hiding place. "Seeing as how the Confederates were clearly defeated by the Union, I doubt France will admit they ever made any attempt to aid the South. Any such admission would undoubtedly harm their present position with the United States. No, Tess, I don't think anyone will challenge our claim."

He rose from the table and, catching her hands in his, pulled her to her feet. "As soon as the situation with Gairmo is resolved, we can turn our full attention to finding that lost gold. Just wait and see, Tess. Soon we'll be rich."

Tess watched the shadows lighten from dull pewter to ash. It would be dawn soon, and Zach would be on his way to the Apache reservation. If his prediction was correct, she'd soon be rich, although no closer to her heart's desire. She didn't need gold or silver, fancy clothes or costly jewels, grand homes and exotic travel. What she wanted—needed—was right here beside her. Finding the gold meant saying goodbye to Zach. There would be nothing left to bind them together. Their paths would diverge; each would forge a life apart.

She turned onto her side and stared at his sleeping face. Sleep smudged the sharp planes and angles, making him appear softer, vulnerable. Dark blond stubble covered his jaw. Even in the dim light she could see the faint smattering of freckles like a sprinkling of gold dust across the bridge of his nose and along the ridges of his cheekbones. Having known him, loved him, how would she live without him? The thought brought unbearable pain and sadness.

What would it be like, she wondered, to have his child? A child with brilliant green eyes and a smile that could melt stone. A fierce longing seemed to materialize out of nowhere. She yearned for a son who would never walk in the shadow of bitter memories, never be fettered with anger, hatred, or resentment. A son who was free to love—and accept love in return.

Yielding to temptation, she reached out and traced the sensual curve of his mouth. Just thinking about his mouth and how hours ago it had traveled over her body, nibbling, kissing, sampling, caused a warm flush to spread through her.

Suddenly, Zach reached out and caught her wrist, causing her to gasp in surprise. He playfully nipped the pad of her finger, then tugged the tip into his mouth and sucked. Tess felt heat curl in her stomach and seep between her legs. She closed her eyes as a ragged sigh escaped. When she opened her eyes again, she was staring directly into Zach's bemused gaze.

"Tess, darlin'," he drawled, his voice rich and warm as molasses. "You're testing my willpower." He took her hand and held it against his loins. "Feel what you do to me."

With a throaty purr of satisfaction, she stroked the steel-like shaft of his manhood. "I wish we could spend the day together—in bed."

His mouth curved in a rueful grin. "You don't know how tempting that sounds, kitten. But as much as I'd like to, we both know I can't."

"I wish you'd take me with you."

"We've been over this before." He grazed her cheek with the back of his knuckles. "It's best you stay here. Take Gairmo and hide him at the mine until I get back. If anyone comes by, tell them he's gone."

"Please be careful."

"Promise." He swung out of bed and reached for his pants.

Tess watched unabashedly. She would never tire of viewing his naked, magnificent body.

"Go back to sleep." He gave her a knowing smile

from over his shoulder. "It's early yet, and I kept you awake most of the night."

"I need to check on Gairmo first." Yawning, she started to throw back the covers.

"Stay put; I'll do it."

Tess didn't argue when he pushed her back down, kissing her.

Moments later, he returned. "The boy's fine. He's sleeping as though he's been drugged."

He kissed her again, hard and swift; then he was gone.

All vestiges of sleepiness vanished. Wide awake now, Tess listened as Zach rode off. "Strange," she murmured. One minute she had been ready to fall asleep; the next she was wide awake, every sense alert. Something nagged at the fringes of her memory and wouldn't let her rest. Slipping into her dressing robe, she walked outdoors and stared toward the east. Dawn smeared the horizon with a palette of rosy hues. But this morning she was too distracted to enjoy the pretty sunrise. Turning, she slowly made her way back inside, her head bowed in thought. In her mind, she replayed everything Zach had said before leaving. Then, her head came up with a snap.

Sleeping as though drugged.

Zach had used the phrase to describe Gairmo's deep sleep. It was the identical phrase Lily had used the previous day. Exhausted from his ordeal, the boy often fell into sleep so deep that nothing disturbed him. At times he slept for hours without stirring. The same deep sleep to which her mother would succumb after her nightly dose of laudanum.

Sleeping as though drugged.

Tess, too, had slept that soundly on Zach's final night at Gettysburg. *Dear God,* she whispered in horror. It finally made sense. The final piece of the puzzle had clicked into place.

That long-ago night Tess had had every intention of spending with Zach and Jed. All day she had chafed that the hours passed too slowly. Even as a young girl, she had a hopeless crush on the dashing Southerner. She knew he would be leaving soon to rejoin his unit, and she wanted to spend every possible minute in his company. But plans had gone awry.

As was her habit, she had waited until she was certain that her mother's sleeping draught had taken effect before slipping from the house. That particular night, Tess had retired to her room, where she waited impatiently for Mary Montgomery to settle down. It seemed to be taking an inordinately long time, and in the interim, Tess had grown sleepy. She had lain down on top of the bed, fully clothed, to wait. When she woke, it was broad daylight. She had raced to the barn, but Zach and Jed were gone. Vanished without a trace. Or a word of farewell.

Tess paced the length of the patio. She recalled feeling physically ill that morning. Her head had pounded mercilessly, and her body felt sluggish. When she had complained, her mother offered to fetch the doctor.

Her pacing quickened. It was almost too horrible to comprehend, but had her mother suspected she was concealing Confederate fugitives? Had she found out somehow, then plotted to turn them over to the authorities? Had her plan craftily included using Tess, her own daughter, as an accomplice, albeit an unsuspecting one? Tess slumped down on a bench and rubbed her throbbing temples. She had tried to be so careful. How had she failed? When?

In retrospect, it probably hadn't been all that difficult. Perhaps she hadn't been nearly as clever—or as careful—as she had believed. Quite possibly, her mother heard her leave the house one night and followed her. Or watched her return. Maybe she had noticed the steady disappearance of food from the pantry and decided to investigate.

How like her mother to take things into her own hands. Mary Montgomery had always tended to be protective when it came to her daughter's well-being. Added to that, she despised the South—and everything associated with it. She would have been livid to discover Tess hiding two Confederate soldiers. It would have been a simple matter to drop laudanum into Tess's drink at suppertime.

Tess pressed her arms against her midsection and rocked back and forth. Yes, it all made sense. But there was no way she could prove it. No way to convince Zach she hadn't knowingly betrayed him. She felt chilled to the marrow by her mother's deceit. Coldbloodedly, Mary Montgomery had somehow discovered Zach and Jed's hiding place, sent Tess on an errand to alert the sheriff, drugged her own daughter, then watched Zach taken prisoner. Though Tess had tried to deny the possibility before, she could no longer ignore the bone-deep certainty of her mother's duplicity.

"Missus?" Gairmo inquired worriedly from six feet away. "You sick?"

Tess forced a smile. "No, Gairmo, I'm fine."

Gairmo wasn't convinced. "You look sick."

Her legs as unsteady as a newly foaled colt, she rose to her feet. She shoved a handful of hair away from her face and slowly approached the boy. "You're looking better this morning, Gairmo. A few more days of rest, and you'll be back to normal." More rest and lots of good food, she added to herself.

He stood straighter, seemingly pleased with her assessment. "Your husband," he said looking around. "He hunting?"

"He's gone to make some inquiries. We're trying to locate—"

"My people." Gairmo's face suddenly became animated.

"Yes," she said, smiling, "your people. But, let me warn you, it may take some time before we find them. After breakfast, we're going to pack some supplies, then take a little ride."

Instantly wary, he drew back. "Where you take me?"

Tess could understand and sympathize with his fear. He had been abducted once before. He must be wondering whether it was about to happen all over again, just as he was on the brink of being reunited with his family. "There's a place close by, an abandoned mine. Zach and I think it best if you stayed there until he returns."

"But why?"

She went into the kitchen and began cracking eggs into a bowl. He followed as she hoped he would. "Some people do not like the idea of an Indian, especially an Apache, staying here. They might come and try to take you. You'll be safer at the mine."

He seemed to think this over, then nodded. "I go with you. Hide where white man not find."

"Well, this is it," Tess announced, trying to inject a cheerfulness into her voice that she didn't feel.

Gairmo slid down from the horse. "Good place," he pronounced after looking around.

Tess dismounted and removed the supplies from the saddlebags. She wished she shared Gairmo's optimism. This was the first time she had returned to the mine since blundering into the cave of bats. Perhaps, she reasoned, that accounted for her present uneasiness.

Gairmo accepted the bundle of food she handed him. "How long, missus?"

"Only until Zach returns. Watch for us after nightfall." She carried a pouch filled with water along with a blanket and led the way into the mine. Ducking her head, she stepped through the low entrance. "It's important you stay out of sight. You don't have to go deep inside unless you see strangers approach. Eat, sleep, rest. Time will pass quickly, you'll see."

She demonstrated how to light the lantern; then, knowing there was nothing more to do, she left him there. Before the trail veered away, she glanced over her shoulder a final time and waved. Gairmo, looking for all the world like a little boy trying to be a man, returned the gesture.

Once she was home again and confident Gairmo was safe, Tess's thoughts returned to the morning's revelation. The more she considered the matter, the more convinced she became that her mother had betrayed Zach's whereabouts to the authorities. At first, her mind had rebelled at believing her mother guilty, but now in her heart she accepted it as truth. Even more troubling, though, was that without proof she had no idea whether or not Zach would accept her account as fact or fabrication.

She was in a quandary. Should she tell Zach everything she had surmised? And if so, would he believe her? He could easily regard her sudden insight as a desperate act by a desperate woman. Dismiss it as an attempt to alleviate blame by shifting it elsewhere. That she would do anything to eliminate barriers between them. Instead of drawing them closer, however, it could drive a wedge even deeper between them.

As she did often, Tess resorted to household chores as the means to take her mind off worrisome problems. Keeping busy, she had observed, provided less time to brood. Laundry offered the perfect solution. She put on an apron, rolled up her sleeves, and went to work. She had just spread the last item over a line to dry when she heard riders approaching. Her heart thudded heavily against her ribs. She froze, her head to one side, listening. Soon the sound was accompanied by the low rumble of male voices.

Not giving herself time to reconsider, she rushed into the bedroom, retrieved her pistol from beneath a pile of undergarments, and dropped it into her skirt pocket. The voluminous apron hid any suspicious bulge. Then she went to greet her visitors.

The delegation numbered six, including Moe Black and Jimmy Jerold. In addition, she recognized Cal Davis, the clerk from the mercantile, and Sam Wilburn, owner of the livery stable, as well as Abner Smith. The final member of the group was a stout, florid-faced gentleman she remembered seeing in town on occasion. All six men shared the same dour, purposeful expression.

Abner Smith, the apparent spokesman for the group, stepped forward and doffed his black bowler. "Afternoon, Tess. That husband of yours around by any chance?"

"If you came to see my husband, Abner, I'm afraid you made the trip for nothing." Tess kept her tone pleasant with effort.

"Is he here, or ain't he?" The ruddy-cheeked gentleman shouldered Abner aside. A wreath of snow-white hair protruded beneath a flat-crowned hat. His pale eyes were magnified behind a pair of wire-rimmed spectacles.

"Easy now, Walker," Abner counseled. "No call to be rude."

Tess took an instant dislike to the man Abner called Walker. Ignoring him, she addressed the lawyer. "Zach had some matters to attend to elsewhere."

She started to close the door, but Walker stuck his boot between the door and sill. "Not so fast, girlie. Since your husband's gone off, we'll talk to you instead."

A sweeping glance at the men told her she would find no help forthcoming. Even Abner looked unusually grim-lipped and determined. "Very well," she said with exaggerated patience, hoping her nervousness didn't show. "Kindly state your business, then be on your way."

Sam Wilburn hooked his thumbs in his belt. "Heard you took in an injun. A renegade Apache."

She gave him a level stare. "I fed a half-starved boy and gave him a place to sleep. He might be an Apache, but I hardly think he can be considered a renegade."

The party exchanged uneasy glances. Abner was the first to recover a measure of aplomb. "Tess, we realize you're new around here, but harboring 'hostiles', as we call 'em, isn't a good idea."

"Since when is it wrong to give food and shelter to someone in need?"

Sam's thick brows drew together. "It ain't, less'n the person yer shelterin' is injun."

Tess tried reasoning with him. "This renegade, as you called him, hardly posed a threat. He was a mere boy. Are you gentlemen frightened of a child?"

" 'Course not," Walker blustered. " 'Cept this one's Apache."

"Apaches killed my brother an' his wife," Cal Davis said, his expression earnest. "They burned his place to the ground."

"Thievin' redskins stole my cattle, my horses. Murdered my best friend." Walker's pale, myopic eyes had a suspicious sheen of moisture.

Sam's eyes glittered with hatred. "Their constant stealin' forced me to sell my ranch, move to town. Nearly lost every cent I owned."

Abner smoothed his glossy mustache. "You gotta understand, Tess. Here in the territory, we do whatever's called for to protect our interests."

"While I sympathize with your losses, gentlemen, your trip has been for nothing. The boy is no longer here." She sent up a silent prayer of thanksgiving for Zach's foresight.

"Gone?" Walker shouted. "Whaddya mean he's gone?"

Tess stared him straight in the eye, and lied through her teeth. "Gairmo left some time during the night."

Sam shook his head in disgust. "Ain't that just like them sneaky bastards."

Jimmy Jerold, who had been listening quietly, asserted himself for the first time. "Why should we take her word for it, gentlemen? She could be hiding the kid somewhere inside."

Furious, Tess turned to him. "Are you accusing me of being a liar, Mr. Jerold?"

"What's the matter, honey?" Jimmy's dimples flashed as he grinned. "Gettin' pretty riled for someone who's got nothin' to hide."

"I say we oughta take a look around," Moe suggested slyly.

"Good idea." Walker nodded in agreement. "If the kid's gone like Mrs. McClain claims, she shouldn't have grounds to complain."

"Seems that's what the men want, Tess." Abner's narrow shoulders lifted in an apologetic shrug. "Mind if we come in and take a look around?"

Yes! She minded a great deal. Tess clenched her jaw to prevent the anger from spewing out. "And if I say no?"

Several of the men had the grace to look shamefaced. The others looked more determined than ever. Seeing Moe Black's habitual smirk, Tess experienced an almost uncontrollable urge to slap it off his face.

"Sorry, Tess," Abner said. "Since you're not being cooperative, I guess we have to take matters into our own hands." He brushed past her into the house, followed by the rest of the delegation.

Tess stared after them in disbelief. She had considered Abner a friend. Why, he had even offered marriage the night of the fiesta, which had seemed strange to say the least. Nevertheless, she hadn't thought him capable of this type of boorish behavior. Where Abner Smith was concerned, she had proven a poor judge of character.

"I'll give you five minutes," she called out, but no one seemed to pay the least attention.

The men fanned out for their search. From her vantage spot on the patio, she could see them peering into cabinets, checking under beds, and rifling though her belongings.

They have no right. No right at all.

Indignation stoked her anger, fanning it into flame until it blazed hot and bright. Suddenly, she had had enough. Time had come to bring this unpleasant interlude to an end. Taking the Smith and Wesson from her skirt pocket, she held it high above her head and fired. The resounding crack of gunfire brought the search to an abrupt halt.

"Now that I have your attention, gentlemen," she said, keeping the revolver at waist level, ready to fire again if need be, "I believe I said five minutes. Your time is up. Now get the hell out of my home!"

Grumbling loudly, the men filed out. None seemed inclined to test her resolve—or her marksmanship.

"Crazy as a loon," she heard one of them mumble under his breath. *Fine,* Tess thought, they could call her anything they liked and she didn't care, as long as they left her alone.

She stood outside and watched them retreat in a thick haze of dust. Then she walked inside on wobbly legs and sank down on a chair at the kitchen table, her back to the wall, her gun in her lap.

And waited.

Twenty-two

Zach shifted in the saddle. After riding sunup to sundown, he had only three wishes: a steaming bath, a hot meal, and a warm welcome. But if only one wish could be granted, he'd settle for the warm welcome. The whole time he had been gone, Tess was never far from his thoughts. He urged his horse into a trot. He couldn't wait to share his news.

The sun had set shortly before he reached Casita de Oro. *Casita de Oro. House of Gold.* Jed's name for the modest little ranch hadn't been an attempt at grandeur, but his dream, Zach realized. His friend had purchased the house and mine, then spent his days searching for a lost treasure. And died before his dream came to fruition. While passing through town, Zach had paid the town marshal yet another visit. But Jed's killer remained a mystery. Frustrating as it was, Zach had to admit that the murder might always remain unsolved.

As he drew near, he slowed his approach and regarded the house with a frown. Something was wrong. At first he couldn't put his finger on it; then it came to him. Not a single glimmer of light seeped through cracks in the shutters. Strange, he thought, usually by this time Tess would have lit at least one of the kerosene lanterns. He had expected to find her reading one of her precious dime novels or scribbling in the journal she always tried to hide from him. But tonight the house was totally dark. No light shining out; no hint of life within. Fear twisted in his gut.

He spurred the horse into a gallop. Upon reaching the house, he leaped from the saddle and, not bothering to stable his mount, tossed the reins over a post and ran inside.

"Tess!" he shouted as he raced from room to room. A feeling akin to panic seized him. "Damn it, woman! Answer me. Where the hell are you?"

He thought his knees would buckle with sheer relief when he heard her voice coming from the darkened kitchen.

Following the direction of the sound, he squinted through the shadows and made out her figure seated at the table, her back toward the wall. He sank down in front of her and peered into her face. "Tess, honey, what's wrong? Are you hurt?"

She shook her head.

Her silence frightened him. Faint light from outside drifted through the open doorway like smoke, painting the room in shades of gray and gloom. He thumbed the brim of his hat back from his brow, his gaze watchful, worried. Her eyes appeared stark and enormous in a face pale as marble. He started to take her hands in his, and encountered the Smith and Wesson in her lap. Very carefully he placed the gun on the table, then covered her hands with his. Hers felt cool, almost cold. "Darlin'," he crooned, "you gave me quite a scare. Sure you're all right?"

"I'm perfectly fine, thank you." She gave him a tight, little smile. A smile that told him she was holding onto her control by a thread.

"I, ah, stopped in town on my way back. Heard what happened while I was gone."

A shudder rippled through her. "Those men had no right to force their way into our home. No right to search through our things."

Guilt rushed through him. Those men wouldn't have gotten through the front door if he had been there. He had left her alone and unprotected. She had wanted to go with him, but he had refused, believing she'd be safer at the house. "I'm sorry, Tess. I should have been here."

She continued as though she hadn't heard him. "I was so angry. If they had found Gairmo and tried to take him, I'm not sure what I would have done." Her gaze rested on the Smith and Wesson sitting on the table.

The significance of that glance wasn't lost on Zach. Tess was a woman who disliked firearms and had voiced her objections loudly and repeatedly. Yet she had found herself in a position where she had been ready to sacrifice her principles to defend a boy she scarcely knew. An Apache. While he couldn't help but admire such steadfast loyalty, at the same time, he felt a twinge of jealousy. If Tess had been that staunch in his defense, his life might have been quite different.

With an effort, he put past hurts aside. "You were very brave today, Tess," he said, gently squeezing her icy hands. "In the future, everyone will think twice before tangling with you."

"Do you really think so?"

"I'm positive, darlin'." Standing, he drew her into his arms. This, he realized, was what he had waited for all day. Simply to hold her. Closing his eyes briefly, he rested his cheek against her hair. Instantly, the sweet scent of lilacs beguiled his senses.

"I'm glad you're home," she murmured.

His arms seemed to tighten of their own volition. "So am I, sweetheart."

To his amazement, Zach discovered that he meant it. For years, he had despised this woman, yet now he resented the minutes he was away from her. When had that happened? When had his feelings started to change? Their lovemaking was great—terrific even, the best he had ever had—but he felt just as fulfilled simply holding her. He wasn't ready, wasn't willing, to explore—much less acknowledge—these changes. Swearing under his breath, he released Tess and stepped back. Worry about her almost made him forget his news.

He managed to find a lamp and struck a match. Instantly, golden-yellow light filled the room. With a supreme effort, he placed his unruly emotions in an imaginary vault and locked them away. Feeling more in control, he turned back to Tess. He was pleased to see that the pinched look had left her face and some color had returned. He took off his hat, rifled his fingers through his hair, and straddled a chair. "Well," he said, grinning. "Aren't you going to ask about my day?"

Perched on the chair opposite him, she smiled, and this time it appeared genuine. "Of course. I want to hear all of the details. Did you find Gairmo's people?"

Zach's grin slipped a notch. "I was afraid that would be your first question. To be honest, I can't be certain. I spoke with an Apache chief, Eskiminzin. I told him all I knew about the boy, but he was suspicious. He would neither confirm nor deny the boy was one of theirs."

"Poor Gairmo." She shook her head sadly. "We're still no closer than we were before to finding his family."

"Don't worry, sweetheart, we're not going to give up that easily. I mentioned that I stopped in town.

Aren't you the least bit curious as to why?" His green eyes danced with excitement.

Canting her head to one side, she studied him thoughtfully. "I can tell you've been up to something. You look like you're about ready to burst."

"I'll have you know my day wasn't a total waste of time." Unable to contain himself another minute, he sprang from the chair, toppling it in his haste. Reaching out, he grasped her hands, tugged her to her feet, then swung her around.

Clutching his shoulders for support, Tess looked at him through narrowed eyes. "Zach McClain, are you drunk?"

He threw back his head and let out a jubilant shout of laughter. "Oh, I'm drunk all right, darlin'. I'm drunk on the fact that we're going to be rich. Richer even than our wildest imaginings."

"Let me smell your breath," she demanded.

He set her back on her feet but didn't let go. "I know where the gold is hidden."

Her fists bunched in his shirt. Her mouth opened, then snapped shut.

Zach relished watching the varying emotions flit across her face: disbelief, hope, excitement, joy. Her lovely eyes shone like liquid silver; her cheeks flushed pink as rose petals. Damn if she wasn't the pretty little thing! She robbed the oxygen from the air he breathed.

Tess captured his face between her palms. "Where? How? Tell me, Zach. Tell me," she demanded.

He knew he must resemble a clown with his ear-to-ear grin, but he didn't care. "Remember Lily mentioning her French maid, Lisette?" At her nod, he hurried on. "Well, since the writing on the map wasn't Spanish, I took a wild guess and figured maybe it was French. I copied down a couple words and stopped by Lil's place and showed them to Lisette."

"And?" She fairly quivered with excitement.

"And . . ." He dragged out the word, wanting to prolong the moment. "I figured out where to look."

"Where is it? Tell me."

"Better yet, I'll take you there."

"When?"

"Tonight."

"Tonight . . . ?"

"Tonight." Turning his head, he pressed a kiss into her palm. "It's there waiting for us, darlin'. I can feel it in my bones. You're going to fall asleep a wealthy woman."

"B-but," she sputtered as reality reintroduced itself. "God, forgive me, but I almost forgot. What about Gairmo? We can't let him spend the night alone in that old mine."

"Don't ask any more questions, Tess, honey, just trust me." He waylaid further argument with a quick kiss. "Before this night is over, we'll resolve the problem of both Gairmo and the missing gold."

With a full moon aiming a bright beam of light on the rugged terrain, Zach had little trouble guiding the wagon over the narrow trail. Tall saguaros stood as mute witnesses to their passage. Under ordinary circumstances Tess would have appreciated the night's beauty, but not this night. She was too tense, too excited, and more than a little apprehensive. Zach had purposely withheld their destination. But now that they were underway, she guessed it instantly. She had become almost as familiar as he with the trail to the mine.

She worried constantly about Gairmo. The boy must be frightened out of his wits at the long wait. She had told him they would come for him as soon as Zach returned. Zach, however, had insisted on waiting until it had grown late. To add to her uneasiness, she saw him glance back over his shoulder repeatedly.

"Do you think anyone might see us and follow?" she asked when he did it yet again.

He shrugged, his eyes on the trail ahead. "Doesn't hurt to be careful."

Tess clutched her shawl more tightly around her shoulders. She couldn't help but notice that Zach had taken certain precautions, sliding extra ammunition into his belt, then taking her Smith and Wesson for additional protection. He had studied the treasure map, committing it to memory, then carefully folded it and tucked it into his shirt pocket.

They rode the remainder of the way swaddled in thick silence. Tess wondered what it would be like to be rich. *Richer than her wildest imagining,* Zach had promised. Ever since her father left to fight for the Union, she had had to struggle for money to put food on the table and a roof over her head. Her single luxury was indulging her fondness for dime novels. If Zach's prediction proved true, before she fell asleep that night she would be rich enough to buy anything, go anywhere. She could have everything except what she desired most: Zach's love. And they were both forgetting that the gold came at a high price. In all likelihood, it had cost Jed his life. No treasure on earth was worth the life of a dear friend.

Finally, the mine came into view. In the moonlight, its gaping black mouth looked evil, sinister. Suddenly she wished she were elsewhere. All she wanted was to retrieve Gairmo and leave.

Not waiting for Zach, she climbed down from the wagon unassisted. "Gairmo," she called, hurrying toward the entrance. She peered inside expecting to find a young boy huddled near a glowing lantern, but she encountered darkness instead.

"Where do you suppose he is?"

She jumped at Zach's voice directly behind her, then scolded herself for being skittish. "I told Gairmo to go deeper into the mine if he heard someone coming. He probably heard the wagon, but didn't know who it was. He'll come out as soon as he realizes we've come for him."

Zach lit one of the lanterns they had brought and handed it to Tess. He lit a second one for himself. Holding it above his head, he advanced into the mine. Tess did likewise.

"Gairmo!" Zach shouted.

"You can come out," Tess called. "It's safe now."

Their voices echoed through the dark recesses of the mine. Still there was no response. Tess gnawed her lower lip and battled an encroaching panic. She never should have left him alone. She should have ignored Zach's instructions and stayed with the boy. What had she been thinking? As Zach was forever reminding her, the Southwest abounded with danger: rattlesnakes, scorpions, and mountain lions, to name but a few.

She swallowed convulsively. "Zach, I'm scared. Do you think . . . ?"

"Don't leap to any conclusions. Gairmo's a clever boy." He gently squeezed her shoulder. "Let's take a look around."

They went a few yards farther, then stopped. Zach raised the lantern high above his head and let light splash over the cold stone walls. He was about to continue when the light fell across a tin lantern.

Tess gasped. "That's the one I gave Gairmo to use."

"Are you sure?"

"Yes, I'm certain. I remember because the base was dented." She pointed to the bent metal.

"What else did you leave with Gairmo?"

"Enough food and water to last until we came for him. And," she added, remembering, "a blanket."

Zach swung the lantern in a wide arc, searching for but not finding the items she had just mentioned. "He must be all right," he concluded. "Don't you see, Tess, if Gairmo had been taken by force, there would be signs of a struggle. Food or something would have been left behind. Instead, everything's gone except for that." He tapped the dented lantern.

She thought it over and decided Zach's theory made sense. Even so, she hated the idea of Gairmo wandering through the desert all alone.

Zach seemed to divine her thoughts. "He's a tough little kid, Tess. He's already endured more than most grown men will in a lifetime. I think he knows he's close to family, and will let nothing stand in his way."

"I suppose you're right," she admitted at last. "Since Gairmo is gone, I guess there's no reason for us to stay." Her experience with the bats had left her shaken, and with a strong sense of loathing for the mine. She couldn't wait to leave.

"On the contrary, our task is just beginning. C'mon." He shot her an enigmatic smile and moved farther into the mine.

Tess was left with little choice but to hurry after him. All the while, she kept reminding herself she had nothing to fear. The interior of the cave was no different now than it was in broad daylight. Day or night, the belly of a mountain was pitch black either way.

"If what I deducted is correct, it shouldn't be much further."

"Are you talking about the gold?" Tess had been so concerned about Gairmo's welfare that she had temporarily forgotten about the lost treasure. "You think it's hidden here in the mine?"

"All this time, we assumed the map referred to the overland route that the soldiers transporting it were supposed to follow. My theory should prove that we were wrong."

Tess ducked under a low beam. "If it's not an overland route, what is it?"

"I'm convinced the map is a crude sketch of the inside of this mine."

"All because of Lily London's French maid?"

"Remind me to give Lisette a nice reward." Zach bent and picked up a broken ax handle. "Think about it, Tess. Word of a gold shipment intended for the Confederacy must have leaked out and Quantrill's men got wind of it. Imagine what those cutthroats would do for a shipment of gold!"

Zach's voice grew animated as he continued. "It all fits with what we heard at the fiesta. I'd be willing be bet that the soldiers sent to guard it were set upon by a bunch of miscreants soon after crossing the border."

"And you think they stopped here?"

"What better place? It's directly along the route north from Mexico and well before they'd reach a town of any size. This would be a perfect spot to defend themselves against attack. It's even possible Quantrill's men posed as friendly escorts before showing their true colors."

They advanced deeper and deeper into the mine, with Tess blindly following Zach's lead. Everything he said seemed logical. Yet the entire episode seemed like something from the pages of a storybook. It suddenly occurred to her that she had been granted her wish. She was experiencing real-life adventure, not merely living one vicariously. This was the reason, she reminded herself, that she had abandoned her staid life in Pennsylvania. Setting her misgivings aside, she concentrated instead on the unique experience. When all this was over, she promised herself she would faithfully record all the details in her journal. It might even mark the beginning of a literary career.

"How do you suppose Jed found the map?" she asked.

"I doubt we'll ever know for sure, but I would be willing to bet he thought the map referred to objects or places above ground, not below. The same as we did at first."

"At the fiesta, the Kemper brothers said people were starting to wonder why Jed was hanging around. He must have known that the gold was nearby and bought property here to stop any talk."

"Someone must have suspected what he was doing—and killed him." Zach's voice vibrated with fury. "I'd like to get my hands on the bastard."

"A secret that size begs to be shared. Jed must have confided, or at least hinted about a map, to someone he trusted." Tess nearly stumbled as a thought struck her. "Do you think it might have been Jimmy Jerold and Moe Black?"

"I wondered that myself. But no one in town remembers seeing them until long afterwards." When the tunnel divided, Zach veered to the right. "Not since they lied about not knowing Jed had been murdered."

The musical tinkle of water barely registered in Tess's mind. "Don't you think that if the gold was really here it would have been found by now?"

"A good question, darlin', but all these years the treasure has been vigilantly guarded."

"Guarded?" She nearly collided with him as he stopped to consult the map. "By whom?"

"You'll soon see for yourself." Replacing the map, he continued along the sloping floor of the mine. "Any of this starting to look familiar?"

Zach's offhand question took her by surprise, caus-

ing her to inspect her surroundings with a critical eye.
She noticed that the pathway had narrowed until it was
barely wide enough to accommodate Zach's broad
shoulders. Then, she caught a whiff of an unpleasant,
pungent odor. Suddenly, everything became much too
familiar.

"Bats . . ." she murmured, halting.

"Steady, darlin'; partners have to stick together. Besides, you don't want to miss all the fun, do you?"

Vivid memories swirled through her mind. Memories of giant bats. Bats soaring and diving about her
as she fled in blind terror. Her mouth felt dry; her heart
raced. "I can't go back in there; I just can't."

Zach half turned and looked at her—really looked
at her—for the first time since entering the mine.
"Sorry, Tess." He dragged a hand impatiently through
his hair. "But you needn't worry. Bats are nocturnal
creatures. They're out right now, searching for food.
We'll have the place to ourselves."

She gave an uncertain nod. "Are you sure the gold
is in there?"

Zach consulted the map again. "Lisette told me the
French word for *bats*. If my calculations are correct,
that's where we should find the gold. Would you rather
wait here?"

"No," she said softly, then cleared her throat. "I
want to be with you when you find the treasure."

He gave her a quick grin and, ducking under a tim-
ber, stepped into a larger chamber, with Tess close behind. Holding the lantern high above his head, he
swung the beam over the rough granite walls. Tess
heaved a sigh of relief at finding the bats gone. All
that remained was the pungent odor and a floor littered
with droppings.

"I don't see anything that looks like gold." Zach's

voice was heavy with disappointment. "Let's just take a good look around since we're here."

Tess, too, felt the keen edge of disappointment. Perhaps, it had been foolish to believe they'd discover a fortune just waiting for them to find it, but she had dared hope. "We still have the ranch, and you said yourself, there's some silver left to be mined," she said, trying to inject a positive note, as much for her benefit as Zach's.

Zach, however, wasn't listening. He had wandered to the far end of the cavern and stepped through an opening which was barely discernible from a distance. Tess, who had watched him disappear, heard him swear softly. Picking her way around piles of droppings, she hurried to see what had captured his attention.

She entered a small chamber, an alcove of sorts. And stood rooted in place.

"Dear God," she gasped.

"Did you ever . . ." Zach's voice trailed off.

Skeletons sprawled across the rocky floor like broken marionettes. She stared transfixed by the bizarre scene before her. As many as a dozen skeletons in various poses were spread about the small chamber. Tattered streamers of clothing draped bare bone. Time had not disguised the bits of bright red and bold blue, brass buttons, and gold braid. Or the miasma of death.

Zach shook his head in wonder. "It must have been quite a battle."

Tess followed Zach's progress with her eyes. He paused here and there to examine one of the skeletons. Yes, she reflected, the battle must have been fierce indeed. The skull of one skeleton had been crushed; several others had blackened, rusty knives protruding between ribs; another still clutched a long-barreled pistol. "It doesn't look as though there were any victors," she said softly.

"I beg to disagree, darlin'." Zach used the ax handle he had picked up earlier to poke through a pile of debris. "At least one person escaped and lived long enough to draw a map."

"Zach," she called, suddenly breathless. Her gaze was riveted on an oblong metal box with a heavy lock partially obscured beneath one of the skeletons. Actually, the odd crouching posture had first drawn her attention to it. "Do you suppose . . . ?"

Zach's thoughts ran parallel with hers. Swiftly he crossed over and, using the ax handle, knocked aside the hunched pile of bones. The bones clattered as they dropped away, sending a shiver along Tess's spine. Using the handle as a lever, Zach tried to pry open the lock. When that failed, he smashed it with a rock. Finally, his efforts were rewarded and the lock sprang open. Tess crowded closer. For a long moment, their eyes locked, alight with anticipation. Tess was light-headed with excitement.

"Ready?" Zach asked, his voice taut.

At her nod, Zach eased open the lid. Tess gasped in awe and sank to her knees beside him. Gold as bright as Arizona sunlight shimmered in the dark cave. Her hand trembled as it reached out to touch one of the gold bars. Surely, she must be dreaming.

"It's real, darlin'." Zach's grin stretched from ear to ear. "And it's all ours."

"Beg to differ, folks."

Tess and Zach spun around at the sound of Jimmy Jerold's soft drawl. Moe Black, wearing his usual smirk, stood behind him, guns drawn.

Twenty-three

"Knew you'd lead us to the gold," Moe crowed. "Just knew it."

"I learned to pay attention when Moe gets a feelin' in his gut. Nine times outa ten, he's right on the money. Pardon the pun, folks," Jimmy chuckled.

Moe nodded in agreement. "My gut feelin's kept me alive more times than I can count."

Tess groaned inwardly. She and Zach had been so intent on finding the gold, they hadn't heard Jimmy and Moe's stealthy approach. Instinctively, she edged closer to Zach. She could feel waves of tension radiating from him and worried he might draw his gun. Even if he did get off a shot, there were two of them with guns already drawn. He didn't stand a chance—*they* didn't stand a chance.

"All right, McClain, toss your guns to the floor real careful like. Both of them," Jimmy said, indicating Zach's Colt as well as Tess's Smith and Wesson, tucked into his belt. "Then put your hands in the air where we can see 'em. Any funny business and I shoot. The lady gets it first."

Zach did as he was told. Moe gathered the weapons, then backed away, smiling all the while. "Always admire a man who follows directions. Shows his brain's in good workin' order."

"Now," Jimmy drawled. "One more little task before you wear out your usefulness."

"And that is?"

"I'm gonna give you the honor of carrying out the gold. After all, that's the least we can do, considerin' as how you found it."

"What if I refuse?"

"I don't think you'll cause any trouble. Not unless you want this pretty little wife of yours to get a taste of lead. Now let's go."

Without another word, Zach bent down and hefted the metal box onto his shoulder, his muscles straining under the heavy weight.

"Allow me to lead the way," Jimmy said. "McClain, if you know what's good for you, you'll stick close behind and not make any foolish moves. Your wife will be the one to suffer if you do. Moe's got a jumpy trigger finger."

"You won't get away with this, Jerold," Zach warned through gritted teeth.

Jimmy and Moe, not the least disconcerted by the threat, laughed. "Oh, I beg to differ with you, McClain," Jimmy boasted. "We'll get away with this, all right, just you wait and see."

Tess bit her lower lip to keep it from trembling. She didn't doubt for an instant that these men had killed before and would have no qualms about killing again. She darted a look at Zach from the corner of her eye. His features looked cast in granite.

"Move, McClain," Jimmy ordered, waving the gun impatiently.

They made a strange procession with Jimmy holding a lantern and leading the way. Zach was next, staggering to carry the box loaded with gold. Tess trailed after them, all the while conscious of Moe close behind with a pistol leveled at her back.

By the time they neared the entrance of the cave, sweat trickled down Zach's face. His breath sawed in and out from exertion. The light outside the mine was only a few shades brighter than that inside. Tess had lost all concept of time, but guessed the hour was well after midnight.

"All right, McClain, set the gold in the back of the wagon; cover it with that tarpaulin; then come back here."

Zach did as he was told and returned to the mine to stand next to Tess.

"Good night's work—for a dead man." Jimmy laughed at his own joke.

At a slight nod from his friend, Moe went over to where his horse was tethered and came back with an object in one hand.

"If you plan on shooting us in cold blood, lawmen will figure out sooner or later who did it and come looking. They'll tear the territory apart trying to find you. You'll both end up with a hangman's noose. All the gold in the world won't do you any good when your worthless bodies are dangling from a scaffold."

"Do we look worried?" Moe casually held up a cylinder with a cord attached at one end, struck a match, and lit the fuse.

"You sons of bitches!" Zach growled. "Blasting powder."

Tess stared transfixed at the sparkling fuse in Moe Black's hand. Zach shoved her behind him, using his body as a shield.

"Further you get from the blast, the better your chances are of stayin' alive." Jimmy's dimpled smile was as friendly as the gun he kept trained on them.

"Until, that is, you eventually die from lack of food and water. You better run, McClain. Run for your life."

Snatching a lantern, Zach grabbed Tess's hand, nearly jerking her off her feet, and ran into the mine shaft.

Moe drew back his arm and tossed the cartridge with the sizzling fuse through the entrance. "Nice knowin' you, McClain." His laughter was joined by Jimmy's.

"Run, Tess!" Zach barked. "Faster!"

Holding her skirt above her knees, Tess stumbled to keep pace over the uneven floor. They ran deeper and deeper into the mine.

The force of the blast knocked them off their feet and sent them flying. Zach rolled on top of Tess as the mountain shook and heaved around them. Timbers groaned, cracked, collapsed. Rocks tumbled and rolled. Debris poured like a drought-ending rain. Then, after the desultory clatter of rubble, quiet descended. A quiet as absolute as death itself.

Tess lay perfectly still, her cheek pressed against the cold, rough stone. She was alive. Zach's heavy weight sprawled on top of her gave a small measure of comfort. At least she wasn't alone. She stirred and called his name. "Zach . . ."

There was no movement, no word of reassurance. Panic beat within her chest like the wings of giant bats. "Zach . . . ?"

Still no response. In order to protect her, he had risked his life. She couldn't—wouldn't—accept losing him. "Damn you, Zach McClain, don't you dare die on me."

Wriggling out from underneath him, she took a deep breath to steady her nerves and choked on the dust-laden air. Coughing and wheezing, she pulled and tugged until Zach lay half-turned on his side. She placed her hand against his chest and was weak with relief to feel its steady rise and fall.

"Dear God," she whispered, "please let him be all right." Her hands shook as they roamed up and down his body, checking for broken bones or gaping wounds. Finding none, she cradled his head in her lap. With a feather-light touch, she traced his features. She smoothed his brow, and her fingers came away sticky with blood from a long gash along his hairline. She took comfort, however, that he was alive. They were both alive, and where there was life, there was hope. For now that was enough.

Tess leaned back against a fallen beam. *So this is how it feels to be buried alive,* she mused bleakly. She had once read an account in a dime novel of a miner who had survived a cave-in for nearly two weeks. She had never appreciated his courage and fortitude more than at this moment.

After what seemed an eternity, Zach moaned, then rolled onto his back.

"Zach, hush," she soothed. "Just lie still."

"What happened?" he asked, his voice raspy.

She gently stroked his hair. "We found the gold, but Moe and Jimmy stole it from us. They set off blasting powder, trapping us here in the mine."

With a groan, he levered himself up on one elbow. "Yeah," he muttered. "The explosion. I remember now. Are you all right?"

"I'm fine." Her voice sounded thready, uneven. "As fine as one can be, trapped by a cave-in."

He started to sit up, but fell back. "My head aches like the devil."

"You have a nasty gash on your forehead, but when I checked I didn't find anything broken."

"Couldn't keep your hands off me, darlin'?" he teased.

Taking her cue from him, she gathered her wits and replied in kind. "Seems I couldn't resist the opportunity to take advantage of an unconscious man. Even though," she added, "I happen to be married to him."

The gravity of the situation didn't allow for prolonged levity. Reaching out, Zach found her hand and squeezed. "We'll find a way out of this, Tess. I don't know how, but we will."

"Of course we will," she replied, returning the squeeze. She wanted to believe him, wanted desperately to hope. "Where do we start?"

He pulled himself into a semireclining position. "I remember taking a lantern before we started to run. Let's see if we can get lucky and find it. The thing must have been knocked out of my hand by the blast."

They crawled around on their hands and knees searching for it. Tess tried to ignore the sharp bits of rock and shale that sliced into her palms and cut her knees. The task seemed an impossible one, a complete waste of effort, but at last Zach let out a cry of triumph.

"I think most of the fuel leaked out, but . . ."

She could hear him fumbling for a match, heard it scrape a rough surface, then watched it explode in yellow-orange flame. The battered but serviceable lantern provided a welcome glow. They stared at each other, mentally taking inventory. Bruised and bloody, dirty and disheveled, they had nevertheless survived.

Zach gave her a crooked smile. "C'mere."

Tess needed no urging. She threw herself into his arms. Zach smoothed her tangled hair, kissed the top of her head, held her hard and fast. There was no need for words.

Then he released her and drew back, his jaw set. "We better get busy. No telling how long our light will last."

Zach went to work clearing rocks and debris. When

they were too large to remove manually, he used a broken beam as a lever. Tess worked diligently alongside him, lifting, pushing, and shoving to create a passageway through the morass of broken granite. From time to time, overhead timbers would creak ominously. They would pause in their labors, straining to hear any noise that might herald further disaster, then when all was quiet once again, resuming their task. Tess was perpetually aware that at any time, more rock could come crashing down and crush them.

Progress was measured in inches. A foot, then a yard, were causes for celebration. Slowly but inexorably they moved forward. Wearily Tess shoved her tangled hair from her face and arched her back to ease the knotted muscles. She cast a worried glance at the lantern. The light was gradually dimming. Soon they would be pitched into total darkness once again. She swallowed convulsively, more frightened than she was willing to admit.

She resumed the arduous task. She envied Zach's stamina, his dogged determination. His shirt was torn and bloodstained, his face black and streaked with sweat, but he never complained. Never admitted defeat. Regardless of what he remembered, Elmira hadn't defeated him, and neither would this.

"Here," Zach said, picking up the lantern, "take my hand and follow me."

They were able to advance a short distance, only to be stopped by another pile of rubble. Tess tried to keep her abject disappointment from becoming obvious. "I don't think the light is going to last much longer," she warned, her voice flat and emotionless.

Holding the lantern at arm's length, he studied their newest barrier. "Someone's looking out for us," he said, his inspection concluded. "This isn't as bad as it looks. It's not a solid wall of rock after all, but a short tunnel of sorts. Way I see, we don't have much choice but to try to crawl through to the other side. Are you game?"

At her nod, he slipped through the narrow opening. "I'll go first."

"Be careful," she called after him. *I love you.* But, the latter remained unspoken, just as it had so many other times.

Zach vanished from sight, leaving Tess alone in the darkness. She could hear scrabbling sounds as he inched forward. Offering up a hasty prayer for courage, she, too, entered the small, confined space. Lying flat on her belly, she crept along behind him. Sharp-edged rocks poked and jabbed. Her cotton skirt ripped. Several times, strands of her hair were snagged on debris and she wrenched them free.

Ahead, the lantern flickered like a friendly glow-worm on a hot summer night. Flickered, faded. Then died.

Zach cursed loudly. All sounds of his progress ceased. "Zach . . . ?"

She heard him swallow, the sound magnified in the stillness. Alarm bells sounded inside her head.

"Zach, talk to me," she cried. "What's the matter?"

He cleared his throat. "I'm not sure I can do this, Tess."

"Zach, unless you tell me what's wrong, I can't help you." The uncertainty in his voice tugged at her heart.

"It's happening all over again."

She forced herself to remain calm, to ignore the razor edge of fear and defeat in his tone. "Explain what it is that's happening all over again."

"Elmira. The sweat box."

"This isn't Elmira," she reminded gently. "And you're not alone."

"I can't stand being confined in a small spaces. I just c-can't . . ." His voice broke like a frayed thread.

"We'll be out of this soon, and it'll be better. You'll see."

"I feel as though I'm in that damned box all over again. It's so cramped in here I can't move. The walls closing in on me like a damn coffin."

"Zach, this *isn't* Elmira. We're trapped in a cave-in, remember?"

His breathing changed, became rapid, shallow. "No light, no air. I'm suffocating, Tess. I can't breathe."

Suddenly, inspiration struck. "Zach," she pleaded. "Listen to me. Take a deep breath, a real deep breath. Can you smell it?"

He took one, then another. "I don't smell anything."

"Try one more time, please," she coaxed.

She heard him inhale, exhale, and prayed her scheme would work.

"What is it you think you smell?"

"I thought for a minute javelina might have wandered into the mine," she improvised. "They leave such a terrible odor behind."

He gave a shaky laugh. "I think you got hit on the head, too."

To her vast relief, he sounded calmer, more in control. "You called it a short tunnel, Zach. We just need to go a little farther."

Stones and rock shifted as once again he inched forward.

"This reminds me of a game I used to play as a child," Tess said, fabricating an imaginary pastime. She desperately wanted to distract him from his memories of the sweat box. "Every year after harvest, the town would hold a fair. People would come from all over the county. The storekeepers would string together empty barrels for us kids to crawl through, then hold a contest. Whoever made it through the barrels fastest won a bag of lemon drops.

"Pretend this is a game, Zach, and you love lemon drops more than anything in the world. Imagine me, right behind you and ready to do anything to win that big bag of candy. You're going to have to move fast in order to win. How would it look if you got beat by a girl? Move. Faster, now. I'm right behind you."

Cautiously at first, then with growing confidence, he crawled faster, steadier, eager to break free from the confining space. "No way am I going to get beat by a girl. My brother would never let me live it down."

Finally she heard him spill out of the tunnel into an open area, and felt strong arms pulling her free and enfolding her.

"We did it," he cried.

Even in the dark, she could picture his jubilant smile. "No, you did it."

"Time to confess, Tess. Was there ever any barrel game?"

She snuggled closer to his solid warmth. She was nearly as relieved as he to be out of that small, cramped space. "No," she said on a sigh, "but if there had been I would have beaten you. Lemon drops are my favorite."

"I'll make a note of that."

She smiled against his chest. "Mind if we rest a bit?"

Together they sank to the hard floor. Strangely enough, as it had the first time they made love, Tess discovered that the total darkness fostered anonymity, lessening restraint and providing an odd sense of freedom. Zach had bravely faced his demons. Now it was her turn to do the same. With the future in jeopardy, she knew there might never be a better opportunity to unburden herself. Tess wanted Zach to hear her account of what happened on his final night at Gettysburg. Whether he believed her or not was out of her control.

"Zach," she began tentatively. "In case we don't make it out of this alive, there's something I need to tell you."

"We're going to get out of here," he said fiercely.

"I'd rest easier if you would at least hear me out."

A lengthy silence was followed by a sigh of resignation. "All right, since you're determined——"

"It's about the night you were taken prisoner. . . ."

"I don't want to listen to lies," he snapped.

Tess recoiled at his harshness. All the old bitterness had seeped back into his tone. It had been absent for a while, but hearing it again cut like acid. She swallowed her disappointment and forged ahead. "I didn't lie when I said I never told the authorities where you and Jed were hiding."

"Then how did they find out, Tess? As I recall, you were the only one who knew."

She linked her fingers together in her lap. He wasn't going to make this easy, but she couldn't delay telling him any longer. "I always believed you had left Gettysburg to rejoin your unit. It wasn't until the night of our wedding that I learned the truth."

"The truth being I was sent to rot in a Union prison camp?"

"Exactly. Even then it took a while to fit the pieces together." Her fingers clenched until the knuckles blanched. "I knew you'd be leaving soon, and I wanted to spend every minute I could with you. Even as a young girl, I——I fancied myself in love with you."

"Really, Tess, why go into all this?" His voice no longer sounded angry, but weary. "Can't we just leave the past alone?"

But she couldn't do that. Now that she had started,

there could be no retreat. "When you mentioned Sheriff Earl Johnson, it brought back certain memories. I remembered all that day I could hardly wait to see you again. I planned to use chores as an excuse to visit the barn, but Mother kept me busy with errands instead. One of those errands was to deliver eggs to a neighbor. She handed me a sealed note and instructed me to wait for a reply."

"I don't see what this has to do with—"

"The neighbor happened to be the sheriff and his wife."

He snorted in disbelief. "You're implying your mother was at fault?"

"I didn't want to believe it either at first. I kept telling myself it was just coincidence. That she wouldn't have done such a thing. That there was no way she could have known you were hiding in our barn."

"Let me see if I've got this straight. You're putting the blame for my capture on your mother?"

"There's more," she persisted. Tess was grateful for the darkness. She didn't want to watch his eyes ice over with skepticism. She smoothed her torn skirt, then nervously pleated the fabric, scarcely aware of her actions. He didn't believe her. The thought made her physically ill. After everything they had shared, he didn't believe her. She never should have broached the subject. The wound was as raw as if it had just happened yesterday. All she had done was rip the scab off a festering sore.

"C'mon, darlin'," he coaxed. "You started this; now finish it."

She drew a ragged breath and continued. "It wasn't until this morning that I couldn't deny the truth any longer."

"What the hell happened this morning to cause your revelation?"

"It was something you said about Gairmo sleeping as though drugged. It was the same phrase Lily London had used at her visit."

"I must have been hit on the head harder than I thought. None of what you're sayin' to me is makin' a lick of sense."

"I remembered once in my life having slept that way—the night you were taken prisoner." She sensed she had won his full attention. "It started me thinking, remembering details I had nearly forgotten. I recalled being unusually sleepy after dinner. Mother's nightly dose of laudanum was taking an unusually long time to take effect, so I lay down on the bed to wait. When I woke, it was broad daylight—and you were gone."

"You're telling me your mother drugged you, then turned me over to the authorities? Why would she do such a thing?"

"Ever since Father was killed at Fredericksburg, Mother hated the South and all it stood for. I think she must have somehow discovered I was hiding you and notified Sheriff Johnson. Maybe she noticed food missing from the pantry. Or maybe she heard me leave one night and followed me; I don't know. It's the truth, Zach, but I realize without proof you have only my word."

"Why should I believe you?"

She found his hand in the dark and wove her fingers through his. "Because I love you," she answered simply, honestly. "I'd die before I let anyone harm you."

Zach made no effort to curl his fingers around hers, uttered no words of encouragement. Disappointment weighed on her, crushing her spirit. Like a fool, she dared to hope for affection if not tenderness. Friendship if not love. Trust and respect. But it appeared she had been mistaken. Their relationship was an emotional vacuum. A black, airless vacuum.

Time lost all meaning. Without the lantern, any further attempt to find their way out would not only have been foolhardy, but possibly deadly. So, they remained where they were and waited. Finally, after what seemed an eternity, sounds filtered in to them.

Sounds of a rescue.

Of boulders being moved, timbers shifted.

When these sounds ceased, two loud blasts from a rifle brought them to their feet. "You in the mine," an unfamiliar voice shouted. "Come out. You are free."

"Hang on to me," Zach ordered tersely.

Arms outstretched to either side, Zach groped his way toward the mouth of the mine. They had gone about ten feet or so when they saw a glimmer of light. Zach walked faster, almost running toward the source. Tess picked up her skirt and hurried after him. Together they emerged from the bowels of a mountain and into bright daylight.

After having been immersed in total darkness, the light was blinding, painful. Tess shielded her eyes behind a raised hand. She knew Zach did likewise. When she finally lowered her arm, she saw a long row of Indians on horseback silhouetted against the brilliant blue sky. Instinctively, she moved closer to Zach.

"Eskiminzin," Zach greeted their leader. "We owe you much."

"You have saved one of ours," the Apache chief returned gravely. "The debt is paid."

Tess's gaze drifted to the boy seated on a sturdy pony with a spotted coat. Gairmo. He acknowledged her look with a slight smile. She felt herself being scrutinized, and her gaze shifted from Gairmo to the man next to him. Spellbound, she stared into eyes blacker than the inside of the mine. The man's compelling presence was impossible to ignore. His angular features could have been hewn with a hatchet. Intuitively she sensed he was a powerful force among his people.

At a nod from their leader, two Apache men jumped from their ponies and came toward the mine. Tess felt her heart leap with fear, but the men ignored her and Zach and went instead toward a pile of rubble flanking the entrance. Her breath caught when she saw the bodies of Moe Black and Jimmy Jerold. Each had been shot in the back.

Eskiminzin addressed his remarks to Zach. "These animals will no longer trouble you—or the Apache."

The bodies, blood still oozing from their wounds, were lifted onto the backs of waiting horses. Eskiminzin raised his hand, then turned and led his men down the mountain. The last two horses in the procession carried the lifeless bodies of Moe Black and Jimmy Jerold. A loud, blood-curdling cry went up from the Apaches as they rode off. The sound made Tess shiver.

Zach observed the departing band. "It's Apache justice."

"What will they do with the bodies?"

"It's better you don't know." Zach stared out across the distant mountains. "Eskiminzin lost two wives and five of his children at the Camp Grant Massacre. The chief next to him, Geronimo, lost a wife along with his mother and three young children in an earlier attack. Let's just be grateful our lives were spared."

"All I want to do is go home." Tess, numb and bone-weary, glanced around and was happy to see the wagon exactly as they had last seen it.

Zach spotted it, too. "Looks like we don't have to walk after all."

He strode to the wagon and looked inside. "Well, I'll be . . ."

"What is it?" she asked, only mildly interested.

"The gold." His teeth flashed white in his grime-covered face. "It hasn't been touched."

Twenty-four

Zach lifted Tess onto the wagon, then climbed up after her and slapped the reins. The wagon rolled down the mountain trail toward home. "I can't believe the gold was still there."

"Why do you suppose the Apaches didn't take it?"

"The box was hidden beneath a tarpaulin and barely noticeable. I suspect the Apaches were more concerned about meting out punishment than the contents of the wagon."

Tess wished she shared Zach's enthusiasm over the treasure. Perhaps it was their close brush with death, but her initial excitement at locating the gold had tarnished. The gold no longer seemed as precious. True wealth, she realized, couldn't be measured by gold or silver. There were many things much more valuable, such as life and health. Love.

"We're rich, Tess." He shook his head, marveling over their good fortune.

Tess refused to cast a backward glance. She didn't want to see the pile of rocks the Apaches had forced Moe and Jimmy to clear from the mine's entrance. And most of all, she didn't want to remember their bloody, inert forms slung over the backs of their horses. They represented two more lives lost in the quest for gold.

"You know," Zach said, his mouth curving in a wry smile, "after the war, I used to dream about going back home to South Carolina. Maybe buy back the family homestead, rebuild."

She turned her head to study him. Not even layers of grime could mar the perfection of his starkly handsome features profiled against a cerulean sky. It would be agony not to see that dearly loved face every morning, every night. Her chest tightened with emotion at their impending parting. Clearing her throat, she asked, "Is that what you intend to do with your share of the fortune?"

He kept his eyes on the trail ahead, squinting against the brilliant sunshine flooding the arid land. "No, not any more. I like the Southwest, so I guess I'll stay put. What about you, Tess?" he asked after a lengthy pause. "Do you ever think of returning to Pennsylvania?"

Was this Zach's way of telling her he was eager for them to go their separate ways? she wondered bleakly. "I'm not sure what I'll do."

She felt his gaze rest thoughtfully on her, but kept hers fixed straight ahead. There was no way she could look at him and disguise the longing she felt—or the desperation. Her raw emotions would be stamped across her face in bold print. For her, finding the treasure marked an end, not a new beginning. She could return to Pennsylvania, or travel to distant lands and, knowing she had left part of herself behind, never be truly happy.

They both lapsed into silence.

Fatigue and depression fettered her spirit like heavy chains. She blamed it for the lack of control she felt. Emotion floated close to the surface, and she fought back tears. Although she loved Zach with her whole heart, never once had he indicated he felt anything more for her than a strong physical attraction. While trapped in the mine, she had told him everything she remembered about that fateful night at Gettysburg. Granted, she had no proof. For Zach to believe her would require a leap of faith. Faith—and love.

As they rounded a bend in the road, the ranch came into view. The small adobe structure slumbering under the hot desert sun seemed a welcome sight as the wagon rolled to a halt in front. Not waiting for Zach's assistance, Tess scrambled down. Zach watched but didn't offer a comment. Instead, he jumped down from his perch and, going to the rear of the wagon, flipped back the canvas and removed the metal box containing the gold.

Tess went ahead of him and threw open the sturdy oak door of the house.

Grunting with exertion, Zach lowered his heavy burden to the parlor floor. "Slide the bar across the door," he instructed.

Tess did as he asked, then watched Zach move about the room, drawing the wooden shutters closed.

"Can't be too careful," he muttered.

Tess didn't need a reminder that the gold had already cost lives, Jed's included. "What do you propose we do next?"

Zach knelt in front of the box and opened the lid. Gold blazed brighter than the light of a dozen lanterns. "Makes a pretty sight, doesn't it?"

"I suppose," Tess admitted grudgingly. "Does Tucson even have a bank? I don't remember seeing one."

"Lionel and Barron Jacobs offer banking services at their mercantile establishment. It's the closest the town comes to a real bank."

"Will it be safe with them?"

"They're honest, hard-working men. It's not an ideal situation, but it will have to suffice until we come up with a better plan. Guess we should think about hiring an armed guard and shipping it to San Francisco."

Tess tucked a strand of hair behind her ear. "Maybe we should call on Abner and ask his advice."

"Excellent idea, Tess." Abner Smith, looking perfectly at ease, strolled into the parlor from an adjoining room. Dapper in a matching brown checked coat and vest and a starched white shirt, his appearance contrasted sharply with their own disheveled state.

"A-Abner . . ." Tess stammered in surprise.

Slamming the lid of the box closed, Zach rose to his feet and positioned himself in front of the gold. "Smith, what the hell are you doing here?"

Abner's luxuriant mustache twitched in a reproving smile. "That's not a very friendly way to greet a guest."

"You'll have to excuse us if we're somewhat lacking in hospitality. We've had a rather trying night."

"My, oh my," Abner clucked, surveying their torn clothes and dirt-streaked faces with obvious distaste. "That's a rather nasty cut you have on your head, McClain. Mind if I ask what happened to the two of you?"

Self-consciously, Tess tried to tame her wildly tangled hair. "We were trapped in a cave-in at the mine."

"A cave-in, eh? Those mines are dangerous places." Removing his gold-rimmed spectacles, he polished the lenses with a snowy handkerchief. "What prompted you to spend the night at an abandoned mine?"

"We—" Tess started to explain, but Zach cut her off.

"I don't believe you ever answered my question, Smith. What are you doing here?" He folded his arms across his chest, his head to one side, and regarded the lawyer with suspicion.

"Hope you folks don't mind that I made myself

comfortable. When I found you both gone, I decided to wait. A cave-in," he mused, changing the subject. "It's nothing short of miraculous that you managed to dig your way out. No one would ever have found your bodies. Sorry, my dear," he said when Tess shuddered. "I didn't mean to upset you."

Zach shifted his weight impatiently. "Surely you can understand that my wife and I have been through quite an ordeal. Tess is nearly ready to drop with exhaustion. All we want to do is get cleaned up and get some sleep. So say what you came to say; then be on your way."

"Yes, yes, indeed." Abner nodded agreeably. "I can understand that; I surely can."

Tess tried to dull the sharp edge of Zach's words. "Zach isn't trying to be rude, Abner. We're simply very tired."

But Abner gave no indication he was ready to leave just yet. "I couldn't help but overhear your conversation before making my presence known. And, of course, I couldn't help but notice that box of gold sitting there on the floor. So there really was a treasure after all," he said softly, as he settled his glasses on the bridge of his nose. "You're a wise man, Zach, to want to protect such a fortune. Gold makes men do crazy thin~~~~~~~~~ steal, even commit murder."

~~~~~~~~ e lawyer's tone cut through her fa~~~~~~~~~ss's attention. She moved closer to ~~~~~~~~~ f them stood guard over the treas~~~~~~~~~ ly overheard, Zach and I were dis~~~~~~~~~ ou for advice."

~~~~~~~~ ar Tess." Abner brushed a speck ~~~~~~~~ of his jacket. "I heartily concur ~~~~~~~~ nsport the gold somewhere safe. ~~~~~~~~ a fact I can attest to from per~~~~~~~~ ~~~~ence. I have the perfect solution to your problem."

While Zach and Tess waited for him to further elaborate, Abner nonchalantly reached into the pocket of his jacket and withdrew a small but lethal-looking derringer, which he trained on Tess.

Tess's mind reeled with disbelief. Reliable, trustworthy Abner Smith, a person she looked upon as a friend, stood calmly aiming a deadly weapon directly at her heart.

"What the . . . ?" Zach took a menacing step forward.

Abner gripped the butt of the gun tighter. "Another step, McClain, and Tess will pay for your rash move."

"Abner, why are you doing this?" Tess cried.

"Your husband asked me why I was here. While it was true I was waiting, I must admit, however, that I was astounded when the two of you appeared. You see, dear Tess, I was expecting Jimmy Jerold and Moe Black. They were due to meet me here hours ago. I was beginning to fear that they had double-crossed me."

"Bastard," Zach growled.

"I've been called worse." Behind the polished lenses, Abner's eyes gleamed with grim determination. "And let me warn you, McClain, in case you get the notion to do something foolish. I'm an excellent shot from close range. One false move and Tess will be the first to pay the penalty."

Tess knew Zach wasn't armed. Jimmy and Moe had taken his weapons earlier at the mine. She was also aware that the closest escape route was behind them and barred with a stout beam. Still, she stalled for time. "All this time, the three of you were partners?"

Abner laughed. "Hardly. The two of them are no more than hired guns. After shooting Jed, I found I don't have much of a stomach for killing."

"*You* killed Jed?" Tess was stunned by the casual

admission. "He trusted you. Considered you a friend, a confidant."

"You son of a bitch!" Zach clenched his fists. A muscle ticked in his jaw, a sign of the tight rein he kept on his anger. "If you weren't hiding behind a gun, I'd kill you with my bare hands."

"By the way, " Abner smiled, not the least perturbed by Zach's threat, "whatever happened to Jimmy and Moe?"

"Ah . . . w-we think Gairmo found his people and led them back here. The Apaches forced them to clear debris from the mine entrance, then killed both of them." Tess fervently hoped Zach was formulating a plan of action. She couldn't seem to think of anything beyond the fact that Abner planned to kill them.

"No matter." Abner gave a dismissive shrug. "I only needed them to keep a close eye on you—something I couldn't do without arousing suspicion. I knew my instincts were right on target when you refused to sell this place at a profit. I was sure then that you were close to finding the gold. How did you know where to look?"

Tess grew increasingly nervous, while Abner remained almost unnaturally composed. "I, ah, found a map hidden between the pages of a dime novel. Zach was able to decipher the words which were written in French."

"You said yourself, Smith, that you don't like killing." Zach fractionally increased the distance between himself and Tess. "There's more than enough gold for all of us. What do you say we split it three ways?"

"No, I don't think so," Abner said, shaking his head. "I happen to be the greedy sort. As for killing, a man can do all sorts of distasteful tasks for money."

Tess surreptitiously wiped her sweaty palms on her

torn skirt. "Do you actually think you'll get away with this?"

"When I'm finished, it'll look like the work of the Apaches. Folks might even decide to retaliate like they did with Camp Grant. I've grown quite fond of you, Tess. Too bad you didn't accept my proposal. As your husband, I'd be entitled to your share. McClain, of course, would have been eliminated regardless."

Tess felt the tension resonate through Zach like the plucked string of a fiddle. He was gauging his next move, she knew. But what were his chances against Abner's gun? The tension was contagious, and she bit her lower lip to keep it from trembling.

Then, everything seemed to happen at once.

Tess, who had been watching Abner, noticed a slight change in his expression. Zach lunged forward just as Abner's finger tightened on the trigger. She shoved Zach out of the way as the derringer spit orange flame.

"Tess!" She heard Zach yell, his voice sounding as though it came from the end of a long tunnel.

The sharp, searing pain caught her unaware. Dazed, she stared in wonder at the blossom of red along the left side of her blouse. Instinctively, she clamped her hand over the site and watched bemused as blood trickled through her fingers.

Another gunshot exploded. Plaster flew from the wall in a hail of tiny particles that stung her exposed flesh like pesky insects. Now that her body had absorbed the initial shock from the bullet, pain dug into Tess with deep talons. She sank to her knees, doubled over. Her head buzzed with a swarm of bees; her vision blurred, dimmed.

Sounds of a scuffle surrounded her. In spite of the pain, she winced at the thud of flesh striking flesh. Cringed at the sickening crunch of breaking cartilage. Gulping back waves of pain, she turned her head. Zach had Abner pinned against the floor, one hand on his throat, the other poised to strike. Splotches of crimson stained the lawyer's once pristine shirt. His glasses dangled precariously from one ear. His face was bloody and battered. He wheezed and gasped under Zach's relentless grip.

"Zach, no," she cried. "Don't. He isn't worth it. Let the law deal with him."

Zach didn't seem to hear her. His fist landed a solid blow to Abner's jaw.

Tess dragged herself closer. "Zach . . ." Summoning the last of her waning strength, she latched onto his arm and held fast. "Enough, Zach. For my sake, please . . ."

It took several seconds, but at last her words penetrated his rage. He blinked away the sweat dripping into his eyes. Gradually, sanity returned. When he noticed her blood-soaked garments, his eyes widened with horror. His heart seemed to come to an abrupt standstill, then race headlong, spurred on by fear. Releasing Abner's limp form like a discarded rag doll, he gently gathered her in his arms. "Oh, my God, Tess. Please, please, be all right."

He pressed his hand over the wound in her side to staunch the flow, but the blood seeped relentlessly. "You're going to be all right, darlin'. I promise I won't let anything happen to you."

Tess tried to smile, but her attempt faltered and she grimaced instead.

Carefully he laid her back on the floor, stripped off his dirty, tattered shirt, rolled it up, and stuck it under her head. Dashing to the cupboard, he pulled out clean white sheets to use as bandages and rushed back, tearing them into strips as he ran.

"You'll be fine; you'll see." He folded a piece of cloth into a pad, which he placed directly over the site,

then wound long strips around her midriff to secure it
in place.

"It hurts, Zach. It hurts so much."

"I'm going to take you into town and find a doctor."
His hands shook as he smoothed chestnut-brown locks
from a face as pale as delicate porcelain. "Be brave a
little while longer, sweetheart."

For the first time since panic set in, he realized the
enormity of her sacrifice. She had boldly risked her
life to save his. Squeezing his eyes shut against an
onslaught of emotion, he kissed her brow. "I'll take
care of you," he vowed raggedly, "just don't die."

Zach held Tess's limp hand in his as he maintained
a vigil at her bedside. From time to time, he searched
for her pulse, needing the reassurance from its faint
but steady beat. If he lived to be a hundred, he knew
he'd never forget that hellish trip into town. Not even
the mattress he placed in the back of wagon could
sufficiently cushion the ruts and bumps in the road.
Each time she whimpered with pain, he had suffered
as well. He would gladly exchange places with her if
only he could.

"Get yourself a hot bath and some clean clothes,
son," Doctor Daniel O'Flynn had ordered after Zach
carried Tess into his surgery. "Nothing you can do
here. I can tend to your wife better without you pes-
tering me."

To avoid wearing a groove in the waiting-room floor,
Zach had taken the doctor's advice, but he returned in
no time. The seemingly endless wait grated on nerves
already frayed. The wait had been nearly unbearable.
He had been about to barge into the surgery when Dr.
O'Flynn had finally emerged, wiping his hands on a

bloody towel. Knowing it was Tess's blood that stained the linen made Zach's stomach churn.

"How is she? Is she going to be all right? Can I see her?"

"Steady, now, boy. It's still too early to tell. Your wife's lost a lot of blood, but it was a small caliber bullet. Far as I can tell, it didn't hit anything vital. 'Course, there's always the chance of infection. . . ."

It had now been twenty-four hours since he had carried Tess into Dr. O'Flynn's waiting room. Twenty-four hours since the town marshal, Francisco Esparza, had arrived to take Abner Smith into custody. Twenty-four hours since Josie Goodbody had volunteered her services.

Josie had proven an unexpected blessing. The best nurse this side of the Mississippi, the doctor had boasted. After Dr. O'Flynn had done all he could, Josie had insisted Tess be taken to her home to be cared for.

Just then, Josie entered the sickroom and, finding Zach camped at his usual spot, gave him a brisk pat on the back. "I brought you a sandwich and a good strong cup of tea." She dismissed the protest she saw forming with a wave of her hand. "You're not going to do that wife of yours any good if you're laid up in bed next to her."

"Do you think she'll make it?"

"She's young and strong. She'll pull through this just fine, mark my words."

Zach's throat worked soundlessly as he struggled to express his gratitude.

Josie smiled and patted his shoulder. "When I come back again, I don't want to find anything on that plate but crumbs."

Zach ate what was put in front of him, slept fitfully on the hard, straight-backed chair, and prayed for a chance to make amends for all his past mistakes where

Tess was concerned. He kept reviewing the confrontation with Abner Smith. Zach had been waiting for just the right moment to make his move, knowing that in all likelihood, he would only have one chance. When at last he saw the derringer shift away from Tess, he had lunged forward. But Tess had seen the barrel of the gun move as well. Heedless of her own safety, she had shoved him aside and caught the bullet destined for him.

Why? he wondered, when all he had given her was grief. He fell asleep, his head slumped forward on his chest, his fingers entwined with hers.

He came awake by slow degrees, aware of someone softly stroking the stubble along his jaw. He opened eyes bloodshot and heavy-lidded from sleep to find Tess solemnly regarding him. "Tess . . ." he murmured, his voice hoarse with emotion.

She smiled. "With that beard, you could be mistaken for a desperado straight from the pages of the *Tip Top Weekly*."

A lump the size of a Georgia peach lodged in Zach's throat at the sight of her lovely smile. He caught her hand, pressed a kiss in the palm, then smiled back at her. Her color had improved. Maybe Josie had been right. Tess was going to pull through after all.

"You're finally awake." He sat up straighter, scrubbed his hand against his chin, heard the rasp of whiskers. "Guess I need a shave."

"How long have I been asleep?"

"For most of the time ever since we brought you here yesterday."

"Yesterday . . . ?" She started to push herself up on one elbow, but fell back against the pillows with a soft moan.

"Easy, darlin', you've still got some mending to do." He leaned forward, elbows on his knees, his expression earnest, and searched her face. "Why, Tess? What made you step in front of that gun just as Smith was about to fire?"

"I told you once I'd die before I let any harm come to you." Gray eyes met green, held them captive. "And I never break a promise."

I never break a promise.

Zach felt as though she had just delivered a blow to his chest with a sledgehammer. Suddenly, he couldn't breathe. All the air had been knocked from his lungs. Tess had nearly forfeited her life to save his. Those weren't the actions of someone who would betray him—ever. She had been only thirteen when she had promised not to turn him over to Union forces. She had been a woman when she promised to protect his life with hers. Both times she had kept her word.

God, what an idiot he had been. What a fool. Could she ever forgive him? He had been so consumed with hatred that he had been blinded to the sweetness, the generosity, the love that Tess embodied. It had taken nearly losing her to realize the truth.

He didn't deserve her, wasn't worthy. He cupped her cheek with the palm of his hand. "I'm a stupid fool, Tess, but one who loves you. Can we start over?"

Tears shimmered in her beautiful eyes. "Then you've forgiven me for the role I played in your capture. If I had only known what was in that note . . ."

"Hush." He placed a finger lightly across her lips. "I think I forgave you a long time ago but didn't know it. I started to love you, too, though I tried to deny it. All the gold in the world doesn't mean a thing if I don't have you."

"The gold?" Tess's eyes widened at the reminder. "Is it safe? I know how much it means to you."

He traced the curve of her lower lip. "You're the

only treasure that truly matters to me. I just hope you'll give me a chance to prove it."

"Umm, I don't know," she said doubtfully, but the sparkle in her eyes betrayed her. "That might take a long time."

"Do you think a lifetime will be long enough?" He kissed her then. A kiss soft, sweet, and tender with the promise of new beginning.

Epilogue

The stylish, well-sprung buggy rolled down the road leading south. Overhead, the sun made its inexorable arc, dragging twilight in its path. The softly muted light painted the tall saguaros in shades of dusky purple.

"Are you sure you feel well enough for a ride?"

"I'm fine, Zach," Tess insisted for the third time. "Stop clucking over me like a mother hen. I had enough of that with Josie taking care of me."

Zach chuckled. "Josie turned out to be quite a gal, didn't she?"

"She certainly did," Tess concurred wholeheartedly. "Never in a million years would I have thought we'd become friends. Deep down inside, Josie's full of love and caring, but with no one to lavish it on she sometimes gets carried away with one cause or another."

Zach gave her a benevolent smile. "You always insist on seeing the good in people, don't you? You even started to feel sorry for Abner when he went before the judge."

"Let's not waste what's left of a beautiful afternoon talking about Abner." She angled the wide brim of her hat to block the slanting rays of the sun. "Isn't this the way to the mission?"

"Mmm," Zach murmured.

"It's going to be sunset soon," she commented, stealing a sidelong glance.

"It certainly is," he said agreeably.

She sighed in exasperation. "Why all the secrecy? And why, when I have a whole new wardrobe, did you insist I wear the dress I bought the day we got married?"

"Because you look so damn pretty in it." He gave her a smile that never failed to make her heart beat faster. "I don't remember if I ever told you that before."

Tess self-consciously smoothed the skirt of the simple white cotton dress embroidered with dainty yellow and blue flowers. Zach had been acting strangely ever since she had recuperated sufficiently to return to the ranch. She had no call for complaint. She couldn't have wished for a more attentive companion. Except that he treated her like fragile porcelain, afraid she'd break if mishandled. Well, tonight she planned to demonstrate that she had fully recovered from her injuries.

"Won't it be well after dark before we head back?" she asked, remembering their previous encounter with the javelina.

"Don't worry about a thing. I'm sure Antonio keeps rooms prepared for travelers who might want to spend the night." He gave her a smug grin; then his expression turned serious. "Besides, I want to visit Jed's grave site. I hope he rests easier now that his killer has been brought to justice."

By the time the mission came into view, the sun had sunk low in the sky. Luscious colors tinted the horizon with shades of coral, peach, apricot, and gold. Even the walls of the mission assumed a rosy glow. Sensing that Zach shared her pleasure made the breathtaking scene even more beautiful.

Antonio, the faithful Tohono O'odham caretaker,

nodded a greeting as the buggy rolled to a stop in front of the mission. Zach lifted her from the buggy, then held out his arm in a courtly gesture. Tess gave him a quizzical look, but accepted his extended arm with a smile. Her hand lightly rested in the crook of his arm as he escorted her toward the entrance of the church.

Tess experienced the same awe that she had felt on her first visit. Even after years of disuse, San Xavier was truly magnificent. The final rays of sunlight glinted off the deep-set windows. A day ended; a night waited to be born. A gentle transition. A time of peace, tranquility.

Beaming broadly, Antonio pulled open the heavy wooden door. Arm in arm, she and Zach slowly started up the aisle toward the altar. It was then she noticed a woman sitting in one of the back pews. A woman with bright yellow curls.

"Lil . . . ?"

Hearing her name, Lily London turned and winked, her eyes suspiciously moist. Tess gaped in amazement. *What is the saloon owner doing here?* she wondered in confusion. And all prim and proper in a dark-blue dress buttoned all the way up to her throat.

Tess turned to Zach for an explanation but he only smiled and continued to propel her up the aisle. Her feet balked when she noticed the front pews filled with people. "Zach," she whispered. "We shouldn't. We're interrupting—"

A soft cry of an infant drew Tess's attention toward a side entrance. Amelia slipped into the church and hushed the baby nestled in her arms. Zach's smile grew wider as he prompted Tess toward the front of the church. It was then she noticed candles had been lit. Dozens of them. And there were flowers. Huge, colorful bouquets of paper flowers, the sort the Mexican women made, were everywhere.

"What . . . ?" She turned to Zach.

Wordlessly, he guided her toward the intricately painted altar. As they drew nearer, the occupants in the front pews turned toward them. Tess gasped in surprise at all the familiar faces. Josie Goodbody. Dr. O'Flynn. Cal Davis from the mercantile. Sam from the livery stable. Even the three Kemper brothers were present, along with others she had met while recuperating in town. Then, to her amazement, Josie's friend, Reverend Tobias Miller, stepped forward, an open Bible in his hands.

Zach took her hands in his and smiled deep into her eyes. "I told you once marriage was only a piece of paper. Well, I was wrong. Tess, I want to repeat the vows we made and start anew."

Tess tried to find words, but speech failed her.

"I love you, darlin'. Will you marry me?"

Tears of joy streamed down her cheeks. Her heart felt ready to burst. Winding her arms around Zach's neck, Tess raised her face for a kiss that would seal their future.

Their guests broke into applause, but neither noticed as two hearts found a treasure more valuable than gold.

More By Best-selling Author
Fern Michaels

Enjoy *Savage Destiny*
A Romantic Series from
Rosanne Bittner

__#1: **Sweet Prairie Passion** $5.99US/$6.99CAN
0-8217-5342-8

__#2: **Ride the Free Wind Passion** $5.99US/$6.99CAN
0-8217-5343-6

__#3: **River of Love** $5.99US/$6.99CAN
0-8217-5344-4

Experience the Romances of
Rosanne Bittner